The Girl Called Ella Dessa

by

Karen Campbell Prough

FIREFLY
SOUTHERN FICTION
LIGHTHOUSE PUBLISHING OF THE CAROLINAS

THE GIRL CALLED ELLA DESSA BY KAREN CAMPBELL PROUGH
Published by Firefly Southern Fiction
an imprint of Lighthouse Publishing of the Carolinas
2333 Barton Oaks Dr., Raleigh, NC, 27614

ISBN: 978-1-941103-85-2
Copyright © 2015 by Karen Campbell Prough
Cover design by Goran Tomic
Interior design by AtriTeX Technologies P Ltd

Available in print from your local bookstore, online, or from the publisher at: www.store.lpcbooks.com

For more information on this book and the author visit: www.karencampbellprough.com

Brought to you by the creative team at LighthousePublishingoftheCarolinas.com: Eva Marie Everson, Carolyn Boyles, and Jessica R. Everson.

Library of Congress Cataloging-in-Publication Data
Prough, Karen.
The Girl Called Ella Dessa /Karen Prough 1st ed.

Printed in the United States of America

To my husband

Thank you for understanding the desire within me to write about a day and time far removed from the one we live in. Your unrelenting support pushed me to continue the journey.

I form the light, and create darkness: I make peace, and create evil:
I the Lord do all these things.
Isaiah 45:7 KJV

Chapter 1

Thursday, September 15, 1836

"Mama, talk to me. I can't do this by myself."

Ella Dessa Huskey's mama sat upright on the bed. "It's too soon. I need help." The lantern's dull glow caused indistinct shadows to shift over the log wall and drift across the woman's thin face and tangled straw-colored hair.

"I don't understand what to do." Ella knew nothing of birthing babies. Her twelve years of life hadn't included that experience. She felt a surge of panic, which caused her stomach to roll. "Tell me what to do."

Mama collapsed back on the flat pillow. Sweat poured down her face. She panted, her blue eyes staring upward. "Ella Dessa, remember," her voice sounded weak but understandable, "I might go to screaming before it's here."

"What do I do?"

"Keep clean sheets under me so your pa can't see the soiled bed. There's more in my trunk." She groaned, twisted sideways, and shifted her narrow hips. "I can't catch my breath. I'm too tired. Ohh ... another one's coming."

1

Her mama grimaced. Ella clamped her teeth on her bottom lip and scrunched her face.

Just as the contraction peaked and faded, the cabin door opened. The morning's meager light slipped into the grim interior. Her pa ducked his head, stepped in with an armful of dried wood, and snatched the door shut with his right hand.

With one swift movement, Ella leaned across the bed and let her disheveled hair hide the side of her face. She placed her lips against Mama's ear. "I'm skeered. He should go for Granny Hanks. Let me ride there myself."

"No—*hush*." Mama's sunken eyes went shut. "It's too late."

"Meara?"

"Jacob?" The callous tone in Pa's voice brought Mama's exhausted blue eyes wide open. Her quivering hands wiped at the sweat on her forehead.

"Is Ella Dessa a help or is she a hinderin' you? If so, I'll kick her outside."

Ella twisted sideways on the lumpy mattress and stared at her pa. Her initial panic doubled, and she clutched Mama's clammy arm.

I won't go, unless I'm told to ride for Granny. She hoped her touch relayed those feelings to her mama. Words couldn't be spoken with Pa glowering at her.

"She's a help. Leave her be."

"Mama," she whispered. "I want to be here. But I fear I might not know what to do."

Unable to answer, Mama shook her head. Her colorless lips twisted with agony. She panted through the next contraction, and her body sagged to the bed. "Don't let it frighten you. Just stand by to tie the cord. Ella Dessa, you're brave. Remember that *always*." Her barely audible words drifted away. Her eyes closed.

Out of the corner of her eye, Ella saw her pa squatting near the fireplace. His large-knuckled hands stacked the split wood. The fire had died to gray coals, and the cabin chilled. She had a hazy grasp on the birth process, and the immediacy engulfed and terrified her.

With her thumb, she rubbed the sweat from Mama's eyelids. "How's the pain?"

"Let me rest."

"Pa?" She clenched her jaw and turned toward him. "She's too weak."

He dropped a piece of wood. His curse sliced through the room.

The irregular flicker of the lantern threw a jumpy, distorted reflection over the sagging bed, and the cabin's one window cast a dull hint of daylight into the room.

"Oh, Lord, give me strength." Mama's voice rose in a whispered prayer. "Let it be a son." She clutched at the bedclothes and moaned through colorless lips. With the mounting contraction, she struggled to lift her head and upper body off the sunken cornhusk mattress.

Ella wedged a rolled blanket behind her back. "Better?"

Mama grasped her knees, pulled them toward the sides of her chest, and strained. A deep groan erupted from her throat. "*Awww. No—awww!*"

Firewood clattered to the clay floor and rolled. Ella whirled toward the sound. "Let *me* go for Granny."

"It ain't needed." Pa pivoted on broken-down boot heels, and his savage kick sent a stick of wood spinning at her. "Yell for me when it's here." He crammed a worn-out hat over his unwashed hair and shoved long arms into his coat. "I'll be at the corncrib."

"Pa, no. I ain't never done this. You ain't gone for Granny. You can't leave me to do this." She ran and grabbed at his worn shirtsleeve. "Stay." Her fingers clung with determination, even though she knew the danger of touching him.

As if they were nasty, he plucked her fingers from his sleeve. His cold inflection spoke of his disdain. "Take yer hands away—gurl. This be jest another untimely birthin'. She's goin' to kill it, ag'in. I got more important things on my mind, like a bear-damaged corncrib to repair." He reached for the door latch and disappeared into the frosty dawn.

His frail wife writhed in pain. But he didn't look back.

Fury and alarm choked Ella. She knew her mama wouldn't kill her babies. Her pa just didn't care. Crisp air rushed in at the wide-open door, and her hands shook as she closed it.

Mama struggled for another hour, growing weaker with each contraction. And Ella cried tears of relief when the blue-tinged baby, resembling a skinned rabbit, arrived. The infant slipped from its mother's tortured body, onto stained sheets between skinny bent legs. A short span of eerie silence filled the cabin. The shrill screams of tormented birthing ceased.

She stared in disbelief at the infant until it gave a pitiful wail. "It's here, Mama. It's ... here." She stammered on the simple words expressing her astonishment. "It's a real baby. This ain't nothin' like the pigs and cows droppin' young. Mama, did you hear me?"

"It's alive?" The woman sank back on the feather pillow, not bothering to examine the baby. Matted hair framed her head. The muslin gown, soaked with perspiration, clung to her emaciated form. Her once-beautiful face lacked color. She shook with chills. "If it's a girl child, I want it named Aileen, after my mam. Aileen ... such a soothing sound." Her blue-veined eyelids closed.

"It is a boy. He's awful little." Ella spoke in hushed tones and marveled at the miniature human and the miracle of birth she'd witnessed.

The baby's concave chest heaved. Delicate arms waved in the air, as his bluish-tinged legs and feet curled and drew tight to his body. He made pitiful raspy noises with every breath he tried to draw into his lungs.

With her eyes still shut, Mama smiled. "Ah, a boy. Let your pa name him."

"Pa's at the corncrib." She shoved sweaty strands of hair out of her eyes. "He walked out." She lifted a square of material and tried to wipe the quivering damp infant.

"Just as well." Mama's voice lost strength.

"The fire went out. He ain't helped with that *neither*." Bitterness welled inside her. She pressed her lips together to prevent another string of heated words.

"Don't fret. The kettle of water will still have warmth."

"He should've stayed!"

"Stop talking of him ... like that. He's done enough by you."

"I don't understand. Done *what* by me?"

"Hush. This be a woman's trial. God's punishment. Clear your brother's throat and mouth with your finger. Has the cord stopped beating? Tie it like I showed. Keep him warm. I need to rest, I'm ... so tired." Sighing, she closed her light blue eyes. "Jacob Huskey can now stop bothering with me. I done paid the price for his name, accepted my duty. I bore him a live one. A son."

"I'm not sure 'bout it, Mama. I don't know if I can cut it." Her fingers trembled. She wrinkled her nose while she concentrated on tying two narrow pieces of cloth about the slippery cord. It reminded her of spilled hog guts at butchering time, and she shuddered.

"You can do it."

"It's makin' me gag." Soft moans of disgust escaped her lips as she used a knife to slice at the shiny, supple cord. "It's done!" She felt as if she had run a lengthy race. "He's his own sep'rate self."

"I knew you'd do it. You're a ... brave child." Mama's bloodless lips formed the low words with short puffs of air. "Ella Dessa, stay that way. Keep faith in God ... alone. Without His touch, we can't stay strong. Don't let no man beat you down."

"I won't." She lifted the pot of lukewarm water out of the fireplace and set it on the clay floor. She used a dipper and poured water into a shallow pan. "I'll clean the baby."

She washed the baby's body and bundled a scrap of blanket close around his trembling form. She felt older than her years as she cuddled her brother and rubbed her nose over the softness of his head. Ella drew in a deep breath. His sweet scent reminded her of baby rabbits plucked from a summer nest of dried grass.

She tucked him into the bend of her mama's blue-veined arm. It took a moment or two of patting and jiggling Mama's shoulder to get her to open her eyes.

"He's right here by you. See?" Ella touched the baby's diminutive hand and caressed each perfect curled finger. "Look at him. He ain't cryin', now."

The baby's convulsing limbs relaxed. His face took on a waxen appearance.

"I'll look later. Ella Dessa, remember ... I love you."

"I love you, too." She leaned to kiss the baby's cool cheek. "This be home, little brother."

"Ella? I feel ..." Her mama grew silent.

"Open your eyes. Don't go to sleep." The chill in the cabin crept closer, surrounding the bed. She took Mama's face between her hands. "Open your eyes!"

A weak moan passed over ashen lips.

"No!" Ella panicked. She threw a frayed horse blanket over Mama's lower body and ran to open the cabin door. "Pa! She's in a bad way. Come quick." She screamed and beat the air with her clenched fists. "Please, hurry." Tears poured down her cheeks.

Her pa jumped from the doorway of the raised corncrib, tossed aside a splintered piece of wood, and jogged toward her. "It's here? What is it? It better—"

"Mama's in a bad way. We need Granny." She shrank aside to avoid physical contact. She wanted to slink into the shadows beside the cabin, but she continued to plead. "Don't let her die. I've done all I were told."

"I figgerd the baby were here. I ain't fetchin' the bossy granny-woman. She let my boy die years ago."

"Mama's strength's gone."

His calloused hands pawed at his unkempt beard, and his left eye squinted shut. "Take care of it, gurl. Women folk knows what to do. You're born with it. Don't tell me ya ain't. You're responsible fer what happens." He stared over her shoulder at the quiet bed and woman.

"No, not me. It ain't my fault. She's gonna die!"

"She ain't gonna die if ya take kerr of things the right way." Pa grabbed her shoulders, shaking her. The back of her head banged against the doorframe. "You an' her God will be to blame fer anythin' bad. Ya stupid, gurl-child." His fingers pinched her thin arms. "Should've left the wildcat to eat ya. I wish it had finished clawin' yer head off."

Shocked by his vicious declaration, she recognized pure loathing in his scorn. He sneered at her scarred neck. She sought to cover the bumpy disfigurement with her hands, but he held her arms too tight. She tried to wrench herself out of his grip while recalling how he slapped and beat her mother.

"Are—are you gonna beat me, 'cause you wish I died?" she yelled, just as a raspy, choking noise filled the room.

6

Pa released her arms.

Ella ran to the bed and jostled Mama's shoulder. "Mama, look at me."

A soft sigh passed between parted lips.

The room grew unearthly quiet.

Ella stumbled away. She opened her mouth to scream, but no sound came out. Her shaky hands covered her mouth, and she thought about running away. But instead, in desperation, she reached for her pa.

Pa's expression changed, showing fear and confusion, and he shoved her sideways. His forceful push sent her into a crumpled heap on the hard-packed floor. "I'm leavin'."

He walked out.

"No!"

A piercing whistle sounded as he called their old mare out of the side field.

"No." Ella whimpered and crawled toward the door. She grabbed the wall, stood, and stepped out into the brisk autumn air. Her breath rose in white puffs. Once again, she felt as if the panther clawed at her, disfiguring her, but it was her heart shredding into pieces.

She staggered through the doorway.

"Git back inside." Pa grabbed a worn bridle off a fence post and slipped it over the horse's head. His right arm spasmed as he doubled the reins over his hand and pulled them tight. "Git back to yer mama."

"Stay. Please?" She held out a hand to him, longing for him to make her believe he cared. "Pa, I'll keep my neck covered so you can't see the nasty scars. Please? I don't want to be alone."

Pa ignored her pleas and stepped atop a log. He threw a long leg over the bare back of the horse and hoisted himself up.

She experienced a sickening wave of shock rise in the back of her throat. It threatened to strangle her. Ella rubbed her face, wiping at tears.

Pa hates tears.

Before he nudged the horse with his heels, he stared at her—wild-eyed. His thin back hunched over the horse's neck and caused his backbone to show through the worn material of his muslin shirt. His booted feet hung below the horse's belly.

Her body sagged against the log wall. She stared in stunned disbelief until frost-tinged leaves of the mountain's foliage hid the man riding away. The glow of the morning sun topped the ridge. It seemed like an evil iron vice gripped her chest, crushing her. She moaned and tried to fill her lungs, even as Pa's hollered curses echoed along the mountain ridge.

"Nooo! You can't leave me. Come—back." She bent at the waist and clenched her arms across her midsection. It wasn't her pa's departure torturing her. The truth hit her. Almost gagging on the realization her mama had died, she dropped to her knees in the dirt and stony rubble.

Not Mama.

Ella fought to breathe, to feel, but a weight of numbness encompassed her while random thoughts flashed in her mind.

Pa's gone. What if Pa don't come back?

He ain't seen the baby.

"He wouldn't have left a boy baby. It's just me he hates 'cause I lived. The others died," she whispered. Now, he'd blame her for Mama's death. "He'd have stayed here, if I'd showed him the baby."

She raised her head, peering through her tousled hair, expecting to see him ride into the clearing. Her fingers furrowed the dirt. The understanding of what Pa's temperament would be like when he returned caused her to quake with fear. He'd make her the brunt of his rage. Mama wouldn't be there to step between them when he reached for the twisted leather strap hung behind the door.

The baby.

He was alone inside. She brushed hair out of her face, stood, and faced the open door. *I'll have to be his mama.* Her thoughts became more rational. She accepted the responsibility and feared punishment. *I'll love him and protect him like Mama did me. I can do it. I'll bear the strap for him.*

Trepidation filled her heart and soul as she slipped into the sparsely furnished room.

Chapter 2

The stillness told her.

His raspy breaths had ceased. Ella trembled.

She knew there was no one to step in and assist her. She dried her tears on the backs of her hands and took on the heartrending task an older woman should've performed.

She had observed mountain women countless times in her short life. No one need remind her life was hard in the backwoods. She knew it dealt out raw deals and equal blows to young and old. She had seen life's handiwork and witnessed agonizing sorrow.

She knelt before the smoky fireplace and stacked kindling and firewood inside the box.

After lugging more water into the cabin, she held back her own gnawing emotions and did her best washing her mama's battered body.

She slipped a tattered, faded brown gown on the baby. It buttoned down the back with pea-sized, needle-drilled wooden buttons and swallowed his tiny form. Ella had worn it, and her mama had saved it for the next child to wear.

Her mama once told her of other premature infants through the years—miniature samples of life—but they all appeared insignificant in Pa's eyes. Each time one was lost, he wrapped it in a piece of discarded cloth before placing it in the cold earth under the pines.

"I never saw them," she whispered to the quiet room. She didn't know how many died. It seemed like there were four—four nameless babies. After each loss, Pa's temper grew more rabid. She learned to dread how the shaking of his right arm heralded his fits of fury.

Or did his temper make his arm quiver?

Of course, there were whispered stories when the valley women gathered to quilt each month. Glances toward her mama, sad ones of fleeting pity, said more than words. Then there were the multi-colored wild flowers, which her mama picked in secret and scattered in woodsy shadows. They marked the infants' insignificant burial holes.

Ella left her mama's corpse undressed because she couldn't lift her. She did the second best and tucked a clean—but ragged—blanket over the lifeless form. Bile rose from the pit of her empty stomach. She talked to the silence pervading the cabin.

"Mama, he ain't ever hurtin' you no more. I hate him. Don't tell me I can't hate him, 'cause I do. There's no feeling in him. God couldn't even like him." Her fingers stroked a length of her mother's blond hair. "Oh, Mama. Now I … I ain't got nobody. He's gonna come back. His arm will start jiggling, and it'll just be me here. He'll center his eye on me. You know he'll blame me. Why'd he say he should've let the mountain lion kill me? Why does he hate me?"

Pa's mean words made her heart fill with glass-like shards. His extreme dislike caused her chest to hurt. But then, she realized he even hated God. His loud curses said as much. With inner resolve, she walked to the hooks on the wall and lifted down one of her mama's dresses.

****

The sun stood straight up and provided an illusion of warmth to the middle of the day. Ella sat on the flat stone sill in the cabin's doorway. She focused her eyes on the steep trail and waited. The beating of her heart seemed almost an audible sound, which flooded her ears and pounded.

She didn't cry. *He might come back.* She licked her dry lips and stared down the trail.

Gone were her bloodied clothes. She had donned her mama's next-to-best dress and pinned up her unwashed hair. A narrow, gathered strip of white material edged the cuffs and offset the faded-brown tint of the dress. It produced the essence of a true ruffle.

Unshakeable weariness enveloped her. She felt as if she had aged—so she deserved the right to wear the adult dress. So what if it was too long? *Mama won't care ... not no more. She told me I'd soon wear longer skirts.* Ella's mother had mentioned cutting apart one of her own three skirts to make her a new dress.

With slow movements, her shaky fingertips explored the top edge of the high neckline. *It hides my ugly neck so people ain't going to see the claw marks. Pa won't be reminded he saved nothin' but a girl-child.*

She scarcely noticed the cold breeze and the hungry gnawing of her empty belly.

She shivered as a horse whinnied. Pa rode up, turned sideways on the animal's back, and offered his hand to the short midwife riding behind him.

"I don't need yer help, Jacob. Ye don't do it out of kindness." Spry for her age, Granny Hanks slid off the horse with her satchel in hand. "If'n the wagon had been hitched, I wouldn't have rode double with ya." Contempt laced her croaky voice.

With hunched shoulders, Ella leaned sideways in the doorway and felt the midwife shove past her. She caught a whiff of crushed herbs, leeks, and grasses scenting the folds of the woman's gray skirt. The tips of Granny's scrawny fingers caressed her bowed head.

That slight touch of unspoken compassion broke her tight reserve—much like a log dam bursting before a flash flood. With sobs skinning her insides apart, she fell forward, crouched on her hands and knees, and wailed out her grief to the forest-covered mountainside.

"*Mama*, Mama, Mama!"

"Stop it. Shet up." Pa's boot came close to her head. "What're ya doin' with yer mama's brown dress on? Who do ya think ya are? You git in there with that stinkin' granny woman."

His calloused hands jerked her away from her blinding anguish, grabbed her at the elbows, and snatched her to her bare feet. She lifted the hem of the long dress and staggered into the cabin—in time to see shock register on Granny's face and transfixed eyes.

The old woman took one sweeping look of the tidy bed and its pale occupants.

Ella realized the midwife hadn't expected to view two corpses laid out in final repose.

"Ach, no!" The woman whirled on Jacob. She lifted a crooked finger to his bearded face, stood as tall as her five-foot stance would allow, and declared, "She's gone. Ye came fer me too late." Her nut-brown eyes grew black as nugget coal. "Too late. I think ye knew it. You're a wretched man!"

Granny's face and bushy white eyebrows could almost make a person believe in witches. Her right eye set lower in her face than the left, her top lip had no curve to it, and her nose twisted to the right—broken by the fall off a frisky mule. Wrinkles cut deep into her tanned, leathery skin and scrunched up her narrow face.

Ella felt awed Granny Hanks dared to lash out at her pa, and she hiccupped with the effort to stop crying.

"You knew the truth in this." The woman, with her coiled white knob of hair shaking on top of her head, railed on at him for not fetching her before the birth. "An' this child shouldn't of had to do the prep'rations alone! Why didn't ye come fer me?"

With growing dread, Ella expected her pa to lose his temper. Would he harm the old woman?

Pa's bad eye squinted. He hooked his big thumbs through his leather belt, and shrugged, even though fear flickered beneath his dark gaze. He drew his bone-thin shoulders up to his neck, amid the midwife's ranting, but he avoided a glance at the lumpy bed. He kept his attention on the open door. His right hand convulsed in an uncontrollable twitch, and the movement extended to involve his lower arm. His thumbs gripped his belt, but that didn't stop the violent spasm.

"Answer me, Jacob Huskey!" Granny stepped closer.

The jerking hand freed itself and bumped against his thigh like a dying chicken.

Silence reigned for a minute. Ella moaned and cowered. *Ohh, be quiet, Granny. He's goin' to hit you.* She slid into a gloomy corner of the room, wishing she could crawl beneath the hard-packed floor.

Pa's bloodshot eyes twitched, but he defended himself and his actions by muttering, "Meara birthed Ella by herself with no help by a midwife. She ain't asked fer ya. She had Ella. Meara knew about birthin'. Don't blame me."

"Well, Meara didn't know 'nough." Granny Hanks snorted the words with outward disgust at him. "I see you'll stand by yer rigid, unrelentin' attitude of denial. Ella Dessa, come here, child."

"Uh-huh." She didn't want to.

Her pa's entire right arm shook with tremors. She wanted to scream a warning. *Granny, he'll see his arm, and it'll make him mad-dog crazy.*

"Come here." The old midwife motioned.

"Granny, he'll bash you with it," she said, but her whispered words went unheard. She positioned her back tight to the log wall.

"Jacob!" Granny shook her finger and continued her tirade. "Yer wife lost wee ones many times, an' she birthed Ella Dessa twelve years past. She were too tired to do this one more time. You men don't know how to control thyself. Can't figger how's the Good Lord made ye like he did, but then I don't question The Maker. *Girl!* Fetch me the baby."

Ella heard the involuntary intake of breath from her pa.

"What?" He half turned toward the bed and snatched the filthy hat off his head. He hadn't known about the infant. "Why you—" His face flushed crimson, and his flat lips twisted with fury as he gnashed his teeth at Ella Dessa.

She realized he wouldn't strike her with the midwife as a witness. His breath became a snake-like hiss. She edged past him and gathered the small bundle. With a wrinkled cloth covering its miniature remains, it could've been no more than a loaf of sweet bread she held, a loaf—wrapped to retain dissipating warmth.

"Didn't live but a short time." Straight-armed, she offered him to Granny.

The aged woman turned back the cloth, lifted the rumpled skirt of the lengthy gown, and checked the gender of the baby. Her seamed face softened. Its worn contours seemed to grow more youthful.

"A son," the midwife whispered.

Pa flinched at the knowledge of the baby's sex. His unreadable eyes rapidly blinked as he stared at the infant. He didn't try to get any closer.

"Ach, such a waste." Granny's large-knuckled fingers moved with reverence, touched the delicate curved ears, and smoothed the downy patch of light hair on top of the perfect, rounded head. The baby was elfin, and she cupped his whole head in the palm of her creased hand. Using the back of her other hand, she wiped at her eyes.

"This baby were too small to live." She placed the baby on the split-pine table and motioned Ella to cover him. Without gazing at Jacob, she spoke. "It be a boy, ye know, but he's gone."

He glared at the midwife as he held his convulsive arm with his left hand, but he didn't react in response to the woman's bitterness nor show the slightest distraught emotion. The knuckles of his left hand turned white with an attempt to hold his spasmodic right arm.

"Yer son, Jacob Huskey. Now, go fetch a death's coolin' board from the storekeeper. Brings it here—right smart. It's nigh on noon. Walter Beckler has one. We need it fer the wake. I'm supposin' ye never made a board in case of a burial. Let people know along the way."

Ella watched Pa use his left hand to shove his salt-marked hat tighter on his head. He ducked through the low doorway, caught the horse's rope bridle, and rode away. Astonished he chose to obey the midwife; she stepped to the open door and watched his weary horse once more disappear down the leaf-strewn path.

She wished more than anything it could be Pa placed on a cooling board instead of Mama.

Chapter 3

$\mathcal{W}$ord of Meara's death spread over the tree-shrouded mountain, through the short cove, and along ridged slopes. People left their chores undone. They came by foot, wagon, mule, and horse, winding upward on the trail. Men brought along numerous types of saws, hammers, and various lengths of boards to fashion a simple coffin.

The late afternoon sun skimmed the tops of trees, lit the sharp ridges, and shone over the rock-dotted field close to the cabin. It caused the autumn foliage to reflect a promise of flaming colors, which would appear after a heavy frost.

The wake wouldn't be elaborate, but it would illustrate everyone's respect for the dead woman. The human contact layered a fleeting comfort on Ella's broken heart. Women set out food they brought with them, or they prepared uncomplicated meals over the fireplace. Men started an outside fire. The open ends of wagons became extra makeshift tables for food preparation.

Voices remained subdued as adults conversed with each other or murmured their condolences to Jacob. Children ran off to play among trees and rocky outcroppings, their lives and emotions not impacted by Ella's sorrow and loss.

The air turned sharper. People donned coats and shawls. The sound of saws and hammers heralded the building of the pine coffin. The muted thud and chink of shovel and pick informed her of the rocky ground's disturbance—its violation—to form a grave. It needed to be ready for the spark of dawn when the burial would commence. It would take place extremely early so families could return to unattended homesteads and animals. The thump, thump of digging jarred through Ella's head until she wanted to cover her ears.

Instead, she sprinted barefooted to the moss-covered springhouse, concealed within the irregular tree line, above the field. She opened the tiny door, ducked inside, and swung it shut behind her. She pulled the hem of her mama's dress between her legs, from back to front, and tucked it under the cloth belt tied around her waist. She meant to keep the skirt off the damp ground inside the log building, which straddled a clear flow of icy water.

With a ragged gasp, she crouched in the protective shelter, breathed the familiar scent of soggy earth, and let the repetitious trickling water wipe out the echo of the metal pick and shovel. A nippy breeze sighed through the gaps in the log walls and shadows grew deeper. She wrapped her arms over her knees and realized she forgot a shawl. Her bare feet grew chilled from contact with the moist soil and decaying plant matter.

Dead leaves blew against the outside of the log wall. They rustled and fluttered as if forcing their way through the gaps between logs in the unchinked barrier. Water sprang through a cluster of boulders, right at the point where the backside of the springhouse came against it. The stream ran across the face of rocks and a stone slab Pa had positioned to construct a diminutive waterfall. With his bare hands and a pick, he had removed surface rocks and hollowed out a deeper pool.

Set in the swirling, clear water, about eight inches down, were stone jars. Their protected necks protruded above the stream. Ella knew one held milk from Mama's cow.

While a jab of regret pierced through her heart, she stared at the stoneware. Water gurgled past them, and a gold leaf bounced along the top of the water. Was it only yesterday morning she saw her mama trudge to the springhouse with a bucket of milk?

Mama had stopped and massaged her lower back. The labor had begun. Mama put off telling Pa because it was too early for the baby. Ella sniffled and wiped at her runny nose with the back of her hand.

I should've toted the milk here.

Although shade collected where she huddled, she could peer through spaces in the log walls. To her right, the sun sat on the adjacent mountaintop. The thin shimmers of golden light reached beyond the irregular parcel of land, cleared of trees and small boulders. The coming sunset would crowd out the green of the pines, darken them, and add a blaze of light to higher trees blanketing the mountains.

The view wrenched her breath away. Her mama would miss autumn's beauty and the fellowship of the women. She could see the broadening gloom envelop the men carrying the finished coffin toward the weather-beaten cabin.

It wasn't a fancy box. It wasn't six-sided. She watched them set the box of death near the door. Smoke from the chimney and the outside fire swirled and united above the men's heads and danced with the undecided wind.

"Oh, Mama, you'd love this gathering," she whispered. "Laura Stuart done brought a sweet potato pie. Mrs. Clanders is simmerin' one of her beloved chickens. I don't know all the folks who've come, but it's so special. You'd be proud to be called their friend. If only you were here."

She shivered and dried her tears. Her consideration turned to the unnamed infant reposing in her mama's arm. A woman she didn't know had suggested she sit and hold the dead baby.

"Mama, she said it'd teach me about life, but Rebecca Foster disagreed, and made her stop insistin'. I hope it don't grieve you none, Mama," she continued, "but he didn't feel the same—the same as 'fore he died. He felt cold, like I feel right now."

A subtle noise caught her attention.

A rock rolled and bounced down the slope, rustling the dried leaves.

She peeked through weathered cracks on the opposite side of the squatty springhouse. Someone giggled in anticipation or reserved nervousness. Two people walked the high ground behind the spring. They came down the hill and headed alongside the building, concealed from the cabin.

Only a gray skirt showed. It swept the matted leaves lying on the ground. Then the black material of a pair of pants joined it. The low sides and extended overhang of the springhouse roof didn't allow her to see faces. She clamped her hands over her mouth and breathed through her nose.

"We need to go back. My father will look for me. It'll soon be dark." The girl's voice became low and teasing. "Want me to get in trouble 'cause of you?"

"Don't worry. You saw how busy he was—talking to the men. I've missed you."

"I missed you."

Two hands dropped into view. A young man's left hand, with fine reddish hair sprinkling the top, gripped the more slender feminine hand. His fingers moved to encircle the wrist.

"You're too pretty to worry."

"Father doesn't like you." Her right hand twisted to break free. Another faint giggle accompanied the struggling fingers. "He says you act too bold, and I'm too young to think of boys."

"Bold? That's not true! What do you say? Besides, he isn't your real father."

"Well, perhaps he's right."

"He's jealous. He wishes he were our age. Please, let me hold you."

"We should go back." The hands fought, fingers entangled. "Please?"

"You turned sixteen in August. See, I remembered." His voice grew muffled, as if he spoke through cloth or something else. "Hmmm, your hair smells like summer sunshine. I bet you never had anyone tell you that. You're my sunshine."

"I want to go back." The voice trembled with uncertainty. "Let go."

Ella drew a rapid breath and held it. She pressed her fingers against her lips and pushed them into her teeth—to keep any sound from escaping. Her crouched position caused her thighs to burn and ache.

"No, I want my kiss." The black legs closed the distance between them. The heavy folds of the skirt seemed to wrap themselves about the legs, enveloping them in gray waves. "You promised me two months ago after the evening service. You said, the next time we saw one another you'd kiss me. So—it's now." His left hand disappeared.

The skirt dipped and moved away but abruptly swung back into position alongside the black pants. "I don't think we should." The teasing tone in the female voice faded, and a frantic tremor took its place. "You're hurting my arms. Please, take your hands away."

The legs stiffened and braced themselves. "No. You promised."

The skirt rippled as if shaken. "Take your hands off me!"

"Give me one kiss. Just one."

"No!" A plain cotton petticoat showed under the swaying hem. The skirt lifted higher and exposed a black stocking and high-cut shoe. "Don't do that. Please. It hurts."

"Quit fighting me." The resounding slap of a hand hitting bare skin echoed like an explosion in the quiet woods. "Keep it quiet. You want your father to come running? Come here." The sound of material tearing accompanied his words.

The hiccupped noise of shocked sobs made Ella shut her eyes, but her ears still heard the girl's hysterical protest. She smashed her face against her bent knees. She trembled and sought to blot out sounds on the other side of the log wall. Fright caused her to feel as if she might wet her clothes.

Oh, God, make him go away. Make him let her go!

"Ella Dessa! Where are ya?" The demand rang in the clear air.

Pa!

A smothered curse followed the shout. The black pants strode away and moved into the deepening dusk under the trees.

The gray skirt swung in the opposite direction, as the girl fell against the side of the rustic springhouse. Two shaky hands grabbed at the dried saplings forming the short overhang. Hoarse sobs died to a muffled whimper.

"Ella Dessa?" Pa's voice sounded close—too close.

19

She didn't budge. She wondered if her pa heard the muted sobs. Where was he? The sun was gone. Only an orange glow showed on the mountaintop. She shook with chills, and her wet toes ached.

The skirt rippled and snagged a mossy log. It made its way along the length of the wall and hesitated at the front corner. Ella heard her pa call again, but he seemed farther down the hill. The skirt fluttered and running legs took it away from the vicinity.

She rose from her cramped position, scrambled to the door, and pushed it open. She ducked under the low header and loosened her skirt's hem from the waistband. Her shaky legs carried her into the cleared field by their cabin, just as Pa rounded the front corner.

He yanked her to an abrupt stop. His clothes smelled of aged sweat and fire smoke. "Leigh's goin' to speak a few words. Where'd ya git off to?"

She gulped for breath and avoided his snappish eyes. "I was in the woods, thinking 'bout Mama."

Droplets of tears slid along her cheeks. Pa's fingernails bit deeper into her arm. The pain reminded her of the hands she saw through gaps in the logs. Immediately, her eyes swept over the silent mourners assembled in the dusky light.

No gray skirt.

More than one man or boy wore dark pants. Who was the guilty one? Was he even present? She winced at the increased pressure on her arm.

"Please. It hurts."

"Don't run off, ag'in." He released her arm and grabbed his right hand with his left, in order to stop its involuntary movement.

With her head bowed, she sought refuge among the women. Their calloused hands reached to comfort her. Laura Stuart snatched her tight to her ample bosom. Ella leaned into the cushiony warmth.

Leigh Chesley cleared his throat. His bespectacled eyes swept over the men, women, and children. After years of filling in when the circuit rider couldn't make a stop, Leigh had recently agreed to be the cove's preacher.

He lifted a hand for silence. "It's always hard to know where to start with a sorrow like this. What do I say to bring comfort? Whilst he walked on earth, Jesus would've placed his hand on our beloved Meara and raised her. But he ain't here. We must face the dismal fact of death, but also the rewards death brings to those who go before us. Then, we must hold fast 'til we see our coming Lord. Hope for peace as you trust in him like the Bible says."

"Amen." Laura kissed the top of Ella's head. "You poor child—so pitiful. May you have peace." Her breath smelled like the chicory coffee she brewed and drank all afternoon.

Ella squirmed and wanted to break free from the hands holding her, but she wasn't quite willing to leave the warm nest provided by the woman's dress and chubby arms. She didn't like everyone gawking at her. She wasn't pitiful.

Her freezing toes hurt. She balanced on her right foot and drew her left foot higher under the dress. She tried to warm her foot by snugging it against the back of her right leg.

"As darkness settles on us, some of you will sit up with little Ella Dessa and our brother, Jacob. A few of you will make your way down dim, foreboding trails to your homes. I'm going to ask God's protection on those leaving tonight and God's blessing on those staying." His next words were softer. "We'll hold Meara's burying at daybreak, yonder on the hill, where the men placed her grave. Shall we bow our heads and thank God that Meara's been released from this earth and welcomed into the wonderful light of Heaven?"

Leigh prayed a short prayer as the inky fingers of darkness gripped and enclosed the clearing.

The prayer ended. Women led little children into the cabin's crowded warmth, but Ella stayed behind. She felt forgotten.

Torches crackled to life and lanterns glowed. The odor of oil and smoke mixed with the strong and earthy bouquet of rotted leaves and horse manure. Two mongrel dogs snarled with exposed teeth and circled each other. Men collected scattered tools and hitched horses and mules to wagons and carts.

She watched torches weave amongst the seven wagons, as a few men climbed into high seats. She shivered and counted three wagons pulling out as a group. They had tight-wrapped torches stuck into hollow poles tied near the drivers. The ride down the mountain would be risky in the moonless night.

Within minutes, the last wagon bumped over rocks and disappeared. In the crisp fall night, the torches flickered through the woods like misplaced summer fireflies.

Silence descended, until a man added logs to the campfire, and a screech owl called from the woods. Sparks and flames brought light and sound to the adjoining clearing. Her body shook with chills, but she resisted the urge to walk past the topless coffin and enter the cabin's warmth.

"Ella?" Rebecca Foster stuck her head outside. "Oh, there you are. Child, what are you doing in the dark? Come in. It's cold. We can't have you taking sick."

"No." She shook her head at the tall, lissome woman with black hair. "A little while longer. Please?"

Seeming uncertain, Rebecca stepped closer and studied her face. "You all right? Katy would like for you to come inside."

Katy Stuart was ten. Normally, Ella would've been thrilled to talk to a friend, but she had no desire to go inside where Mama's body lay. "Tell her I'll be there, right soon."

She watched the door close.

A gathering of eight men and three teen boys circled the fire. They talked and warmed their hands. Most of the faces were strange to her. She mulled over what took place by the spring. Which one of them had attacked the girl? And where was she now?

The cabin door opened.

"Ella Dessa, we need you to come in. Rebecca told me you lingered behind. We can't keep worrying about you out there in the dark. Come here, child." Laura reached for her arm and tugged. "Come. We'll all be with you."

She thought, *be with me? Why do I need you with me?* Instead of asking questions, she bowed her head and submitted to Laura's insistent clasp on her upper arm. But she had hardly turned her back to the fire when she heard her pa's rumbled laughter.

A man chuckled and made a sarcastic remark in return.

With a surge of anger, she shrugged off Laura's hand. "I hate him." Her fingers clung to the door. *How can he laugh? Mama's dead.*

"Ella Dessa? What'd you say?" Laura sounded shocked.

22

"Nothin'."

"I think you did, but I'll overlook it—seein's how things are. Come inside and see if you approve."

"Approve?" She swallowed in an attempt to dislodge the thickness in her throat.

"Of course. Come with me. We placed the cooling board on the table, 'cause of the cabin being small—without much room. I figured we needed seats more than the table."

The heat in the room hit her in the face. The cabin overflowed with downcast faces and sad eyes contemplating her every move. Laura led her to the table. Mama's body lay face up on the narrow board.

Granny had managed to clothe Mama in her faded-blue Sunday meeting dress. Its folds covered her skinny legs. Seven carved wooden buttons decorated the bodice. One large piece of unbleached muslin hid the hole-drilled wooden slab from view, and a sprinkling of embroidered roses decorated one hemmed corner. Copper coins covered the lids of her mama's wonderful blue eyes.

Everyone waited for her to speak, but the clog in her throat grew thicker. Conversation trickled to a stop. An uneasy hush overflowed the room.

"It's … it's very nice." She choked on the words. "That were Mama's finest pretty dress."

The dead infant occupied the stiff bend of Mama's blue-clothed arm. A generous woman supplied a decent shawl to wrap the baby. His perfect white face seemed chiseled out of mountain marble. A miniature bonnet covered his head—a bonnet cut and hand-sewn from a piece of unbleached muslin. With doubled white thread, a line of delicate embroidered roses fanned out along the top. Two scraps of blue ribbon made the tie, and the frayed bow hid the infant's tiny chin.

Ella felt herself tremble.

The ache in her chest threatened to consume her. She pressed her hands to her face and sobbed, and Laura's arms enclosed her in a soft cocoon. Ella wailed until pure emptiness pushed away the throbbing in her heart and the crying stopped, but Laura continued to coo and cradle her as if she were a baby.

Talk resumed.

Granny Hanks moved through the crowded room and laid a bony hand on her shoulder. "Ella Dessa, eat a mite. Ye haven't touched a thing all day. Laura, take her to the chair by the fire."

She sank into the only chair in the room, besides an old rocker moved near the table, and dried her face on her skirt. Her whole body felt drained of strength, but she surveyed the room. Pulled away from the table, one bench crowded the space near the fire. Three girls, slightly younger than her, occupied it. They sat, thigh to thigh. They chatted and warmed their hands, but avoided her eyes.

The second bench remained near the table. Two elderly women used it and kept vigil over the bodies. Three women stood close to the table, talked in whispered voices, and sent searching glances in her direction. A fourth woman sat in the rocker and cradled a sleeping baby. Dark hair covered its round head. A chubby and dimpled hand protruded from a fold in the blanket.

Ella fought tears, swallowed, and averted her gaze from the healthy infant. A borrowed quilt covered her parents' bumpy bed. Six children, varying in age, from crawlers to four years, sprawled together in a mixed fashion—legs and arms entwined—all sound asleep. The fire's flames danced irregular hints of light over their peaceful forms.

Two boys, about the age of eight, sat on her pa's bear pelt. Its shaggy bulk covered the clay floor near the table. With their hips and shoulders touching the wall and their blond heads close together, they played with a stack of her wooden blocks. She couldn't recall their first names. She knew they were twins, orphaned by a winter sickness that took their parents two years before. Leigh and Naomi Chesley, with no children of their own, felt God compelled them to raise the boys.

While bent over the fireplace, Velma Clanders stirred the contents of an iron pot hanging from a hook. She tapped a wooden spoon on the pot's rim and smiled over her shoulder.

"I hopes you're hungry, Ella Dessa." The wide gap between her front teeth showed in the fire's light, and her words always had a slight whistle to them. Her thin dark hair slipped from a haphazard bun at the base of her neck. Little spikes of hair stuck out, resembling a miniature porcupine.

"I'm not hungry."

Ella liked Velma. The woman always treated her like an adult and didn't expect perfection in manners. The summer before, she had walked up to help Mama put in a garden—said it was a relief to get away from her younguns.

Velma, her husband, and five children were considered newcomers to the rest of the mountain families, because back in the spring, they had moved into a vacant trapper's cabin on Pelter's Creek. Friendly, talkative, and talented in decorative stitching, Velma loved to participate in any social gathering. She fast became a regular at Naomi's, where quilters met each month to escape life's hardships.

Was it only last month her mama had sewn a shirt for one of Velma's boys, while others sat around the perimeter of the quilt frame?

"Velma?" She tried to think of a nice thing to say. "Where's your children?"

"Agatha Hood agreed to have 'em all night at her place. She loves children. I knew I couldn't keeps up with 'em. Honey, you're gonna loves what I fixed. Of course, that's besides the chicken. I mixed fresh bear gravy with the last veg'ables from my spent garden. The men'll eat outside and us women inside. Did Granny tells you some of the men will sleep in the barn and in the wagons that remain?"

"No."

"They will. We're much too crowded in here. Can't walk, hardly. Guess you kin takes those girls to the loft with you if they can't stays awake. Us women will stand in for you during the night hours. I can't do less for your mama. Bless her soul. She never complained about her lot in life. I'll miss her quiet comfort and helping hands."

"Thank you." She felt numb to all the kindness. Her eyes chanced another look at the three girls. Laura's redheaded daughter, Katy, sat with them, but the faces of the other two were only vaguely familiar.

Katy gave her an uncertain smile. "We might try to stay up all night."

"That's nice." Ella didn't care what they did.

The aroma of food caused her to feel light-headed, and her stomach grumbled. She wanted to eat, but it seemed unfitting with Mama lying on the table. Squeezing her eyes shut, she hoped to blot the room out of her mind and get control of her thoughts.

What was Pa laughin' about? How can he be so evil?

"Ella Dessa?" Granny shook her shoulder. She held a steaming plate of food with hands flecked with suds—as if she had just taken them out of a pan of wash water. "Velma were askin' if ye wanted a piece of warm bread with yer meal."

"Yes, I'd like bread." She tried to focus her eyes. Had she fallen asleep sitting up? "Thank you." She accepted the plate of sliced chicken and a gravy-flooded mixture of vegetables.

Granny laid dark bread on the side of the plate. "There. Eat an' then we'll fill the plate fer another. There ain't enough of 'em to go 'round." She wiped chapped hands on the apron tied to her bone-thin waist.

"They could have this." She set the plate in her lap. Its warmth felt good on her thighs, but her stomach protested at the idea of eating.

"No. You *eat*." Granny hobbled toward the side of the bed. She spoke to someone in the shadows behind a large piece of muslin, which Ella's mother had hung over a rope, tied crosswise in the corner, for privacy. It made a curtain of sorts when pulled out from the wall. "Fern? What's the problem? Why are ye sittin' back there on the bed?"

"I—I'm watching the babies." A tall teenage girl stood, her oval face lit by the fire's glow.

"The babies are asleep. Ye can leave 'em." Granny tugged the curtain out of the way. "Come, eat with Ella Dessa, an' keep her company."

The dark-haired girl held a crumpled piece of white material in her hands. "I'm also doing mending."

Ella lifted the piece of bread to her lips. But she paused—open mouthed. She recognized the low voice and the full gray skirt. The pale-faced teenager was the girl she had heard by the springhouse.

Chapter 4

"Fern, I know ye can't see behind that curtain." Granny's raspy voice grew irritated. "Git out by the fire."

A child rolled over on the bed and whimpered.

Fern nodded and clutched the material to her fully developed chest.

"Katy, let Fern set there. Go help yer mama carry food." Granny's scrawny arms showed below rolled sleeves. She flailed her hands in the air, letting Katy know she better move.

"Yes'um." The red-haired girl jumped to obey. Her lumpy thick braids bounced. "I'll talk to you later." Her hand caressed Ella's shoulder as she slipped past.

Fern sought a place on the bench and crowded the two younger girls. a beige wool woven shawl hugged her narrow shoulders. A knot held it closed. She fixed troubled eyes on the item in her lap. Her unsteady fingers pushed a needle in and out along a tear extending from the shoulder seam and down the front of a plain muslin blouse.

The younger girls went back to talking.

Ella ignored the hot tin plate balanced on her knees and observed Fern. The white-faced teen finished the hurried stitches and smoothed the fabric with shaky fingers—as if erasing an invisible imprint. Her deep brown eyes swept sideways to meet Ella's.

Ella tried to smile. "My name's Ella Dessa. My mama, she's the one ..."

"I know. I'm sorry." Fern's eyes dropped to the material in her hands.

Even though her heart ached for the older girl, Ella couldn't let Fern know she witnessed the incident.

She nibbled at the piece of bread, but her stomach rebelled at eating the gravy-swamped vegetables. She tried not to act curious as Fern stood, furtively searched the crowded room, and slipped into the shadows by the bed.

With hunched shoulders, the girl drew off the shawl. Her white chemise and pale arms gleamed in the fire's light, and Ella spied muted, lavender marks heralding the darkening of cruel bruises. Fern pulled on the repaired blouse, buttoned it, and hurried back to the bench.

Velma walked to the fireplace, her hands full of a variety of bowls. "Fern can you helps Katy and her mama carry vittles to the men?"

"I thought I'd stay inside." Fern's fingers twisted the fabric of her skirt.

"Humm." Velma ladled more gravy and chunky vegetables into a large wooden bowl balanced in her left hand. "Had to dig this bowl out of my wagon. I keep it for feeding baby chicks when I haves some. I washed it. Naomi also had a couple more bowls." She held the full bowl out to Fern. "Here."

"I—I didn't bring a heavy shawl. Please, let me stay in." Her voice was pleasant but strained. "Here comes Katy, now." She pointed over her shoulder.

Velma acted puzzled by the teen's refusal but handed the red-haired girl the bowl. "Take this, Katy."

Fern rose from the bench. "I'll help fill bowls. Surely, there's something else you need to do." She grabbed Velma's big wooden spoon, tucked her gray skirt under her legs and hips, and squatted by the fire.

The woman straightened and rubbed at her lower spine. Her hand traveled forward to pat her stomach. A grimace distorted her narrow face. "Just sets that bowl on the table so Katy can see it. Spoons are on a towel.

When the men finish eating, I want you and Ella to collects the dirty stuff. You can borrow my shawl. It's double-layered."

"Yes, Ma'am." Fern's shoulders sagged. She filled the bowl, taking more time than necessary.

Only Ella could guess the reason for her reluctance to go outside.

"Fern," she whispered. "I can do it. I don't mind fetchin' the dishes and bowls. You wait inside."

The girl's eyes glistened, but she shook her head. "Thanks. But you shouldn't have to do it."

Curiosity plagued Ella. She wanted to go outside and study each man and boy gathered near the fire. The person who attacked Fern might be with them. She also needed to get out from under the sympathetic looks of the well-meaning women. The log walls had become barriers surrounding her.

"Well, then I want to help. I haven't touched this food. Think we could slip it outside to my pa?"

Fern stood with two steaming bowls in her hands and nodded. "Let me get my shawl off the bed. Pick up a spoon at the table."

"Give me one bowl to hold. My shawl's on the peg beside the bed. Could you fetch it and drape it over one of my shoulders?"

They made it out the door unnoticed and stood in the dark with their backs to the cabin's front wall. By the fire, four of the men sopped gravy with folded pieces of bread, and wiped their lips on shirtsleeves. Others appeared to wait for food.

A chilly breeze swept the darkened hill and rustled the unseen trees. The warm tin plate and bowl felt comforting in Ella's hands. Before she thought better, she said, "Do you see him?"

"Who? Your father? He's to the left of the fire."

She bit her lip. She had accidently referred to Fern's attacker. "Yes, that's Pa. I'll take this to him." She hurried into the yellow circle of firelight and lifted the plate.

"I done ate." The reflection of the fire lit a section of his bearded face. Pa scowled. "Pass it on, gurl."

"I'll take." A skinny man reached for it. His accent gave away his German heritage. His hands quavered. The gravy slopped out of the tin plate and covered one of his hands. "*Ach*, I cannot hold und eat, too."

"Manfred, sit on the wagon bed behind ya. Why not try drinkin' that watery gravy, 'fore eatin' the solids?" Pa waved his hand at her. "Git back inside."

She whirled and retreated to where Fern cowered in the dark. "My pa didn't want it."

"You gave it to my father."

"Oh, I didn't know who he was."

"He's got things wrong with his arms." Fern raised the wooden bowl. "Who do I give this to?"

"I'll take it. I still have this one." Ella skirted the fire's light to the opposite side from her pa. The first teenager she offered a bowl to grabbed it with filthy fingers and shoved a spoonful in his mouth. An elderly man, leaning against a wagon, reached for the second bowl. Someone yelled for her pa to come look at a sore on the withers of a horse. It gave her a chance to run to Fern.

"Thank you." Fern folded her arms and shivered.

Ella decided to let the girl know she had a confidant. "He's not out there. Is he." It was a statement.

"He?" Fern squeaked out the word.

"I hid in the springhouse. Earlier."

With a sharp intake of breath, the girl said, "What? I don't understand."

"I needed to be alone. I heard when you came down the hill." She tugged at her shawl and placed it up on her head. She hoped her confession wouldn't make Fern angry.

"Don't tell." Fern's hands fumbled in the dark and reached. "Please." She squeezed Ella's hand. "I can't let it be known."

"I ain't tellin'."

A heavy-set man tossed a log on the fire. Sparks mushroomed sideways. The sharp scent of pinesap filled the air. The fire's glow illuminated Fern's walnut brown eyes—eyes full of anxiety—and lit the distorted, shadowy view of the empty coffin not four feet from them.

"If he knew, my father would send me away. He'd think I was bad. He's from the old country. He sent my sister away, because Marcy liked an older boy down in Lick Log. He made her go live with his elderly sister in the South somewhere. I haven't seen her for two years. Ma cries at night." Tears glinted on her cheeks. "She'll notice my ripped blouse, even though I repaired it. I was so stupid to go walking with him."

"I won't tell—ever."

Fern took a full-size breath and peered toward the campfire. "I don't see him. He must've left, thinking I'd tell my father."

"Who is the boy?" Ella couldn't hold back the question.

"I'd rather not say."

She wisely changed the subject. "Your father, why can't he hold his plate still?"

"Granny doesn't know. But it's worse. Ma cuts food for him. He's sixty-six. He married my ma after my real father died."

"Hmm." She thought about the jerking of her own pa's arm. "Does the shaking make him yell at you?"

"No, why should it?"

"Just wondered."

"He'll get angry if he hears I was with a boy." She folded her arms tight to her chest.

"Are you all right after what happened?"

"Yes, I'm just ashamed. He didn't—he just tore my blouse. I kept hitting him. He grabbed my arms. He kissed me and touched my ..." Her voice trailed off.

"I wanted to help, but I was skeered."

Fern rested her cheek on the top of Ella's head. "Don't fret. You did the best thing by letting me know you saw it. I can talk to you."

"Wish it were warmer." She hugged Fern's small waist. The cold temperature caused her legs to shake. Her bare toes felt frozen to the ground, and she wiggled them.

The cabin door swung outward. Granny stuck her head out. "Oh, there ye are. Thought the wolves got you." She handed them steaming bowls and pointed. "Take these out an' ask fer empties."

They delivered the last of the hot food, scooted by the circle of men, and collected the used utensils. They slipped unseen to the darkened outhouse and took turns going in it, before entering the stuffy cabin. Both of them sat on the edge of the bed and drew the ragged curtain sideways, so they felt hidden.

A mixture of odors filled the cabin—cooked food, coffee, urine-soaked diapers draped to dry, and human sweat. Behind them, on the bed, the babies and toddlers still slept.

Fern spoke in whispers and asked Ella how she handled her mother's death. Her questions were gentle.

"I hurt. There's a hole inside my heart." She tried to explain the emptiness.

"It's hard to express actual feelings."

"I disremember ever hurtin' like this. It's not my mama on the cooling board. My mama would be helping fix food. She'd be happy 'cause of all the company."

Fern nodded. She eased back the curtain's edge. Her dark-lashed eyes swept the over-filled room. Ella followed her perusal of the activity. One tired-looking woman, with salt and pepper hair, dipped plates and bowls into a bucket of hot water and rinsed them before she handed them off to be dried. Her motions were automatic. She didn't chat with the others.

"That's my ma," Fern said. "She's the one in the black skirt. Her name's Nettie. She keeps to herself, because my father hates gossip."

The splash and chink of the plates blended with the subdued voices of the elderly women near the table. Portions of conversation trickled to Ella. She caught her own name.

Fern dropped the curtain and linked her arm with Ella's elbow. "Women take more comfort in this than men. Men need the wide outdoors, the thick woods, and things they can manhandle. I guess God understands that difference."

"Why does he make men lackin' in feelings?"

The girl expelled a quick breath. "Are you asking because of what happened by the spring?"

"Well …."

32

Karen Campbell Prough

"I don't know the answer. I guess, I'm to blame. That's what I'd be told by my father, were he to find out. I caused it by slipping away and going for a forbidden walk."

Ella scowled. "But you was nice, even when you told him to stop."

"I guess niceness don't count, when you cause a fellow to think he can kiss and maul you." Fern's voice quavered. She patted the repaired blouse and bowed her head.

"I really wasn't talking 'bout you and him. I spoke of how the men stand outside, laugh, and tell stories, while—"

"While your mama's waiting to be buried?"

She nodded. In her head, she also tried to make sense of the way adults ignored death and prepared food for the living. She knew, in a short time, all of them would gather near her mama's body. They'd sit on whatever was available, including the clay floor. The evening and the protracted wakeful night would pass with murmured words, uplifted hands, intense prayers, eating, and an occasional song.

A dark-haired toddler cried out and sat up on the bumpy bed. He caught sight of them, wrinkled his face, and burst into tears. His cries summoned his mother.

Rebecca unbuttoned her dress top and lifted the little one into her arms. "Shh, shh! Quiet, now. Zeb, you've got to stop this comfort nursing." The squirming child took the offered nipple, and his dark eyes shut. A chubby fist curled against his mother's white breast.

One of the older women near the table chuckled. "He'll hav'ta share come late spring."

"I've no milk left. He just wants it in his mouth."

"Ah, proves he's male," Laura muttered, and a twitter of discomfited laughter ran through the group of women.

Rebecca retraced her steps to a place near the table. Her youthful, supple body swayed with the ancient, maternal rhythm of the ages, but the slightly rounded front on her skirt told why her milk had slacked. She expected a second child. Her strong arms rocked her live child not four feet from where a dead infant lay clasped in cold arms.

Ella tore her gaze away from the poignant scene and shuddered. The pitiable cries of her premature brother crowded her mind. Her head ached. She pressed her fingertips against her temple and tried to deaden the dull pain.

I want Mama.

Fern tucked her close under one arm, as if offering physical protection.

"I ain't got my mama, no more." She yielded to Fern's embrace as tears stung her eyelids. "Pa don't like me. He only wanted a boy. Mama said he had a boy by his first woman, but they both died in a fire. I heard Granny tried to save the boy. Then Mama never born him a son. Just me."

"Not your fault." Fern tapped her shoulder and emphasized each word. "God wanted you to be who you are. Don't forget that."

"He—Pa says he wish the painter had kilt me."

"*Panther*, you mean? Your neck. That's what made those red bumpy marks? A mountain lion? I thought maybe a fire."

"No, not a fire."

She covered the left side of her neck with her right hand, closed her eyes, and felt her heart race. A trembling sensation traveled along her spine. In her mind, she heard the scream of the wild cat as it knocked her sideways into the creek. The juvenile panther had briefly entered the shallow water and snarled in her face. She had felt its hot breath fan over her nose and cheeks, and she expected the pain of a torturous death. But the animal's inexperience and hesitation gave Pa enough time to aim and shoot it through the heart.

With a gasping intake of breath, she said, "Its claws got my shoulder and neck. It jumped off a boulder by the creek. Pa shot it."

"He saved your life."

"Yes. Why'd he do that, when he hates me so much?"

"He can't hate you. You're his daughter, not like my father is to me."

"But he says awful things."

"He can't mean them."

"I think he does."

Ella stared at the log wall—two feet in front of their knees. Her mama's sun-faded blue bonnet hung from a hand-carved peg. It was a heartrending reminder of Mama's short life. Its twirled and wrinkled ties dangled against the chinked log wall and resembled limp arms with no life left in them.

Tenderly, the teen drew Ella's right hand away from the scars. The amber glow of the fireplace flickered along the uneven wall and lit Fern's kind face.

"I don't mind the scars. I think you're pretty. I love your freckles. They remind me of specks of dripped honey, and they make you look so sweet. I'm glad you didn't die. I hope we can be friends forever. I know I'm older, but you *seem* like you're my age."

"I reckon I feel older." She smiled.

"You're not old." The girl giggled and whispered, "What's your age?'

"Twelve."

"I'm sixteen."

"I know."

"Yes, I guess you heard." Fern's long eyelashes fluttered and hid her eyes.

"I did."

Rebecca reappeared at the end of the bed. She laid her sleeping child in the midst of other toddlers and infants. He curled on his side, stuck two fingers in his mouth, and sucked. His mother smoothed his fuzzy brown curls and smiled at Ella.

"Child, you look like you're done in."

"My head hurts."

"You need to rest." The woman pointed over their heads at the loft. "Can you show Katy, Abigail, and Faith where they can sleep? The twins, Torrin and Brody, will sleep on the bear hide. Naomi wants the boys where she can keep an eye on them."

Ella slipped off the bed. "Katy? Rebecca says I need to show you my pallet. It's not wide, but we can fold a blanket for more sleeping spots."

"Ella?" Fern followed her. "Why don't you go with them? I'll sit up with the women."

She hesitated for only a second before nodding in agreement. The burden of the seemingly endless day weighed on her. Her head throbbed, and her stomach growled with forgotten hunger. With her lips pressed together, she led the three girls past the table. She kept her eyes averted from her mama's body and reached for the rungs on the loft ladder.

"Watch your heads."

The scent of dried corn stalks greeted them. Beside her pallet, someone had dumped a pile of shucks on the flimsy sapling floor. A borrowed horse blanket covered the crunchy leaves. Nearby, a crazy-patterned quilt waited in a discarded heap.

"We can stand straight up in our loft," one of the girls muttered. She topped the edge and scrutinized the confined space and low headroom. Silky-smooth black braids complimented her dusky skin, but caused her narrow face to appear too long. She shuddered at the sight of the bedding. "Oh my."

"Abigail, don't stop." Katy clung to the ladder below her. "Move! Faith and I will fall."

Ella left her dress on, stretched out on her pallet, and stared at the roof—a mere four feet from her face. Katy crawled over and joined her. Leaves rustled and crunched under their moving bodies.

"Eeek! I'm off the blanket. Faith, scoot." The dark-haired girl shoved the other girl and snatched up the quilt.

Faith, a chubby blond girl, tried patting the springy leaves into a more level pile. "This blanket's none too thick. We will be miserable. Abigail, you're hogging my spot and the quilt. Move sideways."

"Ella Dessa?" Katy rolled to her left side. Her lovely green eyes appeared darker in the muted light. "Are you going down later? I'll go with you—if you want. Just wake me 'cause I might fall asleep."

"I don't know." She studied her young friend's face, inches from her own. Katy's wide-eyed expression showed compassion. She swallowed and fought the surge of hopelessness choking her.

"Well, let me know. You're my friend."

"Thank you. I'm sorry I didn't talk to you earlier, but you was visitin' with those girls. I don't know 'em."

Katy nodded. "That's 'cause you disappeared when we first arrived. I couldn't introduce them."

"I went for a walk."

Ella wanted to crawl to the ladder and climb down. She yearned to wrap her arms about her mama's neck and beg her to come back from Heaven. Abruptly, she squished her eyes shut and tried breathing through open lips. She fought a scream of anguish. It couldn't be true!

I'll soon wake up. I won't be left alone with Pa. Mama will be smilin' and cuddlin' the baby. Please God.

The door to the cabin opened and shut. The clump of heavy boots on packed clay told her a few men joined the women. Below them, a woman's voice lifted in song, tender and melodious. The words to a hymn of faith filled the small cabin. Katy's warm fingers squeezed her right hand. A deeper voice joined in the song, and it became a duet—beautiful and simple.

She listened, almost without breathing. She fought her grief and clung to the childish hand holding hers. She tried to understand the rich words about faith.

My faith looks up to thee . . . .

She wanted to have faith like Mama. She recalled her mama singing the same words.

Tears ran past her ears and dripped to the begrimed pallet under her head. Her left hand dug into the bedding material. The last verse echoed through the cabin and continued, even after the voices went silent.

O, bear me safe above, a ransomed soul.

Chapter 5

The insistent fussing of a baby woke Ella. She rolled onto her stomach and elbows to stare at the busy room below her. The night had seemed unending. Adult voices had kept up a constant murmur, but she didn't go down to join them. She sighed and pondered how she could possibly make it through the burying. Her mind shied and bolted away from the unwanted deliberation.

She sat up, and her head almost touched the barked saplings holding the roof. She studied the three slumbering girls. One of Katy's braids hung loose. Her curly red hair cascaded down her back. Faith had pulled the quilt off Abigail and rolled in it, like a loosely stuffed sausage casing. Her dirty bare toes protruded from one end, and her tangled blond hair stuck out on the other.

The comical image caused Ella to smile.

Her own hair slipped free from the pins holding it on top of her head, and stringy strands fell alongside her face and neck. She dug her fingers through the tangled mess and removed the bone pins. They had been her mama's, a treasured possession, kept in an undersized wooden box. The box had a perfect rose and the initial "M" carved into its lid. Her mama had given the box to her on her twelfth birthday and admonished her to keep it out of Pa's sight. Mama feared he'd break it when he got angry.

She searched under her pallet and lifted the beautiful box to the dim light. With reverence, Ella removed the lid. The scent of cedar wafted from the interior, reminding her of the forest on a warm summer day.

The pins were white, polished smooth, and cool to Ella's touch. As she closed her hand on all six of them, she fought for control over bittersweet memories. Her lips formed words with no sound.

Mama, I'll keep them safe.

She tucked the delicate pins in the box and slid it under her pallet. She combed her fingers through the knotted tangles in her waist-length hair and winced.

In short order, she completed two tight braids, instead of putting her hair up. She wanted to feel like a child, again. With haste, she searched through her meager belongings—wedged under the slant of the roof. She found two pieces of thin leather and bound the ends of each braid.

Hazy air shifted through the loft. She leaned sideways to study the goings-on near the fireplace. Laura stirred a kettle of thick mush while Velma turned browning meat. Adults talked in reverent tones as they picked up their food and went outside.

The door opening and shutting allowed her a quick glimpse of the dim morning light—the day of her mama's burying.

She scooted on her bottom past the sleeping girls to the wobbly ladder. She kicked her skirt out of the way, as her bare toes sought the splintery rungs. No one noticed her presence when she reached the dirt floor.

Self-conscious, she inspected her crumpled dress. It needed scrubbing. Even rubbing her fingers over the thin fabric didn't smooth the creases, and she regretted sleeping in it. She hadn't put much consideration into what she'd wear for the burying. She had no other choice, because she made up her mind she wasn't going back to her shorter little-girl shifts with no collars. She had recently outgrown a dress her mama had fashioned from one of her own. Pa hadn't allowed Mama to purchase or barter for dress material.

"Ella Dessa, ye can't go without eatin'." Granny's sharp-eyed glance spied her bearing for the door. "I know ye didn't eat last night."

Others in the room turned to witness her beeline flight.

"I'll be back." She ducked outside, desperate to get beyond the sight of her mama's body.

The new sunlight filtered through the tops of the pines but left the understory of forest undistinguishable. Ella expected it to be cool outside, a typical September dawn in the mountains, but an odd balmy wind wafted upward from the steep-sided cove. Four men waited near a smoky fire. They drank chicory coffee and paid no mind as she slipped out of the cabin. Two wagons that left the night before had returned.

She ran to the slab-board outhouse and opened the narrow door. The interior appeared foreboding. The meager light didn't penetrate the cracks in the walls. Quickly, she took care of her morning needs and slipped outside. A flock of birds flew overhead and landed in a nearby oak.

Late sparrows, going south, she thought.

Their twittered notes and snatches of song reminded her of happier days, especially with the mild morning. But the welcomed warmth of the day didn't saturate her heart or pacify her spirit. She fervently tried not to reflect on what the day meant.

She spied Pa walking the narrow trace from the creek and hunkered out of sight behind a wagon's front wheel. From her hiding spot, she spied on him. Her mouth fell open at the change in his appearance. His damp, unruly shock of hair was slicked tight to his head. The ends curled without his hat to hold them down.

But what dumbfounded her was the fact he'd shaved his gray-streaked beard.

When he managed to do it, she didn't know, but the astounding transformation took years off his countenance. It made him seem more peaked. He stopped near the fire and plucked his hat from a wagon seat.

She lifted the hem of her skirt and dashed to the cabin door. Her bare feet made no sound. She hated the thought of talking to him. His hearty laughter from the night before recurred in her head and resentment sluiced over her.

Katy, Faith, and Abigail stood near the fire. They each ate from wooden bowls. Laura stood behind Katy, smoothing and braiding her daughter's curly hair. Ella ducked around the privacy curtain, sat on the bed, and impulsively lifted Rebecca's son into her arms. She hugged him and planted a kiss on his pink cheek. The little boy babbled nonsense, reached for her braids, and used them to pull himself to standing in her lap.

"Git-up," he said, his two words ending with a giggle. He bounced in imitation of a horse ride, and his bare toes dug into her thighs.

"You're feelin' right pert." Her hands protected him from a tumble, and his bubbly giggles caused her to grin—until Pa's gruff voice filled the cabin. She jerked the curtain back and peeked out.

"Manfred said one of you women called fer me." Pa removed his hat, bunched it in his large hands, and awkwardly waited for an answer from the unsmiling cluster of women. The indent from his hat showed as a ring encompassing his wet head.

Ella tried to squelch the profound dread she felt. All the people would leave after the burying. She'd be alone with him. The child in her lap chewed on the end of one of her braids, but her attention stayed on Pa. She crumpled the edge of the curtain in her fingers.

"Leigh said it's light enough under the trees." Laura left off braiding Katy's hair, braced her dimpled hands on her stout hips, and faced him. "He wants to start up the hill and requires the coffin brought in. Abe Hanks carved the writing for the cross." Her whole stance portrayed her extreme dislike of him, but her next words were a compliment. "By the way, Jacob, you look younger without the beard."

"Young enough to fetch me a new wife? A pretty woman?"

A gasp of horrified disbelief came from most of the women, and they shrank away from him.

"How dare you," Laura hissed. Her jaw jutted forward, and her heavy bosom lifted with her indrawn breath.

Pa whirled and left the cabin, his hat clenched in his shaking right hand.

A pretty woman? With Mama not even in the ground? Ella dug the nails of her right hand into her palm—in an attempt to staunch the twisting pain in her heart.

"I don't know how Meara made it so many years with the likes of him." In disgust, Laura tossed her head and rolled her eyes. Her auburn curls bounced and threatened to slip loose from where she had piled and coerced them into a fluffy clump. "Granny, you can recall how he mistreated his first wife—what, nigh on thirteen years ago? Sakes alive. Poor soul yearned to die. To get shed of him."

Ella pressed a hand to the side of her forehead. Pa's first wife *yearned* to die?

"But the fire took her and the little one. Perhaps, one ought to call those deaths a blessing." Laura plopped her heavy hips on the bench and reached for a hunk of bread on the table. "A real blessing. Katy, back up here, so I can finish with you."

"Don't go diggin' up dead dogs. Best left buried," Granny said.

"Some think Meara's father had a bit to do with Jacob marrying her." Laura chewed on the heavy-crusted bread and ignored the midwife. "Them being new to the cove, and no one knew Meara's past. They wed so quick."

"You're talkin' of the dead." Granny tapped her forefinger on the table. "Stop, now. We don't need to speak of it at this time."

There was instant silence. Laura raised her reddish eyebrows and gave the other women a knowing smile.

"Enough said." Granny eased out of the rocker and rested her hands on the table. "Ugh, stiffness seizin' my joints." She lifted the sides of the muslin sheet under Mama's body. Crossing and tucking the material over mother and child, she encased them together. But when Jacob and the other men came through the doorway, Granny stepped back. The men balanced the pine coffin between them. Women scurried to shoo children out of the way, and the men carefully lowered the coffin to the hard-packed floor.

With her heart skipping beats, Ella observed Pa draw away from the empty coffin—even though Granny motioned him forward. Instead, Rebecca's young husband, Lyle Foster, and Leigh reverently slid their work-callused hands under her mama's shrouded shoulders and legs. They removed her thin body from the cooling board and lowered it into the waiting coffin.

The two men lifted the box and maneuvered it through the doorway.

Naomi Chesley's face flushed as she faced Jacob. "Go outside with your wife." She brushed past him and drew her shawl around her shoulders. "We're ready. Anyone seen Ella Dessa? I'll search outside."

"No—no." Ella's breath came in rapid jerks. She let the curtain fall back into place. She didn't want to go up the hill to the deep hole called a grave. It would take Mama from her.

"Ella Dessa?" Fern eased behind the curtain and hugged her. "I thought I saw you slip in here. I gave you privacy. You feeling bad?"

"My legs won't carry me to the burying spot." She set the dark-haired tot on the floor and stood. Her legs shook.

"They will." Fern linked an arm through her elbow. "Come, they need you for the service."

"I ain't washed my face." She hung back and shook her head. "My—my dress is filthy." She flicked her fingers at the wet marks caused by her tears. "I'm not ready."

"Shh, just wait here." Fern got a wet rag. "Let me wash your face. Your braids are slipping loose." She used the rag, dampened, and coaxed the hair into place. "You're very pretty. Don't worry. No one will notice the dress."

Ella tried to smile, but her lips wouldn't curve upward. Her body shook. Her right hand fingered the sensitive bumpy skin on her neck. She remembered Mama's tender hands smoothing Granny's herbal salves over the inflamed gouges.

Fern whisked Zeb into her arms. "Hey, big boy, I told your mother I'd get you. Come, Ella Dessa, they're calling you."

"I hear 'em." She felt the finality of it all.

They had taken her mama away.

She ducked past Fern. She stumbled into the sunlight. The coffin rested on the stony ground. Lyle slid the wooden top into place while the men and women watched in silence. Another man bent to grab a wooden mallet.

"No!" She shoved Lyle and fell on her knees. Her hands quivered as she knocked the top aside and drew away the folded muslin. She plucked the large coins off her mama's eyes and flung them to the dirt. All she wanted was to see Mama's face one more time.

Hands tried to pull her away. She savagely slapped them.

"Let her be." Naomi spoke in a firm voice. "Give the child a moment."

Ella ran her hands over her mama's silky hair. Blond tendrils glided between her fingers. "Oh, Mama, it ain't right. You shouldn't have died! Please, don't leave me here." She wiped at the stream of tears blurring the last sight of her mama's face. "I don't wanna be alone," she wailed, not caring who heard her.

"Get her *away*."

Forceful hands gripped her upper arms. The fingers bit and yanked her to her feet. Stunned, she went silent. She recognized the voice and the ruthless hands dragging her away from the coffin.

"Keep her out of the way." Pa whirled her sideways and sent her bumping into Granny. His right hand convulsed with a tremor. He pointed at the coffin. "Nail it."

"No!" Ella cried, but Granny's tender arms hugged her.

Lyle picked the coins from the ground and blew dust off them. His work-roughened fingers reverently laid them over Meara's closed eyes. As he straightened up, he gave Ella a slight nod. Unshed tears filled his eyes.

She hid her face against the skinny midwife, sobs suffocating her. Her stomach felt sick, but she twisted sideways to watch, and Granny's right arm tightened around her waist.

With stony expressions, Frank and Lyle repositioned the top. They pegged it into place. The sound echoed into the woods.

No one spoke.

The drifting, repetitive two-note whistle from a bird in the woods died away. A heavy silence cloaked the thick forest and the mountainous terrain surrounding them. The sighing pines held their breath.

Even the littlest child went quiet, sensing the turmoil of withheld emotions among the adults. Women demonstrated their dislike of Jacob Huskey by giving him cutting stares. They covered their mouths as if to block remarks. Three turned their backs on him. The mountain men kept their heads bowed, seemingly fearful violence might erupt if they dared to look the man in the eye.

Nothing could be gained by a fistfight before a burying.

"No." Granny pressed her colorless lips together and reached for her husband's boney arm. She muttered the single word under her breath, as if she sensed the old man seethed with fury and was about to approach Ella's pa. "Abe, don't fritter away yer breath on the likes of him. He ain't worth it. Come on, child."

She made Ella walk beside them, and they joined the subdued procession hiking to a cleared space under the huge pines. The yawning hole in the ground waited for the body to be delivered into its smothering embrace. Clay-stained stones, dug and pried from the ground, were stacked in a tumbled heap. One man carried coiled lengths of rope to lower the wooden box into the ground.

Ella's bare feet dragged. "Granny, I can't."

"Ye can make it, child." Her arm encircled Ella's waist. "Death's only the creation of fresh life. Yer mama's happy, now. She holds that new infant son hugged in her young arms, an' the trials of life ain't goin' to reach her no more. Why, she's even got her other babies with her."

"Granny, Mama's *gone*." Ella vehemently shook her head. "I can't see her no more!" As her legs threatened to collapse, the midwife held her closer.

"Yes, ye can. Child, look at the heavenly sky. It's the eternal shade of her eyes—cloudless blue. Her face'll be imprinted in every soft cloud ye see. You'll feel her no matters where ye go. God's blessin' her by fetchin' her home. Now, listen to what old Abe says. Lift yer head, child."

Her fingers gripped Ella's chin.

"Granny, I'm breakin' inside!"

"Listen to my old husband. He had schoolin', so Leigh asked him to commence with the buryin'. It's only fittin' since Leigh's new here." Granny pointed at her husband.

The short, bent man stepped to the head of the open grave and raised a tattered Bible in his spidery-veined hands. "Beloved, we're here to lay Meara Huskey in the arms of her God." Abe's quivery voice grew stronger with each word. "The Bible says the Lord of everlasting peace will give you peace during life's walk. I think it means peace even in death. Meara isn't without His touch. She's at peace, but we must still seek *inner* peace here on earth."

A chorus of soft amens lifted from the small crowd of people.

"We can't bring our beloved sister back nor would she long to return to the drudgery of this life. We're the ones left with longing—and sadness. But it doesn't have to be the way of our days." Abe cleared his throat and held the Bible closer to his face, almost touching his undersized nose. "It says here … now the Lord of peace himself give you peace always by all means." He rubbed at his watery blue eyes. "You may read it in Second Thessalonians, in the third chapter."

Ella wondered how he could speak of peace while her heart cracked into a thousand shards. What did peace mean? She didn't even feel God's presence in her life. Shouldn't God's closeness equal real peace?

Abe reverently closed his Bible and tucked it under one arm. "When we stop and remember Meara, we must reflect on God's mercy. His child has gone home where we all long to be. My dear Eleanor knows not to grieve when I pass. For I shall pass into everlasting life and peace." He held his arthritic hand out to Granny. "Love, come stand by me. My legs are weakening."

Without blinking an eye, the old midwife left Ella and stepped close to Abe's shaky form. She wrapped her arm around his thin waist. He thanked her with his watery eyes and a sad smile. The aged man spoke once more, bolstered by his mate's strengthening presence.

"Shall we pray, one and all, the Lord's Prayer?"

They spoke the prayer in unison.

It was over in no time.

The men used ropes to lower the coffin. They pushed and shoveled the soil into the hole. The women leaned on one another and wept in muted sobs and sighs, which blended with the unnatural warm wind murmuring in the pine boughs. The plopping sound of reddish dirt clogs foretold their own future as mountain women.

They knew life was short, birthing was dangerous, and love was a sacrifice. So much could be taken from them. All the while, the women became prematurely bent and gray. Their husbands continued to dream about a future piece of landholdings—straight away over the next mountain, through the next valley—a hunk of gold or piece of rocky soil to carry out their lifelong dreams.

Perhaps, the women saw new life in the individual forms of their loved ones, the children gathered between them, and the dark hole in the ground. Only God sustained them in the bleak, thorn-filled life they fought to hold onto. Each of the women gave more than they'd ever get back from the unforgiving land or their careworn families, but they went on loving and trusting. Their weary, trial-etched countenances portrayed the dreaded and lengthy winter months and the hardships of the mountain people.

Not one of them would voluntarily hike out of the cove or the mountains, even if given the go-ahead and the whereabouts. Their way of life was injected into the interwoven pulsing veins and arteries of their work-hardened bodies, making them part of the surroundings—an element of God's handiwork.

Ella stood straighter. A solid resolve filled her heart. *I'll make Mama proud of me.*

The sun slid behind a cloud. A rumble of thunder started in the bottom of the curved cove and rolled up the tree-hidden mountain. Startled at the deafening noise, men and women reacted with alarm and called for the scattered children. If they meant to beat the storm, they needed to leave right away. The men hastily stacked a double layer of gray and russet rocks on the grave.

"That's unusual," Velma muttered, still facing the grave.

"What ya talkin' about?" Her husband, Gust Clanders, glowered at her. "Rocks are always used." His narrow, pockmarked face flushed with annoyance. He acted ashamed of her and turned away, shaking his balding head.

"Gust, I *meant* the storm." She grabbed at her unbleached muslin bonnet. It threatened to take flight in the wind, like a crazed, flapping bird. She tugged on the threadbare ties and tightened them under her pointed chin.

Lyle's curly light-brown hair blew about his forehead. He snatched the pile of rope from the ground and tossed it to another man. He shouted with the next rumble, "I knew it were too muggy. We got a bad storm coming. Let's go." He mashed his hat tight to his head, collected a shovel, and started down the moderate slope. His long legs ate up the distance. Everyone followed, waved children on ahead, and hastened to the wagons.

Gloom, formed by heavy clouds, boiled up and crept sideways throughout the elongated curve of the cove tucked below them. It emphasized the dire conclusion of two lives, but Ella miraculously felt life and hope unfolding in her heart. God's presence covered her pain. She stood tranquil as the others scurried to wagons. Her eyes remained riveted on the rocky-mounded grave, but her tears dried in the high wind.

Life would continue for her.

Her mama schooled her to be strong. The claws of a mountain lion taught her to be strong. The disgusted glares of a harsh father told her she *had to be* strong. Pa's trembling fingers had a way of digging into her arms. It made her more determined to stay strong, survive, and love life, in spite of him.

Katy scrambled back up the slope, her blue skirt whipping in the wind. She snatched at Ella's arm. "Come on. I'll walk you. Fern's carrying Rebecca's boy."

In front of the cabin, women congregated and gave Ella quick hugs. They whispered their inner reflections and honest promises of prayers. While the coming storm whipped the tops of trees, five of the women handed her small items, wrapped in paper or burlap. They gave tokens of mothering and signatures of grief they couldn't explain in mere words.

Ella's dress snapped in the wind, tangled about her legs, and swept the tiny stones at her feet.

With wistful longing, she watched Fern's family wagon roll away. The teen's mother sat ramrod straight beside her tall husband. Lightning flashed and thunder crashed closer. Huge raindrops splattered the thirsty ground and dampened her cheek. Manfred Stauffer had been in a hurry, barely giving Fern time to put Zeb in the Foster wagon and run to Ella for a final hug.

The dark-haired teen twisted sideways in the back of the wagon and waved her shawl. "Ella Dessa! I'll see you at the next quilting bee. Please, be there."

Ella waved in response, a smile tugging her lips.

"She won't be there." Fingers bit into her upper arm and forced her to turn.

"Yes, she will." She clutched the gifts to her chest, peered over her shoulder as the last wagon disappeared from view. "Fern said she'd see me. I believe her."

"*Pshaw!*" He pulled his hat low over his squinted eyes. Big drops of rain pelted his shoulders and his newly-shaven jaw. His right hand jerked against her shoulder, but his fingers tightened. "Someone done tolt on her—gave her pa an ear full about seein' her on the ridge with that dratted, red-headed McKnapp kid."

It felt as if a rock plunged into her stomach. Pa couldn't be telling the truth. She searched his cold eyes for a clue that he lied. "McKnapp?" Rain mudded the dirt at her feet.

"That's what I said, McKnapp." He let her go. "The boy were seen hightailing it through the ravine after gettin' whatever he wanted from her." With his beard gone, the bones of his jaws showed through his skin. It gave him an emaciated, skeletal appearance. His coal-black eyes crinkled at the corners, but not from years of hearty laughter.

Without thinking of the consequences, she blurted out, "It weren't of her doin'. She tolt him to stop!" She hunched her shoulders against the splattering rain and tried drying her face on her arm.

"How come ya know 'bout that?" He bent forward. "Huh?" His face came within inches of hers, and his hat brim hit her forehead. His breath reeked of the pipe he smoked, Granny's seasoned sausage he ate for breakfast, and the tang of whiskey.

Ella stepped backwards.

"Gurl, is that why I couldn't find ya? I went there and saw movement. Were ya spyin' on 'em? Gettin' yer eyes full, eh? An' couldn't answer me?" He snorted. "Maybe, you ain't so *innocent* as yer mama thought."

Before she could react, his shaking hand flashed forward—wet fingers spread wide.

Her head jerked as the large palm made contact with the side of her head. Stunned, she dropped her gifts to the mud and staggered away from the reach of his arm. She raised her hands to protect her face, expecting another slap or worse. Her ear rang. Tears stung her eyelids, and she fought for control of her breath.

Thunder rumbled. Icy rain soaked through the bodice of her dress. She wiped her eyes and stared at the muddy ground.

Don't cry! Don't let him see you cry.

"Jist 'cause yer mama's gone, don't think I'm goin' to stand fer sass from the likes of you. You're growin' up. An' there's more you're gonna learn about bein' a respectful female. I'm the one to teach ya." He pulled his hat brim lower and pointed. "Git inside!"

She ran to the cabin with the rain pushing her. Her heart hammered so hard she thought she'd faint dead away. *Pa saw Fern and that boy.* Her friend was in trouble, and she couldn't warn her. Would Manfred send away another stepdaughter?

Thunder vibrated the log walls. Gloom filled the inside of the rectangular building, but she didn't care about a lantern or the sting of the handprint on her cheek. She scrambled to the loft, just as the heaviest onslaught of rain hit and clattered on the sundried cedar-shake roof. She curled in a ball on her pallet and willed the roar of the thunder and the drumming of the rain to beat the ache out of her soul.

She heard him come in.

When the cabin door bumped shut, she slid sideways to peer down. Pa cursed and tripped over one of the misplaced benches. Lightning seemed to pass through the walls, illuminating the inside, but she knew the flashes of jagged light actually burst through the small window.

She rolled over on her pallet, to stare at the roof.

Soon, dampness soaked through the parched shakes on the roof. Cold droplets filtered around the layers and dripped on her. Ella turned over and stared at the single square window, with oiled animal skin serving as glass. It was the only item Mama ever begged Pa for during the past summer.

Before that, the cabin had been windowless. Begrudgingly, her pa chiseled and cut through the logs. The square of blessed light became reality. A wooden shutter could be latched shut during the winter. Mama had called it her one bright spot, besides her daughter.

Ella smiled, rolled to her back, and twisted her wet hair into a bun. She closed her eyes and let memories of Mama take her away from the rugged log walls. The drumming of the rain echoed the thump of her heart.

The rain would damage the small tokens the women gave her, but she didn't grieve over them. They were material things, a tiny loaf of bread, an edged handkerchief, or a scented packet of dried summer flowers.

She heard Pa throw his boots against a wall, all the while, cursing the downpour. But his flaring temper and the thunderous storm failed to shake her. After softly repeating a calming prayer Mama had taught her, she reflected on how happy her mama must be walking in Heaven.

"I wish I could leave here and be with you." She imagined Mama bending to listen to her wish. Ella remembered Granny's words on the mountain—how her mama now held and snuggled all her babies. "Mama, I want to be in Heaven. I want to hug the babies with you."

Chapter 6

During the lonely week following her mama's burying, Ella watched her pa with uneasy silence. She sensed bewildering changes in his behavior. He acted preoccupied, like a man wrestling with a hitch or deep inner thoughts.

Each morning, she'd brace herself for whatever ill-tempered treatment he might have in mind. She kept busy if he lingered inside the cabin, only relaxing when he went outside. She used a muslin sheet and managed to cut out a simple shift for herself. She hand-stitched it together and felt tickled to have another dress to wear.

"Now I can wash Mama's dress." She even considered the greater task of selecting one of her mama's blouses and fitting it to herself. "If I take in the waist of all three skirts, maybe I could wear 'em."

****

But nine days after her mama died, the tense routine changed. That morning, Ella knelt beside the fireplace with an iron poker in hand. She scraped back the gray ashes and exposed chunks of glowing coals. Within a short time, she had a hot fire and extended her chilled fingers to the blessed warmth.

Movements came from behind the corner curtain. He was awake. Did he miss her mama?

She poured icy water from the wooden bucket into a kettle and considered what thoughts, if any, troubled Pa's mind. Did he regret not fetching Granny in time?

Ella struggled with the weight of the heavy kettle, but managed to heft it to the hook over the fire. She pushed her mama's flat cooking rock close to the fire and wondered how many years the blackened surface had served as an elevated base. Mama once told her it belonged to her own mother.

Mama would knead pliable dough early in the mornings. She'd brush her white hands together, to knock away loose flour, before arranging flat biscuits on the rock's hot greased top. The vivid image in her mind caused Ella to pause and close her eyes.

A curse came from behind the curtain.

Hastily, she pushed aside memories and searched through the dry goods. Supplies were low. It meant asking Pa to go to the secluded narrow settlement of Beckler's Cove.

I dare not do that.

Pa jerked the curtain aside, sat in the rocker, and shoved his stocking feet into well-worn boots. His hooded eyes never lifted to acknowledge her timid presence. He smelled sweaty.

"I were thinkin' you'd like mush with milk? We have dried blueberries," Ella said.

"No."

"Ah, bits of ham with eggs. I can fix—"

"No!" He pointed a long finger at her. "Leave off yer askin', or I'll take the battling stick to ya. I got things on my mind. An empty belly will hasten my decidin'. Don't talk to me, if ya know what's good fer ya."

She dropped her head and studied her stocking-clad feet. A hole showed one toe.

Pa left the cabin and milked their two skinny cows, which was usually her job. He set the half-filled pail by the table and went back out. She felt jittery. It was worse than anticipating a horrific episode of his arm shaking.

What was he deciding?

Taken aback by the oddity he now exhibited, she kept busy. She strained the small amount of milk. The skinny cows were drying up. The loss of milk would eliminate their butter supply, and she liked to churn butter. The repetitive movement lulled her qualms.

The sound of a heavy axe informed her where Pa was in the woods. She had once overheard him tell Mama he never dropped a dead tree after he found it. He said that once on the ground, they rotted too fast. Mama hadn't replied, but her expression said he wasted time just sitting on the fence with a pipe clenched between his discolored teeth.

With a forceful sigh, she set aside the milk pail and studied the one room, which was now the center of her life. Everywhere she looked were reminders of Mama—the broken spinning wheel tucked in the corner, a pine needle container her mama had worked on, and the woven grapevine basket full of baby garments.

The little gowns had been cut from unbleached muslin during the first part of Mama's pregnancy. Mama refused to sew them together until she passed her sixth month, for fear she'd lose the baby. Now, Ella didn't know what to do with the delicate garments. She walked across the room and covered the basket with a scrap of material, so she wouldn't have to see the miniature clothing. She nudged it with her knee and pushed it against the wall.

The constant chop of the axe stopped.

Curiosity soon pressed her to go see why things remained quiet. As she rounded the back corner of the building, she saw Pa urging their horse to pull another lengthy tree trunk into the side field. Rigging and dangling lines trailed from the horse to the log, and sweat dampened its back and skinny sides.

Ella climbed the crooked worm fence, sat balanced on top of it, and tucked Mama's dress under her bare legs. Pa set the tree trunks on wedges and proceeded to saw them into shorter lengths—short enough to split for the fireplace. It was hard work. His long-legged, lanky body worked with a furor, and his actions made her think of a man racing against time and an invisible deadline.

She looked about the neglected homestead. Another light frost had fingered the tops of the mountains, deepening their fall colors. The day was crisp and clear. Autumn had arrived, along with the last days of harvest and gathering. Nature prepared for a change. A fat groundhog waddled up the slope behind her, and he paused to chew on morsels of yellowing grass and exposed roots in her mama's dried-up garden.

A breeze moved the treetops. Their subtle colors mingled in a swirling pattern, much like a crazy-patterned quilt. One heavy frost would set the hillside ablaze with profound reds, fervent yellows, and pumpkin-orange leaves. September would fade away to October's final blanket of superb color.

The high sun laid warm hands on Ella's shoulders and back, and a bobwhite gave one lonely, unanswered call from the high grass near the woods. She could hear the creek bubbling over rocks. The fresh scent of dried plant life drifted in the air, reminding her of Mama's love of harvest time.

From down in the cove the exuberant baying and persistent trail voices of hounds drifted upward. She lost track of time as the harmonic noise faded away.

How many times had she seen Mama's face battered with blows from Pa's large fists? Mama always took the beatings in order to keep him from hitting Ella's smaller frame.

Pa's head turned.

She took a shallow breath and held it with lips parted. He had spotted her perched on the fence like a timid brown sparrow.

"Ya ain't got better things to do?" He stopped the sawing and removed his hat. "I can suggest somethin'." He wiped his sweaty head and glowered at her. His sinister, bushy brows almost hid his black eyes.

For a second, she felt stunned he actually spoke. Then, knowing she ought to acknowledge his question, she jumped off the fence. "Yes. I need to fix our meal."

She ran, pushed through the entangling grass, and wished she hadn't let him catch her daydreaming. As she rounded the corner of the cabin, tears trickled down her cheeks, but she angrily swatted at them.

Cryin' don't help.

She knelt beside the hearth. She washed some potatoes and chopped them into chunks, with the skins still in place. She dropped the pieces into a small amount of boiling water, and added leftover portions of salt-cured ham and chopped leeks. When the potatoes felt soft, she added the fresh milk and a gob of butter.

Then she sat and waited. She didn't dare call him away from his chores.

With her stomach growling, Ella waited as her mama had in the past. She amused herself by counting how many logs went into the making of the walls. Mama had used them when teaching her to count.

The number reached thirty-four, and he came through the door—reeking of sweat and the outdoors.

He removed his hat, brushed sawdust from his filthy hands, and sat on one of the benches. With reservations, she slid onto the opposite bench. Pa lifted his knife and surveyed the tabletop. It was bare except for the steaming bowls of soup.

"No flat biscuits? Yer mama would've fixed me a half dozen. Straggly-haired gurl, you're worthless."

Ella bowed her head. She hated to tell him they lacked flour for biscuits, long sweetening, or anything else. The flour bags were without substance, except for a dusting of flour.

"I'm sorry, Pa." Her chest hurt. She bit her lip and waited for him to curse her or punch her from across the table.

"*Hmmph!*" He seized his spoon in his fist.

Breathe, she told herself. Her lips parted, and she bowed her head. *Oh, please, dear Lord, don't let him hit me. Thank you for this food.*

He spooned the soup into his mouth and sputtered, "She didn't teach you nothin'." The liquid from his spoon dripped to the table—a whitish-clear blotch on the worn pine board.

But that was the extent of his interaction with her. He slurped with each mouthful of soup. He paid her no heed—as if dismissing her existence.

She had anticipated beatings, expected indifference to her feelings of loneliness, but it was as if she no longer existed. That part was somewhat welcomed. Still, she desperately wanted to talk to someone. She toyed with her dented pewter spoon while he drank the milky liquid in his bowl.

"There ain't no flour in the poke. Velma left her kettle here. It's her best one. She uses it for chicken. I washed it. I'm supposin' she needs it."

She again held her breath and waited—gauging his reaction. She hoped to have a real conversation.

"Then I reckon Velma will hav'ta send her lazy drunk husband to fetch it." He set his wooden bowl down with a loud thump and wiped his mouth on a stained shirtsleeve. "He ain't good fer much, except begettin' more addlebrained offspring."

Quickly, she nodded her head in agreement. She didn't dare act shocked or disturbed by his callous words.

He ran a grubby finger through a dollop of soup on the table. He rubbed at the liquid until the spot dried—darkening the old wood.

Mesmerized, she watched his flat-tipped finger move back and forth. Dread built with each movement of his large hand. She had witnessed the same hand choke her mama for a minor mistake.

Would she be next?

"The flour, I'll git when I ride to the settlement. I've someone—things to tend to. Got me a friend to see, 'cause I've made my mind up 'bout somethin'. I hate livin' on this mountain. Tote water an' heat me a tub tonight." He stood to his feet and snatched his hat from the wooden peg by the door. "I've got splittin' to finish."

****

Later that evening, Ella lay in the loft listening to water slop and splash in the wooden tub. Pa cleaned himself with water she had toted from the creek and heated over the fire. Because she failed to start early enough in the afternoon, the full silvery moon had burst over the treetops as she lugged the last pail to the cabin. Fearful a panther watched from the edge of the woods, she had almost flown along the moonlit ground. The water had splashed her skirt and dampened her legs, causing gooseflesh.

Now, her arms and shoulders ached. Most of the time, Mama could get Pa to fetch all the water. In the past, he filled the barrel outside the cabin door. Apparently, it was now her tiresome job.

After drawing the ragged quilt over her shoulders, Ella snuggled deeper into its comforting weight and warmth. Cool air blew through neglected cracks and holes in the clay chinking. She felt it touch and drift frosty fingertips over her cheek.

What's his sudden hankerin' for a bath?

Her mama often complained about Pa's lack of bathing. He'd let himself go without washing during the late fall and winter months. And he used the chilly mountain creek during the hot summer, but only once or twice a month.

What changed his habit, a little over a week beyond her mama's death?

Chapter 7

Sunday, September 25, 1836

The next morning, after the first blush of the Sabbath, Ella watched her pa slip the leather bridle over the horse's nose. He wore a clean shirt and his newest coat. He had smoothed his curly hair back off his high forehead. Water dripped from one dark curl and traveled the side of his shaven jaw. A red scrape showed where his straight razor had slipped. A dab of dried blood remained.

Is he goin' to the Sunday service?

"Won't be here tonight." In the frigid air, his puffs of breath ascended between them.

She blinked her eyes a couple times and tried to comprehend what he meant. "Not tonight, then—when?" Disbelief washed over her. *He's leavin' me alone?*

"Don't know. An' don't ya go gettin' skeered."

"I won't be skeered." She hid her inner panic. "Remember the flour? Some meal?" She stopped speaking and clenched her freezing hands in the folds of her shift.

He slipped the rifle sling over his head, opposite his powder horn, and then lifted his hat from atop the post. He patted his wet hair and pushed the hat over the flattened curls. "I'll git flour tomorrow."

"Take me?"

"No." His thin face pinched up. His eyes narrowed. "You're goin' to hav'ta learn to be alone. Ya ain't my wife—never will be. Can't deny I ain't debated it, but decided other things are fairer game."

Confused by his odd words, she gulped tears and murmured, "It's just I ain't never stayed alone at night. When you comin' back?" Her teeth chattered. She folded her arms across her chest, mentally warding off his rebuff. She wished she had thrown a shawl about her shoulders and covered the lightweight shift.

He looked down at her. A sneering grin stretched his wide mouth sideways. "I've no plans to be back no time soon. As far as stayin' alone— git use' to it. With that scarred neck ya got, you'll be lucky the scrawny-necked chickens don't up an' leave ya. No man'll ever wed you proper like."

Shock caused her eyes to smart, but she clamped her teeth together. The dull pang in her chest mushroomed. She wanted to drop to her knees, crawl away, and become part of the forest floor.

He threw a double-folded blanket over the horse and mounted the animal's narrow back. "Gurl, you'll see me when I top the trace. Don't slack in coopin' the chickens at dark. I clipped their wings an' flushed 'em into the forgin' pen. Saw a wolf on the ridge last night."

"I heard him." Ella felt a lump building in the back of her throat, threatening to explode in livid, hateful words. She wanted to wound him verbally, the way he hurt her. By biting on the insides of her cheeks, she fought the urge to spew the same curse words he habitually hurled at her and Mama.

What would she do at dark? The harvest moon would still be bright, but it wouldn't keep her company.

The idea of sleeping in the cabin alone felt daunting. Her bottom lip quivered. She willed herself to stare at his broken-nailed hands lifting the leather reins and not at the smirk on his face.

He clicked his tongue and squeezed the sides of the horse with his bony knees. The pitiful animal dropped her head and obediently plodded for the trail. Her ragged hooves crunched on small rocks scattered in the clay and dirt.

He didn't turn to wave. There was no use calling him back. Instead, Ella sprinted barefooted through the stiff, frosted grass, along the hill, and to the grave. She cried out for Mama, but she didn't succumb to tears. She sat under the pines, near the mound of rocks and stones. The recollection of her mama's kind voice reciting scripture soothed her temper.

She pushed her spine against the trunk of the tallest pine and welcomed the pricks and pokes of the uneven bark. Slowly, her breathing grew calm and thoughts rational.

"Mama, I think I can't bear no more. He's done left me alone." She twisted her chapped hands in her lap and rubbed them together to create an indication of warmth. "Come nightfall, I'll bar myself in and practice readin' your Bible. Pa said he done seen a lone wolf." She wiped at a single tear. "I know God'll see no harm comes to me. You always tolt me to wait on the Lord. I just don't know how long to wait *or what* I'm waitin' for."

She stood and whisked leaves and dirt from her shift. She peered down on the only home she had ever known. Filmy smoke curled from the crooked stone chimney and drifted sideways. It hugged the cedar shake roof of the building and then faded away, carrying the scent of charred hickory and the promise of warmth.

But the homestead appeared forlorn and shabby, even with the inviting smoke and the backdrop of color-tinged leaves covering the rolling ridge. Ella squinted and tried to imagine the slender, used-up figure of her mama standing in the doorway, cupping her hands to her mouth, and hollering for her daughter.

Ella Dessa!

A shadow moved to her right.

She ducked behind a tree and peeked around it.

With relief, she spied a red fox—not a wolf—trot out of the forest. He followed the v-shaped hollow. He disappeared and reappeared as he headed for the penned chickens. His little feet patted along in silence. Before he reached the clucking fowl, the brown chickens spotted him and scattered in the forging pen. They let loose warning cackles.

"Hey!" Ella screamed. "Get away from my chickens!"

She lifted her shift well above her knees and burst from her hiding place. She broke into a run, letting her bare feet carry her along the cleared slope as fast as she could go. It felt exhilarating to abandon all decorum and be a child, again.

The fox skidded to a stop, hesitated, and looked from the alarm-raising chickens to the angry human barreling at him. He flipped head for tail, legs churning and belly low, and bolted back through the hollow. Once over the hill and at the fringe of the forest, he trotted up the slanted trunk of a fallen tree and turned to watch Ella pursue the squawking chickens in circles. She could see him sitting atop the log, ears up, and attention focused.

"You ain't gettin' 'em! I *know* you'd like to drag one off. You thief!"

The fox's ears twitched at the sound of her voice. He licked his jaws, yawned, and plopped himself—belly-down—on the log. He remained there, the sun's fresh rays reflecting on his brilliant fiery coat of fur and white-tipped tail. A crimson maple leaf fluttered to the ground, perfecting the picture and blending with the fox's splendid orange-red coat of fur.

Annoyed that the fox appeared innocent, she grabbed a stone from the ground and threw it in his direction. "I'm goin' to kill your sneaky ways right now! Ya no-account chicken thief."

The fox pointed his snout upward and yawned wide, one more time. His teeth snapped together.

With an exasperated sigh, she shooed the six hens into the chicken house. They ran through the feathery clippings of their own wings and mingled at the rear of the tiny dilapidated building. They clucked and voiced their displeasure. The chickens weren't happy about being cooped, preferring to scratch and peck at the soil and dry grass, but Ella didn't want to take the chance of the fox helping himself to a meal. A large owl had gotten the rooster and one hen two weeks before. Her pa had promised her mama he'd build moveable enclosed pens out of saplings.

He never did it.

After collecting two eggs from the nest boxes, Ella latched the small door, and waved a hand at the attentive fox.

"Go. Slink back to your den!"

Immediately after entering the cabin, she boiled the two eggs and ate them. They weren't much, but it was all she wanted. The single room seemed huge and lonely. She stared at the wooden tub sitting near the fire, the water scummy and gray. A bath would feel wonderful, but it meant emptying the water Pa had used, bucket by bucket. Then she'd have to carry water from the creek. But as she studied the tub, the more the thought of a bath appealed to her.

****

Almost two hours later, Ella stripped off her soiled dress and sank into the tub of hot water. Sitting doubled up, she folded her arms on top of her knees and bowed her forehead against them. Her tears made no sound as they dripped to the steamy water.

She remained in that position until the water temperature cooled. Only then did she reach for a rag placed on a nearby bench. With vigor, she scrubbed and washed her body and hair. It felt good to imagine that she might eliminate all her troubles by cleansing her skin.

High above the cabin, on the mountain, a wolf howled. The drawn-out, forlorn noise gave her gooseflesh, and she stood to her feet. Through the one opaque window, the full moon was able to cast a narrow path of light along the floor.

She dressed in a shift and a pair of long woolen socks. Reluctant to leave the fire, she made herself a soft pad of quilts in front of the hearth.

"There's no one to care what I do."

****

Ella's supper was a simple affair of boiled meal with a bit of honey and milk. Even though the cabin felt cozy and warm, she fought overwhelming loneliness, which prompted her to get her mama's Bible and read.

She sat with legs crossed and reverently opened the leather-bound book. She turned the fragile pages. It was the Sabbath, and her mama had always read to her, but she wasn't sure what to read.

Between two pages, a folded piece of paper came to view. Watermarks splotched its creased and yellowed appearance. They resembled teardrops soaked into the paper. With utmost care, she unfolded and smoothed it flat on top of the book of James. Written in a looping and artistic handwriting was a letter—addressed to her mama.

With awe, she read the words aloud. "Dearest Meara, My friend, Logan, promised to deliver this missive to you this evening. I cannot slip away. I have the night watch over the new mining equipment. We leave in one week for North Carolina. Logan laughs at a teacher working in a questionable gold mine, but it is what I must do, right now.

With every fiber of my being, I yearn to have you as my wife. There will never be another woman who will fulfill what I am as a man. Tomorrow, I am coming to ask for your hand in marriage. Parson Wheedon said he could marry us on Saturday.

I will bring the hairpins to you. I have finished the carving on the box. It is my wedding gift to you, along with what is stored inside it. Keep it safe. It is our future.

I have to know you are my wife before I leave. It will be my last trip. I promise. I just need to fulfill my obligations with Barringer, the mine owner. I dislike the lack of restraint showed by all when flakes of gold are discovered. I will not waste my life on the love of gold.

God's gift of art and teaching anoints my talents.

When I return, I will take what I have placed in your hand for safekeeping and buy a piece of land for us. There, I will build you a wonderful home and dig wild roses to plant around it. I will hide it from all eyes, so we can cling to one another. We'll be concealed from the world. The scent of the roses will not surpass the way you take my breath away. I will go back to teaching, and you will lovingly nurture our children. Yours forever and ever, Miles Kilbride."

Ella was stunned to realize another man had once loved her mama. Tucked in the old Bible, wedged between pages of a book her pa wouldn't be tempted to read, the secret had remained hidden. Her mama never mentioned the man's name to her or talked of a love letter.

No date had been added to the letter.

While she stared at the tender words, her childish heart ached. Her mama had endured beatings and punishments, all undeserved.

Why hadn't she married the man named Miles?

She refolded the delicate paper and took it to the loft. She pulled the carved box from under the pallet and held it up. The fire's dancing light reflected on its surface. The rose, carved into the lid, held a sweeter significance. She lifted the lid and fingered the polished bits of bone, shaped into narrow hairpins. Now she knew who fashioned their tapered tines and why her mother cherished them. With care, she placed the folded letter in the box for safekeeping.

A smile played about her lips. She wished to be loved the way Miles Kilbride had apparently loved her mama. Her fingers fumbled, as she braided her damp hair and wound it on top of her head. The six pins did an excellent job of holding it in place.

Back at the fire, she dropped to the quilts and lifted one of them over her shoulders. In the moving flames, she saw her mama's face—free of bruises and sorrow. "Mama, I know you're with God, but you think of me. I found the missive from Miles. He writes words like what's in Solomon's Song, and I understand Pa never cared like that. Now, God can comfort you."

After rubbing aside a tear, she set the Bible in her lap and searched for a passage to read. A New Testament book, with a man's name, caught her eye. She started with the first chapter and read how Paul called the youthful man his son. In the fourth chapter, she read where Paul told Timothy not to let anyone look down on him just because he was young, but to set an example for other believers in speech, in life, in love, in faith, and in purity.

Ella contemplated the words. She wanted to be all the things listed—an example in life. Her heart yearned to be what God designed for her. She closed her eyes and told God she felt sorry about all the anger she held toward her pa.

As the evening slipped away, she stared into the flickering flames and wondered how Pa could hate her. She whispered another prayer. "Dear God, please soften my feelin's toward him."

<h1 style="text-align:center">Chapter 8</h1>

Monday, September 26, 1836

The next morning, as Ella chased the chickens out into the gleaming sunshine, Leigh Chesley rode up the trail on a horse.

"Just here to inquire of you." He grinned from the saddle, lowered a cloth-wrapped pie, and held it out to her. "Naomi sent along a minced meat pie. Fresh baked 'fore sunup. Nice flavored."

"Ohh!" She eagerly wiped her hands on her dress and reached for it. "Tell her I love minced meat."

"So, you *are* by yourself." He dismounted and adjusted the wire spectacles on his nose.

She frowned and shrugged. "Pa went to the cove."

"I know. We all saw him last evening. He rode by when we came out of the service." His voice sounded strained. It was as if he tried to be cheerful, but felt otherwise. He pulled a wrinkled and folded piece of paper from his pocket and tried to straighten the creases. He presented it to her. "Here. It's addressed to you and hand-delivered to us three days ago by Nettie. I knew you'd want it."

"Nettie?" She held the paper in one hand and the pie in the other. She gave him an intent look, not quite believing him. "I—it's a letter from her?"

"No. It's from Fern. I can read it to you, if you wish."

She raised her chin higher. "I can read." She gripped the precious item in her right hand and hid it in the folds of her skirt. She wanted to read it after he left, and her heart pounded with anticipation.

I got a real letter.

Leigh squinted at the cloudless sky. "The day's turning out nice."

"Yes, it feels warmer."

Her fingertips tingled, wanting to unfold the letter. She could feel the wax seal under her thumb.

He removed his hat and scratched his head. "My wife said to let you know Velma's in the ... family way, again. It'll be born in the spring." He appeared uncomfortable delivering the message to her. "Naomi figured you'd want to know, 'specially it being about a friend."

"That'll be six. I hope she figgers how to cut shirt patterns with Mama gone."

Her chest tightened. She dropped her head and fought tears. It hurt to say Mama was gone. A picture played out in her thoughts—her mama sitting in a corner while other women crowded a quilting frame. A rumpled, half-finished shirt covered her lap. A needle dipped and stitched the shoulder seam on a child's shirt.

"Your mother showed kindness to Velma."

"Yes. Velma's brood goes through clothin', much as water strained through a straw basket."

He nodded. "My Naomi was pure upset to hear the woman's husband has abandoned her. He joined men working a new vein of gold, southwest of here."

"I didn't know."

"Yeah. Reckon he'll be gone for the winter, foolhardy soul. These men leave their womenfolk behind for others to see to and chase after mammon."

"Mama told me it's the root of all evil. Only a godly man might turn away from its pull. It's in the Bible."

Leigh raised his eyebrows as if surprised at her knowledge. "Yes, so the Good Book tells us. I've seen nice men go bad following after money. Gold fever wrecks homes—much like other things." He pushed his hat down on his head. "Child, is there anything you need?"

"No."

"Then I'll be riding on. Got some sick folks to see." He stepped into the stirrup and swung his leg over. "When Jacob gets home, make sure you tell him I dropped by."

"I will."

She wasn't about to tell Leigh Chesley she didn't know when her pa would return or how fearful she felt. While she clutched the letter, Ella noted his troubled gray eyes studying her from behind the wire-rimmed glasses.

"You all right?"

"Yes. Tell Velma I'm happy for her. Also, her kettle's still here. Shall I fetch it?"

He nodded. "I'll take it to her."

She ran to get the kettle, placed the pie on the table, and tucked the letter under the edge of the tin, so it couldn't disappear.

When she returned, he said, "I'll go by Velma's on the way home. Got to see what we can do for her. I'd like to go hunt up Gust and pound—talk sense into his head," he muttered.

"Here's her kettle."

He bent from the saddle and reached for the wire handle.

"Ella Dessa, me and my wife, we'd welcome your presence for the winter months—if your father doesn't ever come home."

"Why?" She felt confused. *Why wouldn't Pa come home in a few days? Where else could he go?*

"Well." He balanced the iron kettle on the saddle in front of him. "The twins leave my wife no extra time to do her duties. She'd love help corralling them. I caught both of them standing on top of the chicken house last night."

"I can't. Pa'll be comin' back." Leigh meant she could live with them and help care for the boys. The thought of her pa's anger, if she did that, shook her.

"Just saying … if he don't." He tipped his hat and rode away.

She dashed into the cabin and snatched up the letter. She sat on a flat stone outside the open door, where she'd be in the sun. Her trembling fingers loosened the wax seal and unfolded the paper. She held the first letter she had ever received. With the tip of her tongue, she moistened her lips and whispered the written words.

"My Dear Friend, I am being sent south, to St. Augustine, to join my sister at my Aunt Katarina's home. My stepfather will not relent. He does not believe what I say. He even went so far, I am ashamed to write, he fears I am with child. He believes I have shamed him. My poor ma is sick at heart. I do not know if I will ever see you again. I fear not. I worry about the Indians in Florida. Please, pray for me, and do not forget me. As soon as I am settled, I will try to post a letter. Stay safe. I pray for you every night. I know your sorrow is great. May God stay close by you. Your friend, Fern Abernathy."

Ella tested the sound of the long name. "Aber … nathy." She hadn't known Fern's last name, having thought of it as Stauffer. Slowly, she reread the letter, sounded out the words, and felt a quiver of sadness at each syllable.

Her new friend was gone.

She went to the loft with a heavy heart and tucked the prized letter into the carved box. She wondered how she could write to Fern without paper and a way of posting the letter.

An abrupt wave of sorrow swept over her. She descended the ladder and ran to the isolated grave. After slipping to her knees, she stared upward. Because of her seclusion, only the wind-filled pines, whose sprawled roots had embedded deep in the rocky hillside, heard her words.

"I wish I might see straight to heaven. I need to see you. Mama, the leaves are turning. It won't be a moon's growth, 'til they burst with more color." She paused, wiped her hand over her face, and smeared her tears. "I got me a letter today—a real letter from a new friend I met at your buryin'. She had to go far away. Naomi sent by a pie, and Velma's in the family way again."

The pines whispered in the wind. *Hush, hush, hush.* She labored over her emotions, tried to control her inner turmoil, and fought to think of things besides her lonesomeness.

"Mama, we never named the baby. Pa wouldn't do it. Can I call him Timothy, like in your Bible? I were readin' of Timothy, and I were thinkin' it might fit." She fixed her eyes on the deep-blue cloudless sky. She felt the autumn breeze on her face. "God, please keep Timothy warm and Mama happy."

She asked nothing for herself.

As she meandered down the sunny slope, through frost-nipped golden grass, she spied her pa riding the last hump of the trail. She walked slower, dragging her bare feet, and wondering what type of mood he'd be in when he saw her.

His step seemed lighter, more youthful, as he jumped off the horse and headed toward the cabin. He wouldn't have noticed her, except the old horse spotted her. It lifted its head and whinnied.

Pa jerked off his hat and stared up the hill.

She advanced and stopped ten feet away, hands clasped behind her back.

"You're the spittin' image of your mama." An unfathomable, leering expression lit his face and dark eyes—a glint of unusual interest at the sight of her. "You're lookin' older today." He slapped his hat against his pants leg. "Bought ya a gift."

"Me?" Her eyes flickered to a leather saddle on their horse. "You got a—a saddle."

"Yep, paid fer it this mornin'."

"You bought it?"

"Yes, gurl, but it ain't none of yer dealin's. I had need of it." He reached for a cloth-wrapped package tied to the saddle, undid the string, and handed it to her. "Yer mama's shoes ain't fittin' ya. I got these. Grease 'em down 'fore they get wet. They'll feel good in the winter."

She went speechless. Her shaky fingers pulled aside the material and unwrapped leather boots. She stared. Her bare toes curled in the gritty dirt. Tears blurred her vision, and she hastily blinked them away. Never once had Pa given her anything. Clutching them to her chest didn't still the irregularity of her heart. She attempted to form words of thanks, but her lips couldn't shape the sounds.

He gave her another strange look and grunted. "Not stayin' the night." He removed a second package from the saddle. "I brung a venison slab, cornmeal, bag of salt, an' flour. That's all." He pointed a finger at her and wagged it back and forth. "After today, don't look fer me."

He walked away.

She nodded her head and barely heard the significance of his words. She remained standing in one place. The solid boots felt wonderful held to her chest.

"Thank you, God." Joyfulness filled her heart. She longed to giggle and dance in circles. The boots signified a miracle to her. She was afraid to put them on her feet—afraid they might disappear.

After slipping into the cabin and placing her new treasure on the table, she informed him of Leigh's visit. "And Naomi sent a minced meat pie." She knew it was best to keep Fern's letter a secret.

"He ain't needin' to bring no handouts here. I won't eat it." He sliced a hunk of venison from the cloth-wrapped meat, dropped it on the table, and hung the remainder under the edge of the loft. "Warm that." He pointed at the meat, sank into the rocker, and fixed his stare on her.

Pa's cold eyes became unreadable.

His large hands slid back and forth on the arms of the rocker, in a slow and methodical rhythm. The right one quivered. The thumb drummed against the wood arm in hollow thumps.

Ella swallowed and felt an uncomfortable churning in the pit of her stomach. She had to break the silence. "I doubt he'll be back."

"Who?" His unruly eyebrows rose with the one word.

"Leigh."

"What else did he say? I don't think I like him moseying 'round you. He's got a pretty wife."

"He didn't say much." Fern's letter was her special secret.

"*Hmmph!*" A low growl occurred deep in his throat. "He's got no business up here."

His jerking hand caused her a pang of anxiety. She turned away and propped the cabin door open with a rock. She acted as if the open door was to let in the sunlight, but in reality, she intended it to be a way of escape—should he reach for the strap. She feared her mama's absence would make him turn on her.

"He said he saw you in the cove last night." It was on the tip of her tongue to tell him what Leigh said about her helping with the twins, and then she thought better of enraging him. She also knew not to mention Velma expected another baby.

"He needs to mind his own household." He glowered at her and rubbed his unshaven jaw. "You're a mess. That dress is wrinkled like an old goat's hide. Besides, I don't like seein' you prancin' about in Meara's clothes. Find somethin' else to wear 'sides her dress."

"I outgrew my—dress." Her voice squeaked and broke.

"Well, git out of her dress 'fore I rip it off ya!" Pa half rose from the rocker. His narrow face twisted with an emotion more sinister than anger. His disturbing eyes moved down the length of the dress, and his hand lifted—as if to touch her.

"Yes." Ella gulped in air and sidled away from him. She ran to the ladder. Her fingers seized the irregular rungs, and she climbed as if he chased her.

She crawled to her pile of clothes, alarm causing her to whimper. The selection was pitiful. She grabbed an old muslin shift and crept to the rear of the loft where he couldn't see her undress. She changed in a hurry, but felt vulnerable in the shorter thin shift, so she snatched up a shawl to throw around her neck and shoulders.

Her thoughts drifted to the blouses and skirts her mama kept folded in the trunk. She'd have to cut them apart and see what she could do with them, in order to have more clothes to wear—decent grownup clothing. Mama had promised to do it, but the pregnancy had kept her drained of energy just trying to get through each day.

With her clothing changed, she turned her attention again to cooking.

Ella cut up potatoes and heated them with slices of the smoked venison. She broke the meat apart with a fork. By adding a little water and flour, she produced gravy from the grease in the kettle. She formed two flat cakes and laid them on the rock shoved into the glowing coals. While she did the preparations, she avoided his eyes.

Once they had eaten the silence-filled meal, he disappeared behind the curtain around the bed. She cleared the bowls and set her boots on the table. She applied bear grease to them, wiped, and rubbed it in with her fingertips. A shaft of sunlight beamed through the open door, shone along the tabletop, and caused the greasy leather to shimmer.

"Mmm." She sniffed the inside of one boot. At the same time, a familiar noise caused her to turn toward the curtain drawn along the foot of the bed. The lid of her mama's trunk had been lifted. Its rusty hinges squeaked in protest.

Why was Pa opening the trunk?

She knew it contained her mama's personal clothes, wedding sheets, and delicate items her mama treasured from before she got married. She tiptoed to the edge of the curtain, held her breath, and dared to peek beyond it.

In the dimmer light, Pa squatted in front of the round-topped trunk. He carefully lifted folded sheets and blouses out of the way and dug into the depths. He pulled out a small light-colored item, resembling muslin rolled and secured with a string. His right hand and arm trembled as he untied a knot. The material unfurled like a flag. A folded bit of yellowed paper fluttered downward. It landed in the shadows near the foot of the bed.

A bag hung from his fingers, and he loosened the drawstring at the top. Pa held it by the bottom edge, shook it, and poured the contents into his left hand. He used one quivering finger to poke the stuff in his cupped hand. A smile lifted his sunken cheeks.

"Thank ya, Meara. The rest of this'll pay me back in full. Better than a son," he muttered. He managed to refill the bag and stuffed it into his pocket.

Better than a son?

Ella ducked out of sight and scooted to the bench. She stared at the boots, her mind spinning with questions. She tried to breathe slower and not exhibit any emotion. The muted thump of the trunk's lid heralded his appearance. Pa slipped past the curtain. His arms held clothing and a quilt off the bed.

"Move those boots."

She jumped, clutched the boots to her chest, and watched him. She hadn't understood what took place behind the curtain, but now, she figured he had lost his mind. Why did he dump his clothes on the clay floor by the table?

He spread the ragged patchwork quilt on the table and situated his chosen belongings in the center. Ella edged crosswise the room and sat in the rocker. She saw him collect hand tools and more small items. She swallowed the question on the tip of her tongue. Without a word of explanation, he folded in the corners of the quilt and tied it all with a thin strip of leather.

His arm stopped shaking.

To her, the quilt reminded her of Granny lifting the sides and corners of the sheet over her mama's body for a shroud. Shuddering, she placed the boots on the floor and left the cabin without speaking to him.

Why'd he pack all his clothes?

Ella felt it best to avoid him, and she trotted to the springhouse. She climbed rocks above the gurgling creek and sat on a flat-surfaced boulder. Although the sun dappled the slate gray rocks, she shivered. The spots of sunlight shifted, as the breeze caused the nearby branches to dance. She clasped her arms about her knees and tucked her bare toes under the full shift. She puzzled over Leigh's words and the offer she live with them.

She felt the big man knew things he didn't tell her.

Things about her pa didn't make sense.

"He's goin' to stay in the cove and not come back?" She tested the question aloud, because it tumbled through her mind. It would explain why her pa gathered his clothes.

What will happen to me?

A new sound reached her ears. Someone whistled a lilting tune.

What now?

She slid off her perch and crept barefooted through the woods. She watched Pa tie his belongings to the new saddle.

"That's strange." She couldn't recall ever hearing him whistle. A realization caused her to catch her breath.

He *did* plan to leave for good.

She scurried down the hill. "Pa? Wait."

He raised his head and watched her approach. "What do ya want?"

"You're—you're leaving. Not comin' back?" She felt dizzy. The lump in her stomach made her want to throw up.

"Not returnin'." He stepped into the stirrup and slipped onto the creaking saddle. His hat set low on his forehead and shielded his harsh eyes from her scrutiny. "Don't ferget to feed the chickens an' cows."

"But you *can't*."

"I can't? What I won't do is stay here an' see to the likes of you. I spent a fair share of these years waitin' fer repayment—a son—fer givin' ya my name. Now, I've only taken what's owed me. I figger I ain't duty-bound to the likes of ya. 'Sides, I like grown women, not a skinny, no-curve girl."

She didn't understand his rambling remarks.

"You got in Mama's trunk. You stole from her." Shocked at her own blunt accusation, she edged out of reach. "I saw ya."

"No, it's my past dues." He swung the horse sideways and leaned from the saddle. His thin lips curled in a cruel, mocking smile.

She saw disgust in his shadowed dark eyes.

"Yer mama weren't nothin' but a tramp. I give my name to her offsprin', at her pa's pleadin', in exchange fer this." He waved a hand at the cabin and land surrounding them. "This stinkin' land ain't worth what I done. This is." He padded his pocket.

"You shouldn't talk of her like that. My mama—" Tears burned her eyes and she choked on her words.

"Shet up." He jerked on the reins and turned the horse toward the narrow trail. "I'll be stayin' in town."

She shivered, wanted to disappear in the forest and die. The urge to run until her lungs burst and life faded away made her groan. Numbness settled in.

He was gone.

****

Hours later, after she tended to the chickens and two cows, Ella changed back into her mama's brown dress, even though creases and permanent stains marred the material. The ragged hem dragged the ground. She crouched near the dead fire, uncovered hot coals, and shoved balled deer moss into them. She layered the kindling and wood. Carefully, she put the minced meat pie close to the fire to warm.

No one would share it with her.

While her evening meal heated, she lifted the boots and returned them to the table, side-by-side. The sight of them was still incredible. She never owned anything so grand or expensive. She examined the leather ties and ran her hands over the oiled surface of the dark leather. It didn't matter they looked more like boy's boots than a girl's. They were beautiful. She couldn't bring herself to put them on her unclean feet or wear them outside on the dirt.

Besides, her bare feet were callused and tough. She could take the cool weather a bit longer.

"I should've thanked him." Her shoulders sagged. She spoke to the empty room. "Pa's probably mad 'bout that, but I couldn't think how to say it." She heaved a sigh and tried to come up with ways to excuse her pa's churlish behavior and cruel words. Her mama just always forgave him. Then she remembered the paper on the floor.

It was still there.

She snatched it from the dirty clay floor and opened the two folds. Her mama's precise handwriting greeted her. *These nuggets belong to Miles Kilbride. If he don't return before my death, they're to be given to Ella Dessa, my daughter.*

"Nuggets?" Ella whispered. She turned to the trunk, started to open it, but spotted a sparkle on the hard-packed floor. A dusting of fine powder held a golden shine. *Gold.* Her pa had taken a bag of gold nuggets out of the trunk—gold belonging to another man.

"He had no right." She clenched her fists and stared at the telltale sparkle. Anger held her. Her mama named the rightful owner, the man named Miles. Having her mama's written request ignored caused her more grief than the theft of the gold. She folded the paper and slid it into the Bible.

"Hello, the house. Hey, come back here!" A man's deep voice bellowed the strange greeting and caused her to jump.

Chapter 9

$\mathcal{E}$lla cautiously tiptoed toward the door. Laughter erupted and grew in volume. She inched the door open a crack and placed the side of her face close to the coarse wood.

She saw a wide-shouldered man, with curly white hair, tugging on taut reins. The reins belonged to a determined pack mule. The roan-colored animal laid her ears back, planted her hooves, and stiffened her legs. She stretched her neck with the effort and pulled in the opposite direction, which could've taken her backward down the steep trail.

"Sada, you blame fool. Stupid mule. Stop pulling. Come here! You're going to fall off this mountain someday." The man made the mule advance the last few feet of the steep trail, until the ground leveled off in front of the cabin. It was the area her mama had always called "her yard."

Much like the rush of tumbling debris in a wild stream, a cluster of people poured around the stubborn mule. They made their way into the yard. Most of them were children—a passel of healthy kids—numbering eight in all and varying in age and size.

A thin woman brought up the rear. She shook her head in apparent amusement. "Ephraim, one of these times that mule's going to take you off the mountain."

Her pleasant laugh caused Ella's heart to ache. It brought remembrances of her mama's bubbly sense of humor.

"Do you think she's here?" the man asked.

A dark-haired teen turned to stare at the cabin's chimney. His generous mouth widened in a lopsided grin. "Someone's here. The scent of *food* is in the air."

"Jim, do you always think of food?" A girl with two auburn braids punched him on the arm and squeezed past him to stare at the cabin.

"Peggy, do you have to ask that question?"

Ella heard her giggle.

"No."

He cupped his hands around his mouth and called. "Hello?"

She wondered why they chose to stop in front of her cabin, but she felt giddy with the joy of seeing another human, let alone such a large passel. Her footsteps faltered as she slipped from the cabin. She pawed at her hair, her fingers catching in knots and tangles. Grimacing, she stared down at the discolored spots on her mama's dress.

Two of the younger children pushed each other out of the way, apparently to get a better look at her. The lithe woman stood in their midst. Her dark hair, twisted into a neat bun, showed prominent gray streaks.

"Good day to you, young lady." She waved. "We wondered if we could visit with you."

Visit with me?

Her heart hammered against her ribs and caused her legs to go weak, but she lifted her hand in response. "Yes, stop and visit." As she said the simple words, she burst into tears. Shocked at her own astonishing behavior, she grabbed her skirt and wiped her face. "I'm sorry," she wailed.

"Oh, child." The woman pushed through the cluster of children and smothered her in a hug.

"I'm sorry." She melted into the tenderness of the motherly hug.

"There, there! Cry it out. We don't mind one bit."

The woman's clothes held the aroma of newly baked bread, and Ella wanted to remain cuddled in the arms forever, but she pulled away. She sniffled and faced the others. She knew they saw her messy hair, freckled face, and bare grubby feet showing under the frayed edge of the adult dress. She pulled upward on the neckline and attempted to cover her scars.

"Sorry, I didn't reckon there'd be folks comin' by." She swept away her remaining tears and wiped her nose with her fingers.

"Oh, we came without an invite. I'm Inez McKnapp." The graceful woman's hazel eyes overflowed with kindness. "We wanted to offer our love and God's comfort to you at this extended time of sorrow." Her careful words spoke of education and a place beyond the wilds of the haze-covered mountains.

"Thank you." Ella ducked her head, overcome with the squeezing hurt in her chest. She fought to keep from crying. "My pa left earlier. I don't know—when he'll return." She scuffed her big toe in the dirt at their feet. A puff of reddish dust landed on the woman's sturdy brogans. She winced. "Sorry."

"Shh. They're old shoes." Inez's cool hand pushed strands of hair away from Ella's face."

Ella inhaled and realized the woman's fingers and roughened palm smelled of raw leeks—exactly as her mama's used to when she cooked. She wanted to grab the woman's fingers and hold them against her nose.

"We don't need to speak to your father. You can tell him we called on the both of you. Come, my brood wants to meet you." She nudged her toward the smiling offspring. "What's your given name, child?"

"Ella Dessa ... Huskey." Her curious eyes flickered over the distinctly different faces of the children assembled before her—four girls and four boys. She recalled seeing a couple of them during infrequent trips to the cove. "My pa's name is Jacob."

"Yes, we've met him. This is my husband, Ephraim." Inez pointed at the stocky man still clutching the reins of the restless mule.

Ephraim McKnapp removed his hat and nodded at her. His shocking ice-blue gaze swept from her bare feet to her eyes, but no cruelty lived within their depths. "It's nice to meet you, miss. We were sorry to hear 'bout your mother." He was much older than his wife was and two inches shorter. He had a large nose and a nice smile. "We've been praying the Lord would be with you and your father. We didn't make it for the wake and burying, 'cause half of us were down sick."

She stole a fleeting look to the left, up the slope to her mama's rock-mounded grave. The sun's persistent late rays cut through the foliage and touched the rugged cross where it stood—wedged into the disturbed soil. The cross bore the carved name Meara Huskey and the dates, 1805-1836. No mention of the baby, buried in its mother's arms, engraved the wood.

"It ain't no fun bein' sick," she murmured, not knowing what else to say.

"Thankfully, we're all well, now." Ephraim tightened his grip on the impatient mule.

The animal twisted its thick neck sideways and seemed to peer at Ella. With long ears pointing forward, it stood still. Wrapped bundles and lumpy saddlebags occupied its sweat-darkened back, signifying they'd just returned from the cove and Beckler's General Store.

The girls laughed and someone said, "Sada likes her."

Inez nodded. "My husband keeps a grip on Sada or we'll lose all our goods over the mountain's slope. She gets frisky and wants to rid herself of packs. Rubbing against a boulder is her way of doing that."

"We can't let it happen. I'm too tired to climb downhill and collect it all." The man chuckled and smiled affectionately at his wife.

"We all decided to take the walk to the cove, instead of Ephraim going with our old wagon." Inez nodded toward the children. "Our offspring are like stair steps."

Ella frowned, not understanding.

Inez appeared to read her expression. "I mean, there's lots of them, one after the other in age. The Lord's given us much to be thankful for, because I lost three babies to begin with. This is Grace, our oldest, being close to twenty." She linked her arm through the girl's elbow. "She's getting married near Christmas, and I'm going to cry at her wedding."

"*Oh, Mother.*" The girl rolled her chestnut brown eyes and smiled. "Hi, Ella Dessa."

"Hi." Ella stared at the girl's eyes, rimmed with long curved lashes. They were the most gorgeous eyes she had ever seen. They reminded her of a newborn fawn she once discovered hidden in ferns near the springhouse.

Inez pointed to the right. "The tallest of our family is Jim, our eldest son. He just turned eighteen. Duncan's two years younger in age. He's my strong-willed child. You can tell by his red hair."

Everyone, except the redheaded teenager, nodded.

"Our third son, Samuel, is thirteen. Peggy and Josephine are the giggling ones—at ten and six. Anna is eight. She's holding Phillip's hand. He's my baby and will be three in four months."

"I thank you for stoppin' in." With swift movements, Ella used the heel of her hand to wipe unbidden tears. "I never saw so many younguns, except at Mama's wake, and they wasn't all related." She swallowed the unexpected urge to giggle.

Ephraim's deep laugh showed his delight at what she said. "We're quite a bunch to sort out. We're like beans mixed with peas. Jim, hang to the mule for a minute." He handed the reins to the eldest son. "I want to speak with the Lord."

They all watched the man limp up the incline. Ella noticed he favored his right leg or knee. He stopped under the pines, faced the grave, and clasped his hands at his chest. He bowed his head.

Awed, she watched him and said, "I gave my mama's baby a name, even though he passed on." When no one said anything and Inez only gave her a sad look, Ella added. "It's Timothy."

Inez nodded. "A very nice name."

"My mama read it to me from the Bible." She studied the man standing by the grave. He wasn't like her pa. She would almost bet his arm didn't twitch, and he didn't strike his woman.

"I like the name Timothy." The oldest son pulled on the thin-limbed mule and stepped close. His brown hair parted in the center. Long on the sides, the ragged duck-tailed ends curled behind his ears. The faint line of a darker mustache shadowed his straight upper lip. He resembled his mother, except for the color of his eyes.

Ella's attention locked with his unusual slate gray eyes, and for the first time in her life, she felt a blush stain her cheeks. Unexpectedly, she remembered the book in the Bible her pa forbid her mama to read aloud—

the writings of King Solomon. Love between a man and woman had been a forbidden subject to mention in Pa's presence.

Shocked at her unexpected thoughts, she tore her eyes from Jim's smiling face and reached to stroke the mule's white nose. The deeper roan coloring of its coat started far above the soft nose. It had a lighter-colored mane, sticking up between its ears and along its neck.

Jim chuckled. "Ole Sada likes to be rubbed under her chin. Watch this." He scratched the mule's whiskered chin. She extended her neck and closed her large liquid-brown eyes. Her soft pinkish lips vibrated with enjoyment. "See, what'd I tell you?" He winked.

Her face went warm, and she dropped her head. "She doesn't seem contrary like a mule we had two years ago." With him standing in front of her, she knew what he saw—bumpy red lines above her collar. Immediately, she covered the left side of her neck with her right hand.

The younger children swarmed close to Ella and the mule. They laughed at the reaction Jim got from the pack animal, and Grace spoke to Ella.

"Sada's a big baby. We've had her ever since Duncan was born. She's part of the family." She lifted her brother, Phillip, to her right hip.

The tow-headed boy shoved his thumb in his mouth and gave Ella an intent look of curiosity. He blinked his eyes, but didn't say a word.

Ella smiled. "His eyes are so green." They reminded her of a summer pond filled with new lily pads.

"That's our Papa's Irish background, I guess." Grace squeezed the little boy and grinned at the way he patted her cheek with one little hand.

"Oh?" Ella studied the beautiful older girl and fervently wished she could be as elegant. "You sure got a big family."

Grace nodded. "I know. We've been blessed in many ways. Papa says God lays more blessings on us than we can receive. I truly believe him." She touched her lips to Phillip's head.

Their mother got close enough to pull the boy's thumb from his mouth. "Don't. You're too big for that. No."

"He's spoilt." Grace planted another quick kiss on Phillip's head. "Mother lost a baby boy after Josie—we call her that for short—was born. So, we've spoilt this one."

"Every single one of you is spoilt." Ephraim joined the children and took the mule's reins. Grace's mock astonishment caused him to laugh and kiss her cheek.

Ella couldn't help but grin at the man's bellowing laugh. She felt breathless, not knowing what to say. Peggy crowded in and shoved a damp peppermint stick into her hand.

"Can I share this with you?" The girl's reddish-brown braids had bright curls springing free to frame her narrow face in ringlets.

"Oh!" Ella fingered the sticky candy and raised it to her nose. The scent brought back memories of the only trip she took with her pa to Lick Log. She had been about seven. "It smells so good."

"You can have it." Peggy wiped her sticky fingers on the front of her loose gray dress and shrugged with indifference. "I get candy all the time."

"Peg, don't give her a half-eaten piece." The sturdy boy named Samuel pushed forward. "Here, take mine." Nudging his sister out of the way, he held out a full piece of candy. He matched Ella in height and boldly stared straight into her eyes. His unusual bluish-green eyes twinkled with mischief and fun. "And, you can keep hers, too."

"I can't keep both." She giggled, accepted his piece, but offered the sticky candy back to the girl. Peggy refused it.

"Keep them both." Jim stepped to the mule's pack, pulled on a leather strap, and whipped open a flap on one side. "I'm giving her mine and Duncan's. Got them right here."

Within minutes, she held seven pieces of candy. Phillip wanted the eighth. He substituted it for his thumb and drool soon dripped from his chin. Ella fought tears. The family's generosity overwhelmed her.

"I never had so much." She wiped her eyes and resisted the urge to stuff the candy in her mouth.

Inez pulled her close and kissed the top of her head, before facing the children. "You make me proud. Ella Dessa, it's their gift to you out of their own hearts. It's all yours. Just don't make yourself sick. Now, we must make our way down to Palmer's Ridge. Herding this crowd along that old Indian path will make it close to dark before we get home. Honey, will you be all right until your father gets home?"

87

Honey?

Confused, she studied the woman's face. Why'd the woman call her that? She was also astounded a stranger would be concerned for her welfare.

"Pa's gone for the night. But I know how to care for things." She proudly lifted her chin.

Inez and Ephraim exchanged inexplicable, fleeting glances, and Jim busied himself with the mule's pack. The redheaded son, Duncan, stood close by with the sleeves of his muslin shirt rolled to the elbow. Ella heard him muttering under his breath. The look on his face wasn't pleasant. He abruptly folded his arms.

Ephraim cleared his throat and hitched up his beltless trousers. "Inez, we need to get across the ridge. Pullin' this mule along the trail in the dark won't be safe. We didn't bring a pitch torch. Let's head out."

"At the livery stable today, I heard men say her father's got a new woman. He stayed at her cabin last night—near the west end of the cove. We saw him with her." Duncan hissed the statement through clenched teeth, and his green-eyed stare locked on Ella's face.

Everyone froze. Audible gasps came from Samuel and Grace.

Stunned, Ella stepped backward.

"Duncan!" his mother cried out.

Jim's face flushed. He pushed past the others to face his brother. "Duncan, you had no earthly right to tell her." His fists rose in front of his chest.

"Step back." The father laid a large hand on the teen's shoulder. "I'll handle this." He placed himself between the brothers. "Duncan, you shouldn't repeat unfounded rumors. I think you need to apologize to Ella Dessa. Then git over by that tree." He pointed to a bent pine edged out over the bumpy path, reminiscent of an ancient Indian trail marker.

The boy pressed his thin lips together. Tinges of crimson dotted his smooth cheeks and his eyes flickered toward Ella, as if judging her silence and reaction.

"It's no matter," she blurted out and surprised herself. She didn't want Duncan forced to apologize. All she longed to do was to scurry away and hide. *How could it be true?*

"Duncan?" Ephraim pointed one more time.

The redheaded teen chose to defy his father. In a show of agitation, he rubbed a hand over his face and his hair, but kept his narrowed eyes on her. "I don't like him. Maybe, his daughter needs to know what a skunk he is. He's a liar!"

"Duncan *McKnapp*," his mother said, obviously mortified.

Ephraim's large hands grabbed Duncan by the shoulders and sent him stumbling toward the bent tree. "You do what I said, boy!"

"I'm sorry, Ella Dessa." The woman's face paled. "Our son, Duncan, has been upset lately about a girl he liked. She had to move away, so he's miserable." She wiggled her hand at the younger children huddled close by. "Go with your papa. I'll catch up."

Ella's head ached. She couldn't speak—only stare at Duncan's rigid back. Her thoughts spun in circles. *Pa's got a new woman? Who?*

Inez unknotted a heavy shawl looped about her waist, lifted it to her shoulders, and tightened it across her narrow chest. Her hasty movements said she fended off more than the chilly breeze signaling the setting of the sun.

Grace momentarily paused and told Ella good-bye. Her lovely eyes showed regret for what her belligerent brother had done. "Pay him no mind," she whispered. "He's always in trouble."

Ella grudgingly realized Duncan's frank words helped her understand her pa's strange absence. She had known a tight spot, out of the ordinary, ate at him. He had said as much—stating he had to make a decision. It explained his preoccupation and his final gift of the new boots. The boots had soothed his inner debate between right and wrong. An involuntary shudder skittered over her shoulders. She hung her head, shielding her eyes and feelings.

Her pa had stolen gold out of her mama's trunk and commenced to move on with his life. It was as if she ceased to exist, not worth any consideration. Instead of expecting to be slapped or yelled at after the funeral, she had accepted her pa's deliberate silence and absence. Now, for the first time, she couldn't decide which was worse—fearing abuse or the knowledge she was of no importance.

Inez's hand rested on her shoulder, but Ella didn't acknowledge the compassionate touch. Instead, she lifted her head and considered the children clumped together in a somber huddle near their father. Most waved, but Anna just stared at Ella, her wispy blond hair blowing across her face.

"Ella Dessa, you were alone last night?"

Another woman? Who? Mama's jest buried.

Questions swirled in her head. She felt nauseous.

"Honey?" The woman's fingers pressured her shoulder.

It felt as if a log crushed her lungs. She gulped a shallow breath. It hurt—hurt to suck in air.

"Please, go." She didn't care how rude she sounded. "Pa'll be home soon," she said, ignoring the lie.

Her head hurt. She sought to understand it all. He said he wasn't coming back. But would he bring the woman to live in their home? What were his last words? Her mama was a tramp? A person owed him a debt. Her mama? But he had said he wasn't obligated to—her mama's offspring.

"Ella Dessa?"

"I'm fine." She moved her head from side to side and erased the shattering questions. Her pa's final words made no sense.

Inez insisted on hugging her one more time. "We'll be back to check on you. Understand? Is there anything you need right now? Food? We have plenty on the mule. It's in wrapped packages."

She pushed away. "No, we've—I got food. Pa brought some home today."

"That's good." Inez's lips formed a quivering smile. "You're a beautiful, brave girl."

Jim still held the mule's reins.

His mother's hand touched his shoulder before she walked away.

The family group disappeared. The air grew cool. Clouds enclosed the leftover sunlight spotting the ground.

"Your family has gone." Ella shivered.

"Do you need someone to talk to?"

"No." She bowed her head, avoiding his searching gaze.

Her heart was shredded. It felt the same as when the inexperienced panther had ripped open her flesh. With Granny Hanks' herbal knowledge and her mama's unwearied attention, she had escaped a death-threatening infection.

But what about now? She had no one.

The scars wouldn't go away—ever.

Now, dissimilar scars would disfigure her heart and soul. How much more could she endure? She longed to run to the top of the hill, fling herself on the rock-strewn grave, and die.

"They're leavin' you." She took two steps toward the cabin.

"Listen to me. I'm sorry for what Duncan said. He shouldn't have blurted that out, and I'd like to beat him with my own hands."

"That'd be *stupid*." She glared at him over her shoulder. "He's your brother."

His eyes darkened to a charred gray, mirroring his heated mood. "He don't have a lick of sense when it comes to people's feelings. I might give him what he deserves, after I get him trapped in our barn. That's how we take care of our *brotherly* differences."

"Don't do that."

"You're a pretty girl and shouldn't have to be hurt by Duncan or anyone."

Flinching, she covered the scars with her right hand. *Wish he'd walk away with the rest.* She never felt uglier or more rejected.

He touched her arm.

She whirled on him, her bare feet kicking stones. "I knew 'bout Pa and his woman." The barefaced lie felt good.

"You did?"

"Yes. He's bringin' her here—soon. Tell your family I said 'thanks for the candy.'" With pretended poise, she lifted her chin. Unexpectedly, she wanted him to think of her as unshakeable. Once again, she intentionally turned her back on him. Her left hand still clutched the precious sticky candy.

Jim clicked his tongue to the mule.

Tears dripped off Ella's chin.

The large family vanished like a dream. Not even their mixed voices floated on the wind.

She ran toward the cabin, paused in the doorway, and stared at the deserted surroundings. She hadn't dreamt the whole episode. The candy told her it had happened.

Ella tried to catch a hint of distant voices. But all was quiet. Pa wouldn't be home. However, she could pretend. She could tell herself it was just too late for him to ride a horse along the treacherous, cliff-edged path.

She laid the candy on the pine table and licked her fingers. The sweetness tasted heavenly, but she resisted gobbling the candy. She secured the door for the night and pressed her sticky palms against her cheeks.

"Poor, Mama. I hope she don't know 'bout Pa and his woman."

The growling of her stomach caused her to think of eating the minced meat pie. She knelt on the floor, stirred the hot coals with a charred stick, and added split logs to the glowing embers. The forgotten pie had charred on one side. She pushed chunks of deer moss and strips of peeled bark under the smoldering wood and blew on the coals.

Flames licked upward and ran along the curling bark until they caught on the side of a dry log.

She dug at the pie with a fork. The edge opposite the fire remained edible.

Her thoughts turned to ways to get through the winter. The low stack of firewood, wedged between two saplings, wouldn't be enough for the cold months. Pa hadn't split all of the felled trees. Full logs still lay haphazard on the uneven ground outside. What he had split would last a couple weeks. It posed a problem she didn't know how to solve.

She counted the days since the burying. Eight? Slowly, she tapped her fingers on the palm of her hand and recounted. No, ten. It was almost October. The first flush of color in the leaves would deepen in the cooler weeks ahead. Winter loomed.

The fire's light left the corners of the room dim and chilly. She pulled on a ragged coat, discarded by her pa, and lit a tallow candle. After placing the flickering light in a holder, she sat on the floor near the fire and ate the soft parts of the pie.

The radiating heat felt soothing. She pulled her bare feet under the full skirt of her dress and snuggled deeper into the oversized coat. Its weight over her shoulders felt much like a friend's arm draped about her. She sighed and laid aside the burnt pie tin and her fork.

Her thoughts drifted over the events of the afternoon and the surprise visit of the McKnapp family. The older son's face readily came to her mind. She hugged herself and smiled. Jim had been very nice.

The family's big.

"There's Grace," she spoke aloud. "Jim ... Samuel and little Phillip. That makes four. Peggy, Anna, and Josie. Then Duncan. Eight." Her words accompanied the snapping of the fire.

I wish I were older. Jim might think I were pretty, if'n I kept my scars hid.

She stared at the flames. In her head, she still heard her mama's trembling voice as she read scripture. The evening of her twelfth birthday Mama waited until pa left the cabin and then disobeyed his strict order about Bible reading. She read the sensual words of "The Song of Solomon" aloud to Ella. Tears had imprinted red lines the whole length of her mama's bruised and swollen face.

"This is real love." Mama had ignored a bloody cut on her bottom lip and whispered, "A man and woman are made to love this way. Don't accept less, like I were bound to. My pappy wouldn't let me wed the man which loved me."

"Why?"

"Pappy forbid him to come near me. He brought Mam and me up here in these hills to hide. Jacob, your pa, lived over the ridge. He came 'round, staying to visit. He were older and kept staring at me. Pappy knew he wanted me. There weren't no one else because I had shamed my family. Jacob married me." She gave a hiccupped sob.

Ella had snuggled up against Mama's shoulder, careful of the new bruises down the length of her arm.

Her mama had continued to talk. "Pappy and Mam died three months after, while crossing Halfpenny's swollen creek. I never got forgiveness from Pappy. Then you were born. Life got worse." Regret had etched her words with pain. "My true sweetheart wouldn't have hit me. He loved me like what this says." Her finger had tapped the forbidden pages of Solomon's writings.

"Will a man love me, Mama? With the scars on my neck?"

Mama had cupped her face with warm hands. "Yes, and he'll never belittle you about them."

Sliding her fingers over the disfiguring scars on the left side of her neck, Ella tracked them downward, to where they ran across her collarbone, and curved toward the breastbone. She could hide most of the scars with a high-collared dress, but she only possessed one. There remained a few of her Mama's skirts and blouses. They were much too big. She didn't feel skilled enough to rip out seams and take them in.

She could try wearing her long hair draped across the left side of her neck and shield the scars from inquiring eyes, but it meant she'd never wear her hair up, like a grown woman. Sighing, she tugged her fingers through a clump of tangles. She felt ashamed the whole McKnapp family had caught her appearing so unkempt.

Grace was elegant, and her name mirrored her movements. Her exposed white throat had revealed no painful blemishes.

Ella wrapped her arms around her bent knees and watched the orange and scarlet flames. She knew a forlorn and cold pallet awaited her in the loft, but her heart took comfort at the remembrance of her surprise visitors.

"They don't lack for talkin', with so many. Why, they must talk way into the night. I wish I had a sister—a girl like Fern." She paused and thought of her friend, but her cozy reflections shattered as she recalled part of the earlier conversation.

Inez spoke of Duncan's girl being sent away.

Her pa mentioned a name. *McKnapp?*

The voice was the same. The hand holding Fern's slender wrist had reddish-blond hair sprinkling the top. The sight of Duncan's hand and bare forearm—as he rubbed at his face—flashed into her mind.

It was him. The black pants!

She whimpered as her fortitude crumpled. Why did Duncan want to hurt her with words? Why had Pa abandoned her? God seemed to have left her alone to suffer.

"Mama, please help me!"

Chapter 10

The sputtering metal lantern hung from a misshapen iron hook on the wall. Jim led Sada through the doorway of the barn, and distorted shadows hopped sideways along the rough interior. He tied the mule in an open stall and watched his papa fork dried corn leaves to two half-grown calves secluded in a square pen.

"Papa, the steep path to Huskey's cabin wasn't kind to Sada. She limped home. Perhaps, we need to use one of the other mules for packing."

The older man grunted. "She's like me. Got leg problems." He set aside his pitchfork and went over to pat the mule's skinny rump. "I'm going to trade the two young mules and get horses. We'll keep Sada because we love her so much."

Papa pushed Sada to one side in the narrow stall and loosened the hand-woven strap under her belly. He shoved his hands and muscular forearms under the makeshift collection of leather bags and sacks and lifted the jumbled assortment. With a grunt, he tossed all of them over the top of the short wall and faced Jim.

"Keep her in tonight. I heard a wolf on the back slope. Most likely an outcast and loner. I'm not worried about the other two mules. They got kick left in them—not like me and Sada."

"Papa, I think the red wolf's injured."

"Makes him more dangerous. He can't hunt. He's starving." His papa patted the leather bags. "Why don't you fetch these to Mother, since Duncan's made himself scarce?"

"He hides when it comes to work, plus he knows he hurt that girl. He's ashamed." Jim scratched the mule's forehead, nervously cleared his throat, and spoke what was on his mind. "Papa, Jacob left Ella Dessa alone last night. And most likely tonight."

"Seems so." Papa's thick eyebrows wedged themselves into a crowded frown. "I don't care for the man's innards. Jacob's soul is dark. Can't see how any woman would want him. I know the Good Book says to love thy neighbor, and he just buried a second wife, but that man's been a problem since he came here, almost fifteen years ago. Just like last winter when we all helped him clear his side field. He borrowed my dry land sled. He didn't return the favor when Stauffer needed logs hauled. He's lazy."

"Duncan hates him. Jacob's seeing another woman—with his wife barely cold in the ground."

"But it gives Duncan no reason to treat another person bad, such as he did Ella Dessa. It's awful Manfred believed Jacob's sick story at the time of the burying and sent Fern packing. I never saw such a heart-broken woman as Nettie Stauffer is now—having lost another daughter to her husband's pride. The woman's wasting away with grief this week."

"Manfred's strict." Jim tinkered with the sweat-darkened halter on Sada's head. "But Papa, there's more to the story."

"What? What are you not telling me?"

Jim realized he had slugged open a hornet's nest, and the outcome wouldn't be nice. He wished he hadn't started the conversation. "Well, Jacob talked to the men at the time of the funeral. And then …" He kicked at a pile of matted corn fodder and turned away from the stall. He knew the time for keeping his mouth shut was past.

"Spit it out, Jim. I know you can't hold things in. Not even *your* temper. Spit it!"

Jim folded his arms across his chest, half against the cold creeping through the walls of the barn, and half against the sick feeling in his stomach.

"Jim, does this have something to do with Duncan?"

"Today, while you and Mother stopped to call on Velma, us three older ones went to Beckler's General Store. Grace went inside to purchase dress material. We stood outside. Jacob swaggered past us with that *woman* on his arm! Duncan made a snide remark to me about Jacob not waiting until his wife was cold."

"Ahh, Duncan didn't. Why would a son of mine say that? It's none of his business."

"Well, Jacob heard him. There were men nearby, talking to the smithy. Jacob got in Duncan's face, yelled, and spouted off about what he says he saw near the spring the day of the funeral. He then told everyone it was Duncan with Fern."

His papa faced him with hands knuckled-down on his wide hips. "One of my sons harmed her? Took advantage of her?"

Jim shrugged and muttered, "That's Jacob talking. But I just wondered about it. That day of the burying, Duncan left here when the day chores were done, right after the morning meal. Everyone else was sick." He saw his papa's face redden and swallowed his next words.

"Go on."

"Well, he came back while you helped Mother tend to Peggy and Phillip's fever. Near about dark, as I remember. He came down here to the barn and started plaiting a new whip. I saw the light from the lantern, so I walked out and helped him straighten the leather."

"He didn't say where he'd been?"

"Naw. He acted uneasy, quieter than usual."

"Why didn't you tell me?"

"At the time, I didn't pay much mind to it. I was still feeling sickly. He takes off quite often, and he had completed his chores. I just figured he'd been out hunting or such."

"Tell me Jacob's *actual words*. What did he say today?"

Jim hung his head and hated to tell his papa. "Jacob said Duncan was ripping the girl's clothes off, kissing her, and ... having his way with her in the woods by the spring."

"Enough!" His papa slammed a big fist on top of the stall and shook his head. "Now it's time to deal with it." His lips went pale under his white mustache.

"Papa, give Duncan some slack. Listen to his side. Remember, Jacob's a liar. We all know that. What if there wasn't even a fishing yarn's truth to it? What if he did see someone with Fern, but it *wasn't* Duncan?"

Papa stepped out of the stall and headed for the barn door. The cords on his neck bulged and stiffened like an old bull's neck. He threw open the door and bellowed Duncan's name.

Jim groaned. He knew Duncan would make him pay for revealing the details. Even so, a part of him rejoiced in his brother's probable whipping. He started for the door, intending to make his escape before Duncan came in, but Papa threw out a sturdy arm and blocked his way.

"You're staying. Duncan ain't backing out of this. When you're done with tomorrow's morning chores, I want you to take a bundle of goods to Meara Huskey's little girl. Check on her. See if Jacob came home. She's skinny as a cattail, and her amazing eyes appear huge as an owl's."

Duncan stepped out of the night and into the barn. A waning moon showed over his shoulder. He squinted as his eyes adjusted to the light from the single lantern. "What'd you need?"

"Did you dishonor Nettie Stauffer's daughter?"

The teen's startled green eyes jerked sideways to search Jim's face. "What do you mean?"

Ephraim raised his fist and shook it. "You heard me. Answer—now!"

"No." Duncan swallowed. "Papa, I found out she'd be at the burying. I went to see her."

"Is that all?"

"We took a walk above Jacob's springhouse. I asked her to kiss me."

"And?" Papa limped closer to him. His fist leveled with Duncan's nose.

"I got carried away. I admit I held her tight and took kisses she refused to give. Something came over me. I didn't do what Jacob said. I didn't dishonor her. He lied. He got Fern in trouble for nothing. He wasn't there."

"He says he saw—"

"He didn't see anything from that distance. I didn't get a chance to tell Fern I was sorry. I ran into the woods because Jacob yelled for his girl—the one we met today. No, I shouldn't have run and left Fern to face it. Manfred believed what that hateful man told him." Duncan was as tall as his papa, but at the moment, he looked like a five-year-old. "I heard he's sent Fern to where her sister lives in Saint—"

"*Saint Augustine*," Papa bellowed.

"Papa, didn't I say maybe Jacob lied?" Jim grabbed his arm. "Duncan, I told him that." Jim had never seen their papa so livid. Regret hit. He was sure, at any second, his younger brother would get the worst beating of his life.

Duncan's heavy-lidded eyes searched their papa's face. "Papa, I've told you the truth. You gotta believe me. That rotten man's lying. He left his girl child on the mountain alone the last couple days, while he frolicked with the cove's worst woman. And he didn't just start doing it since the burying. He's no good. Papa, look at the source of the remarks. *Jacob Huskey.* You ain't never had this kinda trouble out of me."

"You're right." Papa dropped his arm and flexed his large-knuckled fingers. His chest heaved. He pushed one hand through his thick hair and nodded. "You boys haven't given me reason to believe the likes of Jacob."

"Whew." Duncan stepped forward and grabbed Papa in a bear hug. "I figured I'd have to fight my own Papa." He gave a weak chuckle and flashed a pleased look at Jim. "Brother, you heard it all. If'n we could talk to Fern, she'd tell the same. It's just her stepfather thought it would shame him. He believed a lie."

"Duncan, don't you ever mistreat a girl or woman, again. That goes for little Ella Dessa. You were *shameful* today. I was disgusted to hear your disregard for her and to know you were my son." Their papa wiped his face and head with his work-toughened hands as if cleansing the problem out of his mind. "I raised you better. I'm going to think things over. I might have you go tell Manfred the truth and beg him to bring the girl home for Nettie—that you'll stay away from her. And—you *will*." He lifted the assorted packs to his shoulder and pushed open the barn door. "I'll take these."

"Papa, I'll bring them." Jim eyed Duncan, judging his brother's temperament.

"I'm taking them now. I know the path, even in the dark. You boys don't dawdle. Mother's probably got supper on."

The wind whistled through cracks in the board walls and swept in at the open door. The lantern fluttered as Jim lifted it off the hook. "You coming?"

"No." Duncan stood with head bowed. He kicked at the clay floor and scattered the litter of grass and leaves. The heavy scent of animal droppings drifted with the air movement. The summer calves jostled each other and bumped against the wall.

"Angry at me? I spoke to Papa about things, when I shouldn't have."

"So? Jim, I'm thinking of leaving here and striking out on my own. Maybe go south and find Fern. I need to tell her I'm sorry. She might consider marrying me."

"Marry you? Naw. I bet she hates you. Besides, Papa said he's not putting up with the way you wander off here and yon."

Duncan ignored him and jerked his thumb at the calves. "You cleaning it out?"

"It's your turn."

"No. You owe me."

Jim handed him the lantern. "Your words hurt Ella Dessa today. You stay and clean it. I won't tell Papa you're thinking of running out on him and the family, just when winter's ready to set in. We need you." He walked into the crisp night. The light in the cabin window and the lopsided moon guided him along the path to the steps.

****

Two hours later, after supper and the evening Bible reading, Jim lay on his back in bed. He stared at the dark ceiling. He couldn't sleep. The lopsided moon shone through the only window and dimly lit the bed. He wondered about the petite girl on the mountain. What had she eaten? Was she lonesome? Was she safe? He folded his hands behind his head and closed his eyes, but sleep evaded him.

The round cornflower-blue eyes of the girl kept bursting into his mind. He could see her sun-streaked hair lift with the breeze and wave across her thin face. Her hand moved, ever so slowly, to push a wayward strand of hair out of the way. The awful scars showed—revealed to his view. Bumpy and red, they engraved an appalling design into her delicate skin.

He wanted to reach out, trace the tracks of the scars, and fit his fingers in the lines disfiguring Ella Dessa's neck. He wondered what caused them. He tossed and turned on his lumpy mattress. What did that to her? *Her father's own hand?*

An animal? He raised his right hand in the dark, spread his fingers, and then snatched them down across his neck and chest. His elbow hit the cornhusk mattress. "Yes!"

Duncan groaned and rolled over. His knees prodded Jim's side. "Go to sleep. You woke me with your muttering and bouncing. Give me more of the quilt!"

"Sorry." Jim turned to face the log wall. The air was cold, but the quilt was a big comfort. And Duncan's solid body next to his added warmth. He felt sorry for Ella in the dilapidated cabin higher on the mountain.

101

Chapter 11

Tuesday, September 27, 1836

$\mathcal{J}$im watched his mother put whole potatoes and dried beans in one burlap sack and wrap a piece of muslin over a loaf of spiced pumpkin bread. The scent of breakfast hung heavy in the warm kitchen.

"Here's the bread. I'll put it on top so it isn't crushed. I packed a small hunk of ham in the bottom. This other bag has two apples." She wrapped a bundle of onions with a piece of yarn and tied it. "There, that does it. I have to tend to my bacon."

"I think it's a bit much for one undersized girl." He left the bundle on the table and smashed his felt hat on his head. He lifted a long-barreled rifle off iron hooks above the fireplace.

"Remove your hat."

He pawed the hat off his head. "I'll be gone most of the morning."

"I know." His mother bent over the fireplace. With a metal fork, she pierced and turned thick strips of bacon in the iron skillet. She gave a loud sigh and laid the fork on a nearby stone. "Maybe Jacob went home last night." Her eyes appeared troubled, and the frown lines on her forehead were more prominent.

"I doubt it. After hearing all the rumors—"

"I wish I had known her mother better. She didn't come off the mountaintop much, but I heard she did join the women when they quilted. You know I'm not much of a quilter. I missed meetings and failed to get to know her."

"Mother, what made the scars on Ella Dessa's neck?"

"A young panther. Over two years ago."

"How come I never heard about it?"

"I would think you had." She thought for a second or two. "Well, none of us knew about it at first, and I guess you had your feelings set on a pretty girl at that time." Her hazel eyes twinkled. She pointed a finger. "Remember? You always hiked down to see that little redhead."

"Hmmph. That was a waste of time. She's gone. Her family left for Virginia. So, what about the panther?"

"Well, from what I heard, it attacked her by their creek. Jacob shot it. But it was the old circuit rider, Brother Cassel, making a visit to their cabin, who found out about the incident. Meara feared she'd lose her only child. Ella Dessa had ran a high fever, and the scratches got infected. Jacob refused to go for Granny and prevented his wife from seeking help."

"He's crazy." Jim felt his face flush with anger. "He deserves to be hanged."

"Watch your talk, young man."

"So, what did Brother Cassel do?"

"He got word to Granny. She rode her old mule to the cabin and bullied her way in. A skinny, immature panther had tried jumping the girl, but instead knocked her in the creek. Its claws only gouged her skin. Otherwise, she'd have died. Granny doctored the poor child, but it was months before she recovered from the infection. Jacob wouldn't allow Meara to leave their homestead during that time. Guess he figured his wife might talk bad of him. So, talk of it died away—at least it did when Jacob was within hearing."

"Why?"

She sighed. "You know why. Most people don't like to rile him."

"Unbelievable." He gritted his teeth. "That man's lacking in normal human feelings."

"Tut-tut. Let's leave off the condemning." Inez ruffled his hair.

"Don't." He tried to duck out of her reach.

"Son, not everyone is as wonderful as your father. You're blessed. All of us are."

"Mother, when was the last time you saw the girl and her mother?" He ran a hand over his thick hair and smoothed it to his head.

"Oh, let's see. Meara came to the only quilting bee I attended this past summer. She brought Ella Dessa with her, but we didn't talk. Meara spent time cutting out a couple of shirts for Velma's boys, instead of quilting with the others. From what I hear, she had a heart of pure gold and a knack for designing patterns of all sizes."

The heavy outside door opened. Duncan and Josie came in, bringing a draft of cooler air with them.

"Hmm, smells good," Josie said. "Can I have a piece of bacon?"

"When we all sit down." Inez waved them to the table. "Where's your papa and the others?"

"Coming. Grace is dressing Phillip. He's ornery today." She tossed her long hair over her shoulder. Its brown waves shimmered, crimped from the tight weave of a single braid during the night.

Jim asked one more question of his mother. "Did Jacob beat his wife?"

Duncan gave a loud snort and mumbled, "Do porcupines waddle?"

Josie giggled. "Yes."

"Hush, Jim—Duncan." Mother's voice dropped to a whisper. "That's not a subject we should discuss." She moved away from the table.

"Maybe, that's the problem," Jim said. "Men like him can treat their wives as if they are nothing but a dog."

"Just make sure you never treat a wife that way."

"Not getting married." He snatched a piece of bacon from the iron skillet and nibbled at it. "Ouch, that's hot." He had already eaten, but the thick crunchy-sided slices were too tasty to ignore. He lowered his voice. "It's too bad about the girl's neck. It's shocking to see."

105

"Yes, I know. I need to explain it to the other children so they don't ask her about them. I was surprised no one did yesterday."

"I am, too. But you brought us up to not hurt another's feelings." He gave Duncan a meaningful look. "She's a tough girl."

"That she is." His mother smiled, and tears welled in her eyes. "And so skinny. You wouldn't think of her as tough. Jim, let her know she's welcome to come stay here." She wiped at her eyes. "I wish I could go with you, but Leigh sent word Velma took a fall. Little Scott had to go for help. They think she broke her wrist. Granny Hanks requested I prepare a meal for the family."

"Gust just left yesterday morning for the mines. Maybe, she didn't fall on her own."

"Hush, Jim."

"Well, people wonder about her unusual injuries." He stepped to the table, ignoring Duncan's dark scowl.

"Have fun hiking while I work," Duncan muttered.

Jim chuckled, enjoying his brother's dark scowl. "Why, thank you, brother." He collected the sacks, shouldered the weapon, and bent to kiss his mother's soft cheek—cool where tears had flowed. "Mother, I do believe you're getting shorter and shorter."

"Quit being a smart face." She made a fist and punched him on the upper arm. "You're just outgrowing your pants. Get along with you. Please give her my love. Make her understand we care."

Duncan spoke up. "Why do I get stuck sorting traps and plowing under the field? And he gets to traipse up the mountain?"

"It's because you'd get lost following the trail to the top." Jim grinned over his shoulder. "Have fun oiling those traps." What he wanted to add was—*you didn't exactly make friends with Ella Dessa.*

He went to the barn and got a backpack his father had constructed from worn leather saddlebags. He flipped it open and slid the burlap sacks of vittles into its depths. After adjusting the straps, he fitted it to his shoulders.

With the gun in hand, he jogged the first part of the trail.

An unusual, heavy frost had turned the mountain pines into tall white sentinels. The morning was dreary and cold, more wintery than fall. He pulled the brim of his hat lower and watched his breath float upward.

He dreaded winter. It meant miserable, short daylight hours. More than any other season, winter ate at his soul. His parents shook their heads at his complaints about tending to penned cattle and sheep, watching for predators, and hauling in cord after cord of split wood for the fire, not to mention treacherous hikes to the spring for water. It wasn't his idea of fun. Plus, nights of marauding animals and daylight hikes to check trap lines along rocky streams didn't appeal to him.

The innumerable cases of jangled nerves, sickness, and cabin fever brought out the worst in all family members—especially when it rained and the temperatures dropped. He hated it when their large clan had to stay crammed between solid log walls. Now that they were older, it felt like suffocation.

Before he topped the trail at the Huskey homestead, he saw and caught a whiff of wood smoke. It drifted low to the ground, like a fog crawling among the trees. The coarse log building, secluded under the pines, came into view.

A weighted plume of smoke rose from the stone and clay chimney, curled snake-like, and drifted toward the ground.

"Morning! Hello?" He respectfully stopped six feet from the moss-edged structure. No breeze moved the surroundings while he waited. His lips felt chapped. His fingers had grown stiff, even while stuffed in his pockets.

The warped wooden door eased open. Ella Dessa had a tattered, multi-colored quilt draped over her narrow shoulders. Gray stockings showed below her muslin shift. Her light-colored hair fell disheveled about her narrow shoulders, emphasizing her stiff posture.

"I weren't expectin' you back so soon."

"Mother sent me with staples she thought you could use. We've more than we can eat. May I speak to your father?"

"He's not here." Her blue eyes had purple circles under them.

107

"Mother sent food." He shrugged the pack off his back and leaned his gun against the exterior log wall. His cold fingers fumbled with a buckle on the pack. "Look, fresh pumpkin bread." He held up the muslin-wrapped loaf. "Mother baked it before daybreak. I saw her scraping the pumpkin. Still feels warm to my freezing hands."

With her eyes on the oblong bundle, the girl stepped back and motioned him into the cabin's dim interior.

The heat from the fireplace hit him and reminded him of sunburn. He set the pack and bread on the table and grinned. He saw the girl's wide-eyed look of delight—because of a loaf of bread.

"Hmm." She unwrapped the bread, gripped the loaf with both hands, and held it under her nose. "It smells like heaven," she whispered.

He laughed. "Well, go ahead and taste a bit of heaven. May I sit by your fire? It *feels* like heaven in here."

"Yes." She laid the bread on the table and snugged the quilt tighter about her small frame. "I'll be back." She slipped behind a bit of frayed sheeting hanging from a rope.

Jim added more wood to the fire and poked at the glowing coals while he eyed the contents of the cramped living space. Only the barest of essentials filled the one-room cabin. A rough-sawn pine table, with two benches, took up the most room. A rocker and chair sat to the left of the fireplace, and a broken spinning wheel leaned against the far wall. A basket of jumbled clothes stood near the curtain, which blocked his view of the bed.

By the table was a pile of flour sacks, mostly unfilled. Two wooden boxes seemed to overflow with straw or cut grass and a damp odor drifted from them, mixed with the scent of rotting potatoes. The thick scent of mold and dampness clung to the interior and reminded him of a cave he once found in the side of the mountain.

The only source of light was the fire and one dismal window—a two-foot square opening. Filtered light fought its way through an oiled animal skin.

The curtain slid sideways. She slipped into view and resembled a small girl playing dress up in her mother's clothes.

She wore the same oversized, wrinkled dress from the day before. A narrow strip of faded brown material, apparently torn from somewhere on the dress, held her hair away from her heart-shaped face. Her cheeks had grown rosy and her eyes shy. The toes of new leather boots peeked out from under the skirt dragging along the floor.

"Unseasonable cold this morning," he commented, trying not to show the sympathy he felt. "Thanks for letting me come in by the fire."

"Thanks for bringin' this to me." Her delicate hands fluttered over the pack as if not sure what to do. "Thank your mama."

"Go ahead. It's all yours." He could tell she wanted to open it. "We've too much to eat. I should've brought you honey. I found a bee tree two weeks ago. The fair weather combs were capped off and overflowing."

"Did you get stung?"

"Yes. They didn't want to give up their hard work, meant for the winter."

"This is too much." She lifted the potatoes and onions from the pack. Her hands shook as she seized the small cut of salt-cured ham. Grease stained the muslin encircling its irregular shape. "Pa will pay you." Her chin lifted with pride. Her child-like expression met his. "We do have cured venison and flour."

"My folks wanted you to have this. There's new butter in the covered tin." He unbuttoned his coat and tossed it over a lopsided bench by the table. "Go ahead, eat." It gave him keen satisfaction to watch her face light with pleasure.

Within minutes, the skinny girl used a knife to slice the heel off the loaf. She sniffed. "Pumpkin." With an air of anticipation, she spread a gob of firm white butter and took a bite.

Jim heard her murmur of approval.

"I guess I'm hungry." She gazed at the thick slice in her quivering hand. She then cut a hunk of ham and bit into it, not caring breadcrumbs still stuck to her face.

He averted his eyes, puzzled by the ache in his chest, and gazed upward. The half-log mantel over the fireplace had no personal items on it. Instead, crowded together was a collection of kitchen implements, iron hooks, a battered metal pot, a pewter candlestick holder, and a diminutive pine-needle basket.

The basket's lid was open. Jim could see a looped coil of delicate handmade lace. Its intricate pattern, a jarring reminder a woman once called this her home. He felt perplexed by the absence of personal items. The walls and mantel at his home peeked out from behind handmade decorations. His mother encouraged her children to make things with their hands.

The cave-like bleakness of the Huskey cabin depressed him. He knew he must move or flee from its encompassing walls. He rose to his feet.

His swift movement startled the girl. A guarded air of alarm clouded her round eyes. She wiped both hands down the front of her shabby dress and darkened the material. Her fingers trembled. The stark anxiety in her eyes said she realized she had let a stranger come into the cabin—without much thought to danger.

"Can I bring in wood?"

"There's no more split." Her eyes darted to the lopsided pile near the hearth, and she licked a smear of shiny grease from her top lip. "It's gone, 'less I put a big log in—one end at a time."

"That's not safe." Jim felt a surge of fury toward the man who left a child alone with no cut wood. "It's only the start of winter. You won't make it through."

"My pa ain't had time. I've burnt too much the last few days. I was chilled." She avoided his stare and used her teeth to pull a hunk of meat off the ham bone. "I haven't split more. There's logs." Grease showed on her pink lips.

"You shouldn't have to. I'll do it." He reached for his coat and hat. "Where's your axe?"

She pointed to the wall beside the door.

He gathered the axe and a froe. "Stay in where it's warm. I can find the logs."

He held back curses when he saw how Jacob failed to prepare for the coming winter. Logs lay on the ground, stripped of limbs, but not cut into short lengths. He saw one lopsided stack of three-foot logs, which hadn't been pre-cut and split, much less stacked correctly. Under his breath, he called the man several choice names as he wielded the axe.

In no time, he had achieved a pile of short logs. Then he set the cut pieces on a tree stump and swung the axe into the dried wood. Identical halves parted and fell to the ground, and he drove himself to split as much as he could.

Jim knew his father would wonder if he stayed away, just to avoid work, but he concluded he could honestly explain his absence. It didn't take him long before he stood back and eyed the splendid pile of split wood he managed to stack near the cabin's door.

He flexed his sore shoulders and explored the homestead.

The boney cows needed tending, and he forked dried corn leaves to the two penned in the dilapidated barn. Their shrunken udders revealed they didn't have anything to give. They stood in filth on the clay and flat-stone floor.

Jim walked to the rugged chicken house. He had to bend almost double to get inside and chase the small flock out into the mid-morning sunlight. The skinny-necked chickens squawked and ran frantic circles in the foraging pen. He found one egg and took it to the girl.

"An egg?" The expression on her face was priceless. "Thanks for helping. I forgot to shut the chickens in last night. A fox snatched one—carried it off. I saw feathers. Leastways, I think it were a fox. We've only five left. I went out early this mornin' to latch their door."

"Chickens are valuable."

She studied the egg in her hand. "We don't get eggs much. A skunk keeps digging under—to get to the nest boxes. Pa drove wooden pegs between the rocks, but the skunk claws the dirt and clay out around 'em."

"It's late in the year for eggs, anyways. Do you have feed for them?"

The girl avoided his gaze. "No, I guess they'll hav'ta make do with scratchin'. I gave the last of the feed two days ago."

"Two days? Hmm, not much for them to find outside. Bugs are dead or gone with the turn in the weather. Don't you worry. We can spare cracked corn and feed for them. I'll try to bring a sack tomorrow." He frowned, wondering what else to do for the girl. "You'll be all right if I leave?"

"I keep busy." She turned away from his scrutiny and placed the brown egg in a basket. Her narrow shoulders drooped.

"Ella Dessa, I'm believing my parents will suggest you stay with us for the winter. It'd be best."

"No. Pa would come home and find me gone. Plus, Duncan don't cotton to him. There'd be trouble if my pa found out where I got off to." She sat on a bench and folded her hands in her lap. "When Pa marries, he'll bring her here. I have to wait. Guess he thinks I need a new mama." Uncertainty clouded her eyes and altered them to a misty blue.

"Ella Dessa, I wish you'd consider packing clothes and coming with me." Jim gritted his teeth and fought the temptation to tell the sweet girl her father wouldn't bring home a new mother. From all indications, Jacob planned to leave the cove. "We can write a note for your father. He can come get you."

"Pa don't read. Besides, there's no paper."

"Then we'll think of another way. Scratch a picture in the clay floor?" he suggested and grinned.

She giggled. "Mama used to do that."

"See? It's a plan."

"No. I got animals to tend." She dropped her eyes to her folded hands.

"Papa and I will come back for them."

"I ain't goin'." Her chin raised a notch.

He almost grinned. "You're a girl. You don't have supplies to last the winter. We'd all worry about you. Come with me?" He held out his hand.

"No." She stared at his outstretched fingers.

"Then, that's it." Jim lifted his empty pack and cradled his rifle. "I'll be back. Maybe, I can bring word of your father." As he opened the door, she shivered and hugged her own waist. She appeared so fragile. "Bye, Ella Dessa."

Her eyes glistened with unshed tears. "Bye, Jim. You tell your mama 'thanks.'"

He nodded, flipped the pack over one shoulder, and shoved an arm through a strap. *I shouldn't leave her here.* But he couldn't hog-tie her. *She's a little thing. I despise you, Jacob Huskey. You don't deserve a daughter like her.*

Chapter 12

"How was she?" His mother occupied a rocker close to the hearth and a stack of firewood. From where she sat, she could keep an eye on the girls doing schoolwork at the table, reach and toss a piece of wood on the fire, and hardly hesitate in her knitting.

Jim smiled. "Thrilled by the pumpkin bread and ham."

Brown woolen yarn curled and looped across her lap. The wooden knitting needles clicked without pause. "Was Jacob there?"

"Naw."

"So, she refused to come."

"Yes." He crouched on the stone hearth and arranged fresh logs on the hand-forged iron grate. "How can Jacob do this to his own daughter?"

Mother stuffed her needles into the yarn. "Not many men are like your father. A man who lets his natural drives and inner selfishness take over will lose what's most precious in this world. Jacob will lose Ella Dessa. If a man doesn't want God's guidance and help along the path of life, his own desires will cause him to destroy his connection to other people."

He recognized the miniature sermon in her words. He sat on the floor, stretched his legs out in front of him, and crossed his ankles. Tired from chopping wood and the hike home, his anger at Jacob grew.

"What's wrong?"

"I'd like to give Jacob a piece of my mind with my fist. I could take him down. He's stringy and tall."

"Jim, letting your temper solve problems will never get you anywhere. Remember that. It'll cost you. Jacob has a frightful temper. Men avoid him. Rumor has it Meara endured beatings. Perhaps, the girl suffered, also."

"How bad did he hurt Meara?"

His mother looked toward her girls. They sat quiet, trying to catch tidbits of the conversation. She dropped her voice to a soft murmur. "I just caught snatches of conversation and overheard the remarks women made when Jacob rode into town. He never brought Meara or Ella Dessa with him. There had to be a reason."

"Can't we bring the girl here?" He tossed another log on the fire. "I think she'd come if you and Grace prodded her."

"Heard my name." Grace entered, sank to the wooden floor on the other side of the rocker, and crossed her legs under her dark-green skirt. Her hands appeared red and chapped from scrubbing the plank flooring in the girls' bedroom. "Also heard what you said, Jim." She raised her smooth brows. "I think her coming here is a great idea. I'll even go with you—to get her."

"Wow, it's not every day my big sister wants to go hiking in the cold."

Grace reached past their mother's legs and smacked his leg. "It's not an unmarked trail. I climbed it recently. *Remember?*"

From the table, Peggy ignored the school assignment in front of her. She placed her left elbow on the book, to keep her place, and twirled a strand of reddish hair over one finger. "I think we can make space for her in our room."

"We're crowded now." Anna wrinkled her nose. "Phillip's in our room."

"Put him with the big boys," Peggy said.

"No, he's still too little." Their mother shook her head. "The big boys wouldn't wake if he needed comforting during the night. This way, he has Grace until the wedding."

"Mother, she's not leaving the cove." Jim saw his mother's face reflect unhappiness at the thought of her oldest child leaving the home.

"I guess not," Mother said. "I'll discuss it with your father. I'm sure we can find room for such a tiny slip of a girl, even if she sleeps here in the kitchen. But your father needs to tell Jacob. We'll say we can use her as a maid, since he's leaving town."

"Maid?" Grace's oval face showed dismay. "You wouldn't do that to her."

Mother rolled her eyes. "Grace, you know me better than that. It's just what we'll tell him."

"Whoa! He's *really* leaving?" Jim tugged at her sleeve.

"Leigh stopped to talk to your papa, just after you left this morning. It seems Jacob told everyone he's leaving town tomorrow. He plans to wipe his feet of the cove, the mountain, and start a new life in Virginia. Phoebe Windorf is going with him. She has kinfolk there."

"Phoebe Windorf! Why, she's a—"

"Jim!" His mother's eyes flashed an unspoken warning. "Grace, where's Phillip?"

"I left him sleeping on my bed. He needed a nap. Mother, we know girls Anna's age have worked the back room of the store, but Mr. Beckler and his sister, Agatha, treat them good. They even board there. How about asking them?"

"Yes. Walter has a kind heart."

"I think one girl's name is Lessie." Grace smiled. "Agatha teaches them to read and sew. It's a good place for them to be."

Jim spoke up. "Agatha only takes in orphans."

"She might make an exception with Ella Dessa." Mother stood and laid her knitting on the rocker seat. "This subject is closed for now. I have to see to our meal. The others should be back soon. We'll discuss this later. Grace, go wake Phillip."

Jim snatched up the knitting and slumped into the rocker. His thoughts whirled.

The door opened, and his papa, Duncan, and Samuel entered.

"I'm froze." Samuel made a beeline for the fire, shucked his coat, and dropped it to the floor. He held reddened hands toward the flames. "We walked half the mountain checking animal trails, tracks, and traps. I'd rather do homework all day."

Jim studied the irritated look on Duncan's face. It told him his middle brother still fumed about being left behind to do the trap line, but he really didn't care what Duncan liked or disliked.

"Who died?" Their papa shut the door to the dogtrot. "Everyone's so serious." A half-grin uplifted his full lips and bushy mustache. He winked at his wife and slipped off his coat. "It wasn't me, I'm still here. See?" With one cold-cracked hand, he playfully patted his wide chest.

"I told them what Leigh said to you." She took his hand, turned it over in hers, and shook her head. "Honey, you need to put bear grease on them."

"No time. What's wrong?"

"The children think we should go get Ella Dessa."

"They do?" He placed an arm along her shoulder, grimaced, and leaned on her. "Do they realize this place can't hold more younguns? Where'd she sleep?"

"She'd sleep with us girls." Grace proceeded to wipe three slates clean and erase spelling words written by the girls. "Phillip will bed with the boys. Samuel's a light sleeper. He can watch out for his little brother."

"Hey, wait a minute! Don't I have a say in this?" Samuel sat cross-legged near the fireplace. "I'm a light sleeper because of the noise level in that room. Phillip won't sleep at all with Jim and Duncan serenading him all night. Ouch!" he yelped, as Jim's boot connected with the side of his right thigh. "That hurt."

Grace ignored them. "Papa, Ella Dessa can sleep on the pallet Phillip uses in our room. I'm sure she won't mind. Or I'll sleep there, myself." Her tone was gracious and pleading at the same time. "I bet Jacob wouldn't even care if she came here."

"I agree." Jim clutched the knitting in his fists. He knew his papa quite often let the majority rule in a family discussion.

"Jim, that's not the issue." Papa shook his head. "Daughter, you've a kind and loving spirit. I'd like to slip the child down here and hide her, but I need to answer to a higher calling. I must try to do it the right way, 'cause

Jacob's her parent. Besides, he and Duncan have tangled. So, I got to tread lightly. Leigh also said he and his wife would take her in. We've a small community of people who'll band together and protect the child."

"I'd give up my pallet if it wasn't for her having to sleep near Duncan and Jim." Samuel snickered. "She'd need cotton stuffed in her ears." He lifted a book from the floor and opened it. "I read at night because I can't sleep."

Duncan advanced across the room in two strides. He grabbed Samuel under the arms and lifted him to his feet, which caused the book to drop to the floor. "I think Jim and I will carry you out to the barn for the night. You'd learn how good you have it."

"Duncan, he's joking." Grace frowned as their red-haired brother released Samuel and gave him a playful shove.

"They both snore like woodchucks." Samuel picked up his coat and hung it on a peg. "It sounds like two saws in our room." He held his nose and produced noises with his throat to prove his point. He got giggles from Peggy and Josie.

"Stop!" Their mother raised her hand. "Hush and quit the nonsense." She rescued her knitting and put it in a grapevine basket near the hearth.

"I agree." Ephraim pointed at the table. "Let's partake of the evening meal. In the morning, I'll go to the cove and speak to Jacob myself." He hung his hat on a peg behind the door and groaned. "I have to sit. My knee seized on me today." He limped to a bench at the table and bent to remove his boots.

The girls scurried to assist their mother.

Jim knelt and helped remove the boot. "Papa, you should've seen her face when I gave her the pumpkin bread. We've just *got* to help her."

"Son, I'll approach Jacob if he'll talk civil to me. And if I can make it down the trail." He grimaced and gritted his teeth as Jim pulled on the boot. "Ahh! It hurts."

"Papa, can I leave my chores and go get her first thing in the morning?"

"Jim, be patient. I don't want Jacob fuming mad and coming after us. He'd do that if we go get her without him knowing."

"He'll give you the girl." Duncan used his fork to shove food sideways on his plate. "He don't want her. But he might think of it as a deal. That she's to work for us. He may insist on you sending him money." He lifted his slanted green eyes and gazed at them over his fork.

"No, he won't." Their mother's words rang firm. "She'll be treated the same as any of you. Ella Dessa won't be a paid servant or even an unpaid one. What little work she'll do, will support her room and board."

Papa pounded the table with his right palm. Plates bounced. "Listen. I'm tired enough to want this chatter stopped. Jim, you hike up the trace tomorrow. Check and see if Jacob came home. Samuel, you want to go with 'im?"

"Sure would. I can help carry things when we *tell her* she's moving."

****

Jim elbowed Duncan over on the bed. Samuel slept on a pallet next to the wall. The girls and Phillip slept in a larger room connected to his parents' bedroom. The large house was a blessing. It had been built to Mother's specifications and wishes. Grace would soon get married and move out. But now, Ella Dessa might move in. That meant the girls' room would remain crowded.

A gust of wind buffeted the sturdy log walls. Duncan's snores mingled with the sound of Samuel's quiet breathing. Jim found comfort with his family within the walls of their home. What must it be like for Ella Dessa left alone?

"Oh, Lord." He closed his eyes, pushed his personal spiritual doubts away, and whispered a prayer of protection for her.

He wasn't one to ask God for things. Prayer couldn't be listed as one of his strong points. He only prayed at the table when his parents asked him to say the blessing. Never once had he let them know how he resisted their strong fundamental beliefs in God's will for their lives. He struggled with his parents' staunch beliefs and battled his temper. But he wanted to please everyone, and that kept him busy playing a game of pretense.

His irritability was his worst enemy, and only Duncan knew the full brunt of it. Jim rolled over and resisted the temptation to jostle Duncan awake because of the erupting snores.

****

118

Ella Dessa used a pointed stick and warmed the last bit of smoked ham over the fire. She rummaged through the food Jim had brought and chose two potatoes. Tomorrow, her food supply would be less. She'd have the small amount of pumpkin bread, the squash, an egg, and the old slab of venison hanging from the loft.

She eyed the moldy venison. It turned her stomach. She figured she'd live on the stored potatoes. The corncrib held no corn within its walls—not even winter fodder for the two cows.

It was late. She rinsed the potatoes with cold water and turned them in her chapped hands. *Why cook 'em?* She liked them raw. The leftover pumpkin bread would be good for morning. Content with her meager fare, she sat near the warmth of the fire and munched on a raw potato and the hunk of ham.

"Guess this is a lazy girl's meal. No cookin'." She spoke to hear her voice over the crackling flames. After swallowing the last piece of the potato, she reached for the second one and bit into it. When it was gone, she remembered the sticks of candy.

While she enjoyed the sweet candy, she stared at the cold dark loft. "No, I won't sleep there."

Within a short while, she banked the fire, pushed aside the muslin curtain, and crawled into her parents' bed. It sagged in the middle and molded to her body as she turned to watch the flames toss shadows on the log wall.

She tried to keep her wild thoughts at bay and fought them the way a bear swats off a pack of dogs. But the more she pushed them away, the more they attacked her.

The wind grew in force. It found places to whistle through the chinking in the walls, especially in the loft above her head. She burrowed deeper under the layers of ragged quilts. She didn't want to hear the noise outside. She knew it meant a bitter wind blew over the forlorn grave on the hillside.

While besieged by an aching heart, she prayed, "Dear God, keep Pa safe wherever he is. I don't care if he stole the gold, or he thinks I need a new mama. I want him to come home. I can be friends to a new mama. I don't want to be alone. Please, help her to like me." Her fingertips inched up to swipe at tears tickling the sides of her face. "Thank you for the fine folks who gave me food and for Jim's kindness in fetchin' it. Help me to do good when the new mama gets here."

She swallowed sobs and pulled her knees and elbows tight to her body, warding off the loneliness. Her thoughts turned to Fern, and she wondered how the older girl felt when her stepfather sent her away.

It must've hurt real bad. I'd hate to forsake Mama alone on the hill.

Jim's face, with the dark traces of a youthful mustache, came to mind. She thought he was handsome, with the older ways of an adult. He had acted concerned about her, and it gave her some comfort.

She smiled, remembering the partial loaf of pumpkin bread. It lay near the fireplace, wrapped tight to keep it from drying out. The thought of it almost caused her to throw back the quilt and go cut a little piece. It tasted so good. But memories of their cabin flooded with the scent of food, prepared by her mama, kept her where she was—because the past hurt too much.

"I mustn't think of myself all the time. I got to think of others." She scrunched her eyes shut and tried to imagine what the new mama would look like. Would she be old—young? Who was she? There weren't too many single women in the cove.

Restless, she flipped to her back and stared into the darkness. *What if I walk to the cove?* She just had to follow the trail. "Yes, that's what I'll do. I'll get up early and feed the animals. I'll wear my new boots and go meet the woman who's going to be my new mama."

Chapter 13

At daybreak, Samuel and Jim headed for the Huskey cabin. No frost sparkled, and the air felt warmer. Both of them carried empty packs over their shoulders. They intended to use them to transport anything the girl might want.

Jim slung papa's gun on his back and adjusted the homemade leather sling. He chuckled, as they hiked side by side on a wide section of the trail.

"What's so funny?" Samuel asked. The rim of his floppy black hat hid his expressive eyes from view.

"Ah, just imagining Duncan plugging away at our chores—mine for a second day.

"He weren't too happy at breakfast."

"Nope, he sure wasn't smiling."

Samuel's brow furrowed as he leaned into the slope. The trail circled a cluster of piled boulders—pewter gray against the rusty soil.

"What's wrong? Need to rest?"

"No, thinking about Papa. His knee's worse. I saw red swelling." Anxiety flooded his adolescent voice.

"I noticed it." Jim remembered the disquiet on their mother's face.

"I think he hurt it squatting and kneeling in the woods, inspecting spots where he thinks we'll set traps. He talked like he's putting Duncan in charge of them for the winter."

"Really? He usually wants to do it himself. Duncan hates setting and checking traps. I wonder what Papa's thinking?" Jim studied the bumpy path under their feet. He didn't like it when unusual things cropped up. It set him to worrying too much, just like the constant fretting over Ella. Once a thought took over his mind, he had a hard time shaking it.

Samuel tugged at his coat sleeve. "Do you think Papa isn't feeling good, besides his knee?"

"I think he's weary." He wanted to eliminate his brother's qualms.

"How old is he?"

"Why?"

"Duncan called him an old man yesterday. Right to his face."

"*What?* He shouldn't disrespect the man. He might find out how strong our papa really is." He shifted the satchel on his back. "Papa's sixty-one. He ain't old. He's just got white hair."

Samuel nodded in agreement. "Why's Duncan so …?"

"Defiant?"

"Yeah, that's the word."

Jim stopped in the trail. "Let's take a breather." He had set a fast pace over the last low hogback, a slope covered with dark evergreens. Samuel's shorter legs struggled to keep up.

"Good. I need a rest." The younger boy bent over and braced his hands on his knees.

"Samuel. Our brother wants to leave and explore the world. Papa wouldn't let him go work in the gold mines this fall, and Duncan doesn't think he should have to work the farm." He drew in a deep breath and stretched.

"How can he think that? He's part of the family."

"He's itching to wander, explore, hunt for gold, and he's more moody each passing day. He'll disappear one day and break Mother's heart."

"I don't want to ever leave." Samuel gazed at an ancient rocky knob above them. "*Never.*" His stance was relaxed and easy, his childish face glowing with health. "Even in the winter, I love the mountains. I'd be content to live here always, but I don't want to farm. I want to teach."

"Teach? Are you that serious-minded?" He smiled at Samuel. "Well, I can see you doing just that. You're not lacking in verve or math. By the looks of it, with you teaching Phillip, he'll know how to read before he's three." He whipped his hand sideways, knocked his brother's old hat to the ground, and ruffled Samuel's hair.

"Hey, what'd you do that for?"

"Felt like it." He dodged his brother's ineffectual punch. "Let's go. We're near the ridge."

When they topped the trail and could observe the secluded cabin, a jab of alarm fired through Jim's veins. He instinctively crouched, jerked Samuel sideways into a clump of trees, and peered through the orange-tinted leaves. No gray column curled from the stone chimney and the door hung wide open. He pulled the gun forward, lifting the sling off his shoulder and chest.

"What is it?" Samuel squatted on his boot heels, knees bent to his chest.

"I don't like what I see. The place seems deserted." His heart throbbed in his throat, choking him, while he surveyed the hushed, dreary surroundings. As their heavy boots scuffed the thick layer of leaves under the trees, he could smell leaf mold. But the air was absent of smoke. There hadn't been a recent fire in the cabin.

"It's too quiet. Did Jacob come get her?" Samuel said.

Nothing stirred. The cows weren't anywhere to be seen.

Samuel slipped forward into a kneeling position and pulled aside the branches. He removed his hat and peered through a space in the lower bushes. "She might be in the barn. You think?"

"There's no smoke, and I split plenty of wood yesterday. She'd have a fire. Tell you what. You stay here. I'm going to the cabin alone. Watch for any movement. Give a low whistle if you see anything. Stay put. But run like an Indian if someone grabs me."

Cautiously, he held the gun shoulder high and inched across the open space in front of the low-profile cabin. When he neared the unfastened door, he paused and held his breath.

Silence permeated the interior. His nose caught the arid scent of old wood ashes.

"Ella Dessa?" He whispered her name and stepped over the stone threshold, gun ready, finger on the trigger.

The girl wasn't behind the curtain or in the loft. The cabin was tomb-like and silent. He felt spooked, not expecting her to be gone when they arrived. He motioned to Samuel and waited until his brother—with shoulders hunched and head low—sprinted the distance between them.

"She's not in here. Stay behind me. We'll search the outbuildings." He tried to act braver than he felt.

"It's scary."

"Shh, go quiet." Jim's fingers cramped as he gripped the gun tighter, knowing he'd have to make one shot count.

The barn door was barred, but he gritted his teeth and swung it open. The two boney-hipped cows extended their brown necks over the stall's top board. One gave a low, expectant moo, and Jim's nerves jangled as the forlorn sound echoed in the dank interior. The odor of urine and piled cow dung, testified to the fact they hadn't been outside that morning.

"She's not in here. Let's try the chicken house." He nudged Samuel with his elbow.

As they warily slipped along the side of the squatty building, Jim noted the door wasn't bolted on the outside. Had Ella Dessa failed to fasten it? It was made to open inward, to keep chickens from flying out when someone entered. He put his hand on the short door and pushed.

It wouldn't budge.

Scowling, he handed the gun to Samuel and slammed his shoulder against the wood entrance. His shove met resistance.

A muffled scream killed the silence. Chickens squawked and cackled in panic, and one burst through the partially open door. It flapped into the early morning sunlight to run in a circle—just as something tried to push the door shut.

"Ella Dessa?" Jim snatched the gun from his brother. "Are you hurt? Let us in."

Broken sobs could be heard. Filthy fingernails appeared on the edge of the sagging door. It opened wider. The scent of chicken droppings and damp earth wafted outward.

She scrambled through the opening and over the raised wooden threshold. Her momentum sent her reeling into Samuel and knocked them both to the stony ground.

"Ugh!" Samuel's wide-brimmed hat went flying. His arms caught Ella Dessa about the waist as she sprawled on top of him. While tangled in her long loose shift, they tried to separate and get to their feet.

Jim sputtered with laughter, laid aside the gun, and grabbed the girl under the arms. He lifted her to a standing position. Samuel rolled sideways and gained his feet, sheepishly brushing at his clothes. The girl covered her red face with her hands.

"I never had that happen before." A good-natured grin lit Samuel's flushed face. "*Whew*! Thought a giant chicken had attacked me." A reddish-brown feather hung from his hair.

Chuckling, Jim plucked the feather from his brother's head and touched the girl's shoulder. "What were you doing in there?"

"There was a wolf."

He surveyed the tree line and field. "He's gone."

Ella Dessa rubbed her face with filthy hands. Her fingers left muddy streaks circling her blue eyes and marking her freckled cheeks. "Durin' the night he was here." Her voice sounded hoarse. "I saw him in what's left of the moon, before I got in with the chickens."

"What? Last night? You spent the whole night in there?" Jim stared at her.

"Yes. It was cold." Her hair hung past her waist, disheveled, and dirty. The scooped neckline of the nightshift exposed purplish-red scars on the left side of her neck. They disappeared downward toward her breastbone. Her fingers clasped the thin material and pulled on it to cover the marks. "I heard sounds when the wind died down. I got the lantern and came to see. He were diggin' under."

"Where?" Jim turned toward the building. "Sure 'nough." Claw marks and a pile of soil marked the hole started under the initial log.

125

Samuel squatted and bent closer, hands on the dirt. "He didn't finish."

"No, I skeert him. He ran, but circled back at me. I jumped inside, shut the door, and put my back to it. He'd come back to commence diggin'. I screamed and banged on the door. Now, it hurts to talk. Plus I was cold."

"You didn't have a gun?" Jim felt sick to his stomach. She had traipsed out in the dark with only a lantern.

"Pa took it."

"You're a bit peaked, but braver than most girls." Samuel grinned and regarded her with apparent admiration. "I know none of our sisters would do that."

Ella Dessa hiccuped and forced a slight laugh. "I'm not brave. It were stupid." She held the shift's material against her neck and started for the cabin. "I need to go inside." Her cold-reddened feet and ankles showed as she hurried away.

Jim and Samuel shooed the chickens out of the coop, retrieved the lantern, and scooped dirt back into the hole. They packed it down.

"Think he'll come back?" Samuel dropped a hefty rock on the soft-packed soil.

"Strange behavior. Yes, more than likely. I bet it's the lone wolf Papa saw by our place. He's limping and starving. If he'd show himself right now, I could shoot him."

"Kind of sad. Less and less wolves in these mountains."

Jim rolled his eyes. "I don't consider it sad. Look what this one did."

"I think he's unable to hunt."

"Well, they kill livestock and even people. It'll be good when they're gone. Leigh lost five lambs to wolves this past spring. We lost three to some wild animal."

Samuel palmed his hat, brushed at it. His calm, green eyes held something unreadable. "They were in the mountains before man."

"So? Does that mean we feed them? Let them kill our stock? No. They're of no use. So, when they're gone, we'll all be safer. There will be more deer. We can feel at ease walking trails or even working in our fields, especially during the winter."

"I don't see it that way." The younger boy's chin lifted, ready for a dispute.

"You wouldn't, Book Man." He affectionately patted his brother's shoulder. "Hey, she flattened you. You should've seen your face. You resembled a bullfrog with a boulder landing on him."

"No, I didn't."

"No, you didn't. You had both arms wrapped about her middle, hanging on for dear life. I had to make you let go of her. What were you *thinking*?"

"I wasn't hanging onto her." He swung his fist and pummeled Jim's left arm. His face went crimson. "She fell into me—knocked me flat."

Jim laughed and dodged his brother's next wild swing. "Missed. Hey, stop. Let's do what we came for—see if we can talk her into going with us."

The girl opened the door to Jim's knock. Her face and hands glowed pink from a good scrubbing, but a deeper flush covered her cheeks. She had removed the filthy wrinkled shift and put on the smudged dress from the day before. Jim took note that her hair hung down her back, past her waist, brushed and neat.

"Thank you for …"

"For rescuing you from the chickens?" Jim asked, teasing her.

"Yes." She smiled. "I slept ag'inst the door."

"We think alike." Samuel's incredulous look said more than words. "I would've done the same thing. Slept against the door, that is."

Jim jumped right in with the problem at hand. "I see your father hasn't showed up. Sam and I came to carry you to our house—until he returns, that is. Even Leigh Chesley said they'd like you to stay with them."

"I don't want to leave Mama." Her cheerless blue eyes welled with tears. "I want to be near so I can talk and visit her grave." She wrung her hands and refused to meet their eyes. "My pa'll come back. He's bringin' a new wife."

Jim took a deep breath, fearing to shovel more bad news on top of her. "I hate to tell you this, but there's rumors in the cove that he's *leaving*. He's told people he's getting married and moving to Virginia. He wants someone to take you for hire. It's mean saying it like this, but I got to tell you the truth."

She went pale. Her freckles stood out against her skin, like speckles on a wren's egg. She closed her eyes and remained perfectly still. Her lips moved, but he couldn't hear her words. He frowned at Samuel, wondering if his brother could hear what she whispered.

Samuel shook his head and shrugged. *Praying*, he mouthed.

"Ella Dessa?" Jim touched her forearm.

She opened her eyes to gaze at his hand. "I'll go with you."

He heaved a sigh of relief. "Mother's making arrangements for where you'll sleep. You'll have to get used to a crowd." He chuckled. "I'd suggest you bring only things you'll need in the next couple days. We'll come back for the rest."

Ella Dessa rolled her meager collection of clothing into a ball and gave it to him. He stuffed it in his pack. She slipped her arms into a man's ragged coat and hugged a tattered leather-bound Bible and square wooden box to her chest. She didn't have anything else for Samuel to carry, but she mentioned her mother's trunk, the chickens, and the two cows.

"May I go say good-bye to Mama?" Her blue eyes grew luminous with unshed tears.

Jim left off adjusting the straps on his backpack. "We'll take care of things. You go and speak to your mother. Want me to put that wooden box in Sam's pack?"

She carefully set it on the table and nodded. Her fingers trailed over the carving on the top. "It's special."

"We'll be careful."

Samuel edged closer to her. "Do you want me to go with you?"

"No." She gave him a wan smile.

They followed her outside, and the girl almost ran up the slope to the isolated grave. Jim saw her drop to her knees, lay the Bible in her lap, and bow her head.

Samuel's shoulders slumped. "I feel sorry for her. She's barely past burying her mother."

"I know, but we can't just go away without her. Come on. Snatch that loop of rope off the wall inside the cabin. Let's catch those chickens before she changes her mind and wants to remain here. We'll tie the chickens' scrawny legs together and secure their wings, so they can't flap. I guess we'll just hang them over a shoulder. I'll take two, since I'm carrying her belongings. You'll have to take the other three."

"Will the chickens survive the trek down the mountain?" His brother continued to watch the young girl's still form kneeling under the pines. Her loose hair flowed over one shoulder.

"They will. Plus we'll take the two cows with us. She can lead one of them, and you get the second one." Jim grinned. "Tell you what let's do. Let's tie the chickens together and drape them over the cows' backs. We'll have to bring a wagon back for the trunk."

"Couldn't we carry it between us? It small and seems to mean a lot to her."

He sighed and rolled his eyes. "Okay, little brother, let's go see how heavy it is."

"It isn't big."

"But it means she'll have to lead the two cows with chickens on their bony backs. What a sight that'll be."

Samuel chuckled. "Guess it's an adventure we'll remember."

"Hmm, we'll remember or *you* will remember? Getting sweet on Ella Dessa? You haven't taken your eyes off her the whole time I've been talking."

The boy faced him. "Not me, Jim. You're the one who'll soon be looking for a wife. You're getting old." His lips curved into a sarcastic smile.

"Samuel McKnapp." He playfully tapped his brother's chest. "I don't plan on marrying a child your age. I'm almost six years older than her. Besides, that new family, the Walds? They have a girl closer to my age. I plan to introduce myself."

They both watched Ella Dessa stand, tuck the Bible under one arm, and brush clay soil from the skirt of her dress. The pines, standing guard over the rock-covered grave, shadowed her forlorn figure.

But then she moved and stepped into the gilded sunlight.

For just a minute, the girl paused—poised on the gentle rim of the slope. She looked down to where they both stood. With a cool breeze lifting her hair and tugging at its flowing length, Ella Dessa raised one arm and waved to them.

The beautiful youthful picture her figure created, and the promise of the woman she would become, jolted through Jim. He didn't wave back. He watched his younger brother's countenance change to adoration.

Samuel lifted his right hand and beckoned to Ella Dessa.

Chapter 14

Ella held ropes connected to the two cows and watched the brothers lower her mama's trunk to the dirt by the porch. In unison they groaned and straightened, relieved of the unusual burden. Even though she witnessed them—especially Samuel—struggle with the trunk while coming down the trail, she found it hard to believe they had done it. No one ever cared what she wanted, except her mama.

"It was heavy." Jim examined his left palm. "I thought for sure I had a blister. Sam, you look tired. Sorry, you're shorter than me. I know you're hurting."

"I can't move that trunk another inch. My arm's pulled away from my shoulder." Samuel bent over and placed his hands on his knees. "Whew! There's blisters on my hands. I just don't want to look. The right one's especially bad."

Ella cringed. Where Samuel's right hand rested on his knee, she could see a raw piece of skin rolled back on its side—rubbed off from contact with the leather handle on the trunk. A smear of blood transferred to his pants. His injury was her fault. She stepped forward, meaning to tell him how sorry she was, but Jim tapped him on the head before she opened her mouth.

"I'll take the cows and chickens to the barn. You take Ella inside. Here, Sam." He pulled her bundle out of his pack and handed it to his brother.

Samuel nodded and straightened to accept it.

"Don't forget. Her box is in your satchel, and you put her Bible in there. I'll get Duncan to help me take the trunk up the steps." He smiled at his brother, as he reached for the lead ropes.

Ella handed them over without a word. He bobbed his head once toward her and turned toward the barn—cows and chickens in tow.

"Let's go inside," the younger brother said, his voice sounding exhausted.

She left off watching the older brother and faced him. "Thank you, Samuel."

He gave her a sweet, lop-sided grin. "Anytime—but just for you."

"I'm sorry 'bout your hand." She fought tears. "I wish it hadn't happened."

He stared at his bloody right palm. "It'll heal. Come, let's go in." He opened the door for her. The wonderful aroma of roasted turkey and fresh bread flooded her senses.

"Oh, my," she murmured, as she reluctantly took a step over the threshold and entered the large square room.

From a table across the room, heads turned or leaned sideways to gawk at her. It seemed the room overflowed with curious pairs of eyes. Much like a frightened chipmunk, she wanted to dash back up the mountainside.

She whirled and bumped square into Samuel's chest.

"Whoa! Got to go forward." He steadied her with his left hand. "No more knocking me down. I'm one-handed, and I've suffered enough for today." But he smiled with sympathy as though he understood her fear. "Turn around," he whispered. "They don't bite."

Like an obedient child, she turned and saw his father rise from a chair at the right of the oversized table. He hobbled toward her, but the wife got to her first.

Inez held out both arms. "Ella Dessa! Welcome to our home." A collection of voices affirmed the woman's statement.

She found herself enveloped in a motherly hug, her face pressed against the woman's warm shoulder. "Thank you."

Over Inez's shoulder, she recognized the faces at the table.

Peggy, with the red-brown hair, grinned from ear to ear and waved one arm in the air. Grace rose from her place on a bench and smiled a welcome. Phillip was in the process of rubbing a white, mushy substance into his blond hair, and Josie twisted sideways on the closest bench to get a better view. The girl named Anna gave her an intent look, but her oval face showed no welcoming expression.

"We're so happy you came with the boys." Releasing her, Inez turned to Samuel. "Where's Jim?"

"He's taking her cows and chickens to the barn. We also dragged a trunk with us. It's outside."

"A trunk? Clear down the mountain?" his father asked. Ephraim hobbled passed his wife, looked outside, and chuckled. "Sure 'nough."

"Yep, I got blisters to prove it." Samuel blew on his sore fingers.

"You will live. Welcome, Ella Dessa." The white-haired man patted her on the back. "We've been waiting for you to get here. Glad you made it, despite my two sons."

She felt herself blushing. "They were nice to me."

"Good." His wide smile crinkled up his eyes.

Peggy waved a hand in the air and gestured. "Come sit here with me."

Ephraim pointed at the table. "Grab a seat and be prepared to eat quick, 'cause Samuel will wolf down everythin' in sight. He calls it 'part of his animal instincts.'"

"Ah, that's not true." Samuel dropped his pack to the floor and laid her wrapped belongings on the rocker. He faced the pine table, with two long sets of benches lining each side, and grinned. "I see you saved us a little food."

Peggy waved, again. "Ella Dessa!"

Inez sighed. "Samuel, mind your manners. Ella Dessa, would you like to wash your hands before Samuel does?" She led her to a large bowl on an undersized wooden stand. On one side of it, a towel—with blue embroidered flowers—hung from a rod. "Here, let me take your coat. I'll hang it right here on this hook by the door."

"Yes'um." She slipped out of her pa's old coat and hesitated beside the bowl of water.

"Here." Inez handed her a square cake of opaque white soap.

She dampened her hands in the water and rubbed the soap over her fingers. She felt ashamed at the grime rimming her ragged nails, but she couldn't help but sniff at the soap. A wonderful scent she couldn't identify wafted from it. Embedded in the soft soap were bits and pieces of purplish plant matter. She rinsed her hands and dried them on the towel.

"Is that all right?" she asked, anxious to please.

"Oh, yes, sweetheart. Samuel you're next." The woman beckoned to him. "Come, honey, hurry up."

Honey?

Why was the woman calling her son that? She watched Samuel gaze down at his sore hands and grimace.

His mother pointed at a vacant spot on the opposite side of the table. "Ella Dessa, that's where you'll sit—in Duncan's space. He left earlier to carry a food basket to Velma and the children. Jim will be sitting beside you when he comes in. Peggy, stop waving your hands like a flapping goose."

"Ouch, ouch!" Samuel yelped, causing all of them to turn. He shook his dripping hands. "That hurt."

"Oh. He's got blisters." Ella moved toward him but stopped, feeling out of place.

Inez lifted Samuel's wet hands and examined them. "Well, as much as it hurts, it's best you wash them. Pat them dry, instead of rubbing your hands with the towel. Press the skin back in place on your right palm. I'll put salve on the blisters after you eat. Ella Dessa, you can go sit down. Samuel's done causing a scene."

Feeling overwhelmed with shyness, she slipped along the table next to the wall and sat on the bench. She leaned to the right and accepted Peggy's exuberant hug. As she stared at the food-laden table, the tabletop swirled and dipped in front of her. She squeezed her eyes shut and willed it to right itself.

"Is she falling asleep?"

"No, Anna, she isn't sleeping," she heard Grace say, from the other side of Peggy. Then, "You sick?"

She caught her breath and opened her eyes. "No."

"You look pure tuckered out."

"Not much sleep last night." She blinked, aware of Anna's wide-eyed stare examining her and the scars on her neck, but she didn't have the strength to cover them.

"I'm happy to see you." Josie gave her a toothy grin. Her brown curls bobbed beside her round face. "That's Duncan's plate, but we'll let you use it."

"Thank you." She inspected the white china. Her trembling fingers caressed the cold surface of the plate. She had never seen anything so smooth. A metal fork and a spoon rested beside it.

"We'll return the blessing now." Ephraim's loud voice stopped all chatter at the table. "Jim can say his own when he comes in. Let us bow our heads."

She followed their lead and clasped her hands together as the man's voice boomed out a prayer.

"Our Heavenly Father, we thank You for this bountiful meal and for our new guest. Please, be with Ella Dessa during this time of change. Show her Your love. Amen."

A chorus of "amens" followed. Even after she heard the chink of silverware and the steady murmur of voices, she kept her head bowed. Hearing her name spoken in the man's prayer sent tingles of astonishment the length of her back.

"Would you like a piece of bread?" A tentative hand touched her right arm.

She raised her head and saw Peggy's sympathetic brown eyes. "Yes, please." She took a warm slice of honey-colored bread and bit into it. The center was soft and yielding to her teeth, not like most bread she ate at home. The flavor evaded her for an instant, but then she recognized it.

Pumpkin.

She licked the tasty crumbs off her lips and took another bite. Her stomach rumbled.

"Could you pass this to Papa?" Peggy still held the plate. "We have butter, if you'd like. And we keep honey for a topping."

Her face grew warm. She had learned her first table manner—pass food to the next person. She set her half-eaten slice of bread on the table and took the plate. She leaned sideways and passed it to Peggy's father at the end of the table.

Ephraim caught her eye and chuckled. His cheeks stretched the trimmed white beard. "Eating is a favorite pastime with the McKnapp family. Even the noon meal. Take a hunk of turkey from what Peggy's handing you."

"Sorry," she whispered and accepted the heaping plate of meat.

With a swift peek at the table, she saw everyone was busy filling their plates, passing bowls, and taking bites of their food. Occasionally, someone's eyes lifted in her direction, but no one outright stared.

"Eat as much of this as you can before Jim comes in." Samuel grinned from across the table. His friendly blue-green gaze put her at ease. He held up a piece of the pumpkin bread and wiggled his light-colored eyebrows.

She smiled at him as the cabin door opened outward.

"Oops—too late," Samuel said.

Jim stepped in. "I put Ella Dessa's chickens in with ours and released the cows into the pen on the north side of the barn." He shrugged off his coat. "Do I smell turkey?"

"A good chance you do. Shot it this morning. Wash and take a seat," Ephraim said.

Jim made his way over to the water bowl. "How you feeling, Papa?"

"Not good. My leg pained all day. I didn't get the side field turned under. You and Duncan need to finish it tomorrow. That'll take care of the two fields for the winter.

"Then you didn't get down to the cove?" Jim slid onto the bench on Ella's left.

"Couldn't manage it." His father scowled, stabbed a piece of turkey with his knife, and lifted it to his plate.

"Ella, you don't have much on that plate." Jim pointed at the small portion of turkey breast and nudged her elbow. "You better eat more than that."

"It's all I need." She felt herself blush at the playful touch of his arm.

"Peggy, pass Ella Dessa the sweet taters. I know she worked up an appetite coming here. She ran to keep up with us and stay ahead of those cows she was leading. Should've seen how we did it."

Ella giggled as she accepted the bowl of sweet potatoes from Peggy. Jim went on and on, giving a much-exaggerated, hilarious account of their downhill hike.

"Had her chickens hung over the backs of the cows. What a noise they created. I made Sam help carry Ella Dessa's trunk, even though I could've managed."

"What? You *made* me?" The boy sputtered and almost choked on his corn. He wiped his mouth on his sleeve.

While they all laughed, Ella ate and mulled over the morning's events. During the walk along the trail, she had enjoyed listening to the good-natured banter between the two brothers. Jim had been unmerciful with his picking at Samuel, but the boy showed his pleasant personality and accepted the teasing. Each time they put the trunk down and rested, they talked with her about their large family, until Ella felt she knew all of them personally.

She recalled they considered Peggy the sweetest of the girls. Her gentle and friendly ways mended squabbles between the younger siblings. She felt thankful the girl sat beside her.

Peggy nudged her in the ribs. "Jim likes to be the center of attention," she whispered. Dark auburn lashes lined her eyes, emphasizing their deep-brown color, but strangely contrasting her bright red-tinged hair. "Did you eat all the candy we left with you?"

Unable to stop a giggle, she nodded and whispered, "It was good." She hated to admit how soon she ate it all.

Samuel interrupted Jim's wild account of their day by leaning forward to speak to Grace on the other side of Peggy. "Looks like Peggy and Ella Dessa are sharing secrets."

"What secrets?" Grace raised her perfectly-arched eyebrows.

Before anyone could reply, the door burst open. Ella's pa stood within the dark framework. Ephraim tried to jump to his feet but fell sideways, his bad knee giving out. He caught hold of the table edge, groaned, and sank to his chair.

"Jacob!" Inez rose from her end of the table, one hand over her heart.

"What are you doing busting into our house?" Jim stumbled around the crowded table and stopped in front of the taller man. He held his clenched fists chest high.

"I came fer my gurl child. I heard she were brought here. You were seen. Ella Dessa, git outside." He thumbed over his shoulder. "Now!"

She hurried to obey by lifting her right foot over the bench, but she kicked Peggy's leg in the process. "Sorry, Peggy."

Peggy's expressive eyes filled with tears, but Ella knew it wasn't from having her leg bumped.

Inez stood with her back ramrod straight. "Jacob, we must talk—"

"You're askin' to be shot." Ephraim interrupted his wife. "Jim, get my gun from the fireboard."

"No guns!" Inez told Grace to hold Phillip and she went to her husband's side. The tips of her fingers turned white when she squeezed his thick shoulder. "Jim, move away—back up. Your father and I will handle this. Ella Dessa, remain where you are."

Pa's narrowed eyes watched Jim.

"Mother, no man has a right to force his way in here." Jim gritted his teeth and held his ground. A vein throbbed at his left temple.

"No man has a right to steal my gurl." Her pa issued a line of filthy cuss words.

Inez left Ephraim's side and grabbed a broom from the wall. "Jacob Huskey, you *will not* use that language in my house or in front of your child or my children. Jim, do as I say. Step back."

Ephraim rubbed his knee and raised his voice once more. "Jim, mind your mother. Jacob, if I could stand right this instant, I'd knock you out that door and off my porch. As it is, I'm askin' Jim to fetch my gun. I'm gonna kill you."

Cowering, Ella thought about sinking below the tabletop. She hadn't expected the appearance of her pa. She felt Peggy clinging to her right hand and pulling, trying to make her sit.

Jim reached for a long-barreled gun on the mantel and passed it to Ephraim, butt first.

"Pa! I'm comin'." She made a quick decision. She couldn't let him be shot.

"Then git out the door." His words hissed between his discolored, broken teeth. Unreadable eyes locked on her face. "*Move.*"

"No!" Inez walked straight to him and stepped close enough to smack him with the broom handle. "Ella Dessa, your father's leaving. Stay where you are."

"Mother, get out of the way." Jim got closer and tugged at her arm. "Papa's got him covered with the gun. He better leave!"

Almost blind with horror, Ella gasped. Her pa's right hand convulsed and the tremor shot up the whole arm. She ducked past Inez and sandwiched her body between Pa and Ephraim's long gun.

"Let's go, Pa." She gazed upward and eyed his rigid, half-crazed expression. "I wanna go with you. Please?" She hadn't thought it'd come to this.

She winced as his left hand clamped on her shoulder and propelled her forward. She tripped over the raised wooden threshold. A frantic look over her shoulder gave her a peek of Jim's clenched jaw and flushed face. She heard Ephraim's heavy breathing and saw the barrel of the gun drop.

Inez followed with the broom clutched in her white-knuckled hands. A stiff autumn breeze wafted through the covered connection between the two shadowed buildings. Ella didn't resist as her pa yanked her to the right—in the direction of the wide steps.

"Ella Dessa!" Samuel pushed past Jim. His hands held her mama's Bible.

She silently shook her head in warning. Her last backward glimpse met with Samuel's green-eyed look of compassion. Her lips trembled as her mama's long dress tripped her on the steps. She shrank away from Pa's outstretched hand.

"Git on the horse." He clutched the reins and held the pitiful horse still.

"Wait!" Inez handed Jim the broom and ran down the wooden steps. "Jacob, please—let's talk. You and I. I know you'll be sensible."

"Sure, 'bout what? How yer ole man's goin' to blow my head off?" His eyes raked down the length of her slender form, and his thin lips curled in distain. "He sends out a woman to bargain?"

"Please. We'd like your daughter to stay with us." Her warm hand rested on the top of Ella's head. Gently, her fingers smoothed loose strands of hair. "Please?"

Ella trembled under the brave woman's reassuring touch.

"No." He shook his head. "She's under my heed."

"But you want to be free of that care. Right?"

"I found someone she can work for." With one swift movement, Pa wrenched Ella away from Inez's touch and shoved her against the horse's solid chest and neck. "Stay put. Don't give me any sass," he warned.

"Not sassin'." She held her breath. Her shaking hands calmed the startled old horse. She didn't want to witness how her pa would treat Inez.

"Woman, if you think I'd let—"

"Pa! I want to stay. Let me stay with 'em." She shoved herself between him and Inez. She didn't want the woman to take her punishment, so she dared to make the unthinkable request—to counter her pa's anger and bring the focus back on herself. "It wasn't their fault. I *begged* to stay. It were lonely up on the ridge. Honest, Pa."

His fingers were swift to bite into her shoulder and make her whimper. The pain caused her to twist sideways. Without wishing to do so, she reacted and silently appealed to Inez for help.

The woman's hazel eyes darkened and flashed. Her facial muscles stiffened. "You *will* remove your hand from that child's shoulder, or I'll yell for my oldest son to bring the gun. You don't want that, because I'll shoot you myself." Her voice turned icy, but her stern eyes were backlit with fire. "It's *your* decision."

Pa's fingers loosened. His right arm convulsed, and he grabbed at it with his left hand. "I've attained a job fer her. An' she's goin' to earn her keep. I'll not be beholden to anyone, an' I won't have her livin' under the same roof as yer red-headed, no-good son." A sneer distorted his wide mouth and showed his yellow teeth.

Ella inched toward the horse, but Pa followed her.

"Who are you going to bond her out to?" She stepped closer. "Are you so low? Is that what you've sunk to? You've desecrated your wife's memory. Now, you're willing to sell a child? Make her work for someone in the settlement?"

"It's my business." Pa's dark eyes shied away from Inez. He tried to present the impression he wasn't disturbed by the woman standing in front of him.

"Who is it?"

Ella trembled and felt invisible. The horse's warm breath tickled the side of her neck and smelled of chewed straw.

"I won't say."

"Where's your decency, Jacob Huskey? You're abandoning this child. At least place her where she'll be cared for and not abused. Then go your own way."

Her pa shifted his weight as if considering his next move.

Ella studied the dusty tips of her new boots protruding from under the ragged hem of her mama's dress. She felt the delicate unbelievable dream of the whole morning dissolving into a nightmare. She wouldn't be living with the McKnapp family.

Pa let an unintelligible curse pass his lips before answering the persistent woman. "Gust Clanders needs hired help ta stay with his wife this winter—whilst he's gone."

The quivering in Ella's legs immediately subsided at the sound of Velma's name. *Velma? I'm bein' sent to help Velma Clanders? Why? Pa dislikes Gust Clanders.* She chanced a brief peek at Inez's face.

A gleam of relief lit the woman's troubled eyes. Inez lifted her chin, presenting stubborn disbelief. "Gust can't pay for help. He owes people in the cove. That's why he's gone to dig for a fool's dream."

"Ella's pay will be a place to sleep." Pa forcefully closed and opened the fingers of his right hand, trying to conceal how badly his hand shook. His breath reeked of liquor. A new felt hat covered his thick curly hair, and he wore a store-bought shirt of stiff white material.

141

Bought with stolen gold, Ella thought. Her eyes searched his rough face.
"When did he speak to you?" Inez's voice softened.

"Days back as he left fer the mines."

"And when do you leave town?"

His defiant, unsettling eyes flashed from under the brim of the new hat, but he answered her. "Daybreak. Me an' my woman are headin' fer Richmond to be married."

His woman? Ella's arms jerked downward to tighten on her midsection. *They're leavin'?* It felt as if the horse had kicked her stomach. She wanted to gag, but comforting hands once again rested on her shoulders.

Inez drew her against her willowy frame. "Perhaps, Ella Dessa should remain here for the night, since the day is more than half past. My girls hope to visit with Ella. I'll personally take her to Velma's in the morning. I need to carry her a cured ham."

Ella wanted to fling herself into Inez's arms. She longed to bury her face against the woman's flat chest and cry away the pain in her heart. But she couldn't move an inch as long as her pa remained indecisive—standing before them.

"I don't like the way ya think of me." Her pa glared into the distance. His nostrils flared, and he gritted his broken teeth. "I've done my best by her—her bein' forced on me an' all. I gave her my name."

She felt Inez's body tense against her back. She didn't understand what her pa meant. Was he talking about her? She squinted in the bright fall sunlight. *I were forced on him?*

"I don't think I've voiced my opinion of you." Inez spoke quietly. "And I fail to understand what you're talking about. My only question is—will you agree Ella Dessa may stay the night and will you state it out loud, so all may hear?"

With another vile curse, he crammed his hat on tighter and jerked the horse's reins. "See to it that she gits to the Clanders' homestead by mornin'."

Without a word of good-bye, he mounted the horse. Ella watched him ride away. The dust of the rutted road kicked into small clouds under the mare's hooves, and the shade of the pines wrapped themselves along her pa's slumped shoulders.

Inez gave a soft, delightful laugh and opened her arms. "Let me hug you. He's gone." Her lips brushed Ella's forehead. "You see, it just took a woman's persistence. Now, let's go soothe the ruffled feathers in the kitchen. Tomorrow we'll walk to Velma's."

Chapter 15

Ella stretched under the weight of the heavy padded quilt and wiggled her toes, which were cozy inside borrowed woolen socks. She could feel Peggy's body warmth, combined with hers, under the covers. Her eyelids flew open, and sleepiness fled.

She awakened to a room hushed and cloaked in unfamiliar shadows. She smiled, rolled to her right side, and pillowed her head on her arm. The soft timbre of breathing and an occasional sleepy murmur said she wasn't alone. It was a heartwarming fact. Little pings of joy sang through her veins and made her want to burst into uncontrolled giggles. She felt bubbly.

Content, she observed the growing daylight tiptoe through the narrow window and glide across the quilt-hidden forms of the sleeping girls. It brightened their sleep-tousled hair.

This is like havin' sisters of my own. She hugged herself and wished she could capture the feeling forever. Oh, how she wanted to stay with the McKnapps.

She recalled the astonishing evening with the big family. She had laughed, played games with the girls, and listened to Ephraim read from their family Bible. It seemed like one magnificent dream. She'd never forget the precious gift she had been given. She felt accepted into their private family circle, if only for a short night. No one yelled at her, and not one person belittled her. She even forgot about her scarred neck for a short time.

Ella sighed with contentment. The detailed and differing patterns of the numerous beautiful quilts became visible. She never saw so many colors, except in wild flowers.

"You awake?"

"Yes." She rolled over and smiled.

"It's a little chilly this morning." Peggy sat up. Her curly hair had frizzed. A tiny beam of sunlight touched it and made it flame with sizzling color. She shivered.

"I'm comfy," Ella replied.

Peggy burrowed back under the quilt, until just her round brown eyes and wild hair showed. The quilt muffled her voice. "I wish you didn't have to go to Velma's. We'd love to have you as an extra sister."

Giggling, she slipped closer to her new friend, with whom she shared a pallet on the wood floor. Her bent knees bumped Peggy's legs. "I'd love to be your sister, but your family ain't needin' extras. Will Phillip be upset when he learns he was moved whilst he slept?"

"Ah, he loves playing with his big brothers, especially Samuel."

"Samuel must love one and all. He's so nice."

"He can be," Peggy whispered back. "Hey, Duncan sure wasn't happy when he saw you yesterday."

Ella flipped to her back and contemplated the dark rafters. "It's my pa he don't like, I s'pose." She wrinkled her nose and considered Duncan's previous actions. "I think he treated me fine when he returned from Velma's."

"Yes, after Papa gave him the evil eye. Mother says Duncan will someday realize what a big horse's butt he's been."

"Your mama said that?" She jerked her head sideways and raised her eyebrows.

Peggy popped her head further out from under the quilt and rolled her pretty eyes. "Well, Mother didn't use those words."

While sputtering with amusement, she pulled the quilt over her head. Together, the two girls huddled under the covers and giggled. "Shh, we'll wake your sisters." But she laughed all the harder.

"Thanks, you two," a sleepy voice muttered.

Peggy and Ella flipped the quilt edge back. "Good morning, Grace," Peggy whispered.

The young woman rolled to a sitting position, pushed her hair out of her face, and yawned. "Hmm. I'd think you'd both be too exhausted to wake me up early." Her loose dark hair flowed in heavy waves over her shoulders and contrasted with her white nightgown.

"Sorry, Grace." Ella felt ashamed. "It's my fault."

"No it isn't." Peggy slapped at her arm. "I started it."

"Stop arguing." Grace stood and stretched. "Mother's probably setting out breakfast, anyways. So, you two get up and go help her. I'll check on Phillip."

"Be quiet." Anna grumbled the words and jerked her quilt over her head.

Josie crawled out of the bed she shared with Anna. Hunching her thin shoulders against the coolness of the room, she turned to her oldest sister. "Does Ella hav'ta leave today? I want her to stay. I love her, already."

"Yes, she has to go help Velma." Grace shivered, stripped off her long nightgown, and reached for a folded dress at the end of the bed. "Anna, you might as well get out of bed. It's light enough to see in here, so it must be late. Hurry, so you can get in by the fireplace. You were sick last week, and we can't have you taking a chill again."

"You act like our mother." Anna still had her blond head buried.

"Well, I'll soon be married. Then you'll be free of me. Get up."

Ella watched Peggy stand and step over their rumpled quilt. She didn't relish the idea of crawling out of the bed. It was nice under the quilt. Peggy had elected to give up sleeping in bed with Grace—to keep her company on the floor, which was where Phillip normally slept.

Peggy shucked off her nightshift. She tossed it sideways into the air as she grabbed her dress. "I'm not using the pot. So I don't have to empty it! Come, Ella, hurry. We have to beat the boys to the necessary."

147

"Necessary?" She sat upright and reached for her mama's wrinkled dress.

"Yes. Ah, the outhouse? Privy? Don't you have one at home?"

"Oh, of course." She pulled off the borrowed nightdress and shrugged into her dress. "Wait for me."

The girls raced each other to the cold outhouse, giggling and ducking in and out as fast as they could. Their cheeks and noses were pink from the cold when they entered the kitchen's warmth and breathed in the welcoming scent of bacon and fried potatoes.

Self-conscious about her unbrushed hair, Ella quickly twisted it into a knob on the back of her head and tucked the ends in. She joined the line of girls at the washbasin and splashed cold water on her face and rinsed her hands.

Peggy handed her a towel. "Here, use mine to dry. Brrr, winter is coming."

Ephraim was the last one to come to the breakfast table. He limped in, favored his knee, and used a knobby homemade cane. After he said the blessing, he kept his hands folded and studied each face at the full table—as if assessing their strengths and weaknesses. "Jim, lettin you and the boys know I won't be helping today. Pain's too bad. You three must do the chores, and you'll do book lessons after dark. Your mother's taking Ella to Velma's crowded cabin. Grace will handle the house chores and the girls' schoolin'."

Peggy caught Ella's eye and smiled. "Papa, may I—"

"No. I think Ella Dessa and your mother will have enough to think about when they get down yonder by Velma's. Many youngsters there. Just like here. It'll be better if you entertain Phillip."

At the mention of his name, Phillip bobbed his blond head up from a bowl of porridge. He held the spoon halfway to his mouth, impishly wrinkled his button of a nose, and grinned at Peggy. His rows of straight baby teeth showed. He wore a blob of breakfast smeared on his right cheek and plastered in his hair.

"Ohh." The disappointed girl stabbed her fork into a thick slab of bacon and bowed her head.

It dawned on Ella. She hadn't heard Phillip speak one single word. He laughed, pointed, and motioned to get what he wanted, but his lips never formed words.

"Jim, will you bring in the washtub before you head for the barn?" Inez handed Grace a damp cloth to wipe Phillip's messy face.

"Yes, ma'am." Jim leaned on the table and spoke to Duncan, who sat beside Josie. "Duncan, you're finishing that side field, so Samuel can feed the animals and start sorting through the broken harnesses and tools. They'll be ready for us to repair."

Duncan didn't look up from his plate of food. He nodded in agreement and scooped the last of the porridge into his mouth.

"Sam, the harnesses are stacked beside Sada's stall. They're a tangled mess." Jim bit into a golden-brown johnnycake. "Don't let it get you all tied up."

"Humph!" Samuel snorted his reply. "I'll be done in no time. It'll give me time to take a nap."

"A tangled mess?" Their father raised his white eyebrows into twin peaks. "I think it's a tangled knot!"

Ella smiled to herself. She enjoyed the assortment of voices and lively talk.

"Well, I guess Duncan and I kept throwing stuff back there." Jim gave his father a sheepish grin. "It's not that bad." He winked at Ella. "But Sam needs to tell Ella Dessa good-bye before he gets his coat and starts work, because once he plows into that pile of leather castoffs none of us may ever see him again."

Everyone burst out laughing except Samuel. He rolled his green-tinted blue eyes. "My dear, Ella Dessa, you don't know the abuse you're avoiding by not staying here with us. Count it as pure luck Velma needs you." His light hair fell across one eye. He shook it to the side and tipped his head to smile at her.

She smiled back and felt every pair of eyes studying her. She knew they waited for a quick comeback to the silly banter going on, but she couldn't think of anything. She wasn't used to joking and laughing at the table. Her home had been tense and lacking in joy or peace. Meals were eaten in strained, mandatory silence while Mama anxiously watched her pa's face.

The unexpected remembrance of her mama's battered face caused the smile to slip from her lips. She bowed her head and shoved the bowl away. She struggled with instant tears and shame at her lack of emotional control.

Jim broke the uncomfortable hush. "Sam, if you weren't so pretty, we'd make you live in the barn." He tossed the last of his johnnycake at Samuel and caused their mother to protest.

"Whoa!" Ephraim waved his hands over the table. He pointed at each one of them. "Girls, clear the table. Jim, bring the tub and haul water. Duncan, hitch one mule to the plow. Samuel, collect the eggs—water the cows. I'm asking Grace to wrap my knee tight and see if that helps."

"Want to send Jim or Duncan for Granny Hanks?" Inez rose from her chair and walked toward him.

"No, I think time and patience will heal it." He caught his wife's toil-roughened hand and pulled her down near enough for a quick kiss on the lips. "Mmm, an' a little love."

Everyone else ignored the tender, intimate gesture and rose from the table. But Ella gave studious attention to the older couple. They truly love one another, she thought. Her surprised perception caused her heart to twist and ache. She instantly knew she longed to be loved in the same way.

****

After Grace wrapped her father's knee, Ephraim hobbled outside. Jim brought in a large metal and wood tub. He filled it with buckets of cold water while Inez set two kettles of the water to heat over the fire. As they steamed and grew hot, she shooed all the girls and Phillip to the girl's bedroom. She told them to straighten their beds and study in the bedroom. Then she turned to Ella.

"Honey, I heated the water for you ... for a bath. I thought you'd like to also go to Velma's with fresh clothes." Using a folded piece of material, Inez lifted the kettles, one by one, and poured boiling water into the tub.

Ella felt her face flush. "I ain't—don't have nothing else, but there's Mama's skirts and blouses in the trunk. They don't fit. The waist of the skirts is big."

"Well, here's what we'll do. You get in the tub. Let me wash your hair. Then while you bathe, I'll examine the skirts and take in seams. When you dry off, you'll have a new set of clothes. I *promise*."

With hands trembling, Ella opened the small leather-covered trunk and lifted the short stack of skirts. They varied in plain and simple colors. "Here. This is all of them."

Inez unfolded a soft gray skirt and held it up. She smiled. "This'll do fine. Please, get in the tub."

"What about the others?" Ella feared someone would walk in after she shucked her clothes.

"No one will come in until they see the tub sitting outside the door—after I empty it. That's one of our house rules. We all abide by it." She motioned with her hand. "Quick, before the water chills."

Self-conscience and nervous, she stripped off her mama's dress, her new boots, and her undergarments. She lifted one foot and stepped over the high edge of the tub. She felt heady from the depth and warmth of the water, but she closed her eyes and willed herself to enjoy the privilege of a full bath.

"Tip your head back."

She obeyed, even though she knew the movement fully exposed her appalling disfigurement to the woman washing her hair. But Inez didn't comment on the scars as ripples of water washed over her discolored skin.

Ella closed her eyes. She enjoyed the feeling of strong fingers and a cut bar of soap rubbing her scalp and running through her long hair. She pretended it was Mama's hands and forgot about the present. She focused on recollecting the past. Her mama's face felt less distinct, as if a fog drifted over the image, shifted it, made all the details harder to distinguish.

I can't let that happen.

She jerked her eyes open and watched the flames in the blackened firebox, until Inez told her to scrunch lower and dip her head beneath the surface of the water. Obediently, she grabbed the sides of the metal tub and slid downward, only to come up sputtering.

"I hate water in my eyes an' nose."

A soft chuckle came from Inez's throat. "Most people do."

"Makes me remember. I feel the water covering my head like when the painter—*panther* got me."

"Perhaps, if you talk about it, the pain will fade." The woman's kind voice was soft.

She swallowed and lifted her right hand out of the water, to let her trembling fingers travel over the scars. "I feel ugly," she whispered. Her throat constricted, and she fought tears.

"You're not. You will someday be a beautiful woman—one your mother would be proud of. Don't forget that." Inez's fingers twisted Ella's hair into a messy bun, and secured the ends with wooden hairpins. "I'm done now. You may finish washing. I'm going to sew."

"Yes'um." She sat motionless in the tub and studied the kindhearted woman.

After sitting in the rocker, turned sideways to the tub, Inez took a small knife and ripped a seam along the waistband and down one side of the gray skirt. Her fast-moving fingers pulled loose the original thread holding the seams. She then threaded it onto a needle and set it aside.

She used scissors to cut a strip of material from the whole side of the skirt. The scissors cut two inches off the waistband. Skillfully, she gathered the skirt material on the tighter band and stitched the side seam back together. As soon as she finished the waistband, she raised the hem, folded it, and sewed it into place with quick slipstitches. She hummed while she worked.

Ella forgot to bathe. She sat spellbound, as Inez's talented hands transformed the full skirt into a girl's piece of clothing. A blouse came next, changed with the same magical skill Inez possessed. Amazed at the transformation before her, she didn't start washing until she heard boots clump on the porch. With a squeal of alarm, she grabbed the slippery soap floating in the cool, murky water.

Inez laughed at her reaction. "They won't come in until they see the tub outside, but you better hurry. I know that water has to be cold."

Within minutes, she stood in the center of the tub and let Inez wrap her in a cocoon of warmth—a large, towel-sized piece of doubled muslin. It had been draped over a chair positioned by the fireplace. The fabric molded to her body, absorbing the moisture. After stepping over the edge of the high tub, Ella walked barefooted to the fire and dried off. Inez laid the clean skirt and blouse on a chair.

"Ella Dessa, here's the clean skirt and blouse on this chair. Waste no time in dressing. Until undergarments can be purchased or sewn for you, I'm lending you a few of Peggy's. I will take in the other skirts and send them to Velma's. Your dress will be cleaned here on washday. You will then have quite enough changes of clothing."

Ella stood gazing at the altered skirt. It fit perfect around the waist and fell to her toes. The shoulders of the blouse puffed out, and the material set comfortable over her underdeveloped chest and slender waist. When buttoned, the high collar's band hid most of her bumpy scars.

Mixed in with the aroma of the trunk and the clean material, was her mama's delicate scent. She yearned to snatch the skirt to her face and take a deep breath. Instead, she ran her hands along the sides of the skirt and marveled at the perfect length.

"How'd you do it?" Tears filled her eyes and blurred her vision. She knew any moment she'd be blubbering on Inez's shoulder, and she bit her lip to stop the tears.

Inez hugged her shoulders with one arm. "It's not that hard when you have to sew for four girls and yourself. You might call it essential—a God-given gift. We do a lot of repairing of hand-me-down clothes, not to mention what I manage to redo for the boys." She smiled. Her deep hazel eyes glinted with kindheartedness. "You are pretty, Ella Dessa. Let's comb out your hair and smooth the tangles. I'll plait it and fasten it up on the back of your head today. It won't be such a bother while you help with Velma's children. You should practice braiding or pinning it up every day."

Shortly, Inez handed a mirrored glass to Ella. "Look for yourself."

She bent close to see her reflection and whispered, "I can't believe it's me."

"Well, it is. Now, let's scoop water out of this tub and get along down the mountain."

"What about Mama's trunk?" Anxiety prickled along her spine. She couldn't be parted from the small trunk. It held her past.

"We can get Jim to load it on the wagon and bring it within a couple days."

"But—"

"Don't worry." Inez touched her arm, compassion in her eyes. "Jim won't let anything happen to it. Is there an item you'd like to take with you? Something you and I can carry?"

"Yes. Mama's Bible and her special wooden box."

****

Jim saw the empty tub outside the closed door. He pulled the door open and stepped across the threshold. Ella Dessa had just lifted her Bible from his brother's pack. He stood captivated at the change in the neglected child they had brought down the mountain.

She wore a full gray skirt and a white blouse. Her hair had been plaited and coiled on the back of her head. The alteration in her appearance produced a stunning change—it aged her and showed the beauty and elegance she would someday acquire.

"Amazing," he murmured, without realizing he'd spoken so loud.

At the sound of his voice, she spun on her heels to face him, and her brilliant blue eyes blinked with immediate shyness. A blush highlighted her oval face, and her right hand covered the edges of the purplish-red scars, even though they barely showed above the collar of the white blouse.

"I didn't hear you."

"I hardly recognized you. I thought Mother had a visitor from the cove."

"Now, Jim, don't tease her." His mother pushed him toward the door. "Take care of the tub. Where's your father?"

"I just helped him hobble up from the barn. He's sitting on the steps—resting. He insisted on going to the barn to tell Sam what to do."

"Well, help him in here and round up your brothers and sisters. Ella Dessa needs to tell them good-bye. Shut the door, it's not warm outside."

He left the cabin and fled from the strange sensation that took a throat-hold on him. He marveled at the transformation in the girl. He knew he had seen loveliness beneath her bedraggled appearance, but it astonished him to see it revealed.

Within a short time, the family crowded into the building. Jim found it interesting to watch their faces as they came through the doorway. His father chuckled and limped to his chair. "Inez, you've done it, ag'in. Ella Dessa, you're a beauty to behold. I'll gladly claim you as one of my daughters."

Turning pink, the girl pressed her fingers to her cheeks. "Thank you."

Peggy dashed in, roughly whirled Ella Dessa in a circle, and gave her a big hug. "You're lovely! I like your hair that way. I wish my hair would stay put, but it sticks out all over my head—with a mind of its own."

"Like a porcupine." Jim ruffled her auburn hair. "Mother will have to shear you to keep it smooth."

Peggy punched him in the side. "That's not nice."

"Children! Leave off the silliness. Tell Ella Dessa good-bye, so we can leave." Inez motioned to them.

Grace hugged Ella Dessa. "We'll be seeing you real soon. The women gather for quilting next Saturday—a week from now. Come with Velma. Mother and I'll be there, because they're helping with my wedding quilt."

"I don't see how Velma will be able to attend, unless Ella Dessa stays with the children." Inez shook her head. "Gust is gone. So no one can care for the little ones. Having Velma's brood of five running wild, while the women work on your quilt, wouldn't help them sew straight lines."

"What's that I hear?" Samuel entered through the door. "Grace *never* sews a straight line." Without looking up, he deposited an armload of wood by the fireplace.

"Samuel, you don't know what you're talking about." She knocked his hat off, and it fell at his feet. "You're just mean."

"Whew." He lifted his hat from the floor. "Glad you'll soon be gone."

"Sam!"

Laughing, he dodged her outspread fingers as she tried to pull his hair. But he stopped, opened his eyes wide, and gave Ella Dessa an intent look. His mouth fell open. "Whoa, who's that?"

"It's me." The girl touched her upswept hair and the neat plaits. "Your mama did it."

Samuel let out a low whistle. "You sure look dandified." Jim saw his boyish face light with recognizable interest. But as the family hooted with laughter, the boy turned red.

"Did you hear that?" Peggy said and shook Ella Dessa's arm. "You sure look *dandified*?"

"I heard it." Josie giggled. "I think he means she's pretty—like a dandelion?"

There was a timid smile of pleasure on Ella Dessa's face. She liked Samuel's crazy remark. Jim experienced a strange twinge, which he recognized as pure jealousy. He was jealous Samuel pleased the child with an honest remark. Pushing away the unexpected reaction, he moved to his brother's side.

"Dandified? I hope you mean pretty. Sam, do you need glasses to go along with your thoughts of becoming a teacher?"

The boy gave him a puzzled look. "My eyes don't need help. I see things just fine."

The door jerked opened behind them. Duncan strode in. He didn't bother to shut the door, and it banged against the outside wall. Cold air swirled in, filling the crowded room with the faint scent of pine boughs.

"Hey, what's your hurry?" Jim grabbed the door and pulled it shut.

Duncan didn't speak to anyone, but walked directly to Ella Dessa. Even though his face appeared void of any expression, Jim knew his oldest brother felt everyone's direct stares.

"Duncan?" Their mother tapped his shoulder.

He ignored his mother and reached for the girl's right hand. He lifted it and placed a homemade envelope on Ella Dessa's open palm. He wrapped her fingers over the top edge, and his larger hand covered hers for a brief instant.

"Take this." His voice was terse and low.

"What?" Ella Dessa's face showed her astonishment. She jerked her hand away from his unfamiliar touch and considered the crumpled envelope. She turned it over. Her blue eyes studied his face. "It's for Fern?"

"Yes."

"Why give it to me?" Her voice quavered.

"I wrote to Fern, but I want you to know I'm begging her forgiveness."

Mother took a quick breath and covered her mouth. "Forgiveness? Oh, Duncan, you said—"

"What are you saying, son?" A flush of anger darkened their papa's face.

Jim held his tongue and watched as Duncan raised his hand for silence.

"Please, I've something to tell her. Ella Dessa, it had to be you in the springhouse. From the woods, I saw a girl come out after Fern ran away."

"Yes." Her gaze dropped, and her lips pressed together.

Duncan's harried green eyes stayed locked on her face. He ran a hand over his red hair—indicating his edginess. "In this letter, I've asked Fern to marry me. If she writes and accepts, I will go get her, and we'll make a home together wherever she wants to live."

A muted explosion of murmurs rippled through the room, but Jim just grinned, realizing his brother had been stubborn enough not to care what each one heard or what they thought. Not even Mother and Papa's opinion counted. Duncan had surprised them all and plucked at his parents' nerves one more time. Jim had to give him credit for that.

"Ella Dessa, I know you'll be the one she contacts, because Manfred doesn't let Nettie read letters from Fern's sister in Florida. He burns them. So, that's my letter to Fern."

"What can I do with it?" She tried to hand it back. "I may never hear from her."

"Keep it and send it with yours, whenever the time comes." Duncan turned without bothering to acknowledge anyone else. He pushed between Samuel and Jim—his shoulders bumping against theirs—as he walked toward the door. He hit the latch with a shove of his palm, walked through the door, and elbowed it shut behind him with a definite finality.

It was a solid and heavy sound.

Chapter 16

Saturday, October 8, 1836

A week later, Ella awoke to shrieks of childish laughter and a tiny body falling across her back. "Oh, that hurt." She raised her head. "Mae, I know your laugh. Get off my back."

Elbows dug into her side, and the slight weight lifted.

"Why wake me?" She pushed herself upright and brushed hair out of her face.

Mae grinned and sat cross-legged beside Ella. Her four-year-old expression of amusement contrasted the pallor of her heart-shaped face. Brown stringy hair hung in front of her lake-blue eyes. She peered through the messy strands, not bothering to push them aside.

"Remy said wake ya!" She poked Ella's shoulder with one finger and giggled.

"So you did. You mind him better'n your mama or me. Move over, so I can get out from under this cover."

"Remy's a big boy." The skinny girl rolled sideways, plucked at loose threads on the worn quilt, and wound one thread around a little finger. She hummed an unrecognizable tune.

"Mae, where's the others?" The quilt-strewn loft was empty and still in the shadowy morning light.

"We're down here," an energetic voice shouted. "You're lazy."

She recognized the voice of Velma's oldest boy and crawled to the edge of the loft. "Scott, what got you up so early?"

The other four children sat at the uneven wood table. Little Rosemary held a pewter spoon above her head and watched porridge drip from it.

"We had a notion to surprise you this mornin'." Velma straightened from bending over the fire and waved her left hand. She still favored her right wrist, even though Granny declared it not broken. "You've endured one week with my wild younguns! That ain't easy."

Ella picked up a shawl and went down the ladder in her nightshift.

"We want you happy." Mae scurried past her and climbed on a bench to sit, her bare feet not reaching the floor. She made her sister Carrie scoot over. Always exuberant, she usually chattered about nonsense.

"Happy?" Ella echoed. "I'm happy."

Carrie placed her hand over Mae's mouth. "I'm biggest. Let me. She means we're declarin' this your day."

"Declarin'? That's a full-sized word. So, it's my day?"

Velma rubbed her back. "Carrie, git your hand off Mae's mouth. Ella, I knew you'd loves to go to Naomi's for the quiltin' in Grace's honor. So, we're givin' you the day off." Her smile exposed the noticeable gap between her top front teeth. "You're free to go."

"Oh dear." She felt like clapping her hands. She had longed to go, but Velma had been ill with morning sickness all week. "I'd love to go."

"I knew it." The thin woman pointed at the table. "Sit and eat. I feels better this mornin'. It comes and goes."

Ella slid onto the bench and took care to sit lightly on the rough areas. If a body wiggled too much, splinters could embed in the most embarrassing spots and be the cause of great pain. Rosemary leaned sideways and planted a porridge-covered kiss on her lower arm.

"Umm, Rosemary, thank you."

"Kiss!" The two-year-old gave her a wide-open smile, which showed tiny even teeth.

She bent and kissed Rosemary's moist, puckered lips.

Velma laughed. "I'm amazed at how she's taken with you. Why, she don't even like her pappy. Makes Gust angry."

Scott raised his head and laid his spoon aside. A stony expression tightened his childish jaw. He had the same space between his upper teeth as his mother and the same dark down-slanted eyes. His hair coloring matched Gust's sandy brown.

"I don't like 'im, either. He's crazy an' mean," he said.

"Scottie, you don't talks like that." Velma shook her finger in his direction.

"You said Rosemary doesn't like 'im." The boy shoved his wooden bowl across the table. "You don't tell her no."

"She's a baby, yet. You're next to the oldest. You knows better." His mother pointed at the bowl. "You take that to the bucket."

Scott palmed the carved bowl and walked over to the wooden bucket his mother used to soak her dishes. He tossed the bowl into the bucket and water sloshed on the floor. Ella looked Velma's way for any sign of maternal reaction, but the woman ignored the deliberate act of defiance. She caught Ella's eye, raised her dark eyebrows, and sighed.

"Choosin' my battles," she whispered. "It's a wise thing to do." Her thin lips curled in a faint grin. "A seven-year-old goin' on eight—who thinks he's fifteen."

Ella smiled. During the past week, she learned to appreciate the woman's quick wit and strength of character. Velma didn't let her present circumstances depress her, instead she said she wanted to prove—if to no one but herself—that she could exist without a husband.

"Ella?" Scott came back to the table and leaned on it. His mood was surly. "Mama says we shouldn't mention it, but did a mountain cat scratch you?"

Velma gasped and picked up a switch she kept on the mantel. "Scott Clanders, that's enough! You will bend over the rocker—rights now!"

"No, please, I'd love to tell the story," Ella said. She laid aside her spoon. "Scott, sit down. I'll tell all of you the story, and then you'll know why I have these marks on my neck."

****

An hour later, Ella stopped by Velma's rocker and gave her a kiss on the cheek. "I'll be home to help with the evenin' meal."

"Go have fun. I'm fine." She appeared weary and older than her twenty-seven years. She patted the slight bulge in her belly. "It's just that this one's takin' the strength out of me."

Ella flinched inside. Memories of her own mama's lack of strength and the premature delivery were too fresh. She could still see her baby brother's heaving chest, his little lungs struggling to draw in air. She patted Velma's shoulder, as she fought tears.

"Thank you, Velma. I won't stay late."

Carrie, Scott, and Remy played in a corner of the small room, stacking blocks to build a fort and arguing amongst themselves, but Rosemary pulled herself into Velma's lap. Her droopy eyes said she'd soon take a nap.

"She'd like to nurse, but ain't got nothin' for her." Velma patted the child's cheek. Her broken-nailed hand was a sharp contrast to Rosemary's rose-petal skin. "I hopes she don't try hogging back in on my milk afters the baby's born at the end of March."

Rosemary's arms and legs appeared thin and blue-veined—as if she might benefit from nursing. Wispy brown hair framed her delicate heart-shaped face, and her ears stuck out. Her huge brown eyes flickered over Ella's face and then closed. Even as she drifted off to sleep, the child's pink lips worked the two fingers in her mouth.

Ella turned to go, but Velma reached for her hand.

"Child, tonight when the little ones sleep, let's sit, and talk—woman to woman. I might even stir up an apple crumble with sweeten'—just for us girls." Loneliness etched her gentle words.

"I would like that."

The woman gave a large toothy smile. "Go, haves fun. Catch up on the gossip for me, 'specially when it comes to what's goin' on with Duncan an' Fern.

"Why?" Ella scowled at the mention of her friend and Duncan. "Has there been more gossip?"

"I only heard Duncan caused much'a stir with his announcement. It's likely to get back to Manfred. That man'll secret Fern off to another place—other than Florida. He's very stubborn."

"Fern may never write." She thought of Duncan's letter. It remained in her safekeeping. *Will I be doin' the right thing, if there's a chance to mail it?*

****

Naomi and Leigh Chesley's cabin was on the western edge of the curved cove, a swift arrow's flight from the small log structure used as a meetinghouse and a church. Ella lifted her shawl to cover her head and set out at a brisk pace. Her booted toes kicked dust as she let her thoughts drift to Duncan and Fern. She had experienced shock when Duncan laid the envelope in her hand. Even more, she was a taken aback at his sudden change in attitude toward her.

Inez had chosen not to talk about her son's announcement during the walk down to Velma's cabin. She merely called it another one of his spur of the moment actions.

It was difficult for Ella to enter Naomi Chesley's house. Memories of her mama swamped her mind. Many of the same women seated near the quilting frame had attended her burying. There were only a few she didn't recognize. Once she said her "hellos and nice-to-meet-yous," she accepted a chair between Grace and Inez.

"We've missed you." Grace kissed her cheek. "I'm glad you got to come."

Inez reached to squeeze her hand. "Hope you're happy with Velma." Her hazel eyes searched Ella's face. "You look content and well."

"I miss both of you. An', yes, I'm happy."

"Ella Dessa?" A finger poked her shoulder.

"Oh, Katy, I'm so happy to see you. Where's your mother?"

"She's at the end of the table. See? Beside Naomi." The girl pointed and then said, "Hi, Grace. How's your father?"

"Papa's knee seems to be back to normal." Grace stroked Katy's curls and pushed them away from the girl's round face. "You're getting prettier every day."

"Thank you." Katy blushed. "Ella Dessa, I might come see you soon. I just heard you're stayin' with the Clanders."

"I know Velma won't mind if you do. She'd love it."

"Then I'll come visit. Talk to you at the midday meal." Katy gave Ella a parting hug before heading to where her mother sat.

Inez slid a cloth bag across the floor and toward Ella with her foot. "Here's your dress and the other skirts I redid and adjusted to fit you."

She shifted the bag between her feet under the quilt frame. "Thank you kindly. I need them."

Inez squeezed her hand. "We hoped you'd be here. Now, tell me the truth. How's Velma and the children?"

"She tires easy, with no strength. Scott's givin' her the dickens. Rosemary acts puny. Mae's wild, Remy's all boy, an' Carrie ... well, she's a problem in her own." Ella ticked her replies off on her fingers and smiled.

Inez nodded as if in understanding about Carrie, a beautiful nine-year-old with impulsive actions. "Some say she's fey. Is she any better? Or does she still do impulsive things? Velma told me about past incidents." She handed Ella a needle strung with thread.

"Oh, she's not fey or doomed to die." She shook her head while rolling the needle between her thumb and finger. "But no, I don't think she's better. She filched Velma's scissors and cut Remy's hair. Now he's got bald patches. He cried an' cried. Yesterday she plopped Rosemary in the empty water barrel on the porch and put the lid on. I heard her sobbin'."

"Oh, my!" Inez covered her mouth. Dismay showed on her face.

"Has me thinkin' she'd do it even if the barrel were full." Ella studied her needle as she spoke. "I don't like to suppose it'd happen."

"I wonder what makes that child act so outrageous." Grace joined the conversation.

"Don't know, but after her mama flicked her legs with a tree branch, Carrie threw up on herself, and then she cried." With one finger, she traced the wedding ring pattern of the stretched quilt in front of them. "I feel sorry for her. It's like something's making her act bad. And she don't want to be bad."

"All you can do is love and pray for her." Grace rethreaded her needle.

"Prayer is the answer," Inez agreed and patted her hand. "Children can be difficult to understand."

"I'm findin' that out." She shoved her needle into the material and changed the subject. "So, your husband's knee is better?"

"He's walking with only a slight limp."

"And the others?" Most of all, she wanted to ask about Jim, but she held her curiosity in check by feigning concentration on her work.

"They're fine." Grace answered before her mother. "Jim and Duncan do most of the work, letting Papa rest his knee. Samuel did get the barn straightened up after about four days."

Ella giggled as she remembered the conversation about the mess Samuel had to tackle. "An' the girls? I so hoped Peggy would come today."

"Oh, Peggy's *very upset*," Grace said. "She wanted to see you, but Phillip came down with a cough. He fussed and clung to Mother. But, of course, my mother wanted to be here, so Peggy had to stay behind. Anna and Josie couldn't be held responsible."

"Would you tell Peggy and the others that I wish to see 'em?"

"If she doesn't, I will." Inez turned to the quilt frame. "Okay, now girls, no more talking. Let's get to work on this quilt."

Talk switched from one subject to the other while needles tucked and tunneled through the astonishing design on the wedding quilt. Ella sank into the comforting arms of female companionship and tried her best at the quilting. As it had always done—the few times her mama tried to show her about stitching—the delicate handwork caused her fingers to feel clumsy and too big to grasp the slender piece of metal and manage the long thread. Twelve stitches to the inch became the best she could accomplish.

It was a relief to hear time called for the noon meal. Ella's fingers had dotted-red holes pricked in them. "Ooh, my fingers feel like I've been pickin' blackberries," she said to Katy, who had circled to her side of the quilting frame.

"Mine, too." Katy held her hands out for inspection. The blushed tips of her fingers showed scratches. "Why do women want to do this?"

"For the food?" Ella giggled and turned toward the women collecting picnic baskets from along a wall. "I forgot to bring anythin' to eat." She felt ashamed. "Guess I weren't thinkin' of food."

"We have plenty." Grace grabbed her hand. "I think we're eating outside under the trees. It's a perfect fall day and has warmed considerably." The three girls walked together toward the baskets.

"Everyone's basket is decorated?" Ella watched as Grace picked up a folded horse blanket and a sturdy basket decorated with sundried milkweed pods, stained blue and umber. The basket had a short length of pale-blue ribbon tied on the handle.

"Yes, it makes it fun." Grace shifted the basket to her nose. "Hmm, smells wonderful. Mother fried pieces of a rabbit Jim snared. She cooked a meat and onion pie with mashed potatoes in it—with a double crust. It's easy to pick up with our hands. She also made sweet potato pie for dessert. Of course, she left a second one at home for the family so Papa and Samuel wouldn't complain." She playfully rolled her eyes.

Ella smiled and felt the warmth of belonging. "I know that made 'em happy."

"Oh, it did. Come with me. Katy, would you like to join us?"

"I can't. I promised Angela we'd eat together. She got here late, on account of her little brother burned his hand."

Inez joined the trio of girls just in time to hear the news. "Is he all right?"

"Yes, his father took him to Granny Hanks. I think she smeared it with messy oil and wrapped it." Katy slipped close to Grace, touched her arm, and impishly smiled. "I'm going to hide my initials on your quilt. I'm good at embroidery. Maw said I could—to see if you find 'em after you're married."

"Oh, you silly girl." Grace laughed and used one free arm to hug the girl. "I bet I can find them."

"Nope, you won't. Bye, Ella Dessa." Katy whirled and ran out the door.

Naomi Chesley—her graying blond hair coiled on top of her head—came toward them and hugged Ella. "Ella Dessa, you look like you've grown an inch! I was so astonished when I looked across the quilting frame and saw you—of all people—sit down. With your hair pinned up, I almost didn't recognize you, but I saw your mother's beauty in you. I hear you're helping Velma these days."

"Yes'um. She needed me. I know you also wanted my help."

"Well, I did, but that's fine. Those twins of mine run me ragged. Brody's gaining weight. So now I can tell them apart when they're off at a distance getting into mischief. Torrin's still wiry, like his father was. I love them, and God gave them to me, but they keep me fluttering in circles—like a vulture!" She laughed and patted Ella's shoulder. "I am glad you could come help us finish Grace's quilt. Time's slipping away."

"Ahh, I ain't much help with the quiltin'."

"Ella Dessa, every teeny bit helps, and you're contributing to a lifelong treasure. I'm positive Grace appreciates it. God sees your sweet work." She turned to Grace and Inez. "Bride to be, Konrad's a lucky man. No doubt, God's in this union. You're going to make a beautiful bride. The prettiest ever in Beckler's Cove."

"Thank you, Naomi. Speaking of Konrad, he mentioned he'd like to stop in and thank the women."

"Oh, that's so sweet of him. The Lord bless him! Yes, I hope he stops by. I miss not having him stay with us, as he did for a short time. Get a bite to eat, and we'll finish the quilt."

"I like her." Ella watched Naomi walk away. Her mama had always admired the woman's unshakable faith in God and her pleasant personality.

"A true God-fearing woman," Inez said in agreement. "The best in these parts."

Grace nodded. "It's too bad she and Leigh never had children, but I guess God's blessed them with Torrin and Brody—if one can call it a *blessing.*"

As they laughed about the antics of the twins, they headed outside to the warm sunshine. A mixture of blankets and quilts added multi-colored square and rectangular patterns to the layers of crimson, orange, and yellow leaves under the maples and oaks. It completed a perfect presentation of God's handiwork—woven together with the talents of the backwoods women.

Ella took a deep breath and paused. *Oh, Mama, you'd love this.*

The women gathered in small groups and opened baskets, all the while laughing and talking. The sunlight streaked through the leaf-thinned branches of the trees and brought to life the mingled colors. The women sat with widespread skirts, adding muted colors of gray, beige, and brown. The scene was perfect and complete.

"Ella Dessa?" Grace faced her, a slight frown of disquiet between her deep brown eyes. "Your expression changed. Are you sad?"

"No, not sad." She broke away from the spell of wonderment and smiled. "It's all too beautiful to be sad. With all the colors and bright sun, I figger it's what heaven's like. So I thought of Mama."

As they set the basket on the crushed grass and unfolded the thick blanket, she spied a dark-haired man riding toward them on a brown and white spotted horse. He followed a rutted path across the wide grassy field separating the Chesley cabin from the church.

He reined in and asked, "Have you ladies seen a beautiful brown-haired gal, who's looking for a handsome man to wed?"

Peals of feminine laughter and teasing comments filled the air. Grace blushed almost as red as the leaves scattered under her feet. As he dismounted, she wasted no time in running to his side. She ignored the women behind her, raised her face, and accepted his possessive kiss and encircling arms. Many of the young women clapped in appreciation while older women gasped.

"I hope that's her husband to be." Ella giggled behind her hand.

"He is." Inez watched her daughter and the slender man walk toward them. "He's special. I don't believe I've ever seen or talked to a more godly young man. He came to these mountains with a dream of teaching backwoods children. You know he plans to start a school here in the cove? There's talk he'll use the church building. He has an uncle who's backing him with supplies."

"Yes, I heard. Scott wants to attend." Ella didn't voice her own longings about school.

"Samuel thinks he's wonderful and wants to study under him—instead of me."

Grace and Konrad stopped nearby to speak to Rebecca Foster.

"Will that bother you?" Ella deliberately kept her voice low.

"Oh, dear me, no. Samuel has an overwhelming urge to advance his studies and become a teacher himself."

"He'll make a fun teacher."

Inez sat, adjusted her long skirt, and patted the striped blanket. "Come, sit with me."

The two of them watched Grace and the teacher talk to Rebecca. "Rebecca's so pretty." Ella felt a touch of envy.

Inez leaned forward to whisper, "Did you know Rebecca's in the family way?"

"I heard."

"I think her baby will be born about the same time as Velma's."

"Her little one, Zeb, is cute." She noted how Rebecca's skirt front showed a rounding, the same as Velma's did. Her thoughts flashed to the birth of Mama's baby and a shudder crossed her shoulders. "I hope both her and Velma—" She stopped, unable to finish her sentence.

"You hope she and Velma have no problems during the birthing. I understand your concerns. Does it bother you living with Velma because of that?"

"No." She shook her head, not willing to tell Inez about nightmares of delivering another baby without Granny in attendance. She smiled and pointed. "Here comes Grace."

The engaged couple, fingers intertwined, came toward them.

"Ella Dessa, I'd like to introduce you to Konrad Strom, the man to whom I'm betrothed." Grace's face glowed and love lit her astonishing brown eyes. She pulled him down with her, to sit on the blanket.

Feeling shy, Ella held her hand out to the man. "It's nice to meet you."

"I'm happy to meet you." His fingers felt warm as he took her hand and lightly squeezed it. "I was told you recently lost your mother. I wish to tell you how sorry I am. I was one of those who did not make it to the burying." His deep blue eyes accented his thin face, dark eyebrows, and hair. The shadow of a heavy beard showed on his face, and dimples in his cheeks spoke of a sense of humor.

"Thank you." She forced herself to keep her head up, even though she feared he could see her vivid scars.

She felt relieved when the conversation turned to the food Inez had prepared. She watched Grace interact with Konrad and noticed a flush of elevated color made the young woman's face intensify in radiance.

"Shall we ask the Lord's blessing?" Inez smiled at her future son-in-law. "Konrad, would you mind?"

"Not at all." He reached for Grace's hand and bowed his head. "Our Heavenly Father, we wish to thank you for this food spread before us and for all the women who have come together to bless Grace and me with a wedding remembrance. Amen."

"Amen," Grace whispered. She smiled and clung to his hand.

Having never witnessed a man and woman who had pledged themselves to be married, Ella found herself enthralled by the whole idea. Konrad seemed so in love with her friend. She couldn't imagine him ever raising his hand to hurt a woman. His kind eyes never left Grace's face and lips when she spoke or passed a piece of the rabbit and onion pie.

"The wedding is fast approaching." Inez lifted soft and lightly-browned triangles of squash out of the picnic basket and offered them to everyone. They were still in the skins and easy to handle. "Grace and I have much to do and plan. Konrad, how's the cabin coming?"

"The logs are cut. I have the land cleared. Leigh's talking to the men. The weather's been good, and we hope to raise the walls next week. The cabin won't be huge. But it'll be ours."

"I think it'll be wonderful." Grace's elated smile lit her gorgeous face. "Perhaps, we'll have time to decorate?"

"Grace, you may have to decorate after the wedding, honey. I'm sorry for the delay." Konrad's hand brushed a loose strand of hair from her cheek, his fingers slow and infinitely gentle.

"I'm not fretting. We'll have fun doing it together, and I'm sure Mother will help. I've finished the needlepoint on curtains for the two windows we planned. My wedding dress still has extra stitching and gathers to be done on the front." Grace blushed and dropped her gaze to her lap.

"I look forward to seeing it," Konrad murmured.

Grace gave a self-conscious giggle and glanced toward her mother, but Inez was lifting a pie from the basket.

"Mrs. McKnapp, this food is superb." Konrad accepted a handheld piece of sweet potato pie from Inez. "I long for good meals, but don't get them very often." He bit into the pie and winked at Grace. "Now, in the future, I hope to get plenty of home cooking."

Inez smiled. "Grace is a good cook. Here, eat more. It'll save me carrying it home."

"I've about had my fill." He leaned sideways and wiped his fingers on the grass. "It's wonderful. You know, I've been camping out at the home location—in a wagon my uncle gave me."

"Grace informed me of that," Inez replied. "You gave up your room here with Naomi and Leigh. Staying in a wagon must be chilly, especially at night, now that the weather's changing."

"Ah, the wagon's snug. It's got an oiled top over it. Just no fireplace." He grinned and touched Grace's arm. "But I'm right where I can work on our land and house, when not sorting through books for the school. My uncle—you'll meet him at the wedding—is providing the initial school supplies. He has the means and the desire to do so. This hidden-away community here in the cove will be blessed to benefit from his generosity."

Inez nodded. "He must be a wonderful person."

"Indeed. He filled a very big void in my life after a falling tree killed my father. I never knew my mother. She died giving birth to me. He's her brother."

Ella kept her gaze on Konrad, even though she felt Grace's gentle eyes turn in her direction and search her expression. She knew the young woman felt concern Konrad's talk of his dead mother would upset her.

"I'm so sorry to hear you have lost both parents," Inez murmured. "When will the school commence?"

"I plan to start classes at the church right after the first of the year, if the winter is mild. From what I understand, eight children are interested. I think the number will grow. I also realize it'll be a short school year, but it will be beneficial to the students. Is Samuel still interested in attending?"

"Samuel has talked to his father. We're willing."

"Good. I hope he'll take over teaching the more immature children by next fall. I think he's capable. It will be good experience for Samuel. I've spent time with him, finding out how advanced he is. You've done a wonderful job teaching all your children." Again, he winked at Grace. "Including the one I'm marrying. I love her voice. She even sang for me."

Grace laughed and visibly relaxed. She leaned close to him, her chin alongside his shoulder. "You better keep saying things like that after we're married."

"I intend to." With his thumb, he wiped a tiny smear of sweet potato from her bottom lip.

Ella slowly munched on her piece of pie. She kept her eyes riveted on the betrothed couple. The food was good, but the privilege of being included in the small intimate group filled her heart with serene delight. Wiggling, she scooted closer to Grace. She felt grown-up and a part of a real family—as if her pa's rejection had never occurred.

In her mind, she tried to imagine how it must feel to have a man fall in love with you. She watched Konrad's face and drank in the inflection in his deep voice. She felt heady with anticipation that someday she might meet a man who'd love her. At the edge of her thoughts, Jim McKnapp's smiling face floated.

Inez gestured over her shoulder. "Oh, dear. We're still chatting and most of the women have gone inside. Grace, we must join them." She rose on her knees to pack the leftovers but handed the basket to Konrad. "Here, take this with you."

"Thank you. I'll enjoy it tonight for my supper." He bounded to his feet and assisted Inez, before offering his hand to Grace.

Ella stood and brushed crumbs and a stray pine needle from her skirt.

Konrad turned toward her. "Ella Dessa, I'm glad we met. Perhaps, you'd be interested in coming to school as well?"

School? She never considered it a possibility.

"I—I don't know," she stammered. She kept her eyes on the leaf-strewn ground.

Inez patted her shoulder. "I think it's an outstanding suggestion."

"But, I ..." Her eyes traveled over the older woman's face. She yearned for the chance at an education, but didn't see how it could happen. She detected a flicker of inspiration in Inez's eyes.

"I think it could work out, even if you did most of your school work at Velma's and attended class when you got the chance." She turned to Konrad. "Ella Dessa is now living with Velma Clanders, helping her with the children while the husband is away. Plus, there will be another child born in about five months or less."

"You look like a smart girl," Konrad said.

Ella squirmed with embarrassment.

"I bet Samuel could bring you lessons after school—so you could study, even if you don't attend." He smiled at his future mother-in-law. "Of course, that'd be with the permission of Samuel's mother."

Inez linked her arm through Ella's bent elbow. "I think you've found an answer to the situation. I'm sure Samuel wouldn't mind dropping by Velma's and giving Ella Dessa the lessons. She'll be a good student, and I know she'll learn fast."

"Mama taught me." Ella's words burst from her mouth. "I can read and do figuring. I read her Bible."

Konrad snapped his fingers. "Excellent! One day, when you're free, I could help you with testing. We'll see where you are—as far as grade level."

"I'd like that." Her heart hammered in her chest. She wanted to jump up and shout, but she controlled her response and succeeded in acting calm. She felt a blossom of hope in her soul. She always wished to go to school, but her pa had laughed at her and told her school wasn't for females.

Inez took her hand. "Let's get back to sewing."

While seated back at the quilting frame, she found it hard to concentrate on the repetitive stitches. Her mind whirled over the possibility of schooling. Her mama would be proud of her. She wanted to toss aside her needle and thread, flee up the mountain, and kneel beside the grave.

She wiped at a betraying tear, blinked, and bent closer to the handwork. In and out, in and out went the needle, but in her mind she knelt under the pines with her knees against the tiny rocks and pebbles.

Mama, I might get some schoolin'.

****

When Ella Dessa stepped into Velma's quiet cabin, it was late afternoon and shadows stroked the woods. All that remained in the fireplace was dark coals and faint warmth.

"Velma?"

No one answered.

A slight noise caused her to walk toward the bed. In the dusky light, she could see Mae and Rosemary cuddled against their mama's relaxed body. Rosemary sucked on her thumb, but it was the only sound heard in the cabin. She tiptoed past the end of the bed and leaned closer. The pregnant woman seemed to be asleep, her pale face drawn and pinched about the mouth.

Ella moved away and climbed the ladder. "Remy, you up here? Scott?" The dark, cramped loft was empty. She backed down the ladder and ran outside.

The air held a decided chill. The scent of a skunk drifted over the open field to the left of the cabin. A faint sound reached her ears. A child's voice cried out, making Ella's stomach lurch.

"Scott? Where are you?" She turned in circles and scanned the darkened edge of the woods, as thoughts of a wolf came to mind. Nothing moved. "Carrie?" She sprinted for the barn. "Scott, answer me. Remy?"

She pulled the heavy door open and stopped in horror. Above her head, Carrie sat on a thick, hand-squared beam crossing the center of the small log barn. The girl's hands clutched the beam on either side of her thighs. Her short shift had hiked up on her skinny legs.

Scott and Remy stood beneath Carrie. Both spun to face Ella.

"She won't come down." Scott gritted his teeth. "I been beggin'. She's *so stupid.*"

With her heart in her throat, Ella spoke quietly. "Carrie, what you doin'?"

A narrow wooden ladder told her how the short girl got to that height and position. Carrie's cloth doll, a beloved toy she'd never willingly abandon, lay on the packed clay floor. Its body, minus any clothes or bonnet, sprawled with its limbs widespread.

Remy sobbed and rubbed at his red face, which showed streaks of grime and tears. "She wants to die 'cause Mama told her we're gettin' a new baby." His six-year-old voice quavered as he hunched his shoulders and bowed his head. "She might bleed if she falls."

"Shh." Ella tucked him close under her arm. "Let me think." Then looking up, she pleaded, "Carrie? Carrie, won't you come down? I'll help you. It's gettin' dark. So, we gotta go in and eat. Are you hungry?" She motioned to the barefooted child. "Scoot sideways."

Scott leaned close. "She ain't hearin' you. She wants to jump. She thinks Pappy will come home 'cause of the baby. I don't know why she came in here. She hates the barn. Pappy whips her in here." He rattled on, his own nervousness showing in his fast-talking. "He whips her hard. We hear her cry an' squeal like a hurt rabbit. She makes him mad."

"Shh, Scott. Let me think." She took a deep breath and felt woozy with fear. "Carrie, look at me."

What was left of the daylight, coming in at the door, barely reached the beam.

The girl's dull expression didn't change, but her lackluster hazel eyes shifted to Ella's face. Without a word, she swung her legs out in front of her, then backward, rocking her thin body on the beam.

"Carrie!" She hollered. "Don't move!"

Chapter 17

Evening, October 8, 1836

Ella pushed Remy toward his older brother. A clammy chill walked up her spine. Without taking her eyes from Carrie's constant movement, she whispered, "Take Remy and go wake your mama. Tell her to come quick."

"I won't do it. She's not feelin' good."

"Scott, don't sass me. I need help. So, please, fetch her. Take your brother and stay with the girls. Don't come back here."

She heard the boys leave the barn. The light faded in the barn and deepened the shadows. She wished she'd told Scott to send a lantern with his mama.

"Carrie, please, sit still."

A distant owl gave one quavering call. The barn's open expanse magnified the eerie sound.

The little girl moaned and kicked harder, now lifting her hands from the beam and holding them above her lap. Her actions appeared wild and deliberate.

"Stop!" Ella held her breath. She felt sure the momentum of Carrie's kicks would lift the child's body off the beam or toss her forward. "*Don't kick. Scoot on your bottom to the ladder. I'll hold it for you. Hurry 'fore you're left up there all night. It'll be dreadfully dark alone. It'll be so pitch black, you ain't goin' to see a wolf, even if he chanced by the barn door." Tears ran down her face.

"I don't like—the dark."

"Then come down."

She heard a quivering intake of breath.

A high-pitched whine of fear forced itself between the girl's dead-white lips. "I don't like layin' in the fodder." Her legs slowed. Their movement became lessened.

"Please, let me help you down." She stepped closer, almost directly under the girl. "Please?" At least, she'd be there to break the girl's fall.

Carrie's dirty feet dangled above her head, but too far away to touch.

"It hurts so—so much. I don't—like it." The girl's shadowed face took on a dazed expression.

An icy chill crept up Ella's backbone. "Honey, let's go inside by the fire." The back of her neck cramped from gazing upward. "Come, get your dolly. She needs her shift."

"Shift comes off—musn't soil it. Must put your shift out of the way. Do it now!" The little girl's voice grew angry. "Take it off, I said! Got to stay clean." She whimpered and covered her face. "My baby doll fell an' hit herself. She might be dead."

"Stay still. Hang on. Carrie, I hear the doll cryin'. She's right here." With cautious movements, she inched toward the cloth doll and grabbed it from the dirt floor. "Can you see her? She's fine, but she's afeerd of the dark. Your baby needs your hugs."

Ella clutched the doll to her heaving chest and waited as thick minutes ticked by.

Where's Velma? Why isn't she here?

Carrie's outline on top of the beam blended with the deepening gloom. Only the light color of her shift showed. Another owl called from a tree, somewhere on the sharp, rocky ridge. Its lonely call drifted through the cracks of the dilapidated log walls.

"Carrie, look down at me."

"No, no. I don't want to! I want Mama to help me." Carrie's cries sounded bewildered and forlorn. They tore at Ella's heart.

Unable to stand still any longer, she tossed the doll aside and reached for the rungs. She scrambled to the top and gripped the beam with sweaty hands, and stared the length of it. She tried to make out the girl's figure in the shadows.

"This way, Carrie. Move towards my voice. Scoot on your bottom. I'm right here."

"I can't," the girl wailed. "I don't see you."

"Ella? Carrie?" The glow from a lantern bobbed and bounced along the filthy straw-strewn floor and irregular walls. Velma lifted the light over her head. "Oh, God help us."

"Shh, she's scared, is all. Carrie, you can see now. Come this way." Ella held out her hand and gestured. "We need to get in by the fire. It's warm inside."

Carrie hiccupped with her sobs, but her skinny thighs moved sideways. She slid and wiggled toward the ladder. When she came within reach, Ella saw she trembled all over.

"That's it." She grasped Carrie's left wrist. "A little more. Turn. Put your foot on the rung." She stepped down one rung and steadied Carrie. The girl turned and reached the second rung.

"I'm skeered."

Ella gripped the rickety ladder by wrapping one arm around it. She used her free hand to guide the girl's bare feet to the short sapling rungs. "Down one more step. We're almost there."

With each step, she heard fervent, whispered prayers behind her. When they touched the dirt floor, she sent a pleading look over her shoulder. Velma placed the lantern on the floor and ran to grasp Carrie in her arms.

"Why? Child, why?" The woman pushed aside the girl's untidy hair and repeated the question. "Why? Tell me."

Carrie shoved one fist against her open mouth and hiccuped as she whispered, "You're gettin' a new baby 'cause I'm bad."

"No, no, that's not true." Velma hugged her close. "I love you. This baby won't take your place, no more than Rosemary did. I love all my babies. Don't you knows that?"

The girl's hands gripped her mama's shoulders. Harsh sobs of fear burst from her throat.

"Pappy told me if—if you find out—if you knows I'm—I'm bad, you'll get rid of me." Her face twisted and scrunched in disturbing distress. "He told me I'm bad."

"No, never. *Never*. He's wrong—so wrong."

Carrie pillowed her head on Velma's shoulder and continued to sob, but with less intensity.

"Velma?" Ella wiped tears off her own face and picked up the light. The lantern shook in her hands. "Let's go inside where it's warm.

Once they got inside, Ella started a simple meal. Velma cuddled the weeping girl in her lap and rocked. Rosemary also wanted to snuggle, but her mother told her it was Carrie's turn to use the rocker. Without protest, the two-year-old played with Carrie's cloth doll and sat close to her mother's feet, so close—she was in danger of the rocker pinching her.

Ella's hands shook as she prepared porridge and a large slice of ham.

Mae hung nearby, pestering her. The boys amused themselves by stacking the wooden blocks to see whose tower could reach the highest. Scott typically won because he was taller. But Remy pushed a bench over to where they played, stood on it, and managed to beat his big brother.

Mae cheered Remy on with his endeavors.

"I win!" The little boy had spunk and gained an advantage over his big brother.

"So what? Ya beat me." Scott flailed his arms and toppled his own stack of blocks. He made a mock bow to Remy. "There, now ya happy? Besides, you cheated."

Their mother stopped humming to Carrie and glared at her oldest son. The battered rocker creaked and the runners protested the movement.

"Scott, that ain't no way to talk." Her left hand stroked her daughter's pale face, but the girl's eyes remained shut.

Sighing, Scott dropped down in front of the fireplace and said, "I hope Pappy brings lots of gold home. I want a gun fer my birthday."

"Don't count on gold, son. Besides, we has a gun. Pappy only took his new one."

"It's old an' too heavy for me." His stormy eyes strayed to the wall above the narrow mantel. The forbidden gun hung there. "You won't let me touch it."

"When you're older." Her lips rested against Carrie's bowed head. "Now hush about it."

Ella spooned porridge into bowls and onto tin plates. Carefully, she divided the slab of ham. She gave everyone an equal piece. But she knew the little ones would only take a bite or two and then offer it to an older sibling.

"Scott, when's your birthday?"

"October fifteenth."

"Oh, that's comin' soon. We must have a party."

Scott stared, as if not believing her. "We must?"

"Yes. Other people have parties. Why can't we?"

"But how do we do it?" His freckles emphasized the innocence of his reply.

"Ahh, we can make special things. Don't worry. Let me plan." She felt a surge of sympathy for the boy and winked at his mother. "What do you think?"

"Ella Dessa, I think you're sweeter than honey." A tear ran over her sunken cheek. "Please, go aheads an' eat. I think I'll rock a short whiles longer."

****

A while later, after all the children had eaten and crawled into bed, Velma sat in the rocker by the fire.

"Carrie scares me," she whispered.

"Yes, it was awful." Ella sat nearby on the rough floor.

"She's acted strangely for the year. I've hoped an' prayed, but I think she lives in a different world from us." She sniffled and wiped at her nose. "Gust ain't patient with her. He'd just as soon slap her, than remove her from harm or danger. She hurts herself."

"Hmm." Ella didn't reply at once. She instinctively knew Velma didn't expect an answer to be forthcoming. "She really didn't want to fall."

"Then why'd she do that foolhardy thing?"

"I think she's pushed by what's in her head." She squinted at the fire and tried to think of the right words. "Somethin' tells her to do things. She does them, but she ain't wantin' to. We don't hear no one talking. But she does."

"Seems that way." The woman rubbed her rounded belly, which stretched the thin dress material. She kept her head down. A pensive expression shadowed her narrow face. "Carrie was Scott's age when Rosemary was born. There were no worries then. But now, with this baby, I don't know. I'm fearful of what my oldest child might do. She's gettin' worse, more so since Gust left us, like she's on pins an' needles."

"I'll be happy to watch out for the baby." Ella felt sorry for the lonely woman and laid a hand on her thin arm. "Carrie won't hurt the baby with both of us here."

Velma patted her hand. "Oh, you're a sweet one."

"Hmm, don't know 'bout that." She hugged her bent legs. The flames in the fireplace crackled and popped with a life of their own. She felt the heat on her hands and face, and the warmth reached through her skirt to her legs and stocking feet.

"Thanks for what you said to Scottie. We'll think of a gift for him. When's your birthday?"

"Mine?" She was surprised at the question. "I'll be thirteen on the fifth day of November."

"Ah, close to Samuel McKnapp's age. He's already thirteen."

"His big brother is much older." She shifted her eyes sideways toward Velma, tempted to tell the woman how thoughts of Jim filled her mind all the time.

"*Much* older." She unexpectedly tapped Ella's shoulder and raised her eyebrows into twin peaks. The fire's glow reflected off her sharp cheekbones. "Child, what's that I sees in your face?"

Ella dropped her head and knew she blushed. "You said we'd have a woman to woman talk."

"Well, for goodness sakes! I didn't reckon you'd confess you are hankerin' after Jim McKnapp."

"But, I ain't—I haven't."

The woman chuckled. "I see. An' I said I'd fix an apple crumble for us women. Will you forgive me, if'n I don't? I'm too tired. That's why I napped."

"I understand."

"So, you like Jim?"

"He's nice to me."

"Yes. An' he's very han'some—goin' to be a fine-lookin' man." Her dark eyes swept over Ella's face, and she gave a knowing smile. "I guess you do have sentiments for him."

"You think I shouldn't feel this way?" She felt nervous talking about the subject, but she knew Velma wouldn't tell on her.

"Child, no one can stop the heart. Feelin's flare up likes fire. Stomp on the flames an' you spread 'em. Dampenin' it down only makes you miserable. It's how we tend to that fire that counts. Out of control, fires can burn us. Contained fires can make us feel nice an' snuggly."

"I don't think I know what you're gettin' at."

She smiled and revealed the ample gap between her teeth. "You will. Just don't pine after him. Don't let your dreams of him blot out another's true love. There'll be others, perhaps. You're young. But I'm not sayings there won't be a fire, which will grow between you. Jim's had heartbreak, already. That girl moved away. He tends to have a temper. That kind of thing can kill love between even grown folks—if not controlled by the Lord. I know that all right." Her dark eyes took on a haunted look.

"I understand." Ella read deep pain and hurtful truth in the woman's facial expression. "My pa had a temper." She bowed her head and felt the emotions well and spill out. "When he gets in a fit, his hand starts shakin' and then his arm. It makes him mad. He'd hit my ... mama." Ella choked on the words and she tried to continue, "He—"

"Child, you don't haves to tell me."

"I do. I have to." She felt the dam inside her slide, crumble, and part. "If Pa was made furious by me, Mama made him hit her. He'd cut her mouth. Punch her eyes black. He'd knock her down, hit her belly, an' then hate her 'cause the babies died. He said he wanted a boy—not me. Then the new baby died—Mama died!" She dissolved into tears.

Fingers grasped her upper arms. "Come here, child."

She sat wrapped in Velma's loving arms while she succumbed to her own pain and grief. She felt the chair rock, but time faded away. It felt as if her mama's arms held her one more time, comforted her, and sheltered her.

When the deluge of tears ceased, she felt limp and drained. She eased herself out of Velma's lap and sank to the floor. She wiped her swollen face and bowed her head against the woman's skirted legs.

"I'm sorry."

"No needs to be sorry. Don't you feels better?" Her fingers caressed Ella's head. "This is what us women folk are su'pose to be to each other. We comfort one another. Gust hits me when he gets drunk. I have my scars inside an' out. My heart's broken, but not dead." She took a deep breath and sighed as though life had drained out of her. "Ohh, I don't believe he'll come back to us. Scottie senses it. I think Carrie, she dreads his return. She ain't actin' worse 'cause he's gone. She's worse 'cause she feels he'll come stompin' in."

Profound silence hung between them for a small amount of time. Only the crackling of the fire made noise.

"I'll stay 'til he comes back." Ella lifted her head.

"Then you'll be here a long time." A single tear traveled down the lonely woman's cheek.

"Then, you've got one more daughter."

"Yes, I do." She bent forward and kissed the top of Ella's head. "Now, gets your Bible. I'll read a passage to you 'fore we goes to sleep. Tomorrow, we'll attend the church service. Leigh will be preachin'. Afterwards, they'll meet an' talk of the church bein' used as a school."

"It's really Mama's Bible and her mama's 'fore that." Ella got the big book and returned to her spot beside the rocker. She crossed her legs and reverently laid the Bible in Velma's lap.

"You've a treasure here." Velma lifted the black leather cover. With care, she turned a few pages and paused.

When she didn't speak right away, Ella tugged at her sleeve. "What is it?"

Velma met her eyes and frowned. A tendril of hair slipped its pins and hung beside her face. "Ella Dessa, do you haves another name 'sides Huskey?"

"Another name?"

She pointed at the page and said, "This page lists the important things in your mama's life, sech as your birth."

"I never saw that." She leaned closer. "Where?"

"Here."

"That's me. Ella Dessa ... *Kilbride?*" She scowled, confused by the unfamiliar name. "What's that mean?" She paused long enough to think. Kilbride was the name of the man who had once loved her mama, but she didn't blurt out that secret fact. She peered at Velma. "Mama never called me that."

"Hmm, let's see what else is written. Your mama's parents were Aileen an' Clive Finley. It says they died tryin' to cross Halfpenny's Creek. I know where that is, but I don't remembers them. They must've died 'fore Gust an' I settled here. Yes. Here's the date of their death. This is your parents' wedding date. This is your birth date. We'll have to give you a party." She smiled. "Since you're doin' a special thing for my Scott."

"I ain't ever had a party, either. Mama told me about parties. She used to live fancy-like when she was little, but not here in the mountains."

Velma tapped the Bible. "Ella, I didn't know you had so many brothers an' sisters who died. I'm sorry."

"I did?"

"Your mama wrote their names."

"What?" She ran one finger down a list of names and dates she didn't recognize. "Look, Timothy's name. How can that be? See? Timothy Huskey."

"No, child, that's not the baby your mama just birthed. That's another one birthed three years ago. Your mama named all of them."

"Them?"

"The ones—the babies she lost. Those that didn't live."

Pulling the Bible closer, so she could see better, Ella marveled at the undersized, beautiful handwriting. The list included five infants and their names. "Becky, Etna, Clarice, Timothy, and Jonah Huskey. So, Mama named one of 'em Timothy like I did?" Astonished, she ran her finger over the written name. "I need to add my Timothy. There were three girls, plus two boys before my Timothy?"

Velma's finger moved from one spot to another. "Ella?" Her voice was hesitant and soft. "If these dates be set down correct an' the record of your name be true, Jacob Huskey mightn't be your father. That'd explain the strange name."

"I don't understand." She squirmed closer.

"Was your mama married to another—'fore your pa?"

"No. What's wrong?"

"Let me tries to explain. Your mama an' Jacob married on the thirtieth day of May, in eighteen-twenty-three. You were birthed that same year on the fifth day of November. That ain't even six months. It takes nine months to haves a baby that'll live. Did Granny deliver you?"

She thought for a couple of seconds. "Mama didn't say so."

"Granny never said you were birthed 'fore you should've been?"

"Not that I recall."

"Well, this date says you were."

"So? What does that mean?"

Velma's face colored. She acted uncomfortable. "This'll take explainin'. First, are you sure your mama weren't never married to another man?"

"Yes. I mean ... no, she weren't." She shook her head. She knew that loving and marrying were two different things. "Mama would've told me if she had."

****

Later that night, Ella Dessa remained awake on her pallet, keenly aware of the gentle breathing of the other children. Her mind whirled with information clearly scribed in her mama's Bible. It kept her from sleeping. Velma explained completely how human babies came to be, and then she told her to keep quiet about the particulars she now knew. Mama listed her last name as Kilbride. According to Velma, only one explanation clarified the different last name.

She curled into a ball under the thin quilt. She thought about the one fact she hadn't told Velma. Her mama once loved a man with the last name of Kilbride. If what she now knew was correct, Jacob Huskey wasn't her pa.

Chapter 18

Saturday, December 10, 1836

With her own shawl wrapped snug about the both of them, Ella carried Rosemary on her left hip. "You're sure about this?" She matched her steps to the slow stride of the pregnant woman.

Velma nodded. "I'm sure. I wouldn't wants to miss the weddin'." She walked with her eyes on the rough path. Her left hand rested on the rounded mound of her belly.

Their footsteps took them beside the rock-strewn edge of Pelter's Creek and through the bare-limbed woods. The gurgle of water, flowing over slick rocks, accompanied their hike—drowning out the rustle of dry matted leaves under their feet. Mae, Scott, and Remy followed single file behind their mother and Ella, but Carrie took the lead and marched on ahead.

"I could've gotten word to someone 'bout giving us a wagon ride, by way of the cove." Ella dropped back to walk behind Velma. The narrowing of the trail forced them between four boulders.

"No, this is fine. Not bad walkin' weather. The forest blocks the wind. Besides, I don't wants people to talk about me not havin' a farm wagon no more," Velma said.

Ella rolled her eyes. "But they mostly know. We walk to church."

"Don't matter. I want to walk today, not ride."

"But you're not feelin' your best."

The last of the oak, maple, and poplar leaves had shriveled and released their stubborn grip on dark limbs. Fall's brilliant colors had vanished, replaced with monotonous brown and black undertones of the bare tree trunks, gray boulders, and clay-colored rocks holding back the mountain's sharper sides.

Ella hugged Rosemary's feather-light body to hers and felt the girl's fingers dig into her shoulder.

"Me skeered," the child whispered. Her round eyes darted and watched the dark tree trunks along the dim trail.

"Don't be. Mama and me are with you." Then with a sigh of exasperation, Ella called out, "Carrie, wait for us. You'll run into a bear or panther. They like the rocks." She felt a shiver of fear run across her own shoulders at the thought of the stealthy tan animal stalking them.

Carrie flashed a look of defiance over her shoulder. The expression said the nine-year-old was in one of her unpredictable moods.

"I don't know what to do with her." Velma kept her comment low, but it overflowed with anxiety. "She's worse—finds ways to stir up trouble. Can I trust her arounds a baby?"

"I'll keep an eye on her."

"I think Carrie likes you." The woman ducked under a low-hanging branch and held it out of the way so Ella could come through with Rosemary.

"I hope so. We need her to like somebody."

Lightning fast, Scott squeezed past them. He headed toward Carrie, dodged the hand the girl threw out to stop him, and laughed. He whirled and faced the rest of them. With an air of cockiness, he marched backward. The gap between his front teeth showed when he grinned.

"Carrie, you're trapped," he said.

His mother gasped. "Scottie, you watch your steps."

"Now, I'm in the lead." His freckles fanned across the bridge of his straight nose, and his bare head appeared tousled, with sun-touched brown hair sticking out over his prominent ears.

"If you stumbles sideways, you'll flop in the creek." Velma clicked her tongue on the roof of her mouth and gave a huff of breath, showing her frustration at not being able to run and get her hands on him.

"I won't." He checked over his shoulder and slowed his steps until he blocked Carrie from moving forward. The creek hemmed her in on one side, and a pile of wedged rocks formed a solid wall to her right side. She couldn't get past him.

Scott gave a whoop of glee and pointed at her.

Carrie lifted her hands and hit him hard in the chest. Her impulsive attack caught Scott by surprise, pushed him backward, and caused him to lose his balance. He landed on his bottom in the middle of the bumpy trail. The fall carried him onto his back, and his left shoulder smacked the edge of a rock.

Before the astounded expression on Scott's face cleared and he could get his feet under him, Carrie doubled back and hid behind their mama and Mae. Velma stopped and turned. She snatched her daughter's right hand and applied a firm slap to the top of it. The sound duplicated the crack of a branch breaking under the tread of a grown man.

Carrie cried out in pain and jerked her hand away.

Scott rolled sideways and scrambled to his feet. He ran at his sister, his face twisted with anger.

Ella threw out her left hand to block him. "No, Scott. Stop."

"You saw what she did." He used both hands to rub his bruised backside, which brought a bubbling giggle from Mae. "I'm gonna hurt her!"

"Your mama did that. No need for you to tend to it."

Remy stepped past Ella and closer to his big brother. "You was funny sittin' in the dirt. Your legs stuck up in the air."

"Stop." His mother motioned him to shut up and shook her finger at Scott. "Get on with ya. You wanted to be ahead of us—now gets to it. You betta pray there's no bear on the trail."

"I'm not afeered of bears." Scott fingered his hurt shoulder, but didn't tempt his mother to punish him. He turned on his heels and walked ahead of them. He kicked at everything moveable.

Velma summoned Carrie. "Comes here. Ends the cryin'. Walk betwinst Ella an' me."

Sniffling, the girl shuffled along with her head bowed. She rubbed at the reddened spot on the back of her slender hand.

Ella felt sorry for her. She had already figured out Scott's motives. He continually irritated his sister, baiting her into fights—so he could have the satisfaction of getting the girl into more trouble. Gently, she touched Carrie's thin shoulder.

The girl jerked in her direction. Her wary eyes seemed void of any inner feelings, but Ella spied a glimmer of pride.

Velma winked at Ella over Carrie's head. "And to think—I've got one more one on the way."

"Yes, that's so." She grinned. "Velma, when we get to the church, may I go to Naomi's house? I hear that's where Grace will be."

"I'm sure you'd be welcome." The woman pulled her wrap closer to her chest and swollen belly. "That wind's now got a bite to it. Hurry, children." She paused long enough to catch her breath and shoo them on ahead of her. "Go fast."

"Rose, lift the shawl over your head." Ella switched Rosemary to her other hip and ignored the soreness in her arms. "Hug my neck."

While they completed the three-quarter mile hike along Pelter's Creek, the air turned colder, and the breeze stiffened. The modest sized log church was a welcome sight.

To Ella, the interior of the building felt warm and cozy, but as soon as Velma and the children took seats on the rough plank benches, she darted out the door. She ran through the field of dead grass to the Chesleys' sprawling cabin. The workmanship on the square-logged building represented a testament to Leigh's industrious nature.

She ignored the bumpy wagon path. It did a winding loop around the large field, but she was in too much of a hurry. The growing wind snatched at loose strands of her hair and tangled them about her head.

Her noisy knock brought a squeal of panic.

The door edged open. Katy peered around it.

"It's just Ella." The younger girl stepped out of the way and motioned her into a huge room—Naomi's kitchen.

"Ella Dessa, you startled me," Grace laughed. "I thought it was Leigh coming back."

"Come join us." Inez waved. "We're helping Grace get dressed."

The smiling bride stood in her undergarments, with her arms hidden in a billow of dark-blue material. Laura Stuart supported the gathered skirt of the wedding dress. Inez and Naomi lowered the bodice over Grace's full bust and adjusted the long sleeves. Peggy waved at Ella and continued to stir liquid in a stoneware jar near the fire.

The scent of apple cider drifted through the air.

"It feels so nice in here." The warmth from the wide stone fireplace drew Ella. "The weather's changin'." With cold fingers, she pulled the black ribbon from her hair and retied it.

"Okay, you can let the skirt drop," Inez said to Laura. "Ella Dessa, can you tie Peggy's bow? Katy, please set out the baskets of bread."

Peggy laid aside a wooden spoon. "I couldn't reach it, and they're all busy." She turned her back to Ella. "Mother made this new dress for the wedding, because I'm the next oldest girl.

"Peggy, I love your hair pinned up like that. You look older." Thrilled to be included, her fingers trembled as she fashioned a large bow.

"Ohh, Mother had an *awful* time making my curls lay smooth. Do you like my dress?"

"Yes, it's a lighter color than Grace's." The medium-blue material felt like silk in her chapped hands. "I've never seen the likes of it. It reminds me of a bluebird's feathers. There, it's tied."

Peggy whirled and presented her back to Inez. A white ribbon controlled her rebellious auburn curls and secured them in place on top of her head.

"Did she do good?"

"Perfect."

"It's *store-bought* goods—the material, that is." Katy sounded jealous. "They ordered it from Richmond. Konrad has relatives there." Bending closer to Ella's ear, she continued to whisper. "We know they're rich. Who else has weddings like this?"

Ella shrugged and watched Naomi hand Inez a small package of folded muslin.

"Here, I think it's time you arrange this on your daughter's head. We need to walk to the church." Her voice held a tremor of breathlessness. "I'll probably never have the honor of helping a daughter prepare for her wedding. Inez, I envy you. I just have the boys."

Laura sighed. "I dread the day Katy marries. I don't want to lose her."

Katy rolled her eyes, nudged Ella, and whispered, "I already know who I'm marryin'."

"Who?"

"Not tellin'." She sniggered and covered her mouth.

"I bet I know." Peggy wagged a finger at the girl.

"Shh. You're the only one who knows. Oh my! It looks like white frost." She pointed toward Grace.

Inez lifted delicate white lace from the package. Varying lengths of the filmy material hung from a curved bone comb. With a trembling hand, she pushed the teeth of the comb into the beautiful curls on top of Grace's head. The longest section of lace slipped over the bride's glowing eyes and nose. It hid most of her youthful features, except her lower cheeks and curved lips.

Ella immediately thought it a shame. How would Konrad know he married the right girl? She recalled her mama reading a Bible story about a man fooled into marrying the wrong girl—a sister to the one he truly loved—all because her face was hidden.

Feeling a bit confused, she studied the expressions of those congregated close to the bride. Even Naomi smiled. No one seemed sad or troubled about the lace. Ella had never attended a wedding so she kept silent about her uneasy thoughts.

Peggy clapped her hands with immediate approval. She edged in closer and fingered the texture of the lace. "Mother, I want one just like this. Please, tell Papa."

"When your time comes." Inez shook her finger. "It better not be for years and years. I don't want to lose all my girls."

"I can't believe Papa ordered this from Richmond. You did a wonderful job of gathering the lace." Grace's eyes showed through the delicate material as she kissed her mother's pale cheek.

"My child, you make a beautiful bride." Inez sniffled and pressed a soggy handkerchief to face. "Oh, I can't cry no more."

"No, you musn't." Naomi playfully slapped at her arm. "Your daughter wants to recall this December wedding as a wonderful day. Besides, you're not losing a daughter, you're gaining another son. Konrad Strom doesn't know how lucky he is."

"I hope he knows." Inez sniffled and folded the handkerchief into a small square. "He's taking my firstborn from me."

"Oh, Mother." Grace gave her a hug. "You'll make me cry."

Laura pushed the door open a crack and stared across the field. "Don't cry, Grace. You're tears might freeze on your face." Her bulky figure blocked the wind coming in the door. "I've never seen such ornery weather." She shut the door and bent to retrieve a colorful braided basket from the floor. "Here, Katy." She tossed her daughter a gray shawl.

"We must hurry." Naomi lifted a brown woolen wrap from a peg on the wall. "I'm covering my head and shoulders against a chill. If Leigh had known about the change in the weather, he'd have had the wagon waiting outside."

"Will it snow?" Katy said.

"I wouldn't be surprised if we have snow by evening. Did you see the clouds gathering over the mountains? There's snow in them—after such a balmy fall." Naomi patted her chest, where she knotted her long wrap. "Grace, do you want one of my shawls? That wind's cutting a path right through the center of the cove."

With an anxious laugh, the bride shook her head and caused the veil to move from side to side.

"The material in your dress is thin, and Naomi has extra shawls," Inez said.

"No. At the moment, I feel like I could walk through a blizzard barefoot and not feel a thing."

The small group of women and girls laughed and hurried for the door.

"I think weddings are scary." Peggy grabbed Ella's hand. Her breath held a hint of apple cider.

"Why?"

"I wouldn't want to go live with anyone other than Mother and Papa."

Ella nodded. She understood better than most what it felt like to live without parents. But she also observed the expression of pure joy on Grace's face. Intuition told her Grace might miss seeing her parents every day, but she wasn't going to miss living with them.

Jim's smiling face popped into her mind. She wondered how it would feel to walk down the aisle facing him the way Grace would soon face Konrad.

"Ella Dessa, come on. Why are you standing there?" A blast of frigid air whirled in at the open door and compressed Peggy's dress against her legs. "We're being left behind."

"Sorry."

Ahead of them, she saw Grace grab the sides of her dress and raise the dark-blue skirt above the waving yellow grass. Her movements exposed the white underskirt, layered with handmade lace. The contrast of color made it a perfect picture and caused Ella's eyes to blur with tears. If only the seconds could be saved.

Almost running, the bride led the way across the rolling field between the Chesley house and the log church. Her full skirt billowed behind her. Inez and Naomi kept up with her, their heads bent to the wind, but Laura lagged behind them. Her stocky figure hindered her from moving any faster.

"Go on, I'll catch up," Laura yelled.

Ella and Peggy sprinted past her and caught up with Katy. The freezing wind gusted over the clearing and flattened the grass. No one tried to talk. They concentrated on moving as fast as possible.

"We made it." Grace went up the steps, as the wind moaned past the corner of the building.

"And not too soon," Naomi muttered.

Grace stood close to the wide door and lightly tapped on it. "I hope they heard my signal. I can't hear anything but the wind." She placed a hand on her head and held the lace.

"Oh, it's cold." Ella gasped for breath, tucked her chin into the folds of her shawl. Her teeth chattered. They mounted the steps and followed the bride's mother, but Peggy's grip on her hand didn't loosen.

"Girls, get in close to Grace," Naomi said.

The brightness of the sun failed to provide ample warmth. Naomi locked her elbow with Inez's as Laura joined the group. The women huddled on the steps, protecting Grace from most of the wind. Bunched lines of hoary clouds poured over the mountain and filled the cove.

Peggy squeezed Ella's cold fingers. "I'm so glad you came."

"Me, too. Velma wasn't feeling good walking here."

"You walked?"

"Yes. It felt warmer then."

Peggy shivered. "I wish they'd let us in." She bent her head and cuddled close. "My hair's getting fuzzy!"

Despite the cold, Ella gave Grace a smile. "Konrad won't figger it's you behind the lace. He might be scared it's a strange woman comin' to marry him—like Leah in the Bible." The wind caused the fragile veil to flap and move. She caught a glimpse of the bride's flushed cheeks and bright eyes.

Grace laughed at her. "He won't be scared. I feel like it's a dream. I'm finally becoming Mrs. Konrad Strom. I'm going to be *married.*"

"Yes, my dear, that's why we're standing here, freezing, and waiting to enter the church." Inez tapped Ella's shoulder. "You better scoot on in. Velma might need help keeping the children quiet. That way they'll know we're out here."

Ephraim pushed on the door just as Ella tried to pull it open.

"About time," he whispered. He tucked Grace's hand through the bend of his elbow. "Let's get my baby girl out of this cold."

Ella ducked into the warmth of the log building and squeezed between Scott and Mae, appreciating the heat from their small bodies. Konrad stood at the front of the church. He gazed at his bride clinging to Ephraim's elbow, as Inez and the others found their respective seats.

Leigh nodded his head, indicating it was time for Grace to come forward.

Ella saw Josie and Anna sat with their four brothers. Jim held Phillip on his lap. Her heart beat double time when he caught her eye and winked. Samuel stared at Grace. His face held such a sad expression, Ella felt sorry for him.

He's worried about losing his sister.

A collective gasp and a sigh of amazement whispered through the crowded building. The tall trim woman fulfilled her name. The home-sewn gown of dark blue had delicate tucks and pleats extending from the neckline to the slender waist, which opened downward and became a full long skirt. The hem swept the rugged wood planks of the floor. The bodice had no collar, but managed to be both modest and beautiful with a high, curved neckline.

The final touch, which caught everyone's eyes, was the ornate white lace encircling Grace's up-swept hair. It barely covered her blushing cheeks in a gathered wave of fragile stitching. Its richness wasn't something usually displayed in a wilderness town, let alone a small cove, miles and miles from a populated city or bigger settlement.

No doubt, she was the most gorgeous bride Beckler's Cove had ever seen.

Ella's eyes switched from Grace to Konrad. *His eyes say she's beautiful.* Her own fingers strayed to the collar of her white blouse and fingered the bumpy scars.

****

Samuel's feelings fluctuated as Grace went to stand beside Konrad and his papa sat down. He clenched his hands at his sides. He silently groaned at his inability to yell for her to stop. In truth, he felt happy for her and excited about the new teacher becoming his brother-in-law, but he longed to grab his big sister's arm and pull her out of the crowded building.

He clenched his top teeth down on his bottom lip and watched Grace freely reach for Konrad's hand.

Grace was his sister, the one who used to read him stories before bed, the one who showed him how to find the best blueberry bushes on the high, sun-filled ridges. She had always been in his life. For him, her leaving home would be as if she died.

Why do things have to change?

Home wouldn't be the same without her gentle laughter. Emptiness might fill the house. Their mother would be lonely.

He heard the scripture and the words Leigh recited. *Why does anyone have to leave his or her parents? What does it mean to cleave?* The only time he heard it used was when his mother chopped a chicken breast into two pieces.

It made no sense to him.

With an upturned face, Grace spoke soft words of forever. Konrad slipped a silver band over the fourth finger of Grace's left hand and clasped the delicate hand in both of his. The preacher's mouth formed words Samuel no longer heard. It was over—his sister had allowed herself to be stolen.

Leigh ended the ceremony. "Konrad, you may kiss your wife."

Grace lifted the veil, revealing her lovely, pink-cheeked face and shining eyes.

Samuel stole a sideways peek at Ella Dessa. The girl's face glowed with attentiveness. Her curved lips parted, as she observed the couple's first kiss as man and wife. In that split second, her vivid blue eyes blinked and turned in his direction. Their gazes locked and held for only seconds, but it was enough for Samuel to feel his heart gallop in his chest.

He saw her press a hand to her scarred neck, before turning her attention back to Grace and Konrad. Everyone laughed, clapped, and cheered. People moved into the aisle and jostled one another to be the first to greet the newlyweds.

Samuel frowned. He lost sight of Ella Dessa as everyone elbowed him.

Because of the chilly December weather, an indoor meal had been planned. He knew borrowed tables filled Leigh and Naomi's house. All the women had baked and brought food to add to the collection. He ducked past the adults congratulating his sister and new brother-in-law and headed toward the door.

Worrying about losing his sister was now a moot issue. Food became more important than lingering in the church and doing mushy things like kissing and hugging. Samuel pushed open the church door and ran for the Chesley log house.

Four older women barely looked up as he burst through the door. They had shed their shawls and busied themselves with opening baskets of food and setting the items on two tables positioned side by side. Chairs and benches encircled and occupied the edge of the outer walls, to make room for the arriving crowd. A comforting fire danced in the massive fireplace.

He slipped in and warmed his hands while he eyed the abundance of delicious food layering the tabletops.

"Samuel McKnapp, I know why ye snuck off an' got here first. Son, keep yer distance from the food—if ye know what I mean." Granny Hanks shook a blue-stained wooden spoon at him.

He eyed the waving spoon. *Blueberry cobbler, for sure.* It had to be his mother's recipe— made from berries dried for the winter.

"Do ye hear me?"

"Why, Granny, I only thought I'd come help you." He grinned at the scrawny woman. She reminded him of one of their chickens.

"A buncha help you'd be!"

"Ahh, you know I can be of help."

"Yes, you'd help yerself."

He heard voices and laughter. The door burst open and flooded the room with wintry air. Leigh ushered in the bride and groom. He stepped onto a bench as the place filled with people eager to get out of the cold. His hand waved above the gathering and motioned for silence.

"Welcome! Thanks to all who stayed to partake dinner with the new couple. We'll ask God's blessing on the food at this time. Shall we bow our heads?"

Samuel bowed his head, but his eyes searched for Ella Dessa's slender figure.

"Our Father," Leigh cleared his voice, "we ask Your touch on Grace and Konrad as they start their life together. Give them blessings abundant. Thank You for this food of which we are about to partake. Amen."

The group echoed the preacher's "Amen." The bride and groom sat in two rockers near the fireplace. People handed them gifts and covered their laps with homemade tokens of love. While they opened the presents, people drifted to the tables, filled plates, and visited.

Samuel ducked between adults and soon acquired a full plate. He sought a spot along one wall. It was underneath the tacked hide of a mountain lion, and he sat with his back against the squared logs. Using his fingers, he shoved a huge piece of venison into his mouth, just as Ella Dessa stepped in front of him.

She balanced a plate of food in her hands. "Konrad said you'd be willin' to bring lessons to me?" Her sparkling blue eyes watched him desperately stuff the meat into his mouth, but her calm expression didn't change, and she didn't laugh at him.

He felt his face redden. He almost strangled on the dry meat, and he chewed faster. "Yes. I told him ... told him I could." He swallowed, coughed, and covered his mouth. "Oh, that almost got stuck."

"I might need help."

"Help?" he repeated, his voice squeaking. "You?" He tried not to cough.

"Yes, with lessons. I won't be at school to hear Konrad teach 'em."

"Oh, I see. Of course—I'll help you." He cleared his throat and wiped his fingers on the front of his clean shirt. "You want to sit down?" He pointed at the space beside him.

Her eyes drifted to the golden-brown hide on the wall. He saw her shudder and switch her uneasy gaze back to his face.

"It won't hurt you."

"I know that." She pulled her gathered brown skirt to the side and sat close to him. Her bent knee bumped his.

"It can't hurt you. It's been dead a long time."

"I know." She set the plate on the floor in front of her. "Will Jim go to school?"

"Jim?"

"Yes. Will he go?" She broke a piece of bread in two and turned to face him. As she took a bite, crumbs fell and trailed down the front of her plain white blouse.

"Huh?" Samuel forced his gaze away from the crumbs on her faintly curved chest. "Naw, he finished his schooling with Mother. He's needed at home and besides—he's too *old*." He moved as if by accident and pressed his leg closer to Ella Dessa's thigh. He grinned at her, and knew she had no idea how his heart hammered his ribs.

"Oh, I guess I should've known that. Your pa's knee is better, right?"

"Yep, he just limps now."

"He walked fine with Grace."

"He did. But I bet he's trying his best to walk without limping."

Peggy appeared and tugged Katy with her.

"Katy, you can sit on the other side of my brother." She knelt beside Ella Dessa and balanced her plate in her right hand. She reached across to snitch a piece of sweet blueberry bread off Sam's plate. "I didn't get one of those."

"Hey, that's mine." He grabbed, but missed the stolen tidbit.

"No more," his sister mumbled. She rolled her eyes and stuffed the morsel in her mouth.

"I'll share mine." Katy handed him one of her two pieces. She smiled expectantly. Her attentive gaze never left his face. Two dots of crimson colored her rounded cheeks.

"Thank you, Katy." He groaned inside and carefully took it from her fingertips, all the while, wishing she'd stop gawking. She was pretty, with her soft red curls and huge green eyes, but he considered her a pest. He was three years older.

"You're welcome, Samuel." She continued to study him.

It irritated him—he had hoped to talk to Ella Dessa alone.

Peggy leaned past Ella Dessa. "Sam, your eyes, and Katy's eyes match— *perfect*."

He fixed his gaze on the plate in his lap and muttered, "I never noticed."

"No, Samuel's are more bluish-green," Ella Dessa said. "Like the wings on a dragonfly."

He lifted his head and felt a surge of hopefulness. He smiled. "Wow, I like that. I'm a dragonfly?" *I'll be anything, just so long as you talk to me.*

"No." She corrected him. "The *color* of your eyes are—"

"Sam, doesn't Katy's hair look beautiful?" Peggy wasn't going to be ignored. "Her mother let her wear it up for the first time. I like the pretty curls hanging by her neck. I wish my hair looked more like Katy's and less like fuzz on an auburn sheep."

"Ahh, sure." He gave a fleeting appraisal of Katy's hair and a thought struck him. "You know what? Her curls remind me of fat red worms we dig in the spring for fishing."

"What?" Peggy yelped, her mouth wide open. "Sam, that's not nice."

Katy's expression was a marvel to behold.

Her eyebrows rose. Her eyes widened and resembled two marshes covered in summer-bright lily pads.

He feigned innocence. "Whaddaya mean? I like those worms."

At his side, Ella Dessa made odd humming noises in her throat. She hid her face in both hands.

He shook her arm. "Are you choking?"

"She's fine. Samuel, you hurt Katy's feelings." His sister glowered as if she wanted to punch him in the mouth. She slammed her tin plate on the floor. Food bounced onto the wood planks. "Why, I ought to—"

"I didn't hurt her." He turned from Ella Dessa to Katy. The instant he saw tears in Katy's eyes, he knew she hadn't taken his words as a compliment. "What I mean is, they look *wonderful.* Just like red worms are wonderful for fishing."

Katy turned away from him and stared straight ahead. Blotchy, purplish-red spots covered her pale cheeks. Her chin quivered, and one huge tear glided down her face.

Ella Dessa reached across his plate of food and patted Katy's arm. "Katy, don't be upset. That's what Samuel meant. I've seen them kind o' worms. Why, they shimmer a pretty reddish color, and they coil up right nice."

Katy clutched her plate of food and jumped to her feet. With a sob, she headed for her mother.

"Now, look what you've done." His sister also stood with her plate. "You ought to be ashamed, comparing her hair to—to worms."

"I didn't mean anything bad." He watched Peggy follow Katy into the crowd of adults, before a long sigh pushed from his lungs. "I'm in trouble. Puddle-deep trouble. Mother will have my head when I get home." Suddenly, he realized Ella Dessa leaned against his right arm with her whole body trembling. "Hey." He tried to see her face. "Look at me."

She burst into a full laugh and covered her mouth.

"You're laughing?"

"You picked the wrong words to say," she blurted out and faced him. "Poor Katy. I ain't wantin' to laugh. It's just—I keep seeing her face. You're sumpthin' else, Samuel!" She started sniggering again. "Oh, my sides hurt."

"Humph. Everything I do or say goes wrong. I didn't say it to be mean. Honest."

"I know that, an' you know that." Her lips lifted in a delightful smile. Her fingers touched his arm and lingered. "Don't fret. I'm sure your sister will put things right. But Katy may hate you."

He studied her hand and fancied he felt its heat through his shirtsleeve. "Would you hate me, if it was you?"

"No. Well, I'd try not to."

"Good, because I'd never want you to hate me." *Oh, why'd I have to go and say that?*

Her lively eyes searched his face, before she smiled. "That's good. It means we're friends." A girl's pealing laughter caused her to turn toward the tables. "Hmm. What's the name of that dark-haired girl?"

"Sophie. She's older than us—by a little." He noticed a flicker of something akin to melancholy in her eyes. "Why?"

"Oh nothin'. She likes talking to your brother."

"Seems to." He watched Jim lift a piece of spice bread and offer it to the laughing girl. "Or him to her. You're not eating."

"It's stickin' in my throat." She swallowed and stared at her plate of food. "Sorry 'bout Katy gettin' up in such a huff. Maybe she'll come back."

"Do you think I want that?"

"Well—"

"Ella Dessa." Rebecca Foster stopped in front of them. "You look so sweet and grown up."

"Thank you."

Samuel dropped his eyes. He couldn't help but notice Rebecca's belly had expanded to much the same size as Velma's, but was hidden by a draped shawl.

"I hear you're living with Velma and helping her."

"Yes'um. I try my best."

"Where is she?" She rose on tiptoe to look around the room. "Oh, I see her. She's sitting near the door. I'll go keep her company."

Ella Dessa's eyes followed the young woman. "She's so nice."

"And pretty." He finished stuffing a final bite of the turkey sandwich into his mouth. "Of course, I know someone else who's just as pretty," he mumbled and brushed away crumbs.

She blinked twice. "Who? Katy?"

"You."

"Me?" Apparent surprise washed over her delicate features. Her right hand slapped itself across the scars on her neck. "I can't say as I believe that," she whispered. Her wistful eyes searched his face.

He made sure no one overheard him and leaned in close. "You need to believe it 'cause I said it. You *are*." His eyes locked on her parted lips.

"Ah, Velma is beckoning to me." With a flush coloring her freckled cheeks, she stood with her plate and walked away.

Samuel watched her bend and listen to the pregnant woman. He had never before experienced the feelings entangling his mind and heart. Girls were pests—giggling nuisances, he always ignored. Now he longed to linger close to Ella Dessa, make her smile, and study the unique expressions on her face. The image of her curved lips floated before his mind.

****

Ella pushed through the crowded room and searched for the children. Velma didn't feel well. Her belly cramped, and she wanted to go home. *How can we walk home in the cold? Velma might lose the baby.*

She saw Jim and Sophie move away from the table and stop near the fireplace. The flickering flames revealed the older girl's smooth-skinned neck. She felt a stab of intense jealousy, but the looming problem erased the girl from her mind.

"Honey, is something wrong?" Inez touched her shoulder.

"Velma isn't well. We need to go home." She swallowed and added, "What do I do? There's no wagon. Gust has it. We can't walk home alongside the creek like we came, 'cause it's freezin', now."

"You *walked* here?" Inez appeared stunned. "I had no idea she was without a wagon."

"Without horses and mules," she whispered. "Or much food, now. We done ate her fav'rite chickens. Don't tell no one." She tried to keep her chin from quivering. "Velma—she says we ain't beggin'. She says Gust will be back, right soon, bein' it's nigh unto Christmas."

"Listen to me." Inez bent close, her lips almost touching Ella's ear. "It'll be our secret. I'll get Jim to bring our farm wagon to the door and take you home. Get everyone together."

"But he's talking to someone." She pointed at the engrossed couple.

"He won't mind."

Ella found Scott dragging Carrie away from a table. He pulled at the sleeve of his sister's faded dress.

"She was stuffin' food in her pocket." He shoved the girl. "She's lucky Pappy ain't here. He'd take her to the barn and whip her for stealin'."

"I ain't got food. I ate it." Stains and crumbs covered Carrie's hands, and she had a blank look of innocence on her face.

"Scott, don't fret. Both of you go to your mama. I got to find Mae."

Ella squeezed past the adults, but felt a touch on her arm.

"Ella Dessa?"

"Oh, Grace! Thanks for lettin' me see you get married. We must go now."

"You're so welcome. It was our pleasure to have you. Konrad's expecting you to start school studies with the rest of the children next month. We also want you to come visit us."

"I will." She turned away. But Konrad laid a hand on her shoulder and detained her.

"I want to introduce you to my family. I don't believe you've met them. This is my uncle, Miles Kilbride, and his wife, Leona." Konrad smiled. "Uncle Miles, this is Ella Dessa Huskey."

Miles Kilbride!

Her breath caught in her throat. She raised her eyes and gazed into the friendly, golden-brown eyes of a man she had seen in the church. "Nice— to meet you," she said and almost choked on the simple words. Her heart hammered against her ribs and pounded in her ears.

She must have misunderstood.

I ain't heard right. He can't be the same man. That'd mean Pa stole this man's gold!

"We are happy to meet you, Ella Dessa." His attentive gaze lingered on her face, even as he touched his wife's arm. "This is my wife, Leona."

Leona's deep, dusky coloring and unfathomable black eyes caused Ella to remember the Cherokee Indians living higher on the mountain, in hidden pockets not known to most white men. They had been friends to her mama and had secretly visited many times.

The woman's smile widened. "Ella Dessa. Such a sweet name. I've never heard it before, but it's perfect for you. My husband remarked earlier how striking your blue eyes were. He spotted you sitting against the wall with Grace's younger brother."

Struck by a foreign accent in her speech and the unexpected compliment, Ella could only stammer, "Thank you. I must go." She whirled to face Grace and Konrad. "I've got to find Mae. Velma's weak. I'm sorry. I hav'ta go." She ducked past them and fought to catch her breath.

Questions, like gold sparks in a fire, exploded in her mind. *Could there be two men with the same name?*

"Mae, come with me." She found the girl on the lap of an old woman, happily munching from an overflowing plate. "Mama's sick. We must leave."

She helped the child slide off the woman's lap.

"Why you breathin' funny?" Mae hung back.

"I'm in a hurry." She clasped the child's hand and dragged her through the room.

Inez met her. "Honey, Jim brought our wagon to the porch. He's walking Velma to it. She'll have to sit on the box seat."

Jim's gray eyes searched her face when she stepped from the house. "It's bitter cold out here. Cover yourself and the children with the horse blankets in the bed of the wagon."

"Thank you."

Carrie struggled to lift Rosemary to the wagon.

"I'll need one of the blankets for Velma." Jim supported the pregnant woman and helped her up on the wagon's box seat.

"Ella Dessa, do you want me to come?" Inez stepped out on the porch and shooed Remy and Scott toward the wagon. "When Jim gets back with the wagon, I can send the others home with their father. They can drop me at Velma's."

"No—no, I'll manage. Go visit with Grace. Carrie, get in the wagon." After lifting Mae over the end of the short-sided open wagon, Ella got in by herself and helped Remy. "Scott, spread two blankets atop us. Give one to Jim. Carrie, get away from the edge and scoot over here."

Inez ran back to pick up a covered basket from the porch. "Jim, take this with you." She handed it to him.

Ella lifted Rosemary to her lap and urged the children to cuddle close. When the team of horses jerked the wagon forward, she grabbed the top edge of the sideboard and hung on. The bitter wind felt like it sliced through her lungs.

"I'm cold—wanna go home." Mae's teeth chattered.

"We are." She tugged the rough blanket over the girl, covering her head and Rosemary's. "Snuggle tight. Keep each other warm."

She scrunched her eyes shut and tried to clear her mind. She felt as if a stupor had settled over her. Dazed, she kept hearing the tall stranger's name—*Miles Kilbride, Miles Kilbride.*

Chapter 19

With her right hand braced against the mantel, Ella Dessa stood by the fireplace. Under her icy fingertips, she felt the splinters and cracks of the dry hand-hewn wood. She fought a sense of panic, because Velma had discovered splotches of blood on her undergarments.

The pitchy scent of the lighter knot she had tucked under the logs filled her senses. The pine pitch snapped and popped. Her skirt moved at her ankles, waving with the pulse of the fire's flames, and the cold draft blowing under the door.

The door opened. Jim stepped in with a pile of split wood balanced on one arm and his mother's basket hanging from his left hand.

"Here." He extended the covered basket by its high arched handle. "Mother insisted it come with us. Just keep the basket until we see each other again."

She accepted the basket and held it close, wishing she had the courage to talk to him about Miles. Perhaps, he knew something about the stranger.

"I need to leave. The family's waiting for me." He stacked the wood and straightened to catch her watching him. His gray eyes matched the wool scarf he had around his neck. Their stirring depths held sympathy and kindness.

"Thank you, for what you've done." A stab of yearning for his undivided attention filled her heart. She wished he'd stay a bit longer.

"I didn't mind."

She wondered if he was anxious to get back to the pretty girl at Leigh's house.

"This wood should hold you through the night." He tapped the pile with the toe of his boot.

"Yes, it should." She stared at the floor.

"You feeling sickly?" He removed his hat and ran a hand through his dark hair.

"No, worried." Ella blinked away the silly desire to touch the loose waves his fingers created as they combed through his hair. "Velma's settled in bed, but she thinks—" She bit her lip and let her words trail off without finishing the sentence.

I can't talk to him about her losin' a baby.

"Thinks what?" he impatiently asked. "You stopped mid-sentence."

"Nothin'."

She switched her jumbled thoughts to the four older children sitting at the table. She hefted the basket and set it in front of them. Their attention had been on wooden blocks scattered along the rough knotty-pine tabletop, but their inquisitive eyes fed on the basket—as if speculating what it held for them.

Jim leaned in close to her ear. "Scared she'll lose the baby?"

His direct question shocked her. It wasn't commonplace for a man to speak about a woman's private situation.

"Yes."

She saw Carrie's head turn toward them, an uneasy frown forming on the girl's heart-shaped face, but Scott and Mae's eager fingers had unlatched the lid to the basket. Their noses sniffed the contents.

"Ella Dessa, no one expects you to handle this by yourself."

"I don't know what else to do."

She lifted her chin. Tiny prickles of fear ran up her spine. The memory of her mama's labor and delivery threatened to overwhelm her.

"Well, I do. I'm going back to Leigh's for Granny Hanks. She can tell you how bad things are or will be." He laid a comforting hand on her shoulder. "Don't fret."

"You'd fetch her?" She wanted to hide her face against his coat. "Your family's waiting. What if Granny's gone home?"

"We'll work it out. I heard Rebecca offer to take Granny home. I hope they didn't leave. If I have to, I'll ride up the mountain."

"She lives way back in a holler." She twisted her hands together. "Granny could sleep here. Velma's beside herself with fear."

"I know." His eyes were kind. "I'll get the midwife here. Papa traded our extra mules and one cow for that new team of horses. Sada's retired to the barnyard for the cold season and not liking it much." He gave Ella a little grin, as if wishing to lighten her mood. "You ought to hear her bray and protest, especially when we hitch the horses. So, anyways, I can get Granny."

"But your papa might—"

"He'll understand." He tightened the scarf around his neck. "I'll take my family home and go fetch her. Old Abe can't bring her. He wasn't feeling frisky enough to attend the wedding."

Ella nodded and turned away from him. "I'll go tell Velma."

"Wait one moment."

"Yes?" She felt Jim's fingers on her arm and wondered why he detained her. His light touch made her heart change beats. She wished she wasn't so young compared to him.

"I found out you had a birthday last month. Velma told me."

"Yes, I'm thirteen." Ella lifted her chin and stood taller, hoping she appeared more mature. "Velma baked a cake. The little ones drew pictures on smooth boards." She pointed at the mantel. "See?"

A row of odd-shaped pieces of pine board—bark still intact—bedecked the mantel. Simple childish drawings of birds, deer, flowers, and unidentifiable objects—done with chunks of coal—filled every bare spot on the boards.

He chuckled. "Well, they did good. Happy birthday–late."

"Thank you." Her heart felt as if it had wings. No gift could mean as much as his spoken words.

"I'll remember next year." He brushed past her and headed for the door. "I'll be back."

After latching the heavy door, she hurried to check on Velma.

"Any better?" She bent close.

"No."

The woman lay on her left side. She had removed her hairpins. Her dark hair fell about her head and shoulders. Streaks of premature silver strands showed in its rippled length. Her resultant silence revealed her unvoiced dread of losing the infant.

"Jim left." She stroked Velma's hair. "Can I get you some water?"

"No. I'm crampin'. It's too soon," she whispered. "It won't live."

Ella held her breath and felt dizzy. She wanted to hide in the most remote corner of the woods—hide from a repeated nightmare. She fought to conceal her fright.

"Jim's fetchin' Granny. She'll know what to do." Her hands fumbled as she tucked the ragged cover next to the woman's shoulders and neck. "You need to rest."

"I needs you to tear a sheet into rags for me. Even with this slight bleedin', I hate to move. I wants to be still ... in hopes it stops. I'm nigh on six months along."

"Shh. Don't talk of it. I'll make extra rags for you."

Velma's hands inched out of the covers and wiped at her cheeks and nose. "I've known things ain't been right with this one. It's been too hard to keep my strength up. Too difficult. God knows best." Her blue-veined eyelids closed. "I'll keep prayin'."

Ella straightened with unspoken resolve. She had to be brave—she had responsibilities. Rosemary sat on the floor near her feet, quietly playing with a ball of unraveling dark-gray yarn. The other children focused their attention on the rough blocks scattered on the table. The crumbs from bread and cheese showed what they had appropriated from the basket.

Scott and Mae fought over who could build the highest stack. She shushed them as she used her hand to scoop away the crumbs. Scott unexpectedly looked daggers at Carrie and reached for a block in front of her. He shoved it under her nose.

"If you ain't usin' it—I'm takin' it. Mae took mine, and Remy won't share."

Carrie banged her hand flat on the table and shook her head. "I want to build a cave."

"You ain't buildin' a cave with our blocks."

"I can. I'm older than you! I want a dark cave to hide in."

"Scott, let Carrie do as she wants. Don't fight." She leaned over the table and helped Remy balance a block on his stack. "That's good, Remy. Now, the rest of you play nice."

****

Thirty minutes later, a quick knock sounded at the door. Granny and Jim slipped in out of the wintry cold.

"It's just us." Jim snatched his hat off his head and stomped his boots against the floorboards, making the closest bench bounce.

Ella grabbed the old woman's gnarled hands. "Thank you for comin'. That wind is filled with ice."

"No need to waste time yakkin' to me. Let me see to Velma."

"She's in her bed."

The elderly midwife's manner was practical. She pushed the shawl off her gray head and rubbed at her face. Her sunken cheeks and nose had flushed purplish-red from the cold.

Ella sensed Jim stood close behind her and turned. Her eyes scanned his calm face for reassurance.

"You can relax, now." He smiled. "Granny knows what to do in cases like these."

The midwife pointed at the floor where Rosemary still played with the ball of yarn. "What's she doin'?"

"Playing?" Ella said.

213

Rosemary had tangled long strands of yarn into a heap on the floor. Her chattered nonsense accompanied the unrolling of the woolen skein.

"Take her over by the others an' then come back."

Ella removed the loops of yarn from the child's little hands and lifted Rosemary to her hip. She carried her to the table. "Carrie, keep your baby sister busy."

"It's getting colder." Jim unbuttoned his heavy coat. "I think I saw tiny flakes coming down. It'll be dark early."

"I'm sorry you had to come here." She clutched the wad of yarn to her chest and watched his long, cold-reddened fingers work each wooden button.

A wide smile appeared on his face. "Don't look so serious." He winked at her as he shrugged off his coat and hung it on a peg near the door. "I got back in time to see Grace and Konrad leave for their new house. My big sister seems very happy."

"She is."

Granny stuck her head around the curtain. "Come here."

"Yes'um." She tossed the yarn to the rocker.

Jim pointed at the door. "I'll be outside."

Out of the corner of her eye, Ella caught a movement.

Carrie headed for a secluded and gloomy corner of the room. Placing her back to the log wall, she slid downward, until she was in a tight balled-up position—her shift covering her knees. She tucked her arms about her bent legs and silently rocked back and forth.

Granny had pulled away the bedcovers. "Velma, I need ya on yer back an' lift yer gown." She caught Ella's eye and muttered, "Just wait nearby."

With a groan, Velma rolled over. Granny gently ran her aged hands over the distressed woman's rounded belly.

Ella stood at the head of the bed, her face averted. Her heart pounded a wild rhythm, and she felt breathless. She tried to ignore her knowledge of what could happen.

"Bring a basin of water." Granny rested a hand on one of Velma's bent knees and bluntly said, "I got to feel inside. It's tetchy to do so, but it'll tell us the worst."

"Yes'm." She scurried to obey, relieved to be doing something physical. There was a pot of water suspended over the fire. In no time at all, she took a bucket of lukewarm water to Granny.

The midwife grunted and motioned her to step to the other side of the curtain. It seemed like an eternity before Granny indicated she had finished the exam.

"Ella Dessa, come here." The elderly woman thoughtfully worked her thin lips back and forth over her almost toothless gums. She washed her blood-tinged hands in the water.

Ella's eyes welled with tears. She took Velma's hands in hers and waited for Granny's diagnosis.

"Well, ye ain't losing it—yet. With bed rest, ye jest might carry it. Bleedin' is slight, not gushin'."

"Oh, praise the Lord." Velma laid a shaking hand over her eyes.

"You must've overworked. A sixth child is a perilous one to carry." Granny shook water droplets off her age-spotted hands and turned her brown eyes to Ella's face. "Can ye handle the lot?" Her bushy eyebrows drew together, and her wide mouth pressed into a severe straight line.

"Yes. I can do it."

"Won't be easy. She's got to stay in bed." She poked a wet finger at Velma. "Flat down or feet raised, 'til I say there's no danger. No liftin'."

"She's reliable." Velma gazed sideways at Ella.

Nodding, Ella assured the midwife she understood. "I'll make Scott and Carrie help with chores."

The old woman used the privacy curtain to dry her hands and pulled the fabric sideways so Velma could view the whole room. "I need ta git home. My old man needs me. Abe ain't so good."

Velma's not losing the baby. Ella bounced on her toes. She wanted to rejoice by jumping up and down. Instead, she gave the frail midwife a grateful smile.

"Watch her," Granny said. "Get Jim."

Ella ran to the cabin door and hollered for him, without realizing he leaned against the cabin's chimney just to the right. "Oh, I didn't mean to yell in your ear. Come in. Granny's ready to leave."

He shivered. "That's good. Daylight's fading. It's cold, and I left my coat in here." He lifted it from the peg and tugged it on.

The midwife surveyed the crowded cabin and adjusted the shawl about her head and shoulders. Ella saw the woman squint at Carrie crouched in the corner.

"I think ye can do it, Ella Dessa. You've got backbone."

She felt thrilled with Granny's unusual praise, especially with Jim hearing it.

He chuckled. "She's strong-hearted. Ella Dessa's been known to spend the night in a coop, just to protect her chickens."

"It had to be done." Ella kicked the toe of her boot against the floor and avoided Jim's teasing grin.

"We still have her chickens mingled with ours."

"Chickens ain't younguns." Granny signaled to Scott and the others. "Leave yer ma alone. Hear me?" With questioning eyes, Mae and Remy edged near the old woman and nodded.

Scott was brave enough to speak up. "I won't bother her."

Carrie continued to rock, not acknowledging the old woman's presence. Once again, the girl seemed wrapped in her own little world—not seeing what went on.

Ella saw Granny's eyes go back to the girl and hastened to say, "She gets like that. It's nothing. It's her way of worryin'."

Granny grunted and tapped one finger to her head.

The movement was so brief Ella wasn't sure she actually saw it, but it made her feel a touch of irritation—like she must defend Carrie's peculiar actions.

"She ain't fey," she whispered. "She has fears about things."

"Hmmph." Granny then pointed directly at Rosemary. "Keep that one from botherin' her ma. She shouldn't be underfoot. It's time she grow up."

"Rosemary? She's no problem. Honest, she plays good."

The little girl apparently understood Granny was displeased with her. She ran across the floor to Ella and raised her arms. Lifting the two-year-old to her hip, she brushed the toddler's downy hair out of her eyes. "Granny, we're glad you come to reassure us."

She fought the temptation to argue with the old woman about the children.

The midwife shook an arthritic finger at Velma's bed. "I ain't foolin' one mite. No gettin' up, 'cept for the necessary. Avoid straining. Ye need to eat in bed, stay in bed. Eat light this night an' then take food regular like. If that no good husband of yers slinks home—he sleeps on the floor. Tell him I said so."

Jim put a hand over his mouth to hide a bemused grin.

Velma waved. "Yes'um."

"I ain't stayin' the night 'cause I think you'll do just as well with me gone. Ole Abe needs me, an' I've been his wife far too long to forsake 'im now—ornery as he appears to others." She turned toward Jim. "Young man, could ye check on this household tomorrow? Or ask another to do it? Git word to me if needed?"

"Yes'um."

"Good." The midwife hobbled to the door, favoring her right hip. "Now take me home before the snow flies. I'm too old to be out in it." Without looking back, she spoke to Ella. "Young lady, prayer is the most help right now—so pray." She tightened her dove-gray shawl under her chin.

"I will." She nodded at Granny's bent back.

Jim winked at her over his shoulder and opened the door. "See you in the morning. Or Mother will. I'm sure she'll insist on coming and leave the little ones with Sam." He waved one hand and disappeared, taking Granny by the elbow.

Ella tried to shake off her immediate feeling of apprehension and bounced Rosemary on her hip for good measure. She gave her a drink of water and a cold biscuit to chew on. With a sigh of relief, she removed her boots and walked across the room in her stocking feet.

"Carrie, it's just us, now." She knelt in front of the girl. "You can come out of the corner." She touched the girl's clenched hand and saw her flinch. "I'm startin' supper. I could use your help. You're hungry, right?"

Carrie lifted her pointed chin and seemed to consider the question. She nodded, and her sad eyes flitted over the room. "I ate bread an' cheese out of the basket. How's—how's Mama?" She acted afraid to look toward the shadowed bed.

"Your mama'll be fine, you wait and see."

"He's not comin' home. Is he?"

"Who? Oh, you heard Granny. No one knows when your pappy will come home. I'm sorry, it might not be for a long time."

After inching forward out of the corner, Carrie stood. "Can I ... can I help you?" she stammered.

"Yes, let's go see what we've got."

She opened the basket and removed bountiful leftovers from the wedding, which now seemed hours in the past. She boiled down a piece of roasted turkey to make a thin broth for Velma while the rest ate at the table. The bed-bound woman thanked her.

"No thanks needed. It's what I'm here for."

"But you've been a blessin' to me, even though you're a child."

"I'm growin' up." She didn't feel young and couldn't remember if she ever did.

The basket held more than they could eat. Rosemary fell asleep, and the other children were soon content, full-tummied, and sleepy-eyed. It had been an exhausting day for all of them. A quick look at the darkened window reminded Ella she still had to feed Velma's old bull and two cows.

She lit a second lantern, bundled the older children into warm clothes, and urged them outside. As soon as the light bounced across the path to the outhouse, Mae squealed in delight.

"Snow!" She tried to capture the white flakes. Her smile flashed in the old lantern's light. "Ella Dessa, it's snow."

"Yes, it is, but we ain't playin' tonight."

She led the children to the nearby outhouse. The light rebounded off the dark tree trunks and showed the delicate flakes drifting past them.

Mae giggled, did a tiny dance, and clapped her bare hands at the moist flakes. Scott and Remy tipped their heads back and stuck out their tongues. Carrie burrowed her chin further into the collar of her ragged cloak, and her hands disappeared deep within it.

Ella swung open the narrow door to the outhouse. Its leather hinges were stiff with the cold. "Scott, you and Remy go first, then run back with your mama. I'll help the girls."

Scott took very little time to do his business. His running feet, clad in broken-down boots, carried him out of sight toward the cabin's lit window. Remy also wasted no time. Then Carrie started to refuse to go in the cramped outbuilding, even with the lantern's light, but Ella insisted.

"I don't want to empty that pot no more than I have to. I'll be havin' to help your mama tonight. Go now. Hurry. It's cold, and the snow's wet. I'll hold the door open so the light will shine in. Then you girls go back in while I go to the barn."

"I like snow." Mae stuck out her tongue, happy with her immediate spot in the world. In spite of the circumstances, Ella couldn't help but giggle at the delight shining from the girl's oval face.

****

Later, with nighttime prayers said, the older children scrambled to the loft. Ella checked on Rosemary in her low bed near Velma's larger one. She smoothed the toddler's messy hair and stood watching her sleep. She couldn't help but think of the baby buried in her mama's arms.

What fun it would've been to have a little brother to love and cuddle.

Quietly, she collected her thin pallet and covers from the loft. She made a bed on the floor, where she'd be close if Velma needed her. She lit a candle and extinguished the lantern before checking on her.

She found her awake.

"Flakes of snow comin' down," she whispered. "The lantern reflected on 'em."

"I'd love to see it." The woman's face grimaced in the flicker of the single candle.

"Are you better?"

"I guess. Pains seem less. No pressure likes before. Not like when standin' at Naomi's house."

"Maybe it were the long walk."

"Could be. Stayin' in this bed will be hard." She squirmed and sighed. "My hip bones hurt, already. But I feel tired. I thinks I can sleep."

"Good."

"You need to go to bed."

"I'm sleepin' down here."

"Bless you." Velma reached for her hand. "I heard Granny tell you to pray."

"Yes."

"I know you will. I'll say a prayer for you." She kissed the back of Ella's hand.

"Thanks." She touched her lips to the woman's cool brow. "You're the one who must rest."

Ella changed to her nightgown and said prayers for the family and the unborn baby. She added extra pieces of wood to keep away the persistent cold. Sparks floated sideways, drawn by the excellent draft in the rock-encased chimney. Unable to sleep, even though bundled in her quilt, her thoughts drifted over the day. It had passed by so swiftly.

Grace had gotten married. She was now Mrs. Konrad Strom. She lived in her own house with a husband.

"Someday, I want to marry." She whispered the words. In her mind's eye, she saw Jim waiting for her at the front of the little church. But the face of another dark-haired man blotted out the pleasant image and flooded her thoughts with turmoil.

She crawled out of her temporary bed, got Mama's Bible, and the carved box. Then she slipped back under the covers and flipped onto her stomach. She braced on her elbows and placed the Bible in front of her. Quickly, she thumbed through the first pages until she came to the list of Mama's babies.

Ella Dessa ... Kilbride. Was it possible? *No, it ain't likely.*

Even as Velma had explained to her, as a slim chance, with what sometimes happens between an unmarried man and woman, it didn't seem likely the man would show up in the cove.

"People sometimes have the exact name," she muttered, trying to convince herself there wasn't a connection to her strangely written name in the Bible, the love letter to her mama, and a stranger in the cove.

She lifted the wooden box, opened the beautiful carved lid, and removed the folded sheet of yellowed paper. She hadn't dared mention it to Velma. It seemed too personal to share—with it being her mama's treasured love letter. It rustled and crackled as she unfolded it. With unease, she reread the neat handwriting and stared at the looping signature.

Miles Kilbride. Can it be the same man? *Is he my real pa?*

With firm resolve, she shook her head. She could never approach the man about the questions in her head and heart. To do so would place a question mark on her mama's character. The secret had to be kept within the Bible and the rose-carved box. She didn't want anything to mar the memory of the woman, whose grave was placed under the swaying pines above Beckler's Cove.

$\mathcal{C}hapter\ 20$

$\mathcal{B}$efore daylight crept through cracks in the haphazard chinking, Ella Dessa forced herself to crawl from the warm cocoon of blankets. She shivered while arranging split logs and kindling over the dimly glowing coals. It would take a hot fire to warm the entire cabin. The night had seemed interminable, but one good thing had occurred. Velma's pains had lessened and faded away.

Ella lingered in front of the fireplace and permitted the generated heat to envelope her body. Her head ached, and she struggled to remember whether she had slept at all. Rosemary had awakened off and on all night, whimpering and demanding attention. At one point, she discovered the child's bedding and nightgown completely soaked. By the time she put a dry quilt over the wet ticking and got Rosemary back to sleep, she felt dizzy.

A quick look in the loft told her everyone still slept. The flames in the fireplace had calmed to a steady crackling burn. She lifted a full kettle of water, hung it on the iron hook, and swung it over the fire. She knew she'd better take advantage of the temporary span of silence to go outside. She pulled on her boots, grabbed her pa's old coat, slipped her arms into the frayed sleeves, and pushed open the cabin door.

She caught her breath in a gasp of pleasure. Accompanying the breaking light of the Sabbath was a pure white layer of new snow. It blanketed the ground and tree branches. The silent world varied in shades ranging from black and gray to solid white. Not an abundance of snow had fallen, but enough to transform the narrow, secluded cove.

Ella thought of her mama's tree-sheltered grave. A sprinkling of pure snow would hide it and soften the heaped rocks and dull brown stones. The innate urge to strike out and hike home caused her to contemplate the snow-blanketed craggy ridges and dark pines directly above Velma's log home and Pelter's Creek. Hidden from view, a trail meandered to the only home she had ever known.

The silence of the colorless world wrapped its lonesome cloak around her—without even a bird breaking the stillness. She knew a visit to her mother's grave wasn't possible. She couldn't walk home.

She overlapped the front of her coat, but didn't button it. It created a protective, double layer across her chest. She battled tears and headed to the rugged outhouse. Her soundless footsteps cut the first yawning tracks in the unmarked snow and left charcoal-colored scars in the white perfection.

She intentionally walked in her own tracks on her return trip from the outhouse, to keep from marring more of the soft blanket of snow. The beauty of the morning caused her to pause once more. The temperature crackled with crispness. Her throat and lungs burned. She pulled the wide collar higher on her neck and face, watched, and waited for an indication life continued beyond the cabin walls.

How could the world appear so untainted and cleansed when life was so tough?

Light eased over the mountaintops, and the new day's illumination fought its way into the deep-hewn crevices and hollows of the cove—like a slow snake numbed by the cold. The growing daylight managed to bring fresh color and chase away the shades of gray, but it lacked the proper intensity. Tentative fingers of the sun struggled to reach across the white expanse. It was as if a cloaked battle had commenced between the sun and the new season—and winter declared an insignificant victory.

Ella sighed, for she knew the day's pitiful sunshine wouldn't be able to heat the coming hours.

She breathed into the folds of the stiff collar and followed her escaping breath with her eyes. It curled in hazy plumes above her head. With another loud sigh, she gave up her tranquil minute of unusual peace and trudged to the barnyard. She had to pour grain into a wooden tray for the skinny bull and cows.

Later, she'd fork fodder from the dissipating pile in the barn to the animals. There were no chickens to feed, and Velma planned to sell the bull or trade him for flour and staples.

Back at the cabin, Ella opened the door to the sound of Mae giggling and pestering Scott.

"You snored last night."

"Can't help it."

"It sounded like this. Snuff, snuff, snuff!"

"Shh, Mae, quiet. Scott, come on down." Ella shrugged off her coat and lit a lantern for the table.

Scott's uncombed head of brown hair appeared at the top of the ladder. Chicory-brown eyes met hers. "Remy an' Mae, too?"

"Yes, all of ya."

Scott turned and descended the shaky ladder. "I'm tired of yellin' at Mae to shut up 'cause she might wake Mama."

Velma rolled over. "Scottie, she didn't wake me."

"Scott, go stay near the fire 'til I fix breakfast." Ella smiled and knew what the woman left unsaid. Scott's own hollering had awakened her. "Mae, come on down. Is Carrie awake?"

"She's sleepin'. Remy's comin'." Mae, with the energy of a summer chipmunk, scurried down the ladder in her nightshift. Her bare feet carried her to the hearth, where she plopped on her bottom, and stuck her feet out to the radiating heat. "My toes hurt."

"They're cold. Mae, you need your knitted socks and a shawl." Ella waited for Remy to join the others before she climbed the ladder to the loft.

Carrie wasn't asleep. She lay in the semi-darkness, staring at the roof just two feet above Ella's head.

"What's wrong?" She knelt and touched the girl's cool cheek. "You sick?"

"No." Her eyes blinked. "Did Pappy come home? Did I hear him or were it a dream?" Her voice sounded dull and hushed.

"No, he didn't come home. Why?"

"I heard noises durin' the night." The girl's hands appeared from under the frayed quilt. One finger twisted and twirled a tress of her long honey-brown hair. "I heard things."

"Carrie, I had to tend to Rose and your mama." She stopped Carrie's finger by wrapping her own around it. "He ain't here."

The girl rolled sideways and gripped Ella's hands with cold fingers. Her troubled gaze narrowed. "Is he comin' back?"

"Some think he won't. Is it what you want to hear—that he *might* not?"

The answer showed in the girl's expression. Fear shadowed her eyes.

"You don't want anyone to know you're skeered of him?"

She nodded, as if frightened to admit her true feelings.

"Then it's our secret."

An insignificant smile quivered on Carrie's pale lips, and her eyes swam with shiny tears of relief. "That's good," she whispered.

Impulsively, Ella bent and enveloped the trembling girl in a tight hug. "Don't you worry. I do understand." She ran her fingers through Carrie's tangled hair. "Are you hungry?"

"Yes."

"Let's go below. You can help me fix potato cakes. I hear Rosemary fussin' and your mama can't tend to her."

Carrie followed her down the ladder. Ella lifted Rosemary from the bed and realized the little girl's skin felt hot to the touch. She chewed at her bottom lip and felt the other's foreheads. They were all cool.

The two-year-old had a fever.

"Oh, dear," she muttered, as the lethargic child lay against her shoulder.

"What is it?" Velma moved in the saggy bed.

"Rosemary's sick."

"Bring her to me." She laid her fingers against her daughter's forehead. Rosemary shook her head no and clung to Ella. "It feels like it," she agreed. "That's why she fussed all night. Do you think it was the cold walk?"

"I don't know. What do we do?"

"There's nothin' to do but wait. Bundle her against chills?"

"I need to fix breakfast."

"You're a sweet girl." The woman's dark hazel eyes mirrored her compassion. "You're just so young—to have to manage this. Now, Rosemary's sick."

"Remember, I'm thirteen."

"Still a child." She said it with motherly tone. "I know you're strong. It's just you can't keep goin' day and night."

"I'm fine." She kissed Rosemary's pink cheek and tried to smile. "I'll fix potato cakes and the little bit of bacon hanging from the loft. I'll bring you a plate."

Someone knocked at the door and Velma jumped. "Oh, who can it be this early?"

Ella pushed the door open. Jim stood there, bundled in an over-sized coat. He held another woven basket in his right hand.

"Jim—come in. I didn't expect you." Pleasure at seeing him caused her to stumble over her words. "Oh, but I guess Granny did ask you to come check on us."

"I will *always* obey Granny Hanks." He gave her a lopsided smile and removed his hat. "It was a pleasant ride down. The mountain is beautiful covered with the light snow." He looked at her face. "You look tired. How's Velma?"

"She's much better, but stayin' in bed like Granny said. Rosemary took sick this morning."

"I'm sorry to hear that." His eyes traveled over the child clinging to Ella's neck. "She looks heavy."

Mae ran across the room to face Jim. Her shift billowed about her skinny form. "Ella ain't lettin' us play in the snow." She did a tiny hop and

227

skip, trying to see what Jim held. "Whatcha got?" A piece of unbleached muslin covered the rectangular basket.

"I can guess what's in there." Ella smiled at him. The faint scent of pumpkin bread surrounded them.

"You think so?" Jim winked and then waved at all the children. "Good morning."

Remy and Scott waved back. Carrie dropped her head and stared at her folded hands.

"I want to see what's in it," Mae said. She lifted the cloth with two fingers, peeked inside, and made a sniffing noise.

"I think Ella Dessa guessed right. It's pumpkin bread." Jim chuckled at Mae's actions. "You sound like a bear dog with all your sniffing."

"Mae quit that." Ella took the basket from him with her right hand, her left arm supporting Rosemary. "Let me put this on the table."

He patted Mae's head but spoke to Ella. "I remember the first pumpkin bread I brought to you. You devoured it."

"I was starved." She grinned and motioned Mae away from the basket. "Wait 'til later."

Disappointed, the girl slipped away from the table and the tantalizing basket.

Jim cleared his throat. "I can't stay. Mother wanted me to see if Velma needed Granny, because I'm headed up to her place when I leave here. We need her—if she can come. Papa's knee is swelling."

"Is it bad?" She could see the worry in his expression.

"Yeah, pain's awful. He can't come down for church today. Doing all that walking at the wedding, without his cane, wasn't good. So, I got to hurry."

She hid her disappointment and patted Rosemary's back as the girl whimpered. "I hope you don't catch her fever."

"I won't. How are the other children?"

Ella pointed. "As you see, Mae's still hopping. Everyone's fine. It's just Rosemary who's sick."

Velma called from the bed, "Hi, Jim. I'm still in bed."

"Lazy?" Jim called out, teasing her. "You're going to get fat."

"Why, so I just might! I heard pumpkin bread mentioned. Your mother's recipe is wonderful."

"I know. I eat too much of it. But it's the last of our stored pumpkins. They didn't do good this year—not enough rain."

"How's your mother since her oldest daughter is gone?" She raised herself to a sitting position on the bed and held a blanket to her chest.

"She's feeling a trifle sad."

"She'll see Grace all the time."

"I know, but I even missed Grace at breakfast. I kept expecting her to walk in and start teasing me about something. Samuel forgot and yelled for her to come to eat." Jim's face held a sad smile. "You should've seen his face when he realized what he did."

Ella giggled.

"Inez has plenty to keep her busy," Velma said, "even though her oldest has gained a life of her own."

"True. It's just that Mother always figured Duncan would leave first. He's so headstrong."

"Tell her I say hello."

"I will." He turned to Ella and lowered his voice. "I can tell by your face and purple circles under your eyes—you didn't get much sleep last night."

She shrugged, laid her cheek against Rosemary's head, and avoided Jim's scrutiny.

"We won't forget that you might need help."

"I know that. Thank you. Take care in the snow."

Rosemary whined and wiggled to get down.

Jim stepped to the door. "I might ride by here to check with you when I take Granny back home."

"Yes, do that." She closed the door behind him and smiled with anticipation at the thought of him returning. "Mae, do you want bread, now? We'll have it for breakfast."

"Uh huh." While bouncing on her toes, Mae grinned and sang, "I like bread. I like bread. I like sweet pumpkin bread." She did a cute twirl. "I like it so much!"

"You better hope you don't get sick. It'll take the bounce and song out of you. Everyone, come have a piece."

While she pushed a knife through the moist loaf, Ella smiled. Her thoughts dwelt on the fact she'd see Jim in a few hours. *I must remember to change my skirt and freshen up.*

Mae pursed her lips, and leaned her elbows on the table. "Why you sighin' and smilin' at the bread?"

"She ain't smilin' at the bread." Carrie slid onto the bench. "You're silly."

Scott walked over, picked up his piece of bread, and went back to the fire.

Ella laid a slice in Mae's extended hand. "I'm thinking 'bout love," she dared to admit. Realizing she blushed, she placed a hand against her cheek and measured the impact of her own words. Was it love she felt for Jim? Was she too young for love? How she wished she could confide in her mama. Her mama would know.

"Love?" Mae wrinkled her turned up nose. "You love bread?"

With a low laugh, she replied, "Of course, among other things."

"Things like me?" Mae mumbled the question around a mouthful of bread.

"No, me," Remy said and took a slice of bread. He wiggled onto the bench beside Mae. "Ella Dessa loves *me*."

Carrie rolled her eyes. "Your other thing ... is it that boy, Samuel?"

Almost choking on a bite of bread, Ella coughed and shook her head. "No, no. I don't love him."

Carrie shrugged her narrow shoulders. "His eyes watch you. I saw them followin' you at the weddin'."

"That doesn't mean love." She laid bread on the table in front of Carrie.

"Oh. Then he just wants to—to tell you to wait—and be in the barn when he says?"

"What? Be in the barn?" Ella was confused. Then the impact of the words hit her.

The girl instantly dropped her eyes. Her expression said she felt ashamed and wished she hadn't spoken. "Nothin'." Her face went chalky. Her pretty eyes widened with raw panic.

Remy forgot to chew and gazed at his big sister with wise round eyes.

Mae twisted sideways and tapped Carrie's shoulder. "Like you had to with Pappy?"

"No, I didn't!" Carrie slapped the side of Mae's face, and the smaller girl burst into tears.

"Shame on you!" Ella glared at Carrie from across the table. "Why'd you hurt your sister? How horrible."

Big tears dripped down Carrie's pale cheeks. She lifted the offending hand and timidly patted Mae's arm. "I'm sorry." She bent closer, pushing her face into the curve of Mae's neck. "Don't cry."

"What's goin' on?" Velma said. "Do I need to get up?"

"No. I'll tend to things." Ella felt horrified by Carrie's reactions and the implications.

Mae continued to whimper, but she clasped Carrie's hand. The two girls clung to each other with their faces touching and tears mingling. The show of tenderness tore at Ella's heart, as she watched the emotional scene. She didn't understand the bond between the two. Forgiveness between siblings wasn't a subject she had ever seen acted out.

Remy dropped his head until his chin rested on the table. He stared at the forgotten crumbled bread in his hands. He swallowed, and his big eyes looked up at her. "What's your other thing?"

Forcing a light laugh, she patted his head and said, "My other thing is—I love *all* of you."

"Scottie, too?" Remy pointed toward his brother. "Even when he's mean?"

"Yes."

Mae raised tear-reddened eyes and replied, "I love you, too." Carrie kept her head bowed, and her left arm encircling Mae's tiny waist.

Ella smoothed the wispy ends of Mae's hair. "Thank you." It felt good to be loved by the little girl, but the emergent yearning in her heart made her wish to hear the words from another's lips.

Chapter 21

Ella recognized the sound of a horse's whinny very late in the afternoon. *Jim!* She lifted Rosemary off her lap, ran to the door, and pushed it open. It was Samuel tying a dark brown horse to the hitching post.

"It's you." Frustration washed over her.

"Yep, it's me. You sound disappointed." He sauntered toward the cabin, tipped his hat at her, and bowed. His actions seemed silly and boyish compared to his older brother's mature ways. "Me and my trusty steed came through the snow to check on you." He pointed at the horse. "Big difference that one—from riding Sada."

"Hurry, I need to shut the door. It's cold."

Rosemary let out a cry of abandonment, and her face crumbled. She latched onto Ella's skirt. With surprising determination, the toddler pulled and jerked at the material. She sobbed and lifted her bare arms.

"Hush, Rose, I'm not goin' anywheres." She picked her up and sighed.

Samuel tracked in snow and pulled the door closed.

"She's sick." Ella patted the toddler's naked back.

"Jim warned me." He smiled, but winced at the level of Rosemary's cries. "She's a loud one, and she looks cold dressed ... *humm, undressed* that way. She needs more than a towel, don't you think?" He pointed to the only bit of clothing Rosemary wore—a droopy diaper.

"She's feverish. I undressed her to cool the fever. Naomi came and said it's best to undress her."

"Don't make sense to me." Samuel frowned.

Ella set Rosemary on her hip and wiped the shivering child's nose with her skirt hem. "Hush, Rose."

"How's everyone else? Jim sent me 'cause it got late. Papa's knee gave out, again. Granny's trying to ease his pain." He suddenly noticed the mess his boots caused. "Sorry."

"I thought Jim would be comin' back." She knew her remark sounded sharp. She felt mean because of disappointment and fatigue.

"Jim stayed home to help Duncan round up our sheep. The dumb animals found two felled railings and scattered over the slope. Their tracks are in the snow. They must be found. We've had trouble with that lone wolf. He's gotten brave about sneaking in close. It's not the harshest winter months, yet. He hasn't bothered the pigs. But, again that's a—yet."

She stared at him. She didn't care about sheep or pigs. With a sigh, she held her hand to Rosemary's forehead, mentally wondering if the child's fever was worse.

Samuel took a quick look at the messy room.

Carrie slid sideways down the bench and edged away from him. Her puckered brow told Ella she didn't want Samuel to speak to her or go near her, and he seemed to get the message.

"How's Velma?"

"*Better.*" She saw him visibly wince at her sharp tone. Rosemary had wrapped her arms about her neck and proceeded to kick. "Stop, Rose!"

Rosemary's bare feet pummeled her belly.

"Ohh. That must hurt." Samuel made a funny face at Rosemary.

The child only cried louder. Tears streamed down her flushed cheeks. Ella shushed her again, turned away from Samuel, and tried to stop the child's persistent sobs. "Shh, Rose, it's only Samuel."

"Yeah, it's *only* me. Why do you keep saying it that way?"

"I don't." She patted Rosemary's back. "Shh, baby."

"Mother was worried about Velma."

"She's better."

"Don't you just love the snow? Did you notice that the layer of snow hasn't melted?

"I ain't had time to think 'bout it."

"Oh, guess you haven't." A glimpse of contrition crossed his face.

With her hot face pressed against Ella's neck, Rosemary continued to whimper.

"Shh, shh, Rose," she murmured. "Samuel, you need to leave before you get ill."

The day had waxed long and tiring, and she longed to crumple to the floor and sob along with Rosemary. She wasn't in any mood to chat with Samuel about the weather or anything else, and she hoped her voice conveyed that fact.

"Do you mind if I stay long enough to get warm—before starting back? It's getting colder." His cheeks were blotched with pink.

"Go stand by the fire." She rubbed her hand up and down Rosemary's back. "Shh, please stop crying."

Samuel tossed his coat over the closest bench and placed his hat on it. Carrie scurried from the table when he got too close. "Hi, Carrie," he said.

She ignored him.

"Carrie's been a big help." Ella tried to nullify the wide-eyed jumpiness in the girl's actions.

The girl gave Samuel another apprehensive look, before hurrying away to sit in the shadows on the floor near her mama's bed.

"I'm not sick." Mae made the announcement of her fitness by coming around the curtain. She stepped over Carrie's legs and waved a hairless doll above her head. "This baby isn't sick."

Velma's voice came from the shadowed bed. "Sam, I hear your voice above the cryin'. Sorry, I can't get out of bed to greet you."

"Hi, Mrs. Clanders. Are you better?"

"I think I am. This isn't a good place to be. You'll get what my little one has."

"That's right. Samuel. You should leave." Ella wiped the child's tears with her free hand and jiggled her up and down.

She felt at her wit's end. The little girl had cried non-stop for an hour. She refused to lie on the little bed near Velma, and her fever seemed worse. She had pushed away any wet cloth placed on her forehead and rebuffed water from a cup. Ella had finally stripped Rosemary to her diaper, in an effort to cool her petite body.

An hour before, Velma had succumbed to her own bout of tears, fretting because she couldn't help with her sick child. And Rosemary's constant crying and refusal to accept her comforting arms upset the pregnant woman.

Samuel stood in front of the fire, hands extended. Ella saw him look over his shoulder at her.

"Want me to hold her?"

"No, that wouldn't help." She stepped closer. "Samuel, please go." Coupled with her disappointment at having him show up, instead of Jim, and the tiredness she felt, she was in no mood to be friendly.

"I don't mind. Phillip likes for me to hold him."

"No. I just want to sit and rock her to sleep."

Before she could react, Samuel deftly plucked Rosemary from her tired arms.

"Hey, what's the problem, baby girl?" He gave her a wide grin, despite her sobs. "You're cold with no clothes on. Look at the gooseflesh on your pitiful arms. Ella Dessa wants to freeze you, much like the pretty snowflakes outside. Does your throat hurt?"

Ella gawked at him, flabbergasted he had actually snatched Rosemary from her arms. She gritted her teeth and hissed, "What *are* you doin'? Give her back." She didn't want Velma to hear them arguing. "Samuel, you ain't helping things."

Rosemary's cries escalated.

"I'm helping. Ain't that right." He bounced the child in his arms and wrinkled his face. "Want to see me make a face like a bear? Grrr!"

Ella clapped her hands over her ears and fought tears. "Samuel, please! Do you think that does any good?"

"I want to see!" Mae ran to him. "Look, Rosemary. A bear."

"What's happenin'? Is Rose worse?" Velma's voice came from behind the curtain. "Ella?"

Scott and Remy got up from where they played.

"Let my sister go." Scott made it a demand and raised a small fist.

Samuel continued to talk twaddle to Rosemary. "Hey, Mae's playing with a doll. See that?" He whirled sideways to let the toddler see Mae standing beside him. "Look, no eyes. That's a pretty doll with no eyes. Yes, it is. Rosemary, where's your eyes? I bet you don't know."

Mae giggled with her hands over her mouth. "She knows."

Ella saw Carrie cower into a ball near the bed and cover her ears.

Still sobbing, Rosemary rubbed her eyes with tiny fists and laid her head against Samuel's shoulder. He tucked the child's face into the curve of his neck, held the back of her head, and jostled her up and down. "Shut your eyes, shut your eyes—little one," he crooned.

Ella pointed at Scott. "Go! Go play—now! Samuel, give her to me."

"Shh, shh."

"Ella, what's goin' on?"

"It's nothin', Velma. Samuel's the problem." She noticed his appraising eyes sweep over her face and rumpled clothes. She glared at him. "He isn't listenin' to me."

"Shut your eyes, lullaby baby. You're my lullaby baby. Shut your eyes ... go to sleep." He moved in a slow circle and swayed Rosemary in his arms.

"You sing funny." Mae tugged on his shirtsleeve. "That's not a song."

"Mae, that's not nice," Velma called out. "Be quiet. It sounds like he's doin' some good."

"Samuel." Ella motioned to him, one more time, with her arms outstretched.

Go sit down, he mouthed, as Rosemary's incessant cries became soft hiccups. "I know what I'm doing, so shut ... your eyes, Ella ... Dessa," he sang. He dipped and circled the room with Rosemary snug against his chest.

"Sure you do. Singing crazy songs." She folded her arms in defeat. She would've willingly punched him—had he not been holding the little girl.

Out of the corner of her eye, she saw Velma shake her head and lie back down. Shame washed over her.

Samuel placed a finger against his lips and pointed at Rosemary's face. He continued his childish song. "Shh, she's shutting her eyes. Go to sleep, go to sleep—" Whirling, he placed his back to the room of staring eyes.

Ella let her shoulders droop.

She gave into the unexpected relief washing over her. It wouldn't do to be angry with Samuel for quieting the girl when she couldn't. She caught his eye, lifted her coat off a straight-backed chair, and pointed at the door. She heard the soft words of another, more familiar, lullaby—as Samuel nodded his blond head in understanding.

He shuffled in a half-circle, but his intense green eyes never left her face.

She recognized true compassion in his gaze.

His heavy boots scraped along the pine board floor, and he held Rosemary's limp, half-nude form in his well-built arms. The tender image softened her heart.

Ella fled to the outhouse and pulled the haphazard door shut on the outside world. She sat and burst into a torrent of tears. She felt like a failure, and the sight of Samuel—a boy—rocking and crooning to Rosemary strengthened her low opinion of herself. He had calmed the sick baby when she failed.

****

Ella slipped into the silent cabin and latched the door. She saw Mae on the floor beside the old rocker, the doll cradled in her skinny arms. The girl placed a finger to her lips and pointed.

Samuel cuddled Rosemary against his neck. His fingertips gently drew circles on her naked back. She slept, limbs relaxed, sweaty hair sticking to her flushed cheeks and neck.

Apparently proud of his accomplishment, he grinned at Ella. "I think the fever's breaking," he whispered.

With a shake of her head, she turned and straightened the disorganized room. She went to Velma's bed. The woman slept with Carrie curled beside her.

"I want to stay here." Carrie's big eyes glistened. "Please?"

She nodded and pulled a blanket up to Carrie's shoulders. With a light touch, she laid her hand against her forehead. "No fever." She experienced a touch of relief. "Take a nap 'til time to eat."

Ella lit a lantern, added wood to the dying fire, and hung a kettle of water over it. Quietly, she prepared their evening meal by peeling potatoes and dropping them into the kettle. She wielded a large knife and cut a skinny slab of salted ham into chunks.

Ignoring the fact Samuel kept watching, she tossed the ham pieces in with the potatoes. *Why can't he look elsewhere? Does he think I can't cook?*

She sighed and admitted to herself that her cooking skills *weren't* good. All she could do was try. She drew comfort from the knowledge there was leftover pumpkin bread to serve with the meal. Soup would do them all some good and stave off Rosemary's illness.

As she shoved another chunk of wood into the flames, she had to admit—Samuel's presence had eased the stress. She couldn't blame him for her selfish irritation Jim hadn't been the one to come back. She knew Jim had responsibilities piled on him.

She pondered the burden of tending to Rosemary during the coming night, especially with lack of sleep. She knew Samuel did the right thing by taking the toddler from her arms. If he hadn't, the girl might still be crying.

God, I'm sorry for my anger at Samuel. Forgive me. No doubt, you sent him at the right moment. I treated him badly.

Ella wiped her eyes and squared her shoulders.

She was her mama's daughter, and her mama had been a strong woman. She wanted to be like her, even though she felt burdened with a lack of confidence in her own abilities and appearance. She ran a hand over her messy hair and cringed at the realization it needed brushing.

Oh my! Now I'm glad Jim didn't come.

The scent of potato soup and ham drifted throughout the room, and her stomach growled. With a touch of shame, she let herself smile at Samuel. She hoped he understood she was no longer upset.

****

239

Samuel kept rocking. He observed Ella Dessa's self-conscious movements about the fire and table. He noted the puffy appearance of her reddened eyelids. She had spent time crying while outside. He could tell she had felt troubled and humiliated. He also recognized her outward show of relief.

He found her attractive. Her waist-length hair loosened itself from the ribbon at the nape of her neck, and blond strands curled about her freckled face. Her lovely hair caught the gold tints in the reddish-orange flames of the fire and shone with what his mother called a strawberry-blond hue. In its depths, he saw the soft color of rich honey.

Once or twice, her weary blue eyes met his, and, finally, a small appreciative smile touched her pink lips.

He relaxed into the curved back of the pine rocker and continued to support the sleeping toddler. Her delicate skin felt hot against his arm. The feverish heat came through the material of his shirt. He started to sweat, but he didn't want to move and disturb her. He felt comfortable with young children. After all, he'd played with Phillip since his brother was a little thing.

Samuel laid his head back, closed his eyes, and breathed in the mixed scent of the cooking food and fire smoke. The gentle, rhythmic squeak of the rocking chair brought a contented smile to his lips. His thoughts mingled the vision of Ella Dessa bent over the fire, with the idea of having his own family. His mind took over and fashioned a life where he was a husband and father, relaxing after a day's work, and cradling his own child.

He and his wife would have a large full-log cabin, built with his own two hands, and tucked under the lip of the mountain. They'd have huge pines to shade it in the summer. There would be a bouncing and trickling creek, running over sun-drenched rocks, for the children to play in. He could see himself coming out of the forest, a deer balanced over his wide, capable shoulders, and his gun slung across his back. His wife would see him. A smile would light her face as she lifted her hand to wave. The sunlight would glint in her blond hair.

Lost in his vivid imagination, Samuel didn't realize Ella Dessa spoke to him until Mae walloped his leg with her doll.

"Don't ya hear her?" She peered through long bangs and swung the soft doll again. "Wake up."

Samuel blinked, rubbed his eyes with his free hand, and noticed Ella Dessa walking toward him. "Ah, did you ... what?"

"I said I'll take her and put her down so we can eat. I gave Velma a bowl of soup. I'm sorry, if you were dozin'."

"I wasn't sleeping. I was just—lost in thought."

Ella Dessa held out her arms. "Please, I'll carry her to bed."

Carefully, Samuel stood and placed the relaxed body of the sick girl in her arms. Soft strands of Ella Dessa's hair caressed his fingers when he drew his hands away. While raising and lowering his stiff shoulders, Samuel examined his palms. He almost fancied his skin tingled where—for just an instant—her hair had rested.

"*Whew.*" He shook his hands at his sides.

"What's wrong? Why you shakin'?" Mae draped the limp faceless doll over one of her shoulders and frowned. "Your face is red. You gettin' sick, too? Is Ella goin' to make you lay down? She peeled Rosemary's clothes off her. Well?" She waited for his reply, and her inquisitive blue eyes never left his face. In their depths, he could see tiny flecks of brown.

"Well?" Samuel copied her. The child resembled a shaggy puppy, and he dropped to her level. "Humph! Nothing wrong, not getting sick, not laying down and no peeling off my clothes. Now, you answer a question. Why do little children stare so much?"

Mae shrugged and pushed her doll into his hands. "Want to rock my baby?"

"Ah, not now."

"She's cryin'."

His fingers wrapped themselves about the floppy doll, and he wiggled it from side to side, making its cloth head bounce. "Oh, look at my head." He used a squeaky voice and Mae giggled. "It's going to fall off!"

Remy ran over to join in the fun. But Scott ignored Samuel and the silly doll.

Ella Dessa returned from shoving the curtain to the side and tucking Rosemary into bed. She smiled at the sight of him playing with a doll. Carrie reluctantly followed behind her. The girl's face revealed the fact she'd rather stay near her mother on the secluded bed. She sat at the table and stared down at it.

He felt embarrassed and stood. "Did she stay asleep?" He dropped the floppy doll into Mae's extended arms.

"Yes. I put a gown on her. She seems cooler." She stood before him and clasped her hands at her waist. "Thank you for what you did."

"I wanted to help you."

Her tired blue eyes searched his face. "I'm sorry for my actions."

"Ahh, I acted like a nut." He smiled at her serious face, hoping to put her at ease. "All is forgiven. We're friends?"

"Yes." A pink flush painted her cheeks. "We are."

"I'm sure glad." He wanted to say more but caught himself in time.

"What will your mother be thinkin'?"

"That I got lost on the mountain?" He grimaced and fixed his eyes on the dark window. "Jim or Duncan will soon appear. They'll figure there's trouble here. I should head out, right now, and meet them along the way." As he said the words, he admitted to himself he didn't want to leave.

"Sit and eat a bite. You can soon be on your way."

The six of them crowded together at the table, spooned the potato soup, and munched on pumpkin bread. He and Ella Dessa talked in muted voices about the snow, Grace's wedding, and the new school—soon to be in session.

Mae seemed more subdued—not her bouncy self—and he noted Carrie ate very little. She fiddled with her spoon, tapped it on the table, and repeatedly refused to look him in the eye. Remy sat beside him, watching, and listening. Scott was glum, eyeing him as if he were an intruder.

Samuel hoped Jim wouldn't show up. He wanted time to talk without his big brother winning Ella Dessa's shy attention.

She handed him another slice of bread. "Eat some more?"

"No, I get plenty at home. Save it for the boys." He left the table and placed three logs on the fire. "I best be leaving."

"We can loan you a lantern."

"That'd help." He didn't relish the idea of riding the trail in the dark—let alone by himself. His coming down to the cove by himself had been a first. It only happened because of the unusual circumstances.

Ella Dessa rose from her seat and went to get the extra lantern. "This one has plenty of oil. It just might be hard to carry on a horse."

"I got to go to the outhouse," Scott muttered to Ella Dessa and pulled on a ragged coat.

Samuel took the offered lantern and set it on the corner of the table. "I'll light it when I leave." He reached for his coat and pushed his arms into the sleeves. "Sure must be pitch-black by now. Scott didn't take a lantern?"

Ella frowned. "Why, no, he didn't."

Suddenly, sobs erupted from outside the cabin door. Samuel saw Ella Dessa's eyes widen in alarm.

"That's Scott." She ran for the door and pushed it open. "Scottie?"

Crumbled within the meager light from the cabin's open door was the boy. He sat in the snow and wept with hands over his face.

"Here, let me." Samuel lifted the lightweight boy in his arms and carried him inside. "Where do I put him?"

"Right here." Ella Dessa pointed at her pile of blankets on the floor.

He lowered the boy. Both he and Ella Dessa knelt beside him.

"Scott? What's wrong? What happened?" She ran her hand over his head and neck. "Did you slip and fall in the dark?"

The youngster buried his face in the blankets. His sobbed words were barely discernible. "Leave me alone."

"Scott, why?" She tried to make him look at her. "Please, we need to know."

"Mama's goin' to die!"

"What?" Ella Dessa gasped. "No! What makes you say that?"

"She ... she's not gettin' up. She don't eat with us." His wails escalated.

"Is that Scottie?" Velma yelled. "What's wrong now?"

Chapter 22

Ella gulped back tears and ran to Velma. "He's upset. He thinks you're dying 'cause you ain't gettin' up. I'll talk to him."

"I need to go to him." Her narrow face appeared as a pallid shadow in the firelight. "Enough of this. I can't takes this bed-layin' no more. I love the child I'm carryin,' but that's my first born son." She swung her scrawny legs and bare feet over the edge of the bed and stood.

"I'll bring him to you."

"No, he has to see me up an' movin'."

Ella felt tears on her own face, as she assisted Velma in donning a heavy shawl to cover most of the gathered nightshift and long woolen socks.

Samuel still crouched on the floor. Scott had wedged himself under the table and shrieked with broken cries. Mae's bare feet dangled near his shoulder, but she pulled them to the bench, out of Scott's reach, and wrapped her arms about her knees.

Carrie covered her ears and scrunched her eyes shut. "Make him stop. He's hurtin' my ears!"

Ella knelt beside Samuel and peered under the table. "Shh, Scott, here's your mama. See? She's out of bed. Please, come out."

His jerky screams hushed. His red-rimmed eyes riveted on Velma's bare feet. "Mama?"

She stepped back so he could see her. She waved to him. "Scottie, what's wrong with you? You've upset us all by screamin' like a banshee."

He crawled out on his hands and knees. "Mama," he moaned. "Don't leave us."

Samuel snatched the wooden rocker and slid it toward Velma. With a look of gratitude, she sank into it. Scott was too large to sit on her lap, her being pregnant and all, but he knelt and clung to her. He broke into a fresh river of tears.

"Shh." She patted his back. "I'm not goin' no place. What makes you think that?"

Scott raised his head and stared at her with red-rimmed eyes. "Sick people—don't get outta bed. They die."

"No, no. I ain't doing nothin' of the sort."

Ella lifted Mae off the bench. With a pale, serious look, the four-year-old hugged her neck. "Scottie scared me," she whispered.

"I'm sorry. He's tired, and I think you're tired. I'm putting you in your mama's bed. Hang on to the doll." She took Mae over to the lumpy cornhusk mattress, gently laid the child on her side, and kissed her forehead. Turning to the low baby bed, she checked on Rosemary. The sick two-year-old slept, despite the noise.

"Velma, Mae's worn out. I put her on your bed." Ella stopped near the rocker and laid her hand on the woman's shoulder. Her fingers could actually trace bones beneath the woman's skin.

"You're a wonderful help." Velma smiled up at her. Bluish-black circles filled the wrinkled space under her sunken eyes.

Remy came over and stood beside the rocker. Carrie slipped off the bench and faded into the darkness along the outside wall. Her distrustful eyes watched Samuel when he squatted before the fire and built it to a cheerful, crackling flame.

"My poor babies." Velma ran her fingers through Scott's messy hair. "Life's hard to understand."

The boy relaxed into almost a stupor, his face against her pregnant belly.

Ella worried about Velma's condition. "Velma, if Scott will lay beside you, shouldn't you go to bed?"

"We can try that."

"Will Mae and Scott bother you if they're both in the bed?"

"No, I'll enjoy them snuggled close." She gently coaxed Scott to stand up. "Go to my bed."

"What about me?" Remy asked.

His mother chuckled. "Come see if you can finds a spot to curl up in."

Ella helped her walk back to the bed. "Don't worry, I'll tend to things. If Samuel's folks come to fetch him, he'll leave. Or he might take the spare lantern and go on his own."

Velma nodded and settled herself between Scott and Mae. Remy crawled up on the other side of Mae. "Ella, try to get some sleep," she whispered. Her fingers caressed Scott's forehead, and her blue-veined eyelids closed.

Carrie appeared at the side of the bed and gripped Ella's hand. "I don't wanna sleep in the loft by myself."

"Try to get in here with us," her mother whispered. "It'll be cozy."

"I don't think the bed is big enough. Carrie, how about sleeping near me? I slept on the floor last night in case your mama needed me. Velma, I'll check on Rosemary during the night." Ella took up the rumpled covers and moved them to a spot along the wall. "Come over here." She covered the girl with a quilt. "I'm goin' to talk with Samuel until he leaves."

Carrie nodded her head and rolled to her side. Her messy hair trailed about her face like brown mosquito net.

"Sleep tight."

Ella sat on the flat stone hearth near Samuel and faced the flames. "Seems like all we do is put more wood on the fire."

Samuel nodded, laid the poker aside, and brushed gray ashes off his hands. "Part of life." He chose a short log and balanced it on top of the burning wood.

Each new piece of wood sent bright sparks drifting and flying up the stone chimney, like spring fireflies caught in a midnight breeze. The hour was late. The room remained quiet, except for the snapping of the fire. For lengthy minutes, neither of them spoke, until she broke the comfortable silence.

"What do you reckon you should do?"

Before answering, he sat back from the fire's warmth and folded his arms on top of raised knees. "I really don't know what to do. I don't know why Jim didn't come hunting me—me being gone so long. I'm a little worried and puzzled." He unexpectedly turned his head and fixed his easy-to-read eyes on her face. "Just the same, I'm glad I came. I think you needed time without a child in your arms."

She considered his honesty. A wash of unexplainable bashfulness struck her. It was as if his words meant more than he actually said. She let a trembling breath slip past her lips before she continued the conversation.

"I'll get the extra oil for the lantern if you wish to go." She watched him out of the corner of her eye, unexpectedly hoping he'd stay. She'd felt melancholy and overwhelmed. His presence now brought comfort.

"I think I'll stay." He grabbed a charred stick and jabbed at the glowing logs, causing a shower of fiery embers to burst from the center of the stack. Logs rolled inward. "I'll tell you something—if you don't laugh at me." His unusual eyes grew darker green in the dim light.

"Won't laugh."

"Well, I'm a mite afraid of going home on my own. There—I've said it."

The powerful set of his jaw indicated he fully expected her to poke fun at him and mock his boyish fears. She nodded. She felt pleased he could trust her to be kind.

"I understand."

"You're not laughing at me? Inside—are you laughing inside?"

She was amused. "No. But you're makin' me feel like it 'cause of the way you're questioning me."

"*Whew.*" With a pleasant grin, he faced her and sat cross-legged. "I was afraid you'd laugh me out of here. I'd have to wander that darkened trail by my lonesome, in the pitch black, worrying about a renegade wolf jumping me and killing my horse—and me."

She giggled behind her hand and tossed her head. "You're so silly."

"I am?" His eyes lit with amusement.

"Well? You could be a storyteller."

"Not storytelling. We've seen that wolf and heard him. He's lame. We had another ewe disappear. Duncan thinks the wolf got it. He saw deep tracks and fresh blood."

She shuddered but kept her eyes on his face. She noticed how his blond hair curled over his ears and down his neck. "Then, I'm glad you're here and safe."

"Me, too." His intent gaze held hers.

"We can talk." She never realized how his jaw line reminded her of Jim's, but his green eyes, with their light wash of blue, were all his own. His looks stood out from the rest of his family. Duncan's eyes were a sharp green with no softness.

"I like this ... talking to you alone. You know we're both thirteen, now." He pointed at her and then his own chest. "You and me. But I'm older—closer to fourteen."

"Yes, of course." Her eyes didn't waver. Her heart rate quickened. She tried to think of something commonplace to say, to keep him talking.

"Ella Dessa?" He made a slight movement as if to reach toward her hand.

She lifted her hand and smoothed her hair. "Why don't you put your poor horse in the barn?" Her actions and words broke the delicate seconds between them.

"Hmm, I will." His voice took on an adult tone. "You should get some sleep, in case Rosemary wakes up. I'll sit here and feed the fire. We can't have anyone else getting sick."

"I'm not sleepy." She instantly realized all her weariness had fled. Everyone was quiet and bedded down. The world seemed tranquil and near perfect. She wanted to talk to Samuel and watch him smile.

"You're not?"

"No."

Samuel chuckled, but he covered his mouth when Rosemary cried out from her bed. They both raised their eyebrows and stared into each other's eyes—waiting—but the toddler didn't fuss again.

Within the flickering firelight, Ella could see the girl's babyish arms hugging a cloth doll. She placed a finger to her lips. "Shh. We better whisper."

"I think I like that idea."

"Want the last piece of pumpkin bread?" She ignored softness in his words.

Samuel nodded. "I'll share with you."

She got the bread, smeared it with a generous glob of butter, and brought it to the hearth. Facing him, she sat with her legs crossed and tucked under her skirt. The toes of her heavy boots protruded. She broke the thick slice into two pieces and handed him the largest one. "I could eat this all day."

"Yep." He bit into his piece and licked butter off his fingertips, seemingly relishing every bit of the taste.

"I wasn't allowed to do that." She watched him and grinned. "Pa forbid it. Mama didn't."

He shifted his position until their bent knees touched. "You miss your mother." His boyish face showed hints of the handsome, mature image he would someday have.

She bowed her head. "Yes, more all the time." She stared at where the hem of her brown skirt encountered his pants leg—dark brown against washed-out brown. Her skirt material was the dull brown. "My life is ... colorless." In most ways, her whole life seemed tedious. It was without any color.

"Colorless?"

"Hmm, like snow." She knew he waited for her to continue. She could almost feel his inquisitive eyes searching her face and scarred neck. She had no need to cover the nasty scars—she felt safe from embarrassment in his presence.

"Snow can be beautiful. Breathtaking. You're just lonely. You are far from colorless. Can you believe me?"

"Yes." She hated to voice her inner feelings out loud. Samuel's gentle qualities eased her qualms.

"What's one thing you wish for?"

Her fingers plucked at a loose thread on the seam of her skirt—her mama's skirt. Waves of longing washed over her. "I wish I could go visit Mama's grave. I haven't been back, since I were to your house. Seems like forever. I felt close to her when I knelt by her grave." She swallowed the lump in her throat, determined not to cry in front of him.

"I know. I figured that out when Jim and I came to get you. Here's one of my wishes." He paused. "I wish ... I could take you to visit her resting place." He pointed at his chest. "Me. I want to."

"Really?" Her heart tripped in her chest and tears welled in her eyes. No one had even offered to take her back to the cabin for a visit.

"Let's plan a hike one day, when the weather's good."

"Thank you." She dried tears with the back of her hand. "I thought I'd have to wait 'til Gust came home. I don't know how long that'll be."

A guarded expression flitted across his face. His gaze faltered and shifted to the fire.

"What is it?" She bent toward him and tried to decipher what she read on his face. She tapped her finger on his left boot. "Samuel?"

"Ella Dessa, men talk."

"So?"

He fiddled with the piece of bread in his hand. "They say Gust intended to walk away from Velma and the children—right from the start—once he got them settled. He wanted to be close to the gold mines. He never planned to farm or hunt. He ain't that type."

"That's awful. Is it true?"

"Men saw him in Lick Log the first couple of weeks after he left here. They told it around the cove how he bragged about his gold findings. He said he found deposits south of here on an unnamed creek near Auraria."

"Then—that's good." She threw her hands wide and motioned at the drab room. "They need lots of things, even besides food. If he found gold, it'll help."

"They think he's a liar. He didn't show them any gold. They say gold makes men do crazy things. They sneak in on other people's land and mines, get what gold they can, and disappear. Drink it up at a tavern."

She nodded. Her thoughts briefly went to the gold her pa had taken from her mama's trunk—Miles Kilbride's gold. "Velma believes he'll come back," she whispered.

"Well, a couple of men at Grace's wedding got to talking after Velma left. I sat and listened. Last week they made a trip to Lick Log—I mean Dahlonega—for supplies. There's now a lot of stores and buildings. They asked about Gust. He wasn't to be seen. No one thereabouts could remember hearing his name or seeing him for weeks during November. He's disappeared. They aren't telling Velma, yet."

"Gold or no gold, he shouldn't have left his family."

"You're right." Samuel's gentle eyes echoed the resonance of his voice. "I wouldn't ever do that to my wife."

"You don't have a wife." She covered her mouth and giggled at her own silly response.

He rolled his eyes and popped the last bit of bread into his mouth. Swallowing, he nudged her boot with his. "Stop laughing at me."

"You sounded so *serious*." She fought a grin and forced a deep frown instead.

"I was serious." He waved his hand and swept crumbs off his pants leg. "Dead serious."

"That's mighty serious."

She broke her remaining piece of pumpkin bread into two bites and offered him one on the palm of her hand. Her pulse sped up as his fingers touched her hand with a light pressure. She met his fantastic eyes and noticed the solemn way he nodded his thanks.

She knew Samuel meant what he said. He'd never leave his future wife and family—not the way her pa slinked off or how Gust disappeared. Samuel would be a man of his word and honest in all things possible.

She fought the crazy desire to have him touch her hand once more. It didn't make sense. She liked Jim—not Samuel. Suddenly, she unfolded her cramped legs. "I guess I better try to sleep, in case Rosemary gets worse.

Go tend to your horse." She rose and shook fine crumbs from her wrinkled skirt. "I'll place a couple of quilts here on the floor for you."

"Thanks, I won't be long." He stood and stretched, hands reaching high above his head. "I'll stay up for a short time and keep the fire."

"Good night, Samuel." She walked toward the pile of blankets in the colder corner of the dim room.

"Night."

Quietly, she removed her boots and slipped under the covers with Carrie. She tucked her brown skirt tight to her legs for warmth. Unwillingly, she closed her eyes and gave into the fatigue she felt. Shivering, after sitting so close to the hot flames, she forced herself to stay still until the layer of blankets warmed her. She needed sleep and felt it softly washing over her.

"Ella Dessa?"

Startled awake, she rolled over, and stared at Carrie's silhouette. Groggy, she swept her messy hair out of her eyes. "What is it?" she whispered.

Carrie's face shone with streaks of tears. "I awoke an' feared you left us."

"No, I'm here."

"But I saw him."

"Samuel?"

"Yes. He's by the fire."

"He won't hurt you." She encircled the girl's left wrist with her fingers. She felt a companionship with the child—despite their age difference.

"I got skeered."

"Shut your eyes, I'm here."

She saw Samuel peek their way. Ella knew he heard the murmur of their voices but couldn't see her open eyes in the dark. If she didn't move, he'd think she slept, even though sleep had fled.

Samuel became a quiet statue. He sat and stared into the fire. His sandy-colored hair caught the fire's fickle light. The flames danced and created strange shadows that leapt and crept along the walls.

What was Samuel thinking? Why did she care?

Ella pressed her fingertips to her forehead and longed to go back to sleep, but two faces seemed etched on the backside of her eyelids. The faces belonged to brothers, each as different as their physical appearance—one fair with blue-tinted green eyes, the other darker haired with unusual gray eyes. The younger brother was humorous, more childlike, and tenderhearted. The older one was serious, handsome, and a hard worker. Each of them now filled a void in her heart.

Chapter 23

It was three in the morning before Ella slipped from her blankets. Samuel rolled into one of the quilts she provided for him. At seven o'clock, he still slept as she prepared a simple breakfast. Remy awoke first and crawled off his mother's bed. He immediately pestered Ella to eat and hovered over thick bacon frying in the pan.

She ran her fingers through his feathery brown hair. "Need to wait for the others."

"I'm hungry now."

"Go change into clean clothes if'n you have any. Then you can eat."

Velma sat up. The cornhusk mattress rustled with her movements. "I don't thinks I can stand to stay in this bed today. I'll go raving mad like a rabid skunk. It's not in my blood to laze around."

At the sound of her voice, Mae and Scott stirred. Mae yawned and rubbed her nose. Scott groaned and covered his head.

Rosemary woke with a coughing spell, and Ella walked over to pat the little girl's back. "By the sounds of things, it won't be a quiet day."

"Is it ever?" Velma threw back the wrinkled quilt and scooted past Mae. "I'm finished with this bed stuff." Her night shift pulled up along her skinny, blue-veined thighs.

"Let me draw the curtain. Samuel's still here. Sleeping yonder on the floor."

"Oh, did he set up, too?"

"Part of the night." She shook off the instant guilt she felt. "While I got a bit of rest."

"That was sweet of him."

"Are you sure about gettin' up?" She watched Velma stand, bend forward, and remain motionless, with her long-fingered hands cupped protectively under her rounded belly.

"Yes, I'll moves careful." She reached for a gray dress hanging on a peg near the bed and sighed. "I can't abides that bed no more. I'm fine. I'll slip this on and join you for breakfast."

"I'll worry."

"Don't, Ella Dessa. This is my decision. I've no husband here to tend to things. I must help care for my livin' babies and leave the *unborn* in God's capable hands. An' I thinks God approves of such a thing. Don't you?"

"I s'pose," Ella murmured, unnerved by the conversation. "I'll be by the fire." She carried Rosemary with her. Remy sat at the table with a spoon in his hand. Carrie stood bent over the pan at the fireplace, turning the bacon.

"Carrie's helpin'." Remy hit his spoon handle on the table. "Make her hurry."

"Oh, Carrie, I didn't hear you. How you feelin' this morning?"

The girl shrugged her shoulders and kept her head bowed. "I'm fine. Not sickly." Her stringy hair hid her face from view. "I figgerd you needed help cookin' this, and Remy was thinkin' he'd help hisself. How's Mama?"

"She's dressing."

"She is?" Carrie's eyes clouded with worry. "She shouldn't."

"She wants to." She placed Rosemary on the bench beside Remy and took the wooden fork from Carrie. "It's done. Let me lift it. How about you? You ready to eat? I think the porridge is done."

"Yes'um." She slid onto the bench across from Rosemary and Remy.

"Do we have milk?" Remy wiggled expectantly.

"Oh, I didn't even think of that. No." Ella's shoulders drooped. "They've dried up. I need to tend to them. I forgot everythin' last night."

Samuel rolled out of his blanket and staggered to his feet. "I forked fodder to them last night, when I stabled my horse." He rubbed a hand across his face and messy hair. "Ohh, did I sleep at all? What was that banging?"

"Me!" Remy shouted, waving his spoon. "See?"

"You slept near about four hours." Ella laid a hand on Remy's arm. "Stop."

"Don't feel like it." Samuel grabbed his hat and coat. "Is it light outside? I'll go tend the animals."

"It's almost daylight. Need the lantern?"

"No." He pushed the door open. A rush of cold air twirled around him and into the room. "Yikes, bitter out here."

"Close it fast!" Ella shivered and tossed another log on the fire.

Velma made her way to the table. She sat beside Carrie and hugged her. "How's my big girl?" Her left hand smoothed the girl's hair out of her face. "There, now I can see your pretty eyes."

Carrie's lips curved upward, and she snuggled under her mother's arm.

"She's not getting sick." Ella gave Carrie a wink. "She helped with the porridge, without being asked to."

"Mama." Remy ran and scooted in by her. He laid his head against her arm and rubbed his fingers over her cheek. "I missed you."

Laughing, Velma planted a loud kiss on top of his head. "Remy, I was rights in the bed, silly."

"I know." He wrapped both his arms around her right arm and hung on. "Can you be out of bed?"

"I'm gonna try."

Rosemary coughed and waved a spoon at her mother. "See? My spoon." Her eyes appeared red-rimmed and watery, but she was recovering.

"Yes, you've got a spoon. I hopes your fever's gone." She shook her head at Ella. "I never heard such screaming as she did yesterday."

A loud knock at the door startled all of them. Rosemary dropped her spoon to the floor.

"Why would Samuel be silly and knock?" Ella shoved the door open. "Sam—oh!" Jim stood beyond the threshold, another food basket grasped in his hands.

"Me—again." Jim gave her a lopsided grin and a dimple showed in his right cheek. His hat, set low on his forehead, didn't quite cover the strands of dark hair framing his handsome face.

"Come in." She instantly felt flustered. He had caught her in the same wrinkled skirt and blouse she slept in, plus her hair hung tangled about her shoulders. She pulled the door shut, accepted the heavy basket, and set it on the table.

Jim stomped the sticky melting snow off his boots. "Ouch, fingers froze," he muttered and rubbed his hands together.

"Mornin', Jim." Velma gave him a cheerful wave. "We weren't expectin' company so early. How's things up your way?"

"Good as can be expected." He removed his hat and held it in his hands. "Hope you're feeling stronger."

"I am, but disobeyin' Granny's orders. I just had to get out of bed to eat."

He nodded with understanding. "I'm sorry to come at breakfast, but we're a bit worried. Where's Samuel? I didn't see his horse outside." A frown marred his wide brow. "We thought he might be here—"

"He put the horse in a stall." Ella swept her hair out of her eyes. "He's at the barn. He offered to check the cows."

"*Whew.* Had me nervous not seeing the horse. When he didn't come home last night, I had visions of him falling off a cliff. We hoped he had stayed here." He loosened his coat. His long fingers traveled down the front and undid the handmade wooden buttons, but he didn't remove it.

"It got dark, and I needed help. So he stayed." She didn't reveal to Jim that Samuel had been reluctant to go home by himself.

"I'm just relieved to know he's here." His curious gaze swept over her face. "You needed help?"

"Rosemary got sick."

"No one else?"

"Not yet." Feeling herself blush at his scrutiny, she turned away and self-consciously ran a hand through her tangled hair. Her emotions reeled with regret. He had caught her resembling a discarded pigling.

It hadn't mattered so much how Samuel saw her.

"We've decided no more can get sick." Velma playfully tapped Carrie on the top of the head. "I needs healthy younguns."

"Papa's knee got worse—went purple. Puffed way out. Granny gave him a dose of nasty liquid that stunk like dead fish."

"Ugh!" Remy wrinkled his tiny nose and groaned. "I'd hate that."

Jim chuckled at the little boy's horrified expression. "Well, it knocked him out. Then she made Duncan and me straighten out his knee and leg. We braced it with boards. He won't be able to walk for a week or more. She wants it to have time to heal and the swelling to lessen."

Velma nodded. "Jim, we'll be prayin' for him."

His fingers rolled the brim of his hat. "I thank you. I sure feel sorry for him."

"He has to wear the boards the whole time?" Ella asked.

"Oh, no. She said he should take them off tonight, but not put pressure on the leg. He's got to let the swelling go down. That means bed rest and no work outside. Duncan, Samuel, and I will do the work, which isn't much right now. We still have a lot of winter repairs to do—fences to mend." He turned toward the door. "Well, guess I'll go out to your barn and prod Samuel into hurrying."

"I'll get Samuel." Before Jim could say no, Ella grabbed her coat. "You can visit with Velma." She ducked past him, slipped out the door, and ran the scuffed, muddy path to the barn. The crunchy snow still lightly covered the ground, but it no longer held any brilliant beauty.

Samuel stood outside the barn, struggling to close the crooked door. He had brought his horse out and tied it to the fence. "What's wrong?"

"Nothing. Jim's here." She stopped in front of him, gathered her long hair in her hands, and twisted it into a bun. With cold fingers, she tucked the ends in to hold it all in place. Because Jim hadn't removed his coat, she knew he wouldn't stay, and she was anxious to get back and spend more time with him.

Samuel turned toward the cabin. "Oh. I see his horse. Ella Dessa, these cows are in bad shape. They need more feed and—"

"I know. I'll talk to Velma 'bout it. Jim's here to fetch you home." She lifted the hem of her skirt well above her ankles. "Come on." She sprinted ahead of him.

When she entered the cabin, she was out of breath. Jim sat at the table, deep in conversation with Velma. Ella noticed he still hadn't taken off his coat. It surely meant he'd leave the minute his brother appeared. Disappointed, she almost shut the door in Samuel's face.

"Hey, let me in." He ducked in and tossed his hat on the peg by the door. With a light tap, he touched her on the shoulder. "You were shutting me out. What's with you running like a scared rabbit?"

"I didn't shut you out, and I didn't run like a rabbit," she hissed, hoping Jim hadn't heard.

"Ella Dessa, Velma has nothing but good things to say about you." Jim's eyes glinted with admiration. "I knew you could handle things."

She shrugged and smiled. "I didn't do it all. Samuel helped last night."

"You bet I did."

Jim stood. "Sam, we worried last night. Now I know why you stayed. No problem. I would've done the same." He winked at Ella.

Samuel's inquisitive glance went from his oldest brother to Ella. "I didn't mind staying. How's Papa?"

"Not good. His knee is swelling. Duncan's cutting small timber on the west side so we can use it for fence posts. That way we don't have to haul posts from the supplies in the barn. You and I have to repair a fence in that area and help Duncan. I told Papa I'd come get you, take you with me, and work until dark. You ready to go?"

"Yes, if Ella Dessa doesn't need help."

She shrugged her shoulders. "I think we'll be fine."

He lifted his old hat from the peg. "When school starts, I'll bring by assignments." He smiled at her. "I won't forget."

"Thanks." Ella returned his smile, but she was conscious of Jim standing close. She wished she were older and prettier, more like the dark-haired girl at the wedding. That girl appeared perfect with her unmarred skin, and she was more Jim's age.

"Sam, let's go. You're stalling. Go get your horse out of the barn." He tugged on his brother's sleeve.

"My horse is outside the door."

"Then get on him." Jim nudged him toward the door. "I hope everyone stays well. Don't get sick, Ella Dessa. We can't spare Samuel to come take care of you." He winked at her.

Embarrassed, she shook her head. "I wouldn't want him to take care of me." She crossed her arms, hiding the stained blouse she wore.

"Hey." Samuel looked hurt. "After all I did for you? You talk like that?" He then gave her a silly grin and plopped the floppy hat on his head. "Don't think I'll ever sit up with you again."

****

Jim and Samuel rode in silence until they reached the steepest part of the narrow, rutted trail. Three bulky pieces of rock had broken loose from the side of the mountain and lay in the path.

"I rode around these rocks coming down." Jim reined in his horse, swung his leg over the saddle, and stepped down. He led his horse closer to the rocks. "If someone brings a wagon, they won't get through. Let's roll these off the side." He looped the reins over a nearby tree branch and turned. "Think you can help me?"

"Are you asking me to help?"

"Sure." He squinted at his brother and realized how tall the boy sat in the saddle. He had lengthened out in the past couple of months, and the added inches made him seem older. "Get on down. We can manage them—between the two of us." He turned to survey the damage. "They must've dropped during the night. Ice probably popped 'em loose."

With grunts and groans, they rolled and shoved the first irregular gray rock off the edge. Samuel grinned, inclined his head, and listened as the rock plunged between leafless trees. It made a rapid and shattering descent. The second one crashed into a pine tree and slammed to an abrupt halt.

"Ouch!" Jim yelped and laughed. "Glad that wasn't me. What a *headache*."

"Don't want to fall off this stretch of the trail." Samuel shuddered. "Now, one more to go." He flexed his shoulders. "Got to put muscle into this one."

"Do you have any muscles?"

"Yeah, let me show you what I got. Come on. I'll let you help."

"If you're going to show me, then you best do it yourself." Jim feigned quitting, but joined Samuel in rocking the stone, until it started to roll. "Look out. Let it go."

They watched the third and largest stone careen between boulders and trees. Samuel snatched off his hat and waved it over his head. "Yee ... ha! Wow, did you see that one bounce? I bet it went ten feet in the air."

"Hmm. If it had been a body, it would've been battered to pieces." Jim removed his hat and wiped a forearm across his face. Their boots stamped out muddy gouges in the trail where the light snow had melted. The sun lifted into the sky, bright and strong. "Snow didn't last long on this stretch. That sun's hotter today. I don't need this coat."

Samuel inspected a scrape on his right palm, caused by one of the rocks. "Oww." Bright red blood dripped to the ground and joined the melting snow.

"Are you going to live?" Jim rolled his coat into a bundle and strapped it behind the saddle.

"Yeah." Samuel pulled off his own coat.

Jim saw a dark smear of blood on the front of it. "Hey, now you're bleeding on your coat."

"Ugh." He threw the coat over the front of the homemade saddle and dabbed his hand on his pants leg. "Jim, this stupid cut won't stop bleeding. I'm dripping."

"Here, use this." Jim pulled a square of muslin out of his pocket. Their mother had neatly hemmed the edges. "It's clean. I haven't used it on my nose." He grinned at Samuel.

"I hope not."

"Listen, Papa's getting worse. The three of us need to help take the load off him, especially when it comes to hunting or anything requiring a lot of walking." He unwound the horse's reins from the tree branch.

"What does that mean for my schooling—when the time comes? Do I have to forget it?" Samuel tightened the cloth over his hand. "Tie this?" He held his hand out to Jim.

"Hold still." Jim shifted the dangling reins to the crook of his elbow and tied the corners of the square cloth around his brother's hand. He knew how much the new school meant to Samuel. "You'll have to do chores earlier in the mornings while it's still dark. And get home fast after school. Otherwise ... no, you can't go. Mother will continue to work with you during the evenings, just as she has with all us older children. Little ones do schooling in the mornings."

"Hmm. I promised to take lessons to Ella Dessa—if I go to school." Samuel showed his exasperation by kicking at the mud. "I can't break that promise."

"That means you'll be going out of your way, riding to Velma's place."

"I know that. It won't take long."

"Better not. Drop them and be on your way up this trail."

Samuel nodded in agreement. "Is Duncan bristling at the thought of more chores?"

Jim laid his forehead against his horse's neck and sighed. "Duncan's never happy. He's not saying much." He turned to face Samuel. "The three of us will have to do all the plowing on the east slope—come spring planting. At which time, you may have to miss school. Papa's knee can't take the punishment of the sharp angle on that slope."

"What made his knee get like that?"

"Mother thinks it's the result of his fall while building Stuarts' barn last spring."

"Yeah. That barn raising wasn't kind to a couple of men. Laura Stuart's nephew broke two ribs with a fall, and ole Abe cut off a finger."

Jim stepped into the stirrup and swung his leg over the worn leather saddle. "Let's get home before Duncan thinks he's left alone to do all the work. He'll run away if that happens." He bumped the horse's sides with his heels, clicked his tongue, and urged the animal over the grade. At the top, he hesitated and reined in his horse. He watched his brother struggle to make his horse stand still.

"Come on, Sam. Need help getting in the saddle?"

"What saddle?" his brother shouted. "This homemade piece of leather? You call this a saddle?" His spirited horse sidestepped and moved in a circle, avoiding his attempt to mount. "You're sitting on the only real saddle anyone owns in the cove."

"It's not the saddle keeping you on the ground, Sam." He chuckled at his brother's red face. "She's got you figured."

"Hey, I have a hurt hand. Stupid horse." The teen hopped with one foot in the stirrup and finally mounted. His horse's hooves kicked stones the whole way uphill. "Easier for you to get on, anyhow. Your horse is shorter."

Jim chuckled. "You just need to grow longer legs." He took the lead and twisted sideways in the saddle to look back. "Has Ella Dessa heard from Fern?"

"Not that she mentioned."

"Probably just as well." He shook his head and faced forward. "Who knows what'll happen when Fern gets Duncan's letter. Her reply will determine our brother's future actions."

"You're right about that."

They rode in silence until Jim asked, "So, you two sat up all night?"

"What? Oh, Ella Dessa and me?"

"Who else?"

"No one else. Just us two." There was a hint of a teasing in Samuel's voice. "Sure did find conversation interesting, for a change. Wasn't like a brotherly exchange."

Jim knew that if he turned in the saddle he'd see a giant smile lifting his brother's lips. He resisted the desire to see if he was right. Sam meant to goad him into asking more questions, so he went along with the game. "And you talked all night?"

"No." Samuel chuckled. "Just for awhile—'til we were all talked out."

"When did you sleep?"

"We took turns sleeping. She was tired and about crying when I arrived."

"So, you comforted her?"

"Why, sure."

"You're a bad liar." A barb of jealousy pricked Jim's chest, and he tried reasoning with himself about it. *She's a child. Why can't I get past that? It must be those soft blue eyes and her helpless appearance.*

"I'm not lying. I rocked Rosemary for her."

"That's not comforting Ella Dessa."

"Well, yeah ... I did that, too." Sam's tone grew smug. "Wrapped my arms around her and gave her the biggest kiss—"

"Now, I know you're pulling my leg. She wouldn't accept that kind of consoling from the likes of you—boy."

"Hmm, that's for you to think over."

"Mmm-hmm." He let a moment pass before asking, "What did you talk about?"

"What's with all the questions?" Samuel caught up and rode abreast.

"Just curious. She's a smart girl." He glanced at their surroundings. The trail leveled out and turned east. No smoky-colored haze covered the mountains. It was a cloudless, wintery-blue sky.

"Too bad she can't attend school."

"Yeah. She might do better at schooling than you do." He looked sideways at his younger brother. "Eh?"

Samuel's face brightened. "I wouldn't mind a bit."

"No?" The clopping of hooves kept tempo with their choppy conversation.

"I'd just ask her to help me with my studies." He swept his old hat off and held it over his chest. "Please, Ella Dessa, I'm falling ... behind in reading. I need help."

"You're amusing this morning."

"I got the most talent in the family." Samuel grinned at him, apparently enjoying their banter of words. "I sang and entertained Rosemary when she cried last night."

"And she cried harder?"

"No, she went to sleep. Ella Dessa appreciated my help." A happy glint lit Samuel's blue-green eyes.

"You like her. Don't you?"

"She's nice." A tinge of pink colored his brother's cheeks.

"Why, Samuel McKnapp, you're turning red as a rooster's comb."

"Hey! What about that new girl at the wedding?" Samuel kicked his horse's sides and rode on ahead. "You sure were sweet talking and spending time with her. What's her name?"

"Sophie Wald?" Jim contemplated his brother's wide shoulders. Samuel would soon pass Duncan in size. Duncan had stayed on the short side, like their papa.

"When do you plan on getting married?" Samuel shouted back at him.

"What? Slow up. You crazy? Married—to Sophie? I hardly know her."

"No, I mean to anyone. If you found someone, would you marry her right away?"

"You ask the craziest questions." Shaking his head, he continued to stare at Samuel's back. "I don't plan to marry any time soon. I'm not eighteen, yet. I'm not marrying young. There's a world to see beyond these mountains. Why?" His horse trotted just behind Samuel's mount.

"Just wondered how soon you'd be out of the running."

He rode up beside Samuel. "What does *that* mean?"

"You're going to lose!" Samuel gave a whoop of delighted laughter and slapped the reins against his horse's neck. The old horse jumped and sidestepped. "Beat you to the finish. Go horse!" His mount straightened up and headed straight for the log barn. Its roof showed over the last rise, between tall pines.

Jim loosened his reins, clicked his tongue, and leaned forward over the flowing mane. "Like fun you will, little brother. Not in this race or any other."

Chapter 24

Friday, April 14, 1837

She felt Velma's curious eyes watch every line of ink in the copybook. Ella realized the lessons Samuel brought to her from the schoolmaster fascinated the young woman. She knew Velma considered schooling very important and did her best to encourage all the children. She didn't put up with much idling when it came to lessons.

"I must copy all six lines." She bit down on her bottom lip and concentrated.

"Do you haves Bible readin' to do?" Velma leaned across the table so she could watch Ella write the looping letters in light strokes along the paper.

"Not tonight. Carrie says she must read five verses. I just have these sentences." She toiled over the last sentence she was to copy.

"I will see that she does it while I nurse the baby."

Ella dipped her goose quill in the cone-shaped glass bottle of charcoal ink and paused. Her thoughts about the birth of the baby interrupted her concentration.

Never had such fear gripped her as when Velma's contractions got closer together. The vicious flashes of lightning had lit the woman's grimaces as she bore down, and thunder obliterated her loud groans. Every crack in the log walls served as an entryway for the pounding rain, and it ran along the walls on the west side of the cabin. There had been no way to fetch Granny down the rain-slicked trail to help with the birthing. The contractions had come so fast and heavy, even Velma lost control of her usual staunch fortitude.

Ella had put the three youngest to bed, with Rosemary bedded down with Mae. Scott and Carrie sat on the floor near the fireplace, which danced and sizzled with rain managing to splatter down the chimney. Their mother's half-sobbed cries and the booming of the storm kept them craning their necks to look toward the bed. The only privacy was one quilt hung from the bottom of the loft.

The lumpy, cornhusk mattress had added to Velma's discomfort. "Ella, if I'm ever rich, I'll haves a goose down mattress! Ohh!" She had reached to grip her legs and groaned with the next contraction. With a gasp, she rolled to her right side. "It's comin'!"

"I see its head!" Ella had reached to steady Velma's uplifted knee, but felt useless as she watched the incredible birth.

With hardly any effort, the woman delivered the chubby dark-haired infant. His angry cries had filled the single-room cabin while thunder rolled down the west side of the cove. Wind then swept the thunder up the east side, and Velma laughed.

"It's a boy!" she yelled out to her two oldest children. "You gots a new brother."

Ella had covered Velma with a sheet and worked with the infant boy. Her hands shook as she cleared his little mouth and wiped his round face. He wrinkled his brow and gave a harsh cry that seemed like music to her ears. She felt wonder at the perfect birth. Velma had almost seemed giddy and joyous as she gazed at her baby.

"Oh, Velma, he's perfect," she had whispered. The new baby's coloring didn't match the blue-tinged baby she had seen born up on the mountain in the dreary cabin. This baby would live and not fight for breath.

Braced on one elbow, Velma had run her left hand over the infant's wet head. "I love this gift, another beautiful child from God. Cut the cord, then we'll let Carrie and Scott comes look." She laid back on the bed. "Thank you, Lord." Tears had dripped down the woman's flushed cheeks.

****

A hand tapped her on the head. "Ella? Where's your mind gone?" Velma stared at her. "You look like you're in a trance."

"Ouch." She wrinkled her nose and giggled. "I keep thinkin' of Adam's birth. He's such a perfect baby." Her hand hovered over the words she still had to write.

"Your writing's beautiful." Velma tapped the upper, right hand corner of the paper. "What is this? I didn't know you could draw."

Ella shrugged. "I shouldn't have drew on the page like that." She turned the copybook around, so Velma could see.

"Honey, it's lovely an' so delicate. A fawn layin' amidst violets?"

"Yes. I drew them from memory. It isn't much, and the teacher might get angry. I ruined the corner of the paper."

"Oh, I should thinks he'll be impressed."

"Thank you. I never got to draw much when I lived with Mama. But I love to draw." She pulled the copybook back into place, pressed her lips together, and made the final looping letters on her assignment. "*Whew*, it's done. And only three blots on it." She considered the spots where her ink had dripped or spread. "I wish it were perfect, but my hand shook."

"I only had schoolin' my grandma gave me." Velma sat with one elbow on the table. She rested her chin on a cupped hand. "That's not much, I guess."

"It's enough. I've seen you help Scott with his lessons. You read the Bible." She waved her hand over the page and waited for the ink to dry.

"Am I botherin' you?"

"No, I'm done for tonight." With care, she blew on the page, closed the copybook, and tied the leather cover shut. She smiled as she put the tiny cork into the neck of the clear glass bottle, careful not to spill the precious ink Master Konrad had allowed her to use. She held it to the firelight and contemplated the bubbled glass and the liquid ink. "He mixed this just for me and told Samuel to bring it."

"Don't let the little ones seize that."

"No, I won't, and I'll make sure Carrie takes it to school Monday. I'm glad Master Konrad saw fit to give me two days to use it. When you were with your grandma, where'd you live?" She wiggled her fingers and tried to work a cramp out of her right hand. "Ouch, I gripped the quill too tight, again. I wish I could relax while writin'."

"We lived nears Richmond. Gust asked me to marry him, which I did. A year later, Carrie was born an' Grandma died. We lived with her, so we stayed on 'til the house burnt the night I birthed Scott." Her voice shook with emotion. "Gust left a lit pipe on the table nears my bowl of yarn. I almost lost my new baby to the fire."

Ella folded her hands on top of the copybook and gazed at the woman. "I'm sorry. That must've been awful."

"We had to rely on help from other folks—much like now. They built us a tiny cabin, but Gust never added to it." Her eyes reflected past sadness. "He drank. I delivered Remy myself 'cause Gust was on an extended huntin' trip. Mae came the year after, and it seemed no time at all for Rosemary cames along. Gust moved us here so he could be close to the gold fields."

"You knew that?"

"Yes, I'm no ninny. We stayed four months west of Lick Log, 'fore I insisted he get me and the younguns away from the squalor. I didn't want to live in a shanty along a dirty stream with gold-crazed men." She stopped talking and stared at the rough pine table. With a broken fingernail, she picked at a loose knothole. "Now, I guess, he's chosen gold over us." Her hunched shoulder bones showed through the thin material of her dress, emphasizing her words of rejection.

"I'm sorry, Velma." She didn't know what else to say. The woman's sudden sharing of the past had taken her by surprise, although she realized it probably served to ease the woman's mind.

Velma patted her hand. "Nothin' for you to feels sorry about. I was ramblin'." She sat straighter and lifted her chin. "Now, I've somethin' to say."

"Yes?"

"I want you to starts going to the school with the others."

"With the others? You're sure?"

"I can watch the younger ones and the baby for that short a time. There's no reason for you to stays home. Adam's five weeks old, now. It's the middle of April. I've got my strength back."

Ella didn't dare breathe. Reality might slip away if she took in a lungful of air. She gripped the edge of the table with her ink-stained fingers. It seemed too amazing to be true. "You said I can go?"

"Yes, on Monday. Scott and Carrie will loves havin' you walk with them."

"Oh, bless you!" She jumped from her seat, ran around the table, and grabbed Velma in what her mother used to call a bear hug. She buried her face against the woman's neck. "I *love* you."

"That's the way I feel 'bout you," Velma whispered, her hand stroking Ella's hair.

"Samuel won't hav'ta bring my lessons to me no more." She lifted her head and smiled.

Velma chuckled and patted her back. "I don't thinks Samuel will be none too happy 'bout that. He loves comin' to see you. He's smitten with you."

"Smitten?" She plopped back on the bench.

"Yep. Slapped rights in the face with wantin' to please you and see your purty smile."

"Oh, that's silly. He does it 'cause he promised Master Konrad." Ella found Velma's remark pleased her. No boy had ever been *smitten* with her.

"No, that young man cares deeply."

"Ahh, I don't see it that way." She fingered the scars on her neck and shook her head. "He doesn't."

"Meet his eyes, and you'll make out his devotion to you. Them bluish-green eyes sparkle like a leaf-covered mountain reflected in a duck pond—especially, when he catches sight of you."

"A duck pond? Oh, you're silly and stringing a real yarn, now." Thoughts of Samuel with sparkling eyes—because of her—caused her to laugh.

271

"No. Not so."

A low whimper came from the cradle near the fireplace. "I'll see to him," Ella said.

Velma waved a hand at her. "I'll go."

Ella watched the young woman rise and maneuver sideways along the bench. Her movements were slow and shuffled. Even more than a month since the baby's birth, she remained weak. Granny said the husky baby boy had taken the strength clean out of Velma.

She pursed her lips. She hated what Gust Clanders had done to Velma. She hadn't repeated the things Samuel discovered about the missing man. She knew the rumors wouldn't comfort her friend, but only make her burden heavier. It seemed best to leave it an unrevealed subject.

For now, she had school to consider. Her mind whirled with possibilities. She felt heady with excitement and anticipation. Perhaps, she could complete all grades and become a teacher or an artist. She had intentionally shoved all hopes and dreams of a future out of her mind.

Velma turned with Adam cuddled in her arms, and Ella left the table to go see him. His chubby fists beat the air over the edge of a small scrap of blanket. Gently, she touched his fingers and felt them curl around one of hers.

"Velma, he's such a good baby." For just seconds, she thought of baby Timothy and her heart clenched with the old ache.

"He's my sweet baby." Velma kissed his smooth forehead, below the shock of fuzzy brown hair. "I was so depressed this week, thinkin' over our meager life, but no more. I feel happier 'cause you picked moccasin flowers downs by the creek and brought them to me. You're a kind-hearted girl, Ella Dessa."

Ella smiled and glanced over at the delicate, slipper-like spring flowers she had found and wrapped in wet moss. She had presented the combination of yellow flowers and gray moss to Velma, in hopes of lifting the woman's spirits. They now occupied a stoneware jar on the table.

"You acted so weary and dispirited. I had to do somethin'."

"Well, you did the right thing." She sat in the rocker near the fire and unbuttoned her dress top. "I must have good milk. He's gettin' fat on it. I should've had twins."

Ella laughed, tickled at the woman's buoyant sense of humor. "Oh, don't wish that on yourself."

"No chances of it happenin' now." Her hazel eyes widened with an unexpressed surge of apparent emotion. It engulfed her, and her chin quivered. "Ella Dessa, I knows he's not set to come back."

Ella faced the fire and bit at her bottom lip. She crossed her arms, hugged her chest, and struggled with whether she should tell Velma or remain silent. But this time, she let go of her original resolve.

"Perhaps, you're right." She faced her friend. "He hasn't been seen by anyone since before Christmas. At least ways, that's what Samuel tells me he heard. Your husband's either missin' or gone elsewhere to pan for gold."

"By missin', they mean—*dead*."

"Some think he had no plans to come back. I'm sorry."

Velma stared straight ahead without blinking. She rocked and patted the bottom of the baby. In the quiet room, the smacking sound of Adam's mouth against the exposed breast seemed extra loud.

"I think he's dead."

Ella inhaled. "Don't say that."

"No, listen to me. I don't feels him in my being. It's as if he's gone for good. Many times, I prayed for God to stop the beatin's. Guess he did."

"You have no proof." She turned to the fire and grimaced, wishing she hadn't broken Samuel's confidence. She pressed her hands to her chest and closed her eyes. She had hurt Velma needlessly.

"Look at me, Ella Dessa."

She obeyed immediately, caught off guard by the sternness in the woman's voice.

"Sorry." A slightly amused smile registered on Velma's thin lips. "I didn't means to make it a command. It's just that, if the worst is found out and he's dead, you'll knows why I ain't grievin'. I commenced to grieve many years ago. My heart was torn from me and laid bare. I never plan to love ag'in. There—I said it." She pressed the baby's hand to her pale lips.

"I'm glad you're not bein' hit no more, but what will you—I mean, what will we do? Foods gone, 'cept what families still bring us. The cows were traded for meal and goods. We ate your chickens."

273

"Oh, I don't know." She hunched over the infant in her lap, as if protecting him from harm and reality. Her thin arms encircled his blanketed body.

"Don't cry." Ella went to the rocker and knelt. "Please, don't cry."

"There's no answer—no answer." Huge tears dampened the woman's worn cheeks, following new wrinkles formed by her drastic weight loss. "God only knows. We have to rely on the good wishes an' provisions of others." A sob shook her skinny shoulders.

"We can't cry. The little ones will see. It'll scare them."

Mae and Rosemary had been sitting in the center of Velma's bed with Carrie's three rag babies. The quiet childish hum of their voices blended as they pretended to coddle real babies. Since the older children started school, the girls had become closer, playing together more often.

"You're so right." Velma wiped at the tears remaining on her face. "What's to be gained by tears? I just don't knows what to do. I do feel helpless."

Ella agreed about feeling helpless, but a thought sprang into her mind. "Would you differ to me seein' if there's a need for help at the store?"

"Help?"

"Perhaps, I could work for Mr. Beckler."

Velma swiped away final tears of defeat. She nodded. "We must try." Her troubled eyes focused on the jumping flames. "We can't continue to be beholden to others. I haves my pride."

"Then, it's settled. Monday I'll walk the children to school and tell Master Konrad I may attend. After school, I'll inquire of Mr. Beckler."

"Ahh, poor Samuel will be so sad he's not walkin' my little ones here and bringin' lessons to you."

"He won't be sad." Ella grinned. "He'll be relieved. Besides, we'll see one another at school, and he can go straight home afterwards."

****

Monday morning, Ella stepped into the simple log building serving as both church and schoolroom. Eyes watched as she walked to Master Konrad's desk and set her leather-bound copybook and the bottle of ink on his desk. She faced the teacher while Carrie, Remy, and Scott took their usual seats.

"Velma says I may start school." She felt almost giddy. Her wide smile caused her cheeks to ache.

"Well, Miss Huskey, we're sure pleased you've joined us." Konrad's dark-lashed eyes swept the room and the fifteen students occupying the backless church benches. "I believe the vacant seat by Samuel will be yours. I don't separate boys and girls like most teachers do. Grades go together. Coats go on the pegs and lunch baskets on the floor underneath them. All written sessions will be done at the two tables. Here's your slate." He smiled at her. "Take your seat Miss Ella Dessa Huskey."

Wiggling his eyebrows as a silent welcome, Samuel tapped his finger on the space next to him and grinned. Ella hung her coat, set the basket containing hers and the others' lunches on the floor beneath it, and went to sit beside him. She felt herself blush at all the eyes watching her, and she tugged at her blouse collar, to make sure her scars remained covered.

Samuel's elbow jabbed into her side.

She peeked sideways at him.

"You didn't tell me at church yesterday." He whispered out of the corner of his mouth, lips barely moving. He managed to keep his eyes on the teacher and didn't look at her.

Ignoring his comment, she lifted her chin a notch and folded her hands on top of the slate in her lap. She enjoyed his apparent surprise and felt a joyous satisfaction in knowing she managed to keep it a secret from Samuel McKnapp.

The hours flew by, and school ended for the day. Her head swam with all the subjects covered, but contentment nestled in her heart. She was where she longed to be—in school—and she had much to learn.

Ella told Carrie and Scott to wait outside of the school. She needed to collect her copybook and makeup assignments from the teacher. Her hands shook so, she had to place her palms on the rough desk and press down. She watched Grace's husband carefully pen out what he wanted her to study and memorize. She felt amazed at his precise handwriting and hoped she could one day write as well and with total ease.

"It's in the Bible, Ella Dessa. Have it memorized for presentation to the class by this Friday. I'm keeping your copybook because I didn't have a chance to go over the assignment you finished."

"Presen ... *tation?*"

"Yes, you'll stand before the class and recite the passages in Psalms I've written down. I require it of all the upper grades."

"But, I ain't—I've never done that." She pressed her lips together and swallowed. Her mouth went dry. She laid her right hand over the few inches of scars visible above her collar and said, "I don't think I can. I can't stand and talk—in front." Her bottom lip quivered. In her mind, she saw all the children staring at her neck as she stood before them. "You don't understand," she whispered.

His kind eyes swept over her neck and up to her face. "Yes, I do. Doing the recitation will be the best thing you could ever accomplish."

Tears dripped down her face, and she shook her head. "No—"

"I have faith in you. You've got courage, and you'll carry out the task." His attractive blue eyes reminded her of an early morning summer sky. "Ella Dessa, don't let your fears hold you back. Speak with confidence, and no one will take their eyes off your face."

"But—" In her head, she chided herself. *Keep quiet about your scars.* She listened to her inner voice and nodded. "I'll try. I need to go. Velma's children ..." She pointed at the door.

He nodded and dismissed her.

She bounded down the steps of the church building and into the warm sun. Samuel stood near the trail with Carrie, Remy, and Scott.

"You waited?" Ella dried her damp cheeks with her hand and untied her shawl. "You didn't have to."

"Thought I'd walk you as far as Beckler's. Scott says you're stopping there."

"Yes, I am."

"A mite warm." Samuel used his hat as a fan—waving it in front of his face. He squinted in the afternoon sunlight. "But with the sun dropping, it'll cool down fast and get cold for the night."

"Are you also stopping at the store?"

He hesitated and put his hat on. "No." He spoke to Ella but gazed directly at Scott. "I wanted to speak to you—ask you something."

Scott stood frowning at him. "Is it private?"

"No." He turned his back on Scott and faced Ella. "I saw a carpet of tiny blue flowers covering the stones by the creek. There must be thousands of them. Do you want to go look at them with me? They practically drip over the stones and into the water."

"Can't. I have business to tend to." She watched other schoolchildren disappearing along different paths. They all carried the wraps and coats that had kept them warm earlier in the day. "I'm goin' to ask Mr. Beckler to let me work for him."

"You? Work?"

"Ain't that what I said?" She pressed her lips together to stop any other clarification, turned, and hurried away. Samuel trotted to catch up and fell in step with her. Carrie and Scott lagged behind them with Remy chattering and kicking stones.

"You sure that's a good idea?" Samuel shoved his hat upward and scratched at his head. His hair appeared sweaty and darker in color where it met his forehead. "I mean, with all you do at Velma's?"

She sighed, trying to master a look of indignation. "Samuel, are you sayin' I shouldn't help her in this way?"

"No, that's not what I meant." In order to face her, he walked sideways—shuffling his boots.

"I know the things I can take care of, 'specially with God's help. It's best I do this." She squared her shoulders and lifted her chin a notch. "We need to get by on our own—Velma and me—without people in the cove helping us. Why, just last night, Lyle brought us a chicken he killed."

Samuel's face brightened. "Hey, Ella Dessa, I forgot! Papa told me last week to let you know I'll be bringing your two cows to Velma's, along with your chickens. The hens will be laying soon—it's that time of the year. A couple will be good brooders."

She almost came to an abrupt halt in the path. "Oh, Samuel. For honest? I never expected them back—after your papa havin' to feed them."

She touched his arm. "That'd be *just* what we need. I'd feel like I were repaying Velma, if my chickens laid eggs and had chicks."

"That's not all. Some time back, Papa said he put our bull in with your two cows. I heard him tell Mother the old bull stood up to them—*right nice*. Bet your cows will have calves."

Ella felt her face go warm, to hear such boldly stated information. "I see. Tell him thanks." She stopped as they reached Beckler's small store. "Well, here we are."

"I don't know as I like you starting school." Samuel shuffled his boots in the dirt and folded his arms. "It'll seem funny not stopping by with your assignments. My feet are accustomed to going that way." He grinned boyishly. "How do I retrain them?"

She realized a lump had formed in her throat. "Samuel, you've been faithful to help me the last few months. I will miss you stoppin' by."

His face brightened with pleasure at her words, and he tapped at his chest with his right thumb. "Oh, I'll miss it more than you."

"Oh, but just think, you'll be gettin' home earlier. It won't be near dark."

He gave a *harrumph*. "That's what I'm afraid of." He fiddled with a ragged spot on the sleeve of his coat and gazed up at the mountain behind the store. "My brothers will expect me to help them."

With a peal of laughter, she waved her hand. "Bye, Samuel." She told Velma's children to sit on the steps and wait for her. She wanted to be alone when she talked to the owner.

It felt cooler inside, and she shivered. Mr. Beckler towered over a short bald man, and the two of them were haggling over the price of some leather gloves. Ella gripped her hands behind her back and waited.

The rear door of the store stood as wide open as the front door. It caused a waft of air to blow through the entire store, from back to front. She could see a reddish bank of dirt and stony rubble piled behind the building. Smoke drifted from a smoldering outdoor fire pit. An iron tripod and kettle straddled it. An old donkey, tethered to a tree stump, stood with his head hung and eyes closed. The dropping sun glinted along his back and scruffy coat.

She breathed in the scent of wood smoke, the grassy smell of twirled hemp ropes, and the familiar aroma of dried herbs. Mixed in was the taint of human sweat. With a slight turn of her head, more scents grew recognizable. There were soaps made from delicate flower blossoms, crisp new cloth, bagged grains, lantern oil, and leather—her favorite scent in the store.

Ella curled her toes in her leather boots and remembered when her pa gave them to her. Even though his last and only gift to her had been a token of his unspoken guilt-feelings, the sight of them always filled her with joy.

Pivoting on her boot heels, she surveyed the room. Tanned leather whips hung coiled and looped over wood pegs on the sidewall. They were part of the store's leftover stock—supplied for cattle drives down to the gold mines.

Three-drawstring bags, fashioned from cured deer hides caught her attention. They hung at eye level, and she moved closer.

Intricate images of deer, bear, violets, butterflies, and a variety of birds graced the golden leather bags. The designs had been cut and tapped into the surface. With her fingertips, Ella traced the patterns and marveled at the minuscule details. The fine feathers on the birds were so delicate they couldn't be felt, only seen with the eye.

She whispered each name as she identified them. "That's a hummingbird, a ruffed grouse, and—"

"Well, well. Ella Dessa, what can I do for you?"

"Oh!" She jumped at the sound of Mr. Beckler's voice and realized his customer had left.

"Admiring the leather bags? They are more than beautiful. They are works of art." The hefty-shouldered man moved to stand beside her. "Shouldn't be hanging in my small store." His pleasant smile widened under the white mustache covering his top lip. "Like them?" He studied her face as if he perused an open book.

"Yes, very much. I like to draw." Self-conscious at his frank scrutiny, she turned her head away and dipped her chin downward. She knew he had seen her scars many times in the past—but not when she hoped to ask for a job.

"I'm selling them for a relative of the schoolmaster. The gentleman delivered them today, along with other leather goods. He says to give some of the profit to the schoolmaster."

Ella's pulse quickened. "Our teacher?"

"Yep, the same. I think the man is his uncle."

Miles Kilbride!

"He brought ... brought this in here?"

"Yes. Konrad Strom's uncle is an artist. My sister's thrilled with his work—her being good at that stuff herself. He even does wood carvings. Konrad told me his mother's brother made a second trip from North Carolina, to bring a bundle of books for the schoolhouse. He's now headed back east. He's a very friendly, likeable man. In fact, he was here this morning."

Her thoughts flashed back to the letter in her carved wooden box.

Walter chuckled. "He teased me about having a mountain cove named after me. I told him it was named after my father, who set up a trading store with the Indians many years ago."

Ella chewed at her bottom lip and eyed the beautiful designs. They rivaled anything she had ever seen, except one particular item. Her thoughts went to the meticulous, detailed flower petals carved into her mama's box. She knew the artist had to be the same person. And the connection must be kept a secret.

Mr. Beckler rubbed a hand over his neatly-trimmed beard and waited, apparently puzzled by her prolonged silence. He nodded toward the rear of the store. "Nice day we're having. It's invigorating. I'm bringing in the good air by propping the doors. It helps build the body's strength." He flexed his arm muscles and grinned. "How's Velma? My sister's worried about her."

"She's fairly well. The baby's growin'." With nervousness mounting in her chest, Ella eyed the friendly face of the storeowner. Then she swallowed her pride and blurted out her reason for dropping in. "She's why I'm here. I need to find a way to help Velma. I want to earn some money for vittles and cloth."

"Oh? You want to help Velma?" He didn't hesitate. "I could use someone to straighten these shelves." He lifted a bolt of material. Its tight-woven, beige finish contrasted his tanned fingers. "If Velma can spare you, can you start tomorrow?"

"Tomorrow?" Her mouth went dry. The asking and the receiving had been quick and easy. "After school, perhaps?" she ventured to ask in return.

"Of course, after school it is." He placed the bolt of material on a shelf behind him and lovingly patted it with his hand. "This here is my finest linen. I don't let folks touch it, unless buying, so remember that. I ordered it from Richmond."

"Yes, sir." Her heart turned flips. She had a job—it would help provide food and dry goods for Velma's family.

"To start, Ella Dessa, at the end of each week you may exchange your earnings for supplies Velma may need." He hesitated and then said, "Plus, I'll throw in a small sack of flour or meal once a week. Feel free to take a piece of taffy to the little ones when you leave on Fridays. If I need you on Saturdays, we'll do an exchange for your time. Is that agreeable?"

"Oh, yes! Thank you." She couldn't think of anything else to say. Her heart overflowed with joy. She paused at the doorway and smiled at him. "I'll work hard."

"Whoa!" Mr. Beckler smacked his own forehead with the palm of his right hand. "Near about forgot. There's a letter for you. The rider dropped it off here last Friday—literally on the run. The man hardly paused. He was heading north."

"Me?" Dumbfounded, she pointed at her chest.

"Yes. Let's see." He opened a shallow drawer in the rough-built counter behind him and pulled out a dirty, folded piece of paper. He wiped it across the front of his shirt. "It has your name but no return address. I was going to bring it to you." His brown eyes peered over his spectacles and showed immense interest. "Must be from far away, it's so soiled. A bit was due on it, but I took care of it."

"Thank you." Her fingers trembled, as she grasped the sealed missive. She didn't want to open it in front of him.

"The courier will ride through the first of the month, on his way down to Dahlonega, and then south," he gave her a slight nod, "if you're hoping to attempt a reply."

"I understand." She clutched it in her hand and joined the children outside.

Scott leaped to his feet. A long stem of wild grass dangled from the gap between his front teeth. "What did he say?"

"I start tomorrow." She answered Scott, but her eyes sought Samuel's beaming face.

"I knew you'd do it," Samuel said. "Nobody can say no to you. Now, if it was me—he'd laugh."

"What's that?" Scott plucked the stem from his mouth and grabbed at her arm. "For Mama?" He tossed the grass and tried to jerk the sealed letter from her grasp. "It's from Pappy?"

"No, it's my *very own* letter—penned to me. *See?*" She pointed at her name on the front fold, fluttered it in front of his frustrated face, and then tucked it in the waistband of her skirt.

"I waited. Can I walk with you today?" Samuel's eyes seemed more blue than green in the afternoon sunlight. "I've never been able to walk you home."

"I'd like that—we'd like that." Ella took Carrie's hand and headed past the small blacksmith's shack.

A chinking noise and the hiss of hot steam coming from the crude structure seemed to add to the sound of her heart thumping in her ears. Exhilaration churned in her veins. The day turned out wonderful—first school and then news of her cows and chickens. To top it off, she had a job and a personal letter to read.

Samuel fell into step beside her. "You're smiling."

"I'm happy."

"Why are these birds comin' back so soon?" Scott grabbed cherry-sized stones from the ground and tossed them at tiny blue-gray birds flitting through leafing tree branches.

"The gnatcatchers must know it's an early spring. They want to build nests. After all, it's nearly half through April. You shouldn't hurt 'em," Ella said.

Carrie frowned. "He always hurts birds."

Ella stopped and pursed her lips. "Spee, spee, spee!" She mimicked the bird's soft and repetitive call. "Why hurt them? There's times when you can call 'em right down out of the trees by doing that. They get curious. My Mama taught—Scott, *don't!*"

Carrie giggled, a very extraordinary sound coming from her. She watched Scott throw another wild stone. "He always misses."

"Shucks, Carrie. I heard that." Bending over, Scott scooped three more round stones. "Watch this." He trotted ahead of them and continued his barrage on the feathered creatures.

Ella shook her head. "That's mean."

Carrie nodded and slipped her hand into Ella's hand. "He *likes* to be mean."

"I want to do that." Remy collected his own arsenal of stones.

Samuel glanced at Ella and chuckled. "I remember doing the same thing."

"When you was a *child,* many moons ago?" she said, with a bit of sarcasm.

"Why, sure. I'm fourteen, now." He took a deep breath and stuck out his chest. "I'm almost grown."

She stopped and faced him, swinging Carrie's hand in hers. "You're taller, that's for sure."

"Head taller than you."

"Ah, huh. Isn't it funny how things change?" She was fully aware of how handsome Samuel had become—how broad his shoulders seemed. The teen boy had made a turn toward manhood, and she felt left behind.

He cleared his throat. "I like changes." His intense eyes said more than his words, as they moved from her eyes to her lips.

She dropped her head, hiding from his frank scrutiny.

Carrie tugged loose of her hand and ran to join the stone-flinging fun.

"I think we've been left alone." Samuel stepped closer.

She felt his hands touch her shoulders and raised her head. "What?" His fingers pulled her toward him.

He touched his lips to her cheek. It was a soft, fluttery caress, and Ella shivered, forgetting where they stood.

"*Hmm.* I better hike up the mountain." He stumbled backwards and tripped over an exposed tree root. His lips curved in a wide smile. "I'm happy for you—for Walter hiring you. I have chores to do."

"Samuel?" She touched her cheek.

"Gotta go." He pointed to a faint trail going up a ravine. "I'm taking the old path. See you tomorrow."

She still felt his light kiss. A lump formed in her throat. Something told Ella her life had turned a corner, much like spring pushing away winter's harshness.

The three children reappeared at the bend in the trail, and Carrie placed her hands on her hips and called. "Are you comin'?"

"Yes, wait for me." She ran to join them—her heart so bubbling full she couldn't stop smiling.

The four of them rounded the last curve in the dirt trail. The sound of the babbling creek grew in volume, and the wretched cabin slipped into view.

Carrie's bare feet came to a stumbling halt. Her fingers clawed at Ella's sleeve, and she made an abnormal whimpering sound. Scott's stones slipped from his fists, and the boy froze in his tracks.

Remy's mouth fell open. "A wagon." He sidestepped toward Ella and crouched on his heels in the dirt. "Why?"

"*Our wagon.*" Scott's words were a mere whisper in the breeze. "He's home."

Chapter 25

"*I*t's Pappy. He's come home." Scott's legs broke into a trot, and he headed for the wagon with two horses tied to a tree. Two more horses, wearing ragged saddles, stood in front of the cabin—reins wrapped about the single hitching post.

Carrie remained planted. Her flat chest jerked with each breath she inhaled. "No, no!" Moans poured from her colorless lips. "Quick! Go back—to the school."

Ella laid her stuff on the ground, encircled Carrie with her arms, and used her own body to shield the child from the sight of the dilapidated wagon. "Come here, Remy." She held her hand out, wiggling her fingers to the younger boy. "I want you close to me."

Her hands patted the girl's back while she looked over her shoulder at Scott. He jumped on the wheel of the wagon, stared into the bed, and then hopped backward to the ground—almost falling in the process. With extra haste, he scampered away as if a snake were coiled within the rotted sides of the wagon.

Then he ran to examine the two skinny horses in the harness. He expertly ran his child-sized hands over their necks, backs, and withers.

With unexpected tenderness, he cupped the one horse's dark muzzle and leaned his forehead against it.

Ella then realized one thing about the hotheaded child—he could show tenderness.

Scott jogged to them and faltered to a stop.

"It's him. And sure 'nough our horses. High Knees is the blood bay. But he's thin, now. Bellows is the black. He breathes funny, but I like 'im." Scott bounced on his toes with dirty fists and arms drawn close to his chest. Nervous energy showed in his movements.

"The horses—they're yours?"

"Ah-huh." He nodded then shrugged. "Least ways, the two hitched to the farm wagon. Wagon's ours."

She stared at the tall red horse with its ribs showing. The sight caused her shudder—as if it represented a dreadful warning. She wondered what to do.

"There's a dead wolf in the back of it." Scott almost shouted it at her.

"Shh!" She placed her finger against her lips. "A wolf?"

"A dead wolf?" Remy's mushroom-brown eyes grew big and round.

Scott nodded. His face had lost color. He nervously licked his pale lips and drew in air through the gap between his front teeth. "Flat dead. Eyes open."

Carrie clung tighter to Ella and whimpered.

"He shot it. The head's bleedin'. Pappy must be in ... with Mama. I didn't hear nothin' though. He's usually yellin'." The uptight tone in Scott's voice said more than mere words could've at that point. He feared for his mama's safety, and he wanted to fight for her. "I got to go in there."

"No, you don't. Let me think." She swallowed. "Stay quiet." She couldn't let the children walk in on an awful situation. Where could she send them? Back to the store?

Remy tugged on her skirt. His uneasy eyes searched her face. "He don't hear Pappy?"

Instantly, she made a decision. "Scott, take Carrie and Remy. Go along the trail to the dead pine. You know the one. Near the angled path to the creek?"

He nodded, and his brown-flecked hazel eyes widened with apprehension. "Ah-huh. The lightnin'-struck one. Looks like a gray haunt." With the tip of his tongue, he explored the gap between his teeth. His lips twisted, and he fought tears.

"Don't follow me." She pointed her finger at the three of them, her voice firm. "Stay under the tree, 'til I come for you. You hear?" She snatched her stuff from the ground.

Scott grabbed Remy's hand and ran. Carrie fled right behind them. In no time, they vanished and dust settled in their small tracks.

Ella proceeded toward the hushed cabin. *Heel, toe, heel ... toe*, she repeated in her head, remembering what one of their Indian friends had taught her about walking quiet-like. One of the horses tied to the post—a brown and white-spotted mare—raised its head. Its tail swished sideways, and it watched her stealthy approach.

Be quiet—be quiet, she silently begged the wary animal.

Near the door, she paused and rested her forehead on the thick wood. She could hear the murmur of more than one male voice, but they didn't sound angry. She sent up a quick prayer for protection and drew a ragged breath of courage. With deliberation, she cradled her copybook in her left arm and opened the door with her right.

Heads turned.

She didn't recognize the two rough-dressed men. They switched their attention from Velma to her. The taller of the two had long dark hair, which shadowed most of his face. She saw his square, smooth jaw line, but not the color of his eyes. Ella blinked in the dim room and assessed the situation. Her senses expanded to high alert. The tang of sweat, unwashed bodies, and dirty clothes permeated the room. She wanted to cover her nose in disgust.

She saw Rosemary sound asleep in the center of the big bed. Velma sat at the table with her arms crossed over her narrow chest, hands clutching the tops of her arms, as if holding her body in a tight embrace.

Mae leaned against her mother's side with two fingers crammed in her slack mouth. Her four-year-old expression said she didn't understand the presence of the strangers. Her blue eyes begged Ella to make them leave.

"Come here, Ella." Velma beckoned with a shaky hand. "Where's the children?"

"I left them outside." With quick strides, she rounded the table, dropped her shawl and copybook to its surface, and placed her hands on her friend's shoulders. "They won't come 'til I call."

"Good." She gripped Ella's hands in her own. Her fingers dug in. "This is Lance Jarvish an' Josh Ragget."

"What's wrong?" *I don't care an owl's hoot about their names.* Ella wanted to know what brought them to Velma's home. She didn't care what her expression said. For once, she wasn't worried strangers would be shocked by her awful scars. She held her head high and locked her eyes on the men.

"Oh, the worst," Velma said.

Adam whimpered from his cradle and kicked his chubby legs. His mother's clammy hands shook, but continued to cling to Ella's fingers.

"The worst?" She glared at the men, ready to pounce, much as a mountain lion once jumped her. She wished the beardless one would step near the window so she could see his face and judge his expression.

"Yes." The oldest man, sporting an unkempt white beard, gave a drawn-out sigh. "We jest tolt bad news to Mrs. Clanders." The immediate slump of his shoulders said he didn't feel like repeating the information.

Velma nodded. Her eyes said she wrestled with inner pain. "They tells me Gust's body were found three weeks ago an' buried."

"Three *weeks* ago?" was all Ella could think of to say. "Three?"

"They fetched home what's left of his things an' our wagon out yonder."

"You waited three weeks to come here?" She hoped they heard the disdain in her voice. The odor of their sweaty bodies caused her to feel nauseous. It brought forth the memory of winter months when her pa didn't bathe. "Where did you bury him?"

"We didn't have to, 'cept his legs. He buried hisself in a collapsed ridge he were digging into—on Yahoola Creek." Lance Jarvish's unemotional hazel eyes narrowed. "We daren't leave our claim to come here on the spot. Had to hide it." His thinning gray hair was combed straight back from his forehead and didn't do much to cover his liver-spotted head.

Ella knelt beside the bench and enveloped Velma in a tight hug. "I'm sorry. They should've come sooner."

"Now I hav'ta tell the children." Her voice broke and quivered on the last word. "That's the worst. We'll wait 'til these good gentlemen takes their leave." She looked intently at the two of them. "I've no money. Can we offer you a meal for travelin' here?"

"No, ma'am." The one named Josh shook his head. A black shock of hair whipped across his forehead.

With compressed lips, Ella stood.

"We've got to ride back to camp—south. Like to make it 'fore dark." Josh fiddled with a faded black felt hat and kept his eyes on it. "See, we got to camp near our stake. That's why—"

"That's why we ain't come sooner," the man named Lance interrupted. "We fight off claim jumpers most every day. Got a trusted friend standin' guard. We felt it our God-appointed duty to bring news of your husband's passing."

"How'd you know he lived here?" Ella almost shocked herself with her boldness, but she continued, "Which one of you killed him?"

Velma caught her breath and tugged at her hand. "No, child, they didn't kill him. Don't speak so."

"They didn't?" She raised her chin, and her heart hammered in her ears. She didn't believe their story.

Josh faced her. His black eyes reminded her of a moonless winter sky. Stunned, she realized he was quite young, no more than Jim's age.

"We ain't killed anyone." His words sounded terse, but the disturbing eyes took on a softer appeal. "No man done the deed. Nature did. We jest found the body after the killin' been done. We gave him a proper burial. There's even a marker. Gust spoke of this place one time when we checked him into Sprawls' Hotel."

"Sprawls?" Velma said in repeat. "Where?"

"A tanyard in Lick Log. Oh, name's diff'rent ... Dahlonega. He drank too much that night. Bein' tossed in a tanning vat speeds up the soberin' process one time and ag'in. We also was directed here by a man answerin' by the handle of Kilbride—who we met headin' east, away from here."

289

Miles Kilbride, again. Ella found her stiff attitude melting in the seemingly direct gaze of the younger man. "Who murdered Velma's husband?"

"I done tolt you—no one," Lance said, almost shouting.

Josh nodded. "The section of a hill he hacked into, while lookin' for a vein or placer 'longside the creek, gave way. It buried an' smothered him. Must'va laid there awhile—days. We came across his feet stickin' out— buried him more proper. Found his wagon an' starving team tied to a tree, near a crude camp. There weren't a shanty. We suspicion he dug into a weak section of the riverbank, a ridge, hoping for a gold signs. Buried alive."

Velma's grip on Ella's hands intensified. A low, sad groan came from her ashen lips. "I knew it ... I knew it."

Mae leaned against her mama's side, and a sob escaped her lips. Horrified, Ella knelt and gathered the child into her arms. "Mae, don't. Baby girl, come with me." She lifted Mae, carried her past the two strangers, and slipped outside.

Not fifty feet away, Scott, Carrie, and Remy stood under a chestnut tree, their troubled faces cast into shadows by the budding branches overhead and the dwindling sunlight. A chill filled the air. Ella hurried toward them with Mae in her arms.

"You disobeyed me."

She felt a flash of anger at the children's blatant disrespect to her previous order, but recognized the childish disquiet etched in their expressions. They all grew tearful as they heard Mae's muted sobs. Ella's initial reaction cooled. Her heart ached for them.

"Your sister's not harmed. Mae, stand here with Carrie." She lowered the girl's bare feet to the pebble-strewn ground. "Dry your tears."

Scott latched onto Ella's arm. "Don't punish us for disobeyin'. We wanted to be near, if'n Mama needed us."

"She don't need you." She muttered the words and placed her hand on Scott's shoulder to calm him. She studied the elongated shadows inching their way from the woods into the cleared field by the barn. "Let's put the horses in the barn. Scott, can you handle them and the wagon—enough to take it over by the barn?"

He nodded, but his eyes widened with surprise at her words. "Pappy don't let me to do that, and there's the wolf. I'm skeered of it."

"You said it is dead. Your pappy isn't here—not in the cabin. Your mama will tell you why. Scott, I'll help put up your horses. The other horses belong to two men talkin' to your mama. Remy—girls, wait for us." She indicated for all of them to stay put. "Carrie, hold Mae's hand."

"I want Mama." Mae's bottom lip stuck out. Her features and haunted eyes showed she didn't understand.

"Soon." With her fingers, Ella wiped Mae's face free of tears and pushed her unkempt hair out of her eyes. "Stand here. No frettin'."

In solemn silence, the three children leaned against one another for comfort.

Scott and Ella went to the horses, and he stroked the smooth nose of the one named Bellows. "What do we do with the wolf?"

She peeked inside the old wagon and shuddered at the sight of the powerless wolf—lain out on its side. "We won't worry about it," she replied. "It's that simple."

The carcass lay stiff and gaunt. Its reddish-brown and blood-flecked coat appeared ragged and dull. Sightless, eyes stared at the side of the wagon. Pointed white fangs gleamed along the open jaws.

Scott made short work of coaxing the horses to pull the wagon close to the log barn. Ella helped him unhitch them and then motioned to Carrie. "Hold the barn door for us. I'll hang onto this horse."

"No!" Carrie violently shook her head. The blood drained from her thin face.

She refused to step toward the shadowy barn and its sagging skeletal door. Her widened eyes switched from the barn to the cabin's door as if she expected someone to walk out the door. With stumbling steps, she backed away.

"No, no."

Scott slapped at Ella's arm. "Whoa, remember? She don't like the barn, even though she tried to jump that time. Let me. Hey, I got an idea."

He left her holding both horses and ran to open a side gate. He then scurried into the murky barn and back out with an armful of moldy dark fodder. Bellows strained against the leather reins. He perked his ears forward and watched Scott.

"What's that for?" she asked.

"Walk 'em this way. They should remember." He went through the gate.

Both horses followed him into the side field surrounded by a split rail fence. He threw the dried corn leaves on the ground.

"That's it. I'll put them in the barn later, one at a time." He sounded grownup and more sure of himself. "They can chomp this. We can dig a hole before school an' plant the wolf."

Ella had to smile. "Good thinkin'. Thanks, Scott." She gestured to all of them. "Let's go—"

The noise of the cabin door shutting drew their attention. The two men strode toward their horses.

"Who's that?" Scott jumped sideways and bumped into Ella's hip.

The older man didn't acknowledge their presence or look in their direction. He crammed a filthy hat on his head and mounted the brown horse, but Josh advanced toward them, with hat in hand. His clothes hung loose on his skinny frame and needed a good scrubbing. His raven-wing black hair curled against his neck and collar and reached past his full eyebrows.

"Miss?" His dark eyes stared at her.

"Yes?"

He flipped hair out of his face and stood with feet planted wide apart. "I jest want to say I'm sorry 'bout your father."

My father? Ella's back stiffened. Her lips parted. *He thinks I'm Velma's daughter.*

Scott frowned and tugged at her sleeve. "What's he mean?"

She shushed Scott with a quick touch. The eyes of all the children focused on her. "Thank you for takin' care of things. I'm sorry I spoke as I did in there."

He nodded and lowered his gaze. "I figger I'd react the same—if I had loved my father." He twisted the hat, played with the squashed shape of it, and flicked dust with one nail-bitten finger. The ragged brim whispered in the cracked palms of his hands, and a festering cut reddened the top of his left hand.

"The news is bad, but now we know."

Josh's thin frame indicated missed meals, and his hands appeared to have been in water and exposed to the elements. Panning for gold did that. A twinge of sympathy welled inside her.

"We mine a spot on the west branch of Butler's Creek, direct south of here, near Lick Log—excuse me, Dahlonega. Got us a bark shanty. If you need—"

"Git on your horse!" Lance turned his mount toward them, whistled, and jerked his right arm through the air. "Time's wasting, and I'll leave ya."

"Got to go. Lance's worried. We left the claim. Now we won't make it back tonight. He drove the wagon this mornin' an' those horses ain't much—not trained good. He's in a bad temper."

"Where'd the wolf come from?"

"Oh. Last night it made a mistake of raidin' our vittles. We camped aways from here, south end of this here cove." He nodded over his shoulder at Lance. "He shot it at first light. An easy mark 'cause it were limping bad. Starvin'. Girl, may I ask your name?" He stepped back to his horse. The twilight creeping between the log barn and the dense woods seemed to darken his eye color. "Please?"

"Ella Dessa."

An insignificant smile lifted his hallowed cheeks. He nodded and set his hat on his head. "Nice, soft ring to it." He walked away. A ragged hole showed in the seat of his faded pants.

"He's creepy, like the woods at night." Scott glared after him. "He kept eyeing you."

Ella's fingers squeezed Scott's right shoulder. "Hush."

"What'd he say about your father?"

"Not now." Seconds later, she watched Josh turn in the saddle and raise his hand but she didn't wave. Uneasiness rolled over her, mimicking the wary expression on Scott's face, but the feeling faded—when the forest hid the two men. They had brought their tale of death and were now gone.

Should Velma even believe them?

Her attention switched to the four children clustered close, and she felt sorrow for what they'd soon learn. "Let's go talk to your mama. Scott, remember I'll need your help buryin' that wolf come mornin'. I've no desire to try shucking off its useless hide." She paused and gave an exasperated groan. "No, we best do it tonight—don't want bears or other varmints sniffing it out. Remind me later. We'll do it by lantern."

Velma didn't pretend great sorrow over the news Gust wasn't returning. She was straightforward with her children—almost unemotional and blunt. Ella watched her cuddle Remy as he cried. She noticed Velma respected the fact Scott refused her comforting arms. He glowered, eyes red-rimmed, but he didn't give way to tears like his little brother. Ella couldn't figure out if he was sad, relieved, or frightened by his own lack of grief.

Maybe, it's anger he feels.

She watched the boy ignore everyone and sit mesmerized in front of the fire. She instantly knew how Carrie felt, even though the girl didn't give any indication of her innermost struggle.

She's creek-jumpin' happy her pappy's dead.

Mae and Rosemary were outwardly unaffected their father had died. Mae had gotten over her crying spell and acted content to go play.

With an exasperated sigh, Ella tried to push all the intermingled thoughts out of her mind. She called to Scott. "We need to tend to the wolf. I bet it's the one my pa saw some time ago."

They buried the emaciated body of the wolf in a shallow grave near one side of the barn. Its rancid odor caused Ella to gag. Neither one of them spoke. They set the lantern on the ground and worked within its yellow circle of light. Distant lightning lit the sky beyond the mountain. It felt as if they buried Gust Clanders, wiping away the family's memory of the detestable and no-account man.

Ella shuddered. She didn't mourn at the knowledge of the man's untimely death—she hadn't known him well enough—she quelled under the realization he had probably never accepted God. He was known as a worthless, fierce-tempered man. Now, most of his own family wouldn't grieve his passing, and in the future, he'd stand before the Lord without salvation. It was a heart-wrenching and sobering thought.

****

About bedtime, a much-needed rain battered the sides of the cabin and managed to leak through the chinking and drip along the shake roof. Thunder rolled down one side of the mountain, across the cove's narrow, curved width, and up the other slope. The floor quivered under their feet. Everything grew damp and chilly, even with a constant fire, which hissed and popped as drops of rain sprinkled down the rock chimney.

It took a while for the children to fall asleep. Ella washed dishes and put things away while Velma nursed the baby. But Ella soon dried her hands on a scrap of muslin, reached inside her skirt's waistband for the letter, and walked over to Velma.

"Are you goin' to tell the cove of his death?"

Velma laid Adam on the bed and diapered him. Her eyes lacked emotion as she tied the piece of cloth around the baby's belly. "Yes, no reasons to hide the facts. They'll see the wagon. I now have no hopes of him returnin' with gold so I can't pay back all I owes."

She gave Ella a sad but oddly amusing smile and caught one of the baby's chubby bare feet in her hand. She kissed the pink toes and then put the foot through the leg hole of a knitted wool soaker. Her face carried a permanent weariness. Her eyelids slanted downward on the outer corners—more than they ever did. At only twenty-eight years old, she resembled a middle-aged woman.

"I'll tell Master Konrad at school."

"Yes. He needs to know." Velma raised Adam to her shoulder and patted his back. His dark head bobbed and curious baby eyes blinked in the fire's light. "He can pass the word."

Ella nodded. In her hand, she clasped the letter. "See what I got today—when I asked Mr. Beckler about hirin' me? He had this."

Velma's eyes shone with expectancy. "A letter? Fern?"

"I hope so."

"What about the job?"

She smiled. "I start tomorrow."

"Oh, child." She used her free arm to hug Ella. Tears shimmered in her eyes. "I hate it you'll haves to work, but it's a blessin'!"

"Yes, it is—God's love."

"Yes, yes! Come, read your missive to me." She headed for the rocker.

Ella sat on the floor. Carefully, she broke the light wax seal and unfolded the paper. The delicate, elusive hint of lavender scented the folds. She held it toward the fire's light. Her lips formed into a smile as she recognized Fern's beautiful signature at the bottom of the single page.

"My Dearest Friend, it says," she began. "I write this while seated on a bench under an oak tree. It has bright new leaves. I'm so close to the great ocean, I catch a whiff of it in the very air I breathe. I taste salt on my lips. This paper feels sticky under my hand. The hot sun peeks through the branches, and it's only March. Everyone cautions me to keep a bonnet on, but right now, it hangs on my back. I cannot bear it. As it is, I feel I shall smother in my cotton dress and underskirts. They say the weather gets much hotter. I've lost my appetite. My sister insists I'm much too thin for the interest of any gentleman, but I don't care to attract such attention.

I miss Ma. Please, if you get a chance, send word to her that both Marcy and I are happy. We miss her. I know I dare not write to her. I feel awful going behind my stepfather's back, but I must let her know how we fare. My address is at the bottom of this page. I could not chance it on the outside. Please, write and tell me how things are with you. Your loving friend, Fern Abernathy."

Velma sighed. "How lovely. Will you write back?"

"Yes. I want to tell her I now live in Beckler's Cove with you. I'll need to post Duncan's letter with mine."

"I wonder what kinds of ruckus that'll cause?"

"Maybe, she won't ever write to him."

Velma nodded and lifted Adam to her shoulder. Her hand patted his back, and he burped readily. "Perhaps, she shouldn't, after what you told me."

"I don't think I could ... if I were her." For a moment, silence reigned.

"Guess we'll hav'ta wait and see." She gave Adam the other breast and went back to rocking. "How was your first day at school? The little ones tried to tell me, but I told 'em I wanted to hears it from you."

"It was fun and skeery. I've so much catchin' up to do."

"You'll make us proud." Velma patted Ella's cheek. "Thanks for comin' to live with me."

****

An hour later, with the rocker pulled close to the fire, Ella sat and tried to collect her thoughts. Her mind felt dog-tired. The rain had washed away the warm weather, and the temperature in the cabin dropped.

Somewhere outside, an owl hooted. Its drawn-out call sounded lonely and questioning. The room remained hushed, except for the snapping fire and the boys' light snores. A movement at her left side startled her.

"Carrie, you scared me. What you doin' awake?"

The girl's bottom lip trembled.

"Come here." Ella's breath caught in her throat. She held out her arms. "Room for us both in this rocker."

The girl slipped into her lap, and they snuggled for a few minutes. There wasn't any need to talk. She understood the stiff waves of emotion the girl rode.

"I hate him."

"I know you do."

Sobs erupted, and the child literally writhed in emotional suffering. Ella held her and offered her presence as a solace.

"Cry, jest cry."

With her mouth crushed against the curve of Ella's shoulder, Carrie muffled her words of torment. The flood of tears went on for several minutes.

When the girl's body relaxed and only random hiccups shook her, Ella started rocking. The unvarying, rhythmic squeak of the wobbly rocker added to the peace sinking into her thoughts. She instinctively knew the same healing flooded Carrie's troubled mind and wounded body.

"There won't be no more fearful waitin'." Her lips touched the girl's head. "The one who caused your pain won't return. God's protection has reached you, and without His touch nothin' is possible."

Carrie stirred and snuggled closer. Three and a half years apart in age, but bonded together by secret wounds, the two of them hugged. Ella knew the younger girl had suffered more in a physical way than she had. Abuse takes many forms, and they had lived through the trauma.

With trembling hands, Carrie sat up and dried her own tears. "I got your neck wet."

A wave of giggles made Ella's sides hurt. "Yes, you washed my scars real good."

Carrie placed warm lips against the bumpy skin of Ella's neck. "There, I kissed 'em, too." The fire's light showed her unique crooked smile. "They don't bother me." Her fingers lightly stroked the ragged lines.

"Thank you. No one but Mama ever kissed 'em." She felt tears on her own cheeks.

"I love my mama."

"I know you do. I loved mine. Still do."

The younger girl wiggled sideways so the fire's light shone on Ella's face. "Never tell her."

"I won't."

"He can't kill her now."

"Did he say he'd do that?" A surge of nausea made her realize how similar their stories could have been.

Carrie's head nodded. "Yes. If I didn't go to him ... in the barn. He'd wait, catch me out by the outhouse, and hurt me. He said I were ... were a dirty girl." Her bottom lip and chin quivered.

"You're not what he said."

Her fingers bit into Ella's arm. "He did things. He told Scott he were whippin' me. Scott heard me—heard me cry in the barn." She whimpered. Tears ran down her pale cheeks and glimmered in the fire's light. "Then he'd go beat on mama and say she ain't spanking me 'nough—that I were full of sin."

"Shh." She laid her fingers on Carrie's lips. "Stop. His wicked voice is stilled. Don't repeat his words." She dropped her hand and studied the girl's oval face. "You're soon to be ten?"

"Yes."

298

"Then, you're old enough to understand it ain't your fault ... him doin' what he did. Right?"

Carrie kept her head bowed. "It isn't?" She lifted her light hazel eyes to search Ella's expression. The refection of the fire danced across the girl's skin and the log wall behind her.

"No." She tapped the girl's shoulder. "*No!* He made you think it was. It was his sin."

"He lied?" Her bottom lip quivered.

"Yes, he lied, and much worse. Your mama would've died to help you. Mine would've. She fought Pa. And made him beat her—'stead of me. It was awful to hear. I wanted to beat him like he did Mama."

"How'd you figger your mama would die for you?"

"She tolt me. I gathered he was hateful. I even saw him steal things."

Carrie again traced Ella's scars, inching her finger along the bumpy lines. "A wild cat did this?"

"Yes. I was near 'bout your age."

"Does it hurt?"

"Not now. It hurt awful at the time. It just makes me want to hide. I feel ugly."

The girl's gentle eyes searched her face. "That boy doesn't care 'bout your scars."

"What boy?"

"Samuel. His greenie-blue eyes say so. I think he loves you."

"Oh, we're friends." She also knew their childish companionship had changed.

Carrie chewed at her bottom lip and murmured, "He won't ever hurt you."

"No, he wouldn't."

"But you like his brother."

Startled, she avoided the young girl's direct stare.

A big smile bunched Carrie's cheeks, and her eyes lit up. "I won't tell. I think you'll someday love Samuel. You should marry him."

"Carrie!" Astonished, she gave a soft laugh. "You're silly."

The girl giggled. "I'm goin' to watch and see if you marry him."

Ella rolled her eyes. "Poor Samuel might disagree with you."

Carrie suddenly yawned. "My eyes are tired."

"Hmm. We need to go to sleep."

"I know. Thank you." The thin girl stood and offered an unusual hug. "I want you to be my sister."

"We're sisters," Ella whispered. "Forever."

She waited until Carrie disappeared up the loft ladder before slipping Fern's folded letter into view. She held it tight in her hands. She would write and let her friend know how things were in Beckler's Cove and in her own life.

Duncan's letter remained safe in her wooden box. She'd send it with her own and let God work out the details between Fern and Duncan. It wasn't her concern.

She couldn't help but wonder what kind of response Duncan expected from the girl he had frightened and degraded. She felt he had ruined his chances of gaining Fern's respect and love. Only God knew how it might end.

Tired and feeling at peace, she banked the fire. Except for the gentle breathing and murmurs of those already asleep, no other sound disturbed her immediate world. It was strange to feel relief, after the awful news delivered that day. The knowledge of Gust's death had given all the occupants of the household a sense of harmony.

"That man can't bring pain and hate back to their lives." The crackling and popping of the fire muffled her whispered words.

She wasn't sure how much Velma knew of her daughter's abuse, but the woman must suspect cruelty had taken place. Perhaps, in the coming months, Velma would face her own child and beg forgiveness. What could she have done to stop it, other than kill Gust with her own hands? Who would've dared to stand beside her and face the man with his filthy lusts? Maybe she never knew the terrible truth.

"Carrie's been released from fear." Ella knew the child's life might've turned out different. She smiled and recognized the fact. Now the little girl would have a chance to heal under God's blessings and touch.

My own life is far different than I dreamt it'd be at the time of Mama's death.

Life, with its many facets, had woven filaments, which connected her to many other people—and as far away as the swampy wilderness called Florida.

"Tomorrow, after school, I start work for Mr. Beckler. God is good."

Without God's touch, the course of her life wouldn't have been altered. She knew the difference in herself and the peace she felt. For the first time in her life, Ella Dessa eagerly awaited the future.

Acknowledgments

I believe God instilled in me the unquenchable desire to write. I know He provided the right people to influence and help me along the journey. Loved ones, encouragers, and fellow writers all have my gratitude. My mother, Leona Campbell, taught me to cherish the old books and storytelling. The many paper dolls she made or bought for me became building blocks, stirring the imagination. My children, Cameron and Stephanie, tolerated a mom who sometimes dressed as an old woman and told crazy stories at church gatherings. My eight-year-old grandson, Connor, refused to help burn old copies of my manuscript in the fireplace, and he curled up in a recliner to read—declaring it too good to burn. My husband, Ed Prough, bestowed unselfish support and true understanding of my need to write. A friend, Marlin Nichols, did the first edits and enthusiastically supported the story's worth. Another friend, Becky DeGraff, read rough drafts and told me how the characters came alive for her. My local writers' group and our superb leader, Daphne Tarango, took time to comment on rough copies. My dedicated agent, Linda Glaz, at Hartline Literary Agency, agreed to represent me and never failed to believe in my writing. She gave encouragement when I felt perplexed or discouraged. Carolyn Boyles, my first editor, astonished me by saying my book would touch the reader's soul. Eva Marie Everson, with Lighthouse Publishing of the Carolinas, continually offered enthusiasm about my storytelling and the characters. From the first time I met her, she gave me gentle reminders that I needed to believe in my writing and hopes for a published book.